Valley of
the Lost

Books by Vicki Delany

Constable Molly Smith Series
In the Shadow of the Glacier
Valley of the Lost
Winter of Secrets

Other Novels
Scare the Light Away
Burden of Memory

Valley of the Lost

Vicki Delany

Poisoned Pen Press

Poisoned Pen Press
6962 E. First Ave., Ste. 103
Scottsdale, AZ 85251
www.poisonedpenpress.com
info@poisonedpenpress.com

Printed in the United States of America

To my children: Caroline, Julia, and Alex

Acknowledgments

This book was written during my year of living (not very) dangerously. I owe many, many thanks to all the people who made it possible.

To Julia and Ron for the spectacular view of the valley and the glacier that helped to get Smith and Winters back on track. To Jerry & Linda for peace and quiet and the inspiration for Lucky's garden. To Maya for a home-away-from-home and surroundings full of art in the Casa Del Soul. To Marika for the solitude of Cedarwood Cottage from which I could watch the snow fall. And fall. And fall. To Karen and Bill, at whose home the snow continued to fall and I accomplished two things: I wrote and I shoveled snow. Smith and Winters' next adventure has to be set in the winter.

Thank you to Alex Delany for the EMT expertise, and to members of the Nelson City Police and the RCMP for giving me a peek into their world: Brita Wood, Constables Dino Falcone and Corey Hoy, and Corporal Al Grant. Particular thanks to Detective Paul Burkart who never tired of answering my questions with good humor, and to Constable Janet Scott-Pryke for friendship as well as advice.

As always thanks to my invaluable early readers Karen Wold, Julia Vryheid, and Gail Cargo.

As has been said before, the town of Trafalgar, British Columbia, and all the people living there, is nothing other than a product of my imagination.

Chapter One

The setting sun had slipped behind the mountains, and in the bottom of the valley, long ago carved out of ancient rock by the swift-moving river, the summer's night was hot and close. The scent of cedar and pine, decaying undergrowth, rich earth filled the air, and further up the street a pack of young people, sounding as if they'd already hit the bars, laughed at nothing at all.

Lucy Smith, known to everyone as Lucky, stood at the back door of the Trafalgar Women's Support Center enjoying a rare moment of peace before walking to her car. It had been a long, hectic day, but a good one, and she was pleased with herself. Today she'd accomplished something. For once, the women seemed to be paying attention to what she'd been trying to teach them.

Lucky drove an ancient Pontiac Firefly. It was parked at the back, in a small gravel clearing chopped out of wild grass and weeds up against the bottom of the mountain. As she unlocked the car door, a soft cry came from the bushes. A cat? Lucky climbed into her car, paying it no further attention. The heat of the day still clung to the worn seats, and as she put the key into the ignition, she rolled down the window to try to catch a bit of a breeze. She was about to turn the key, to start up the engine, when she heard it again.

Definitely not a cat.

It sounded like a baby. How odd.

Lucky reached into the glove compartment and pulled out a flashlight. She flicked the light on as she stepped out of the car, and pointed it into the dense brush beyond the parking area. The thin beam illuminated dead leaves, broken branches, gray and white rocks. A single black sock. A blue can of Kokanee beer shone in the light.

And a small yellow package, lying on the ground about ten yards inside the woods.

Lucky tried to focus; the bundle shifted, and cried out.

She pushed her way through the undergrowth, heedless of branches reaching for her face and scratching at her bare arms. She dropped to her knees, pushing a sharp stone into her flesh. She shifted to get off the rock, and shone her light into the folds of the yellow blanket. A scrunched up white face blinked back at her, trying to shut out the sudden brightness. Tiny fists waved in the air.

"Oh, my heavens. You poor thing." Lucky stuffed the flashlight into the elastic waistband of her short, baggy pants and reached for the baby. "What are you doing out here all by yourself?" She peeled back the blanket. The baby was small, no more than a few months old. He, Lucky guessed it was a he as it was dressed in a blue sleeper, opened his mouth and yelled. He was clean and at first glance appeared to be healthy. His clear eyes were dark blue, his cheeks pink and chubby, his head bald, and his cry lusty.

"We'd better get you inside. They call me Lucky, but you're the lucky one. Good thing I found you, and not a bear or a cougar. Where's your mom?"

Lucky gathered the baby into her arms, and stood up. The flashlight dropped to the ground and rolled over, throwing its light deeper into the woods, touching the edges of a dark shape underneath a large red cedar. With a pounding heart, Lucky scooped the flashlight up. She clutched the baby, now screaming with gusto, to her chest and took a few hesitant steps forward.

A woman lay on her back. Her eyes were open wide, but she wasn't looking at the branches swaying overhead or the stars barely visible through the thick canopy of branches, leaves, and needles. Shifting the baby in her right arm, Lucky crouched down and touched the base of the woman's neck. Her skin was cold, and nothing moved under Lucky's shaking fingers.

Constable Molly Smith's boot slipped in a puddle of vomit. Instinctively her head jerked back to help her keep her balance and the man's fist connected with her mouth. Her head spun, and she tasted hot sweet blood, but she managed to keep her footing. She ducked in case a second blow was coming. Dave Evans grabbed the man from behind and wrenched his arms back. "That's enough of that."

The man was big, about six foot three with the weight to match, and arms bulging with muscle and tattoos. His hair was long, thin, gray, and greasy. The moment Evans touched him, all the aggression fled. "Hey, I'm sorry, buddy. I didn't mean to hit the lady. It was an accident, right? Can't we forget all about it?"

"I don't think so," Evans said, snapping handcuffs on meaty wrists. "You okay, Constable Smith?"

She touched her lip. Her fingers came away streaked with blood. "No harm done," she said, inwardly seething. Nothing Evans would like more than to think he'd saved her from the big bad guy.

The crowd shifted and, sensing that the fun was over, those at the back began to move away. Flashing blue and red lights washed over them, making it look as though they'd all gathered for a party.

Smith and Evans had been called to the Bishop and the Nun, a cheap faux-English pub on Pine Street. Not even nine o'clock, but on a hot Thursday evening in Trafalgar, British Columbia, the bars were filling up fast and plenty of the patrons had begun the night's drinking in the middle of the afternoon.

Two men had been thrown out of the bar, told to take their fight outside. When they did a crowd gathered quickly, eager for excitement. At first the fight consisted of nothing other than a lot of obscenities, a bit of pushing and shoving, verbal threats and aggressive posturing. But as the police car rounded the far corner, colored lights flashing and siren on, one of the bystanders had broken away from the crowd, staggered toward the antagonists, and vomited all over the smaller guy's shoes. He took offense to that, and sent the bewildered drunk to the sidewalk with a strong right hook. One of the man's friends, or maybe just a stranger happy at the opportunity to instigate a good street brawl, ran forward, and the fight began in earnest.

The police rushed in to break it up. Whereupon Smith slipped and the big man punched her in the face.

Everyone stepped back. Once a police officer was involved, the crowd seemed to think, the fight was no longer harmless fun. Someone helped the vomiter up off the sidewalk, and the tattooed man tried to make his apologies.

"Save it for the judge," Evans said.

They stuffed the big man into the back of the car. His original opponent, the guy who'd thrown the first punch, had melted into the long shadows between the buildings the moment the police car came to a halt.

Evans took their prisoner, still expressing his regrets, downstairs to be processed into custody, while Smith went to the women's washroom to check her face.

A thin line of blood ran from the left corner of her mouth down her chin, making her look like Dracula's bride after a feast at the castle. She put her hat on the counter and scrubbed the blood off her face. It didn't look too bad, she thought, studying herself in the mirror, but her lip would be sporting a sizeable lump tomorrow.

She ran her fingers through her short blond hair.

She'd worn her hair long until a few weeks ago, tied into a French braid when she was in uniform.

Graham had liked her hair long; he liked to play with it, wrap it around his fingers, put the ends in his mouth and pretend to chew. She'd kept it long after he'd died, but recently she decided she needed a more professional looking haircut, so she'd ordered the hairdresser to chop it all off.

After which, she'd gone home and cried.

Her radio crackled. "911 call from 317 Cottonwood Street. Lady says she found a body. VSA." Vital signs absent.

Smith put her hat back on her head, and dried her hands on the seat of her pants as she ran out the door.

Most of the clients of the Trafalgar Women's Support Center were young mothers. The center kept stores of supplies for anything a child might need. Lucky had placed the crying baby in a blanket-lined laundry basket, put the kettle on to boil to make up a bottle of formula, and was searching through the storage cupboard for disposable diapers when she heard the siren.

She'd called 911 from her cell phone, unlocked the back door of the center, and carried the baby inside. The face of the woman lying so still in the woods was unmarked, and Lucky had recognized it. Ashley. Lucky couldn't remember Ashley's last name, nor the name of the baby. Something old-fashioned, yet trendy at the same time.

Red lights flashed through the narrow front windows. The siren cut off in mid-note.

Lucky picked up the crying baby and went to the door.

Her own baby was climbing the stairs, talking into the radio at her shoulder. One hand rested on the ugly black Glock at her hip, and the other carried a big flashlight. A street light caught the blue stripe running down the uniform pant leg.

"Mom?" Constable Molly Smith said. "Did you call 911?"

"What I found...It's...she's out back. I told them to send an ambulance, but there's no need. She's in no hurry, now, poor dear."

"Show me what you found."

"Have you been in an accident? There's a cut on your lip."

"Never mind me, Mom. Where's the body?"

Lucky led the way through the center, and out the back door. The day had been hot and humid, but welcome night breezes were flowing down off the mountains. A skunk had defended itself while she was inside, leaving its scent on the night air. She pointed into the woods, beyond the edge of the parking lot. "Through there. She's dead. I checked, Moonlight."

Another siren cut the silence of the residential streets.

"That's the ambulance. Go and meet them, Mom. Tell them to follow me." The strong flashlight threw a circle of yellow light toward the woods.

Lucky watched as Moonlight stepped off the grass into the trees. She tried to act tough, but she was a very new police officer, still on probation, and Lucky knew it couldn't be easy for her coming across dead bodies. Moonlight had never talked about it, but she'd had a hard time dealing with finding Reginald Montgomery last month in a back alley with his head bashed in.

No time to worry about that now. Lucky met the paramedics at the door and sent them out the back. Knowing that more people would soon follow, she left the door open. She changed the baby's diaper, it was a boy all right, and fixed a bottle. While waiting for the formula to cool, she stood at the back door, bouncing the infant in her arms and watching the activity in the woods. The paramedics hadn't come rushing out, bearing a laden stretcher, and Lucky knew she'd been right—Ashley was dead.

She was settling down at the kitchen table, baby cradled in one arm, bottle in hand, when John Winters walked through the door. He wore a pair of loose-fitting jeans, colorful shirt, and black jacket. His brown eyes opened fractionally wider and his neatly-trimmed silver mustache twitched as he recognized her.

"They're all out back," Lucky said, with a nod toward the door. The baby latched onto the bottle's nipple and began sucking for all he was worth.

"Were you the one who called us, Lucky?"

"Yes."

"I have to ask you to stay until I've had a look round and talked to Molly."

She nodded.

"Nice baby," he said.

"Isn't he?"

"I'll be back."

Lucky smiled down at the baby. His eyes were closed and he was sucking hard.

Sergeant John Winters left Lucky Smith nursing a baby and walked outside. Constable Brad Noseworthy was setting up lights at the point where the mountain met the gravel and grass of the woman's center. The RCMP had been contacted and Winters knew they were on their way. He'd left Dave Evans on the street, stringing up crime scene tape and telling the neighbors, politely, to mind their own business.

Molly Smith stood to one side, holding a lamp while Noseworthy decided where to place it. He was the Trafalgar City Police's only qualified crime-scene investigator, but he'd step back when the RCMP forensic team arrived.

"Show me what you have, Molly," Winters said.

She handed Noseworthy his lamp and ducked into the trees. About fifteen yards in, a small clearing gleamed under strong white lights as if ready for its Broadway debut. A body lay on the ground. It was on its back, looking up. Winters crouched down. He felt Smith standing behind him.

"Move anything, Molly?" he asked, his eyes running across the dead woman's body. She wore a sleeveless red cotton tank-top over a multi-colored skirt, and black ballet-type shoes. The clothes appeared to be undisturbed, the skirt folded across her bare legs as if she'd taken a moment to rest before continuing on her way. She was short, probably not more than five foot one or two, and very, very thin. Colorful beads were woven through the strands of her long dark hair. A red and black tattoo of a dragon curled around her right ankle.

The remains of old scars dotted her bare arms. Beside her, a needle lay in the dry, brown bed of leaves.

"Drugs," he said. "Did you move anything, Molly?"

"Nope. Just touched her neck looking for a pulse. She's getting cold. The paramedics came right after me and checked her out, but they didn't move her much. Didn't have to."

"Your mother called it in. She found the body?"

"Yes."

Winters' right knee cracked as got to his feet.

"Recognize her?" he asked. It wasn't a strange question. In a town the size of Trafalgar the police knew almost everyone, particularly the modern-day hippies, like this girl, who hung around Big Eddie's Coffee Emporium, the corners of Front Street, or the bars on Pine Street.

"I think I've seen her. Just around town. Never in any trouble, far as I know. Do you, um, have any idea what happened here, John?"

"I do. But I'm not going to speculate. And neither should you."

Her face tightened and he stifled a grin. Molly Smith had the potential to become a good police officer. But she was sometimes too quick to forget she was very young and very inexperienced. He hadn't liked her when he'd first met her, mistaking her enthusiasm for ineptitude. She'd proven herself. Once. But she still had a long way to go.

"What happened to your face?"

"Street brawl."

"I hope the other guy looks worse."

"No. But he's spending the night in the cells contemplating the error of his ways."

It was fully dark now. Headlights turned into the parking area behind the center. Doors slammed and men spoke and shapes passed in front of the lights.

Corporal Ron Gavin of the RCMP strode over; he and Winters shook hands. The Mountie nodded at Smith. "Coroner's right behind me," he said. "Saw her in my rear view mirror."

"I'm going inside," Winters said. "To talk to the witness." He gestured to Smith to follow him out of the woods. Gavin needed room to work.

Smith pulled off her hat and rubbed at her head. Winters didn't care much for the new short haircut. It was cut about two or three inches long, all over, and either stood out from her head in spikes or was flattened by the hat. She was pretty, tall and lean and fair, with wide blue eyes and hair the color of summer corn. The new hair style made her look even younger, and more vulnerable, than the neat braid. Like the sort of London street urchin Charles Dickens wrote about.

"Is your mother looking after one of her grandkids?" Winters asked.

"My mother? No. It certainly isn't mine and to the best of my knowledge my brother hasn't spawned lately. I assume it belongs to one of the clients. That's what the center's for, mostly. They teach new mothers how to care for their babies, and help them access resources and stuff."

"But they're closed." The sign beside the front door had given the hours and an emergency phone number.

"Someone left it behind, maybe?" Smith said, sounding not too interested.

"Don't make assumptions, Molly. Your mother found a dead woman, and now she's minding a baby. She seems calm about all of this."

"I figured she was busy with the baby."

"Has anyone contacted your father?"

"Not me. Should I?"

"I think your mother needs some care, Molly. She found a body in the woods and she's showing as much emotion as if it had been an abandoned shoe."

Smith pulled out her cell phone.

"Take Dave's place on the street, and tell him to come inside and join Mrs. Smith and me."

"I'd rather…"

"Get Dave." He walked away without looking back.

Lucky Smith sat in a big armchair in the main room. The fiery red head, heavily streaked with gray, bent over the child in her arms. A strand had come loose from the clip at the back of her head and caressed the baby's cheek. At five foot two, Lucky was much shorter, and pudgier, than her tall, thin daughter. You wouldn't think they were related, at first, until you saw the firm set of the chin, the high cheekbones, the shape of the eyes— Lucky's green, Molly's blue.

The Trafalgar Women's Support Center was located in a heritage house. Still arranged like a home, it had a large living room with comfortable sofa and thread-bare chairs, a kitchen, last remodeled in the 1960s, dining room featuring a scarred wooden table with seating for ten or more, and stairs leading to the second floor. The house was old, wallpaper fading, paint chipping, floorboards lifting and carpet edges curling. A cork board, covered with information from government and social service agencies, filled one wall of the kitchen. Beneath a framed print of sky, lake, and flowers in the high alpine, Lucky cooed softly to the bundle in her arms.

Winters took a seat in the couch opposite her. The springs were none too good and they sagged beneath his weight.

"That's a cute baby, Lucky. Whose is it?"

Chapter Two

"I can't believe you missed the whole thing, Meredith. What on Planet Earth were you up to?"

Meredith Morgenstern shifted in the hard-backed chair. She endured the stream of abuse and tried to settle her breathing into her chest. One breath after another. One breath.

He'd told her to cover August's Fourth Thursday. The fourth Thursday of every month in spring and summer, the stores along Front Street put on a street festival. Musicians, wandering buskers, street-side food stalls. Her cell phone had conked out somewhere between interviewing a clown on stilts, and a lady selling homemade jam and chutney. She hadn't heard the order to get to Cottonwood Street and check out the police activity converging on the area.

Only once she'd gotten home and plugged her phone into the charger, did she get the message. By the time she arrived at Cottonwood Street only Constable Dave Evans, as handsome as ever, was there. He'd told her to go home.

She gave him her card, as if he didn't know who she was, and suggested they have a coffee some time when he was off duty. He'd put the card into his pocket and said he'd think about it. Arrogant prick.

Meredith knew better than to relate all that to Joe Gessling, her editor. A newspaper legend in his own mind, Joe held firm to the belief that he could do no wrong. So she cranked out a smile and said "They kept it under the radar, Joe. You know how it is sometimes."

"Sure do," he said.

Meredith doubted that he had any idea at all of how it was. His grandfather had started the paper; his father kept it going, year after year, without making the slightest change. A few months ago, Gessling *Père* collapsed onto his desk while pouring over copy, victim of a massive heart attack. He survived, but barely, and Joe had been brought back from a paper in Picton, Ontario. Wherever that might be. Joe talked long and loud about his ideas to bring the *Gazette* into the 21ˢᵗ century. Whatever that meant. He'd already tried to introduce more color and a lifestyle section. The idea had failed when it turned out that there wasn't enough lifestyle in town to gather advertising revenue.

That might change once the Grizzly Resort began building. Word around town said the resort partners had the huge advertising budget necessary to attract investors as well as persuade the citizens of Trafalgar that the resort would be good for their town.

In Meredith's opinion, the latter was a long shot indeed. The citizens of Trafalgar were legendary for their opposition to anything that smelled of corporate money or government interference. But the resort promised top-of-the-line boutiques, quality restaurants, high-flying clientele, and Meredith was all for it.

"I want tomorrow's paper to have the full story," Joe said. "Front page, at least half the page, devoted to this. We don't get enough unusual deaths in Trafalgar, so I want to squeeze this one for all it's worth."

Meredith registered her boss' idea of 'enough' deaths. But it wasn't her place to suggest that he pretend to have some sympathy.

"You got it." She got to her feet and turned toward the welcome sight of the door.

"You're pals with Constable Smith, I hear."

Truth be told, in school Meredith Morgenstern and Moonlight Smith had hated each other. They'd been bitter enemies, facing off across the gym floor or into the mirrors in the girls' bathroom. Recent events had done nothing to reconcile the newspaper reporter and the police officer.

"Yeah," Meredith said. "We go back a long way."

"Great. Squeeze that for all you're worth, will you." He turned toward his computer monitor. He shook the mouse and the Star Wars screensaver disappeared.

All Meredith wanted in life was to land a real job at a real newspaper and get the hell out of this hick town.

"Half the front page. Tomorrow," he said. "Or I'll know the reason why."

"What the hell happened to you?"

Andy Smith paused in the act of pouring himself a cup of coffee and stared at his daughter.

"Please, Dad. Don't make a fuss. I had an argument with a doorknob."

Lucky looked up from the stove. The edges of the blue plastic spatula she held in her right hand had partially melted years ago. "I've heard that one before," she said. "From the women down at the shelter. Almost every one of them, when they first arrive."

"You mean someone hit her," Andy said. "Is that it, someone hit you?"

Smith dropped into a chair. She'd dared to sneak a look at herself in the mirror as she brushed her teeth, and guessed how her parents would react. The swelling had spread up to her nose and into her cheek. The purple and yellow color did nothing to distract from the effect. She'd carefully checked out each tooth. Fortunately they were all firmly fixed in place.

"You should see the other guy," she said.

A vein throbbed in her father's neck and his eyes began to bulge. He clenched his fists. "He should be strung up in the town square. What kind of a bully hits a woman?"

"I am not a woman. I am a police officer. Calm down, Dad. It's not a big deal." Her face hurt like hell. If she hadn't known that her parents almost prayed for the day she'd come to her senses and quit the police service, Smith would throw herself into her mother's lap and cry for sympathy.

Andy passed her a cup of coffee. "What are you doing up so early, anyway?"

"Like I could sleep."

Once the coroner had arrived, signed the paperwork, and allowed the body to be removed, and Winters had told Andy to take his wife home, and Ron Gavin and his partner were hard at work examining every inch of the forest floor behind the women's support center, Smith had been sent back to the beat, while Evans stayed to keep curious bystanders at bay.

To Smith's surprise, the rest of her shift had been uneventful. Apparently everyone had had enough excitement for the day seeing a female cop belted in the mouth and hearing that a body had been found in the woods.

She'd gotten home at four, and had been woken only a few minutes ago by a screaming baby.

Lucky took a bottle off the stove and squeezed a drop onto her forearm. She reached into a laundry basket on the floor beside the stove and gathered up a pink blanket. Sylvester, the big sloppy golden retriever, sniffed at the bundle.

"Mom, where did that baby come from?"

"This is Miller," Lucky said. "He is not 'that baby', Moonlight."

To her constant embarrassment, Molly Smith's given names were Moonlight Legolas. Her parents had been '60's era hippies, Americans who fled the States for refuge in Canada when Andy received his draft notice. They'd named their daughter Moonlight for the light falling on snow the night she'd been born, and Legolas because they were big *Lord of the Rings* fans. Molly's brother, now a lawyer with a petroleum company in Calgary, endured the moniker of Samwise.

"That's the baby of that woman found dead behind the center, isn't it?" Smith said.

Smoke began to rise from scrambled eggs cooking on the stove. Andy pulled the frying pan off the heat, with a shrug of his shoulder toward his daughter.

Lucky lifted her eyes from the baby. "I remembered his name after you'd left. I'm only looking after Miller until his family can be located."

"Gee, Mom. There are government people to do that."

The phone rang and Andy Smith answered it. "Nope," he said, "she's right here." He passed it to his daughter.

"Hello?"

"Morning, Molly." Sergeant Winters. "As you seem to be up already, how'd you like to come with me to Trail? The autopsy's set for noon."

Smith's chair might have been an ejection seat on a fighter plane. "You bet, John. I'm ready."

"I'll pick you up at eleven." He hung up without bothering to say good-bye.

Smith looked at her parents. Lucky's attention was concentrated on the baby, happily sucking on the plastic teat. Andy watched his wife, his face dark and troubled.

Smith went upstairs to get dressed. Her parents had almost split up recently. But the marriage had held. After all they'd been through it was unlikely a baby would be able to come between them.

Ready well before Winters said he'd pick her up, she went back to the kitchen in search of coffee.

"Where's Mom?" she asked her father.

"Taken Miller upstairs to change him."

"Mom needs some help, Dad."

"Perhaps they'll be able to track down Miller's family today, and someone will come and get him."

"I mean help dealing with this."

Andy Smith looked into the depths of his own cup. "She's fine."

"She's certainly not fine." Smith took a mug off the shelf and poured black liquid into it. "She found a dead woman in the woods. Granted there wasn't blood and gore or anything, but the woman was still dead."

"She doesn't seem bothered by it."

"That's my point, Dad. She should be bothered. She needs to deal with it, and I don't think she is. She should see a counselor. Victim services will send someone out. I'll give them a call."

"Don't." Andy tossed the remainder of his coffee into the sink, and put his mug into the dishwasher. "Time to get to the store. Your mom can't come in long as she's looking after Miller, and we're short staffed without Duncan as it is."

"Dad. Listen to me. Despite appearances, Mom is not handling this well."

"Leave it, Molly," he said, with a sharpness in his voice she rarely heard these days. "You of all people should know that your mother would hardly appreciate any interference from the police, or anyone associated with them." He grabbed his car keys from the hook beside the back door and left.

Smith chewed on a fingernail.

Her parents hadn't exactly been overjoyed a year ago when she'd told them that she'd been accepted by the Trafalgar City Police. But she'd thought they, her father at least, were coming to accept it.

Apparently not.

As well as keys, the hooks mounted beside the kitchen door held raincoats, Lucky's gardening hat, a fanny pack that no one had claimed for several years, three dog leashes, and a pair of mittens left by Ben, Sam's son, on his last visit. Smith grabbed a leash.

"Time for a quick walk, Sylvester."

The dog scrambled out from under the kitchen table, tail wagging, mouth open, ears perked.

Upstairs, Miller began to cry.

"The baby was found only a few feet from his mother's body. If Lucky Smith hadn't heard him crying and he'd been out there all night, it's unlikely he would have survived."

Eliza Winters shivered. "I can't imagine how anyone could be so callous."

John Winters smiled at his wife. "That's why you're such a nice person."

She lifted one eyebrow. "That's why I'm such a perfectly normal person."

"Normal is not a word I'd use."

She laughed and walked behind him. Cupping his neck in her hands she began to work at the tense muscles. He groaned softly and settled back into the gentle warmth. "Down a tiny bit. That's it, there."

She applied pressure to the right spot for just a moment before taking her hands away. "Don't you have someplace to be? Like at work?"

He wiggled his shoulders, disappointed at how soon the neck rub had ended. Time was a massage would only have been second on the list of things he wanted before heading out to work. He looked at his watch. "I have thirty minutes."

She stood in front of him, bent over and kissed him deeply. Her tongue slipped into his mouth, and she pressed her chest against him. "But," she whispered between his lips, as her fingers sought out the skin between the buttons of his shirt. "I don't."

Eliza stepped back and straightened up. She touched his cheek with one finger. "I'm already late. Even considering Kootenay time. Wish me luck." She scooped up her bag and headed out the door.

Winters sighed and turned the page of the *Trafalgar Daily Gazette*. It was a thin paper, more classified ads and concert announcements than real news. Which was, he thought, definitely a good thing. Nothing about the body found last night, or the abandoned baby. Probably too late to get into today's edition.

Eliza's car roared down the driveway. God, but he loved her. They'd been married for more than twenty-five years, and every day John Winters thanked his lucky stars that she continued to put up with him. She'd been a successful model in her youth; now she did magazine ads and TV commercials. The sort of thing, she always said with a twinkle in her eye, designed to appeal to women with a social conscience and encroaching wrinkles. She kept a condo in Vancouver, somewhere to stay when she had an assignment in that city. But a resort development outside Trafalgar wanted to start advertising, and Eliza's agent had suggested she was exactly the woman to be the spokesperson for a condo project aimed at affluent, comfortably retired baby boomers.

It would be nice if she could get work that didn't require her to go away for days at a time.

He finished the paper. Time to pick up Constable Smith. He'd called to ask her to accompany him to the autopsy on a whim. Ray Lopez, his detective and the only other member of the General Investigation Section, was tied up with other business and Winters didn't want to take him away from that. Last time Smith came to an autopsy, she'd run from the room, hand over mouth.

Perfectly normal for a first-timer.

Perhaps he wanted to give her another round of exposure. It took time to build a hard shell, to make one seemingly impervious to all that the pathologist's knife would reveal. Winters had fainted at his first autopsy. The embarrassment of the experience had not been made easier when his supervisor told the whole department, in graphic and highly exaggerated detail, about the thud young John Winters made when he hit the floor.

He tossed back the dregs of coffee. Time to go. For better or for worse he'd invited Molly to tag along, so he'd better go and get her. Hopefully she'd break down soon and buy herself a car. Since her mountain bike had been stolen, she usually got around by borrowing one of her parents' cars.

"No indication of rape. Nor of sexual interference of any kind. No battery. She might have fallen asleep and died. Wrapped in the welcoming arms of Orpheus." Doctor Shirley Lee snapped off her latex gloves and tossed them into a bin.

"Don't be so melodramatic, Doc," John Winters said. "Something killed her."

Molly Smith had pressed herself against the far wall like a martyr facing the firing squad for the duration of the autopsy.

The sights were bad enough, but the sounds… When the doctor had spread the dead woman's legs apart Smith felt her own legs buckle. Russ, the doctor's assistant, had touched her arm and nodded toward the door. Smith gave him a weak smile and shook her head. Russ seemed like a nice guy, with a bit more warmth than the pathologist who might as well be replaced by a robot. Smith and Russ had chatted briefly as Doctor Lee got ready to do her job, and Smith told him about her own mother finding the baby beside the dead body of his mother. Russ had been full of sympathy, for baby as well as mother, and that helped Smith endure the ordeal of the autopsy.

"Heroin overdose," Lee said. "That is, of course, an unofficial opinion. I'll need to see the chemical analysis first. But I suspected it soon as I saw her—the size of the pupils was pretty much a giveaway, plus the blueish color of her fingertips and lips, and the discoloration to her tongue."

"Stupid. Stupid." Winters shook his head.

"You saw the marks on her arm. She'd been a regular user."

"Old marks," he said, holding the door open for the two women. The pathologist was small, not any larger than the body she'd just examined. Smith wondered if she bought her latex gloves at a specialty children's store.

"That's the interesting point," Doctor Lee said. "Other than the most recent injection site, I'd say she hadn't injected for a year at least."

"So she misjudged the quantity needed. Out of practice so to speak, and used too much," Smith suggested.

"What she did or did not do is not my concern. I can only tell you what I observed. You figure out why. You'll have my report soon. John. Constable."

They watched her walk away.

"Is she always so chatty?" Smith asked.

"Sometimes she's reluctant to offer information. But she's good at her job."

They walked out of the hospital and got into the unmarked van. "Your opinion, Molly?"

Smith started the engine. Pleased at being asked, she waited for a mint-condition, mint-colored, vintage Corvette to pass before pulling out of the parking space. "She hadn't used for a while, gave into the temptation one more time, and misjudged the amount. I've read that people who haven't taken heroin for a long time often use the amount they needed at the height of their addiction, and it's too much for them now. Tough about the kid though."

"And the restraints?"

"Restraints?"

"As well as old needle tracks on the arms, there were signs of restraint around her wrists and ankles. Very recent, Shirley thought. What do you think of that?"

Smith swore under her breath. At that vital moment, she'd probably been concentrating so hard on holding onto the contents of her stomach that she wouldn't have noticed the corpse sitting up and pointing an accusing finger at Russ.

"Kinky games, probably."

"If you didn't hear the conversation, Molly, please don't pretend to know what's going on. Ashley, our victim, had been a heroin user in the past, and she went out in one final big bang last night. But the marks of restraint around her wrists and ankles suggest that it might not have been entirely of her own volition."

Chapter Three

The woman smiled at Lucky. "It was kind of you to take the child in last night. I'll take over from here."

Lucky smiled back. "I think it would be best for Miller to stay with me for the time being."

"Don't worry, Mrs. Smith. We'll find a suitable foster family for the child. Until his natural family can be contacted."

"The child," Lucky said, "is named Miller. I'll save you the bother of looking for a *suitable* foster family and volunteer for the position. Didn't I read recently that the province is short of foster parents?"

"I am sorry, Mrs. Smith, but you haven't been approved. Therefore I can't leave him, uh, Miller, with you."

Lucky glanced at the basket in the corner beside the stove. The black head stirred, and the colorful blanket, fawns and bunny rabbits playing, shifted. Sylvester lay beside it, his brown eyes open and his ears alert.

"Miller approves." Lucky got to her feet. "If you'll pardon me, I have things to do."

"You're not equipped to handle a baby." Jody Burke remained seating. She sipped at her tea. She was with Child and Youth Services, and had only arrived in the Mid-Kootenays earlier in the week to take up her new position, a much-needed addition to the existing structure of the Ministry of Children and Family Development. Lucky hadn't met her before, and had taken an instant dislike to the woman. Burke had an aura of cold efficiency surrounding her that Lucky had often run across in people too tied to the regulation book to worry about those they were supposed to be helping. Burke's lips were outlined in a bold red lipstick that did nothing but accentuate their thinness. Silver bangles ran up her right arm, and long silver earrings dragged at her earlobes. She wore a loose flowing dress in shades of orange and red. Her gray hair was cropped short and she was close to Lucky's age.

The kitchen door flew open, the old hinges squeaking as they always did, and Andy Smith staggered in, arms laden with white plastic bags from Safeway. "Hi," he said to the visitor. "I think I got everything you wanted, Lucky." He put his shopping on the counter. Bags toppled over and containers of formula and packages of diapers spilled out. "I ran into several people in town who told me they'd heard that we've taken in this child and will be coming around with their grandchild's cast-offs. I fear we're going to be buried in baby supplies."

"So it appears I am equipped," Lucky said, giving Jody a smile. "Anything else I need, I can get from the women's support center or the second hand shops. I hope you didn't block Ms. Burke's car, dear."

"Nope. I have to get back to work. Flower's not happy at being called in for an extra shift, and I can tell you right now it's going to cost us."

"Mr. Smith," Burke said, "Please explain to your wife that as a representative of the Province of British Columbia, I'm here to claim the child until we contact his family. Which, of course, we all hope will be soon."

"I never explain anything to my wife. She doesn't allow it." Andy opened the cupboard and rummaged through cans of beans and packages of spices.

Lucky smiled at his back. She and Andy had been together for more than thirty years. Tumultuous, passionate years. Two people of strong personalities and stronger opinions. They'd disagreed on a lot of things over that time, sometimes to a fevered pitch. But in all those years, they'd never had troubles such as were propping up recently. She wanted to keep on fighting against all the injustice she saw in the world: he wanted to drift into a contented middle age, heading for a comfortable retirement.

But he'd gone shopping for the baby, and had essentially, but very politely, told Burke to piss off.

A soft murmur came from the basket by the oven. The fawns and bunnies shifted as Miller stirred. Sylvester stretched from claw to claw and stood up.

Lucky opened the door. "If you'll excuse me, the baby needs attention."

"I'm not going to drop this." Burke's red lips were pinched in disapproval, and spots of high color had broken out across her thin cheeks. "I'll be back with the authorities if I have to."

"Mind the bump on the right side of the drive," Lucky said. "It can rip into your undercarriage."

Burke stomped down the steps toward her car.

Lucky half-turned her head back toward the kitchen. "By the way, dear," she shouted. "Did you remember to call the police station and ask Officer Smith if she'll be home for dinner?"

Andy came out to the back porch and draped his arm over his wife's shoulders as they watched Jody Burke escape down their driveway. "Don't drag Molly into this, Lucky. You don't want her to be a police officer, so don't call on that position when it suits you."

Lucky shrugged his arm off. "The baby's crying," she said.

Andy decided not to go back inside for the bag of peanuts he wanted.

"She lived here. And you can't tell me anything more about her?"

Marigold, the woman called herself. "On the outside I'm merry," she'd explained. "And inside I am gold."

"I can see that," Winters said.

"Pure gold." She smiled, wiggling her fingers in the air. She wore a silver ring on every digit. She wasn't overweight, but came close, dressed in a short denim skirt and loose, colorful blouse that left one shoulder bare. Her long dreadlocks, streaked blond from the sun, were stuffed into a haphazard bundle at the top of her head. She talked without looking the police officers in the eye.

"You don't even remember her last name?"

Marigold shrugged. "I never knew it. The baby was cute. Miller. Nice name. He was an active baby, particularly when he wanted to be fed. Didn't sleep much. I read somewhere that's a sign of intelligence. Don't know if that's true or not. I need help with the rent, and Ashley paid up on time. The last girl who lived here? Wow. Can you say psycho?"

Smith leaned against the wall, saying nothing. After they left Kootenay Boundary Regional Hospital in Trail, Winters asked her to accompany him to interview the girl's roommate. He felt more comfortable, he explained, with a female officer in the room when he was questioning a young woman. The girl had given Smith a sideways glance when they arrived, and spoke only to Sergeant Winters.

The apartment was typical of many: an older, badly-maintained downtown house broken up into apartments. Small rooms, low ceilings, a whiff of mold and cooking spices. But Marigold and Ashley had decorated with a colorful hand: bright posters on the walls, multihued afghans tossed over the sagging couches, a woven rug covering part of the stained carpet.

The unmistakable scent of skunk mixed with coffee—marijuana—lingered around the room. Marigold had obviously been smoking pot when the police pressed the buzzer and identified themselves. Smith heard a toilet flushing before the door opened. Winters must have smelled it as well, but they weren't here for a minor pot bust.

"What about her mail?" he asked. "What was the name on her mail?"

"She never got any."

"No bills? No offers of cheap credit?"

"Not a thing."

"Do you have a job?"

"Of course I have a job. I wait tables at The Bishop and the Nun. That's why I didn't mind sharing with a baby. I work nights, don't get home 'till three or four, usually go to bed around six. Ash gets up with Miller." She swallowed. "I mean she got up with Miller early and they usually went out so I could sleep." She pulled a worn tissue out of the pocket of her skirt.

"Did Ashley have a job?"

"She had a baby to look after." Marigold blew her nose.

"She have a boyfriend?"

"Not that I knew. I mean, no one ever came round, least far as I saw. I'm sorry, Mr. Winters, but I really don't know anything about her. She paid her share of the rent and otherwise kept herself to herself."

"You said she went out in the mornings? Where?"

Marigold shrugged. She glanced toward a small wooden box on the side table, presumably where she kept her supply of marijuana.

"You didn't know?" Smith asked.

Marigold's eyes were red and moist and her nose ran. She looked directly at Smith for the first time. "That's quite the face you have there, cop lady. Last time I saw a bruise like that I was leaving home. If your boyfriend's knocking you around, there are places you can go for help, you know."

Smith felt herself blushing. No one would ever assume that a male officer, Dave Evans for example, had been hit by his girlfriend.

"Constable Smith's perfectly capable, Marigold," Winters said, causing Smith to blush even more. "No need for you to worry. Back to matters at hand. Are you telling us you didn't know where Ashley and Miller spent their days?"

"Honest, Mr. Winters. She didn't tell me and I didn't ask."

"She ever go out with you? In the evenings, your days off?"

"I need the money, so I don't take many days off. But no, she didn't. I don't think I ever saw Ash without Miller. Unless the baby was sleeping and then Ash was watching TV and listening for him to cry."

"She take drugs? Be honest with me, Marigold. I'm trying to find out why she died, not bust her for using."

"I never saw her take anything, honest, Mr. Winters. Why she wouldn't... wouldn't use anything."

Smith guessed that Marigold almost said that Ashley wouldn't even smoke any of her pot. Winters pretended not to notice the slip.

"What's going to happen to Miller now?"

"That's why we're trying to find her family. In the meantime, he's being well looked after. Don't worry about that."

He stood up, and Smith moved away from the wall. "Thank you for your time, Marigold. I appreciate it." He handed the girl his card. "If you can think of anything, anything at all. Who her friends were, maybe something she mentioned about her past, call me at that number."

She blew her nose again, and tossed the card on the coffee table. The table appeared to be of good quality, solid wood, careful workmanship. Someone had carved an obscenity, deeply, into the table top.

Smith and Winters clattered down the rickety stairs to the street. Winters' phone rang, and he dug it out of his shirt pocket. He said a single word and snapped it shut. "I have to get back to the station for a meet with Ray. But I could use a coffee first." Winters led the way to Big Eddie's Coffee Emporium and Smith followed, unsure as to whether she'd been invited to tag along or not.

She didn't know what her relationship to the sergeant was. They'd worked together just once, a few weeks ago, and she'd begun to get the feeling that he, if not actually liking her, at least thought she might make a competent cop one day.

He'd joined the Trafalgar City Police recently. A step down the ladder from a high-profile career in Vancouver homicide. Among the rank-and-file officers, only Smith knew something about the near-disaster of a case that had caused him to abandon the big city and seek sanctuary in the small mountain town of Trafalgar. She'd never told him she knew.

He ordered a large coffee, strong, for himself and a hot chocolate with whipped cream and chocolate sprinkles for Smith, without asking her what she wanted. Hot chocolate was what she'd ordered the last time they'd been here. It was a mite warm for hot chocolate today, but as she wasn't paying she wasn't going to object.

"You ever see her, Marigold or whatever ridiculous name she's taken on, around town, Molly?" he asked once they were back on the street.

"She works at The Bishop, that was true. She's there almost every night. She hangs around with an after-hours crowd. Cooks and bartenders and wait staff who are too wired after work to go home to bed. They usually go to someone's house, or have a private party in the back after the bars close."

"Trouble?"

"No. When the bars let out, the staff are generally stone cold sober. There are exceptions, but I haven't heard of the people from Tthe Bishop being among them."

They reached the steps of the police station. The red and white maple leaf flag hung limply in the warm, humid air. "What about Ashley?"

An image leapt into Smith's head of the tiny pale girl, laid out on the steel autopsy table, under the harsh, unforgiving white lights while Doctor Shirley Lee prepared to open her up. "You might ask Dawn," Smith said, referring to Constable Dawn Solway, who, on her own initiative, did a lot of work with the kids who drifted into Trafalgar. Seeking a pot-soaked, neo-hippie paradise and finding sky-high rents, expensive food, and not much in the way of affordable accommodation. And attentive police.

"Good idea." He tossed his coffee cup into the trash bin at the foot of the steps. "Thanks, Molly. You've been a help." He took the stairs two at a time. She crushed her own cup in one hand. But she hadn't finished the drink, and chocolate splashed onto her yellow T-shirt. She swore under her breath. She hadn't wanted hot chocolate anyway, and now she was wearing it. She looked at her watch. Not much more than an hour to go home, change into uniform and get back to town in time for her shift. And she'd been left without a lift. She lived about 12 kilometers outside of town, obviously too far to walk. Her parents' store, Mid-Kootenay Adventure Vacations, was located on Front Street, only a couple of blocks from the police station. She set off down the hill toward town. The sun was hot on her face, but black clouds, heavy with rain, were gathering behind Koola Glacier.

Bloody John Winters.

◇◇◇

Lucky looked up as her daughter staggered in. Moonlight's short hair was plastered to her scalp and the yellow T-shirt clung to the girl's generous curves.

"Raining?" Lucky said.

"No, Mom. It was so hot I went for a swim in the fucking river."

Lucky turned back to the baby in her arms. Miller's dark blue eyes were open wide and he waved pudgy fists in the air. "Mind your language." Lucky said.

"Fuck. There, I said it. Now he's contaminated for life." Moonlight kicked off her shoes. "I need a car. Dad was not pleased at having to give me a lift."

"I thought you were with John Winters."

"Fuck him too." Moonlight stomped out of the kitchen.

Lucky stroked the baby's soft cheek. Miller looked back at her, and Lucky thought she might have seen the trace of a smile.

Angry footsteps pounded up the stairs and down the hall.

Moonlight. Molly. Her poor Moonlight.

"I might as well retire for all the time I'm spending at the store." Andy came through the door. "Tell your daughter that adult children should be living on their own. I was in the middle of signing up a big group for a family-reunion weekend kayaking trip when Molly marched in demanding that I lend her the car. As that would have left me stranded, I hurried through with the family."

"Did they sign up?"

"Thankfully, yes."

"You've found someone to replace Duncan as tour guide then?"

"You know Jeff who fills in now and again for that company up the valley? He's been looking for regular work. I think he'll do. Now all I need is someone to look after the books." He glared at his wife, the office manager. "And to be left alone to run my company."

"I have been," Lucky said, "away from work for precisely six hours. Quite understandably the entire business has collapsed into ruins in my absence, but one must make accommodations. Suppose I died suddenly, what would you do then?"

"Don't joke, Lucky." Andy rummaged through the cupboards. "Ah, there you are." He grabbed a bag of peanuts in the shell.

Overhead, a door slammed.

"As you aren't using it, Molly can take your car to get back to town. I have to go."

"We have to talk, Andy," Lucky said. "About Moonlight."

"Okay. Later. Bye." He ran out, clutching the peanuts.

Lucky looked at Miller. Although the baby resisted, his eyes began to close. Andy's car started up and pulled out of the driveway.

Moonlight slammed another door.

After she'd been injured in the horrible conclusion to the Montgomery murder last month, Moonlight had gone back to work as soon as possible. She'd reluctantly visited the psychologist the police department used for officers who'd experienced trauma on the job. After a week, she'd blown the therapist off as a waste of time, taken leave, and gone to Vancouver. To visit friends, she told her mother. Lucky knew that Moonlight had no friends in Vancouver. Graham's grave was in Calgary, where his parents lived. She suspected her daughter had gone to visit the spot where Graham died. An alley in the Downtown Eastside. Lucky called Terry Richards, a good friend who'd recently moved to the coast, and asked her to go down to the Eastside and look for Moonlight. Terry had found the girl, squatting in the alley, holding a bouquet of deep purple roses, amid the detritus of

Canada's most notorious neighborhood. Lucky'd asked her friend merely to check on Moonlight, but Terry stepped forward and, not saying a word, held out her hand. Moonlight gripped it and allowed herself to be pulled to her feet and led toward the lights of the street. She dropped the flowers into the alley behind her.

Graham and Moonlight had been engaged, waiting until she got her Masters' degree in Social Work from the University of Victoria before getting married. But Graham had died, in a totally preventable incident, working Vancouver's Downtown Eastside. Moonlight quit the MSW program, drifted aimlessly for a while, and then suddenly announced that she was going to become a police officer.

As much as that career decision had horrified Lucky, she'd been slowly, and somewhat reluctantly, coming to realize that the choice might have been the right one for her daughter. Moonlight was regaining her confidence, her strength. And, to Lucky's delight, the girl had begun to think about dating again. Encouraged by Lucky herself into a catastrophic situation, Moonlight went on her first date since Graham, only to be horribly betrayed. At first she appeared to handle it well, and Lucky breathed a sigh of relief. But then Moonlight had her hair cut: the new look startling, dramatic. Andy told her she looked good, but Lucky feared the cut was a sign of something deeper. And then Moonlight went to Vancouver.

To mourn at the site of Graham's death.

Terry had gathered the girl up, walked her to her car, and driven ten hours to Trafalgar to deliver her to her parents' door.

For two days, Moonlight played with Sylvester in the garden, took long walks along the river, listened to music in her room.

On the third morning, Constable Smith put on her uniform, the one with the blue stripe down the pant leg, the badge of the Trafalgar City Police (since 1895) on the shoulder, Kevlar vest, belt heavy with equipment, including the black gun her mother hated so much, and went back to work.

Nothing, Lucky knew, had been resolved.

Chapter Four

As John Winters walked into the GIS office, his partner, Detective Ray Lopez, was carefully removing a few dead leaves from the row of African violets he tended on the sunny windowsill overlooking George Street. He had not been happy to return from his daughter's wedding to find that Winters hadn't bothered to water them. Two of the plants almost died, and Lopez was carefully nursing them back to health, tossing angry glances at Winters every time he did so.

Looking nothing like his name might suggest, Ray Lopez was blue-eyed and redheaded, pale with a splash of freckles across his cheeks. He'd been adopted by a Spanish family. The Celtic looks were a startling contrast to his sometimes casual Latin habits.

Winters dropped into a chair and rolled it across the floor. "Heroin overdose for sure, Doc says." He looked at the painting on the wall. His ugly words a sharp contrast to the scene of a child playing in a mountain meadow filled with yellow flowers.

"Poor kid." Lopez shook his head. He was a good bit shorter than Winters, compact muscle slowly turning to fat on his wife's famous cooking and meals served at their legendary family gatherings. He had four daughters of his own, and a soft spot for young women in trouble. "Regular user?"

"Apparently not. Tracks on her arms, but Lee says they're more than a year old, at least, and she couldn't see anything more recent. Except for yesterday's, of course."

"Only takes one."

"Yup."

"Who was she?"

"There's the funny thing, I don't know. No last name, no friends I can find. No sign of a boyfriend. Gave cash to her roommate to pay the rent, never got any mail. Kept to herself, her and her baby. Lucky Smith said she came to the support center sometimes. I'll pop by and talk to Lucky later, ask if she's remembered a last name since we talked."

"You got any idea where she might have gotten the stuff?"

"I hate to think it might have been here in Trafalgar. Check with your guy if he's seen the dead girl with any of the people he's watching. If so, it's bad news."

Marijuana was plentiful in Trafalgar; plentiful, inexpensive and, according to the users, of the highest quality. Harder drugs were not unknown. Lately a bit of heroin had been spreading through the Kootenays, and the RCMP thought it originated in Trafalgar. Lopez was working hard trying to find the source.

"There may be a complication," Winters said. "There were signs of restraint around Ashley's wrists and ankles, very recent, put there within a day or two, Lee said. And it looks as if the girl struggled against them."

"Sex games gone beyond her control? Maybe she was a working girl?"

"That's what I thought, at first. But the roommate says Ashley never left the baby."

Lopez laughed. A laugh without mirth. "After all these years in this job, John, nothing would surprise me. It's possible she specialized in turning tricks for guys who get a kick out of doing mommy while baby watches. You might want to have the kid checked out."

Winters looked into his partner's blue eyes, and his stomach turned over. But Lopez was right. "I'll get Barb to call a public health nurse to have a look. Ashley paid her rent in cash. Like the heroin, she had to get the money from somewhere. Someone has to know who she is."

Winters rubbed his thumb across the face of his watch. "The paper called earlier, looking for a quote," he said, to himself as much as to Lopez. Winters often thought out loud; he liked to have a sounding board. "Haven't had a chance to call them back yet. We're not letting anything out about the cause of death, or that we think it's suspicious. Just saying we'd like to talk to people who knew her. She went out most days, the roommate said. In the morning." He stood up and went to stand at the window. The sun was shining, but it was raining. A laughing couple, young, happy, ran up the hill, one arm around each other's waist, the other trying to fend off the raindrops. It wouldn't matter if they got wet, he thought, they'd have fun drying each other off. Jolene, who worked at Big Eddie's, came down the hill, the beads in her hair bouncing behind her.

He idly stroked the leaf of one of Ray's violets.

"Step away from the plant," Lopez said, his voice pitched low and slow to make him sound like an American TV cop. "And no one gets hurt."

"Sorry. Forgot." Winters turned back to face the room. "Okay, this is how we're going to play it. You have to remain on the heroin case. We have too much going on to drop it now, and anyway there might be a connection with the girl Ashley. You don't have any more daughters getting married this summer, do you?"

Lopez grinned. "Vacation all finished for the year, boss. Although I do have a ticket in tonight's big lottery. Thirty mil on the line."

"That ticket wins and we'll be closing the whole department. We're all in on it. I'll back you up and take the Ashley case. In my gut, I think she was killed. Tied up and shot full of heroin. Whether the dosage was intended to be enough to kill her's for the courts to decide. But even if she was tied up, quote-unquote, voluntarily," he made marks in the air with his hands, "and took the drug of her own free will, I intend to find out who and where she got it from. We done?"

"Done, boss."

Winters walked down the hall to the office administrator's office.

She was at her desk. Typing with a speed that had her fingers a blur of motion. Barb was the longest serving member of the department. Even more than Jim Denton, the daytime front-desk constable. The young guys joked that over the ages Denton had worn an imprint of his big boots into the floor underneath the console.

"Barb," Winters said, very politely. They were always polite to Barb, otherwise she might report her displeasure to the Chief Constable, who lived in fear of her. "Can you please find out who the Ashley Doe baby's been placed with? Then find a public health nurse and set up an appointment for us to go and have a look at him. When you have a minute, but sooner would be better than later."

"Sure," she said.

"And remind me what the number for the *Gazette* is. For some reason I keep forgetting."

"I'll e-mail it to you," she said. "Or you'll lose it between here and your office."

"Thanks. The cop brain is genetically programmed to avoid any and all contact with journalists. I couldn't remember that number if I tried."

"But you won't try. You haven't told me what you'll be bringing to the annual summer pot luck at my place." Barb turned back to her computer. "I expect the Winters' family specialty."

"We're working on making a decision. It's not easy." He himself couldn't cook anything that didn't involve a microwave, and Eliza was worse. They'd have to buy something, and hope it looked homemade. As always, the thought of his wife lifted his heart just a bit. Twenty-five years of enthusiastic sex verses home cooked meals. He'd always known that he'd made the right choice.

Lucky Smith, nee Lucy Casey, had never had a fondness for the police. Pigs, she and her friends called them in their youth. She'd been arrested for assaulting a police officer at the infamous Democratic convention in Chicago in 1968. When, in her opinion, the police had rioted. She'd worn that arrest as a badge of honor for many years. She'd been a sophomore at the University of Seattle when her boyfriend, a math student who failed his year because he spent more time on campus politics than on math, had been drafted. Andy Smith had asked her to come to Canada with him. Until the day he died, Andy's father, Andrew Smith Senior, had refused to have anything to do with his draft-dodging son.

But Andy Smith Junior and Lucy Casey had settled in Trafalgar where they'd set about making a life and a family of their own.

With one child a lawyer for a big oil company and the other a cop, Lucky sometimes reflected on the irony.

She'd finished feeding Miller, and was settling the baby down for a nap when the phone rang. Sergeant Winters asking if he could stop by to talk about Ashley. Moonlight aside, Lucky still didn't care much for the police, force of habit perhaps, but there was something about John Winters that made her think she could be persuaded to change her mind. He was in his late-forties, early fifties maybe. Tall and lean and long-legged, with short black and white hair and a neat silver mustache. Few men these days could carry off a mustache without looking gay, but John Winters managed. When they were in college, Andy had sported a highly-fashionable "Fu Manchu" mustache that dripped down the sides of his chin. Blond, for heaven's sake. The very thought of it made her cringe.

Lucky heard the car before she saw it, and went to the door to greet her visitors. John had brought company. A short fat woman, with dull brown hair tied in a tight bun and round red cheeks got out of the van.

John was dressed in casual beige pants and a loose brown shirt. The shirt, she knew from asking Moonlight, was worn untucked to cover his gun, baton, and handcuffs.

"Alice," Lucky said with genuine pleasure. "What brings you here?"

Alice Stanton flushed, and looked for John Winters to answer.

"I'm sorry to bother you, Lucky, but I need Alice to have a look at the baby. Miller, is it?"

"Yes. But he's sleeping."

"I'll try not to disturb him, Lucky," the nurse said, giving her an uncomfortable smile. "But, well, it's required, you see."

"He's perfectly fine. You saw him last night, John. I haven't starved him in the meantime."

"You're not being accused of anything, Lucky. Please, let Mrs. Stanton check the child out. I have a few questions to ask you about Ashley anyway. Is that coffee I smell? I haven't had a cup since breakfast."

Lucky stood aside and let the visitors in. She could tell when she was being manipulated. Coffee indeed. Like cops didn't drink coffee all day long. Jody Burke may have sic'ed the authorities onto her, but Lucky knew they'd find nothing wrong with the way she was looking after Miller. However, it did seem rather unusual to find an officer as senior as Sergeant Winters sent out to check on an abandoned child case.

"While I'm here," he said, "I'd like to ask you a few questions, Lucky. If you don't mind?"

Whether she minded or not was irrelevant. "Pull up a chair. I'll get the coffee."

Alice found the baby, asleep in his bed by the oven, without directions. The good people of Trafalgar had gathered enough baby goods to supply every child in Oliver Twist's orphanage. Formula, jars of baby food, clothes, blankets, mobiles, books, rattles, toys. Plus baseball bats, footballs, building blocks, and puzzles. Even a pair of soccer shoes, which would fit a healthy teenager. Everything but a stroller. Fortunately, the women at the support center had found an old-fashioned baby carriage, the type called a pram, with big wheels and a high handlebar. It might have been the height of fashion in World War II, but it was better than keeping the baby in a basket on the floor.

Alice leaned over and gathered the sleeping bundle into her arms. "Why don't I leave you two to chat," she said. Sounding as falsely cheerful as a character in a Grade One school play.

"Sure," Lucky said.

Alice carried the baby into the living room.

"I haven't had him for twenty-four hours." Lucky poured coffee into mugs. "No time to call my coven to gather and practice our child abuse rituals."

"I don't want coffee, so please sit down," Winters said. His eyes were dark and serious, his mouth set in a tight line. "This child was found in highly unusual circumstances. You'd be surprised at some of the things that go on in this world."

She fell into a chair. "Surprised, probably not. I've been around the block a few times myself. I'm sorry, John. I sometimes make inappropriate comments when I'm feeling tense. I made chocolate chip cookies a bit ago, would you like one? I don't cook much any more, what with the store and all my activities, but now that I'm home with Miller, when he was sleeping I discovered an urge to bake. Probably something going back to the stone age—throw that mastodon on the fire while the kids are busy playing with rocks."

The edges of his mouth turned up. "A cookie would be nice."

Miller cried out in the other room, and Lucky's ears pricked up.

"You know Alice is taking care," John said.

"She's a good woman." Lucky got to her feet and pulled a square tin down from the shelf and arranged cookies on a white plate. And tried not to listen to the sounds coming from the next room. Alice wouldn't find any signs of abuse on the baby. But Lucky worried, nevertheless.

Winters took a cookie. It was rich and heavy with butter and chocolate. Lucky served coffee. "You might think you don't need it," she said, "but nothing goes better with cookies than good coffee."

He accepted a cup and added neither milk nor sugar. "Tell me about Ashley. Last night you said you didn't know much about her, not even her last name. Have you remembered anything?"

Lucky nibbled on a cookie of her own. "I've been thinking about it all day. She never gave us a last name, and we don't insist. The purpose of the center is to help young mothers with basic skills—caring for their babies, of course, but also things like preparing nutritious meals for older children. That's what I do there. I give cooking lessons. Nothing fancy; I just try to show them how to prepare a healthy, satisfying meal on a budget, and discuss shopping tips. You'd be surprised at how many of these young mothers think choosing food and preparing their own meals is too expensive. And too difficult. They only need to be shown how much better value, and nutrition, they get from fresh food. We teach them how easy it can be."

"When did Ashley start coming to the center?"

"A month ago, maybe. Six weeks." The girl had been an enigma. Hanging at the back of the group, reluctant to come in. Sometimes gone before Lucky had finished the class. But always with her baby tied to her side in a wrap-around blanket. "She bottle-fed Miller," Lucky said. "We supplied her with formula. It's one of the services we provide, although we encourage the women to breast feed. I remember that because it's unusual around here. Young women these days are so keen on breast feeding. And more power to them."

"Who were her friends?"

"I don't know that she had any."

"There must have been one or two women in particular she talked to. Mothers always seem to hang out together."

Lucky thought of the packs of young women, dressed in long skirts or baggy cargo pants, pushing strollers through town. Laughing women. Laughing children. Fresh faces, shiny hair, colorful clothes.

"I never saw Ashley with anyone. She always arrived alone. She kept to the back of the class, and she left alone, usually early. I try to take each group shopping with me at least once—some of them don't know their way around the supermarket. But I don't think Ashley ever came. I can't recall her even talking to any of the other moms. I tried to talk to her a few times. I ticked Miller under the chin and pretended I wanted a cuddle so I could unfold his blanket to check for signs of neglect or abuse. But the baby was plump and, well loud, if not quite cheerful, color good and eyes bright. The mother was polite, but not interested in making conversation." Lucky let out a lungful of air. "I should have tried harder, shouldn't I?"

"Regrets," Winters said. "If we eat enough regrets we don't need food. You think I don't regret that I didn't follow up on those stolen bikes more aggressively?"

Lucky lifted her eyes from the pile of chocolate chip cookie crumbs she'd been assembling on her plate. She'd never thought for a moment that John Winters would be sensitive enough to understand what effect last month's mountain bike theft case had truly had on Moonlight. Apparently he did.

They watched as Sylvester stretched luxuriously and strolled to his water bowl. The big dog drank with noisy enthusiasm.

"Did you see Ashley on Thursday," he asked. "During the day?"

Lucky thought. "No. Come to think of it, I hadn't seen her for several days. Not since…" Her voice dropped away, and she stared at the pile of cookie crumbs.

"Since?" He prompted.

She looked up. Horrified to realize that she'd completely forgotten the details of her last conversation with the dead woman. "Since she told me she'd seen someone from her past and he'd help her."

"What did you think of that?"

"So little I didn't even remember it until now." Lucky shook her head. Those girls, the lost ones, the young mothers with their babies and no one else, often had some mythical man about to swoop in and rescue them. It wasn't Lucky's role to disabuse them of that notion. Although she sometimes wished she could.

"Are you sure she said it was a he?"

"Definitely. It's always a man, and if it hadn't been it would have had more impact on me."

"Did she say anything about him?"

"No. Just someone from her past. I thought she was making it sound all dark and mysterious to make herself seem important. I paid her no mind. I'm sorry, John. That was foolish of me."

"Don't let it bother you. We don't usually hang on to a person's every word, thinking that we'll be questioned by the police later."

She gave him a soft smile. Grateful for the kind words, but knowing that her failure to dig deeper would bother her a great deal.

"When was that?"

Lucky let out a heavy breath. "Four or five days ago, maybe? Not a week. I just know that I didn't see her again, not until I found her...." Her cookie rose in her chest, and she stopped talking.

"Thank you for your time, Lucky," he said, getting to his feet. "If you remember anything, anything at all Ashley might have said, that last time or any other. Anyone who seemed to be friends with her..."

"I know where to find you." She held her hands to her stomach and began to stand up. "Alice?" she said.

"Oh, right." He raised his voice. "Ready, Alice?"

The nurse came out of the living room, so quickly Lucky suspected she'd been listening at the door. Miller was asleep in the nurse's arms.

Alice laid the sleeping baby into his pram and carefully tucked the blanket around him. "Such a cutie pie," she said. She looked at John Winters and gave him a shake of the head that Lucky suspected she wasn't supposed to see.

Winters sighed and let out a well-suppressed aura of tension. And Lucky realized that Alice wasn't here to check up on her baby care.

She felt tears in the corner of her eyes at the ugliness of the world.

Chapter Five

The bars closed at 2:00 a.m. Spilling into an area of about three city blocks, several hundred people, many of them feeling no pain, staggered out onto the streets.

Constable Smith rolled her shoulders and shifted the considerable weight of her gun belt. Late in the afternoon, when she'd passed the big sign outside the drug store that displayed the time and temperature, it had said it was 42 degrees Celsius, 107 Fahrenheit. Although it was now early hours of the morning, the temperature didn't seem to have dropped much. She suspected that if she were so inclined, she could fry an egg underneath the Kevlar vest, in the gap between her breasts.

"You okay, Molly?" Dave Evans said. "I mean after that hit you got yesterday. Nasty, eh?"

"Open heart surgery was required," she said, through clenched teeth. She'd saved Evan's hide from a fire-bomb not long ago, and about all he could offer in thanks was one condescending remark after another. "But, I'm happy to say," she continued, "I survived the ordeal, and here I am in fighting form. No need to worry, Dave, your back's safe."

He shifted in his size-twelve boots, and wiped sweat off his forehead with the back of one hand.

People began coming out of the bars, moving into the streets. Women laughed, at a pitch high enough to have ravens falling from the trees; young men strutted their stuff. A few people shied away from the watching police officers but most smiled and nodded.

A man left the bar, taking swigs from an open can of beer. Evans walked up to him, and ordered him to pour it into the gutter.

Smith put her hands on her belt. Her bra itched against the skin of her chest. She wanted to dig inside, root around, find the source of the itch and scratch it out.

Which would not be a very professional thing to do.

"Hey, sweet thing. Wanna have some fun?"

Sure, Smith thought, *after I blow my brains out.* The man standing in front of her was young, his black hair cut almost to the scalp. His body formed the perfect male triangle of strong shoulders, compact stomach, thin hips. She'd never seen him before.

He held a homemade cigarette between his fingers. "Nice bruise you got there. Like it rough, do you? What a coincidence, so do I." He lifted his right hand to his mouth, and blew smoke into her face.

Coffee and skunk.

"Are you trying to provoke me?"

"Perish the thought. Aren't you just the cutest thing? Whatca doin' after work?"

Another puff of fragrant smoke.

She grabbed his arm. "Get rid of that, fast."

He drew a deep breath on his cigarette. "No way, sweet thing."

"Let's see some ID."

His eyes opened wide. "What?"

"ID. Now. Move it." She grabbed the cigarette out of his hand.

"What the hell? Back off, lady. That belongs to me."

She pinched off the burning end and put the cigarette into her shirt pocket. "You can't produce identification, then I'm taking you in. What's your name?"

"Okay, okay." He dug through his pockets. Pulling out an Illinois driver's license he held it in front of her face. She grabbed it and read the information into the radio at her shoulder.

"Thank you, Mr. McIntyre. We'll continue this conversation down at the station." She took hold of his arm.

"What the hell?"

She spoke into the radio. "Trafalgar five-one. Outside The Bishop. I need a pickup." Dispatch cracked affirmation. "I'm taking you in for possession of an illegal narcotic. I strongly advise you not to resist."

Evans turned from watching the crowd leaving the bar. "You need some help, Constable Smith?" This time she didn't take offense at his offer of assistance. She would have done the same for him.

The curious were beginning to gather. Two men, also strong and fit with shaved heads, watched but said nothing.

"Can you believe this shit?" McIntyre said to them.

"You going to come nicely, or add to the charges?" Smith said, watching the friends out of the corner of her eye.

They shrugged and looked away, melting into the crowd beginning to gather. Smith saw her old enemy, Meredith Morgenstern, watching them.

"Damn it," McIntyre said.

"We're good here, Constable Evans," Smith said.

A marked car pulled up, and McIntyre, still protesting, but offering no physical resistance, was briefly searched, handcuffed, and loaded into the back. Smith got in the passenger seat, and they drove the few blocks to the station.

Smith did the paperwork. McIntyre had no record, no outstanding warrants, so was released with orders to return tomorrow.

He spat on the floor, barely missing the toe of Smith's boot. "Fascist police state," he said. "I'll tell everyone back home what Canada's really like. I thought you were supposed to be so goddamned liberal."

Ingrid, the night dispatcher, laughed as the door slammed. "B.C. tourism'll be after you, Molly."

"I might set up my own tour company: jails of the Kootenays." She took advantage of the stop at the station to use the washroom before going back onto the streets. Trafalgar had the reputation of being lenient on minor marijuana infractions, but the police didn't take too well to having it flaunted in their faces.

On her way to the door, she walked behind Ingrid's desk to have a look at the monitors watching the cells downstairs. Number three was empty.

"Hey," she said. "Where's my guy?"

"Just left," Ingrid said. "You let him go."

"Not him. The guy in three." Smith pointed to her lip. "The one who bopped me."

"No one there when I got here."

Smith ran to check the files. Brian Atkins had been released first thing this morning. Case dropped. No further action to be taken. She swore with passion. The guy had attacked a cop, assault PO, and was released without even a fine. Sometimes she wondered why they bothered at all.

◇◇◇

"How'd it go?" John Winters asked his wife.

"Well, I think. But you know how it is. You think you bombed and they can't wait to have you, and you think you're a star and they won't return your calls."

"I'll always return your calls."

She laughed, and handed him the newspaper.

"Seriously, it's a heavy money gig. They're prepared to shell out big, big bucks for this campaign."

"Thus they can afford you."

She ignored that. "But…"

Winters looked up from the paper. The headline and half the front page dealt with a woman's body found in the woods in Trafalgar. Below the fold, preparations for the visit of a federal cabinet minister took up the space.

"But what?"

She turned her back and fussed with bread, the toaster oven, butter, and a pot of jam. He admired her rear end wrapped in snug beige shorts. "I don't know if they offer me the job if I want to be on their side of this issue."

He pulled his eyes away from her lovely rump. "Sit down and tell me what's happening."

She sat. "M&C Developments, right? After the M, Reginald Montgomery, died, the C, Frank Clemmins, found another partner. Pretty darn quick, too. An investor from the States, Seattle I think, name of Steve Blacklock. Steve brought in new money, new ideas, and they're going after serious players to invest in their resort."

"And you have a problem with it?"

"I think I do. There was this bunch of protesters standing outside when I drove up. The usual stuff, homemade placards, pictures of grizzly bears, intense people. I stopped to talk to them." She raised one hand. "Yeah, yeah, big mistake. They told me if the resort goes ahead it will destroy the Grizzly habitat, as well as do all sorts of other nasty stuff. I don't know if I want the contract, John."

"So refuse it. We'll move into a homeless shelter, eat out of garbage cans, and I'll have to sell my body on the street. But hey, we can do it."

Eliza didn't laugh. Her eyes burned with a green fire. "There are people who sacrifice a lot for their principles, you know, dear."

He felt like a schoolboy caught with his hand in the church collection box. "I do."

"All I'm saying is that I might have to decide."

His cell phone rang, and Winters flipped it open. Eliza glared at him before reaching into the fridge for a strawberry yogurt. She carried it into the living room.

"Good morning, John," Doctor Shirley Lee said. "Hope I'm not disturbing you."

"Always a pleasure, doc. Surprised to hear from you on a Saturday. What's up?"

"Not much I can talk about on the phone," she said. "I'll have my prelim report ready on Monday. But there is one thing you should know ASAP."

"Shoot."

"Constable Smith said something to Russ before I began the autopsy. I barely registered it at the time. But when I was writing up my report, I remembered."

"What?"

"She told Russ that the woman's baby had been found in the woods, close to the body."

"The baby's fine. He's in care while we try to locate the family. Why are you asking?"

"The woman you're calling Ashley Doe has never given birth."

"Sergeant wants to see you, Molly. Said to go to his office soon as you arrive."

"Why?"

"I forgot to ask. Do you want to wait here while I interrupt whatever he's doing to check?"

"Who pissed in your cheerios?"

"The grandkids are visiting. Haven't slept for three days."

"Good thing you work here then, Jim, lots of chances to get some shut eye." Constable Dawn Solway came out of the lunchroom, wiping her hands on a paper towel.

"If I wasn't so amused, I'd laugh," Denton said.

Smith went down the corridor to the GIS office. The door was open and Winters was at his desk, typing fast with two fingers.

"Jim says you want to see me?"

"Come on in."

She pulled up a chair. "Ray's violets are looking great."

"Please, don't remind me. I'm sure he's going to carve 'plant killer' into my tombstone.

"I have an appointment at three-thirty to go around to Ashley's apartment and look through her things. I would've liked to have done it earlier, but the roommate was insistent that she needs her sleep before going to work at five. But, as it's now three and you're on duty, you can come with me."

"Okay." Smith tried not to look pleased. Her shift was from three to three, and it could be pretty boring out on the streets in the late afternoon. And any chance to be involved in GIS work would do her in good stead, she hoped, if she were to make detective some day. But—she poured cold water on her ambition—she needed to graduate from probationary Constable first.

"This girl, Ashley, is proving to be as elusive as a puff of smoke. Dawn says she doesn't know much about her. She showed up in town six weeks or so ago, baby on her hip. No big deal: many girls here have babies. She didn't go out at night, hang around the bars or street corners. I'm checking with all the guys to see if anyone ever stopped her and asked for ID, but so far no one has. I've had photocopies made from a pic taken at the autopsy, the best they could do considering the circumstances, and we'll be asking around. I'm hoping that a bar somewhere will have carded her."

"She looked very young. Might be underage," Smith said. "Maybe she went somewhere else looking for fun."

"Her roommate says she didn't have a car. No reason that means she didn't have access to one, of course. But without a name, it's going to be hard to find out."

Winters glanced at his watch. "We've just enough time to get a coffee at Eddies." He stood up and put on a light jacket. Smith stood also.

"How's Christa?" he asked.

Smith did not want to talk about it. Christa Thompson, her best friend, her former best friend, had recently been badly beaten by a stalker. "Doing good, although she's anxious about the trial." Smith only knew that because Christa had spoken to Lucky. She hung up the phone if Molly tried to talk to her.

"She shouldn't be worried. We've got him good."

They clambered down the steps of the police station. Christa was not, in fact, doing good at all. She was a mess, afraid to go out, not starting on the new term's university courses. Just sitting around her apartment all day, blaming Molly Smith for all her troubles. As Smith blamed herself. Lucky told her that Christa needed time to heal, mentally even more than physically, and when Charlie's trial was over, she'd be better equipped to deal with her trauma.

Smith doubted it.

She'd eaten before leaving home, so refused Winters' offer of a drink. He drank his coffee on the two block walk to Ashley Doe's apartment, and tossed the half-finished cup into a garbage can outside the door.

Joan Jones had to be the most boring name in the entire world. As soon as she escaped from the stifling environment of the parental home in Winnipeg, she'd given herself the name she'd been born to have. Now she was Marigold. And Marigold was not pleased to have the cops around again.

Dead or not, Ashley deserved the privacy she guarded so carefully. And Marigold intended to respect that.

She opened the door to Ashley's bedroom and stood aside to let in the pretty uniformed woman and the older man in casual clothes. The room was small, but neat. The single bed was made, covered with a tattered beige candlewick bedspread. The only other furniture was an old dresser, the front of one drawer hanging off, another missing altogether. The walls were papered with posters, not of rock stars, but scientists. Albert Einstein, with his big halo of white hair. Marigold thought she recognized Isaac Newton because the dude was holding an apple and looking up into a tree. She didn't know the other old guys in long robes surrounded by stars or primitive scientific instruments.

"She was into the history of science," the female cop said, "that's interesting."

"Oh, those," Marigold's lips tightened in distaste. "The previous girl left those. I told you she was psycho."

Smith, the cop, looked through the things on the top of the dresser. A hairbrush, a stick of deodorant, almost finished, a scattering of colorful elastic bands, three baby bottles, clean. A tin of formula and a blue pacifier.

It was all Marigold could do not to shove the cop's nosy hands aside. These were Ashley's things. She didn't have much, but it all deserved to be treated with respect. Smith opened the dresser drawers while her boss watched. Marigold wondered why a woman not much older than she would be working as a cop. Dressed like a storm trooper, doing what a bunch of old guys told her to do. She felt that Constable Smith was judging her, and Ashley as well, by the way she picked through Ashley's few things.

Not that she'd had much: piles of disposable diapers, sleeper suits, blue mostly, neatly folded. For herself, summer clothes only, long skirts, loose tops. "Do you know if she intended to leave at the end of summer, Marigold?" Winters asked.

She shrugged. "No idea."

Practical white underwear. A single pair of sturdy sports sandals standing against the wall. Smith found six books underneath Ashley's underwear in the bottom drawer. Mass-market paperbacks, well-read, by big name authors. She handed them to Winters and he checked the flyleaf and flicked through the pages. Marigold could tell by his face that he didn't find anything of importance in the books.

A book was half under the bed. Smith bent over and pulled it out. She showed it to Winters. He sighed, heavily. The book was on caring for your baby.

Smith dropped to her knees and peeked under the bed. "It's dark, and hard to see," she said. "Bring me a broom, Marigold, so I can fish around under here."

No point in arguing. Marigold did as she was asked, resentment at being ordered around by a woman her own age building up inside her.

Smith pulled out a crumpled tissue, another pacifier, a small amount of dust, and a crumpled flyer protesting the Grizzly Resort.

The woman handed the flyer to the man. He read it. "Was Ashley interested in this issue?"

Ashley was intensely interested in the Grizzly Resort. It was about the only thing, other than Miller, that Ash seemed to care about. Marigold shrugged. "She said we have to take steps to preserve the environment now or there won't be anything left for children such as Miller to appreciate."

She hadn't, in fact, said any such thing. She'd been interested in the resort, without taking sides. But that's what people who were opposed to the resort said, so Marigold repeated it. Something to keep the cops happy.

Winters held up the flyer. "Did she go to this demonstration? Or any others?"

She had. And came back unusually subdued. She hadn't said much about it, or what she thought of the protesters' arguments. When Marigold tried to discuss it, Ashley said she hadn't made up her mind. Personally Marigold figured that if the resort went up, the bears would go somewhere else. Plus it looked like there'd be some nice bars and restaurants at the resort, and she was hoping to apply for a job. The tips were bound to be a lot better than she got at The Bishop and the Nun.

She chewed her lip. The people who cared about grizzly bears weren't the type to kill someone like Ashley. And the people who were developing the resort were under enough pressure from environmental groups without having the cops investigating them. They might just pack up and take their resort money to China or somewhere. And Marigold's hopes for a job with them.

"I don't know," she said, looking directly at Sergeant Winters. "She didn't say if she'd gone or not. I didn't think to ask. Sorry."

Winters said nothing. The silence hung in the room. Out on the street, someone yelled and a woman laughed. The room was hot and stuffy and the scent of baby—dirty diapers, baby powder, warm skin—still lingered.

"Look," Marigold said at last, "I have to be getting ready for work, so…"

"We found a key to the apartment on her," Winters said. "Do you know if she had any other keys?"

Ashley kept the key to her safety deposit box inside one of her socks. The cop hadn't felt it when going through Ashley's things. A couple of times, Ashley had gone somewhere for the whole day, and returned with enough cash for the rent and what little she and Miller needed. Marigold didn't know where she went, or who she got a lift with. None of her business. As long as Ashley came back with rent money.

"Nope," she said in answer to his question.

Marigold led the way to the door. Winters was still holding one of the paperback novels and the flyer.

The police walked down the stairs. The bulletproof vest the woman wore must be a nightmare to wear in this heat, not to mention the dark clothes and all that equipment she had to lug around.

Ashley hadn't told Marigold much about her life. She was a private person. But they'd sometimes shared the odd bottle of wine on Marigold's nights off, and she'd confessed that her real name was Jennifer, Jennifer Watson. Not as awful as Joan Jones, but still you couldn't blame her for changing it. She was from Oakville, Ontario, which was near Toronto. Marigold was from Winnipeg, and she figured that beat any city on the boring scale.

If the police managed to discover Ashley's real name, Marigold thought, they'd just hand Miller over to Ashley—Jennifer's—family. Better that the baby find a nice new family to adopt him.

Winters carried the dog-eared paperback and the torn flyer advertising a demonstration against the Grizzly Resort down the steps. A man eyed Smith, in her uniform, suspiciously. He was old, probably her parents' age, with gray hair tied into a pony-tail that fell almost to his waist and a beard to match. His mustache curled up at the edges. She wondered if all that hair was designed to cover up the fact that he had almost nothing on top of his skull.

"What's interesting about that book?" she asked.

Winters stopped walking and flipped the book open to the inside front cover. Smith leaned closer to see. The page was stamped with the faded address of a second-hand bookstore in Vancouver.

"If Ashley bought this book herself, which is a big if, as it seems to have been passed from hand to hand since," he flipped to the front matter and read, "it was published in 1998, then we know she was in Vancouver at sometime in her life. Christ, Molly, every broken-down Canadian kid ends up in Vancouver eventually. This gives us nothing. Absolutely nothing.

"A murder investigation starts with the victim," he said, more to himself than to Smith. "Who hated/feared/loved/had an accident with/even a chance encounter with the victim so that he or she ended up killing her? It all flows from there. But this girl, Ashley? No past, and not much of a present. If I can't figure out who Ashley was, how can I figure out who killed her?"

Chapter Six

From his office window, John Winters could see over the roofs of town, past the rows of houses clinging to the lower slopes of the mountain, and up to Koola Glacier, still snow-topped in high summer, sparkling in the hot sun. He wondered if it was ever possible to get tired of this view.

That Marigold was lying was so plain she might as well have hung a banner over Front Street to advertise the fact. She was probably lying about everything she knew about her roommate. Which might not be significant if, as Winters suspected, Ashley hadn't told her much. But she went into overdrive in the lying department when Smith found the flyer advertising the protest against the Grizzly Resort. That demonstration had been held out of town, on the highway near the construction site, so the Mounties would have been watching. He'd circulated Ashley's morgue photo to the RCMP, and gotten nothing positive back, but he'd ask them to have a second look with the demonstration in mind. Not that it would probably matter much—so the girl was opposed to the development. Most of the town's population under thirty were.

He figured he could have Marigold singing her heart out in five minutes flat—send a car around to her place as she was about to leave for work, bring her into the station for a private chat in the interview room, a uniformed officer present.

The girl could wait.

He rubbed his eyes and went back to his desk.

Ray Lopez had reported that nothing happened last night. The officer they'd brought in to play the sting had, once again, not been approached. Maybe he'd been made. Regardless, soon they'd have to send him back to his regular job. The entire complement of sworn officers of the Trafalgar City Police numbered twenty; no good for undercover work as every drug dealer in town knew where they went for lunch.

Winters had spent most of his career in Vancouver, the later part on the rough streets of the Downtown Eastside. Canada's worst neighborhood. He hated drug dealers with a white-hot passion.

His phone rang, and he picked it up with a barked "Winters."

"My little ray of sunshine."

"Sorry. Just angry at the world."

"You're entitled, sometimes," Eliza said. "Look, as strange as this might sound, we've been invited out to dinner with the M&C Development partners."

"They want to have dinner with me?"

"Of course not. They want to have dinner with me, and reluctantly agreed to include my spouse. That would be you, the ever cheerful Sergeant Winters. José's been invited as well."

"Who's José?"

"My other husband."

"Please, Eliza, I've a ton of problems on my plate and I don't want to play games."

"Okay, okay. José's the male model they want to work with me. We'll be together for shots of a happy retirement couple enjoying the benefits of Grizzly Resort. You know, golfing, fine dining. Of course there isn't yet a golf course, or a restaurant to photograph us enjoying, so they want shots of José and me on the resort location with the mountains and river in the background, and take us to Whistler for fine dining and golf background."

"I thought you didn't want the job."

"I said I'm not sure."

"This dinner's tonight?"

"If you're busy, I'll make your excuses. I want to go. I want to talk to José, because I don't know anything about his portfolio. And before I make a decision, I want to get to know the partners a bit better." Her voice dropped into serious tones. "I know you're busy, and I love you because you care about your job and all the garbage you have to deal with. Dinner's at *Feuilles de Menthe* at eight. I'll leave home at five to. If you can come with me, that's good. If you want to drop by, that's fine, and if you can't face it, that's all okay too." Her voice lifted. "Time to check out the wardrobe. I hope they haven't invited someone to join us who expects to see the face that was on the cover of *Vogue* thirty years ago. If so they're going to be crushingly disappointed. Love you, muchly." She hung up.

He stretched his legs and put his feet on the stack of boxes containing papers from some long-forgotten case. *José, eh?* Most of those male models were as gay as the balloons at a seven-year-old girl's birthday party, but it never hurt to be on guard.

Nine would be a good time to arrive. Let José have a drink, or two, and be feeling comfortable but not too smashed to make trouble.

Before going to dinner, he wanted to make some sense of this Ashley girl. He'd contacted his former colleagues in Vancouver. But with no last name, and a description that would fit a good number of the young white women in Canada, they couldn't do much to help. Her fingerprints weren't on record. Which either meant she was a clean, responsible citizen, or had never been caught.

Maybe someone in town would recognize the photo they had of her. Taken in the morgue, it was impossible to hide the fact that she, poor thing, was dead. He'd sent the photograph to the RCMP, and all the towns in the area. He'd also sent feelers across the country and down into the States looking for info about a newborn white boy who'd disappeared a couple of months ago.

It wasn't just that if he was to find out who killed Ashley, or cold-heartedly watched while she died, he had to know more about her. If Miller was to be returned to what relatives he might have, they needed to find out about Ashley's background.

Ashley Doe had to have some family. Somewhere.

His phone rang again. "Winters."

"Good news, we're ready to go." It was Paul Keller, the Chief Constable, calling from his home.

For a moment Winters thought the boss had found something out about Ashley. But then he remembered that she wasn't their only problem.

"When?"

"Tomorrow afternoon. A nice quiet Sunday in suburbia. The yellow stripes," Keller used the not always polite nickname for the RCMP, "will be joining you, but it's your show. They'll be in position at sixteen hundred hours. They'll have the dog and I've told Al Peterson'll you'll need to take two of his constables to watch the street."

"I'll handle it."

"I know you will. Good luck." Keller hung up.

Chapter Seven

The morning fog was so thick, she couldn't see the building across the street. Still, Rachel Ferguson thought, it was a better view than what she saw in the small mirror she kept in her desk drawer. With a light hand, she ran a stick of pale pink color across her lips and tucked a strand of loose hair behind her right ear. The caramel highlights in her brown hair were beginning to fade and the neat bob was looking a bit ragged. And was that a coffee stain beside the top button of her white shirt? She'd been roused out of bed at three a.m. and had pulled on the blouse she'd worn the day before, not realizing that she'd still be working fourteen hours later. The three a.m. had been easy enough: responding to a call to 911, uniforms had found the ex-boyfriend sitting in the middle of the living room, the gun tossed in a corner, sobbing over the body and saying he was sorry but she'd forced him to do it. There wasn't much for Ferguson and her partner, Al Jacobi, to do but supervise the gathering of evidence. They'd been about to pack it in, and go home to grab a bit more sleep, when another call came in. A drive-by. One dead, a known gang member. And more suspects than would fit into a city bus. That one had kept her on the move most of the day. Then back to the office to finish up some paperwork. She'd been about to pack it in for the day with enough time for a quick nap before meeting her sister for dinner when the phone rang. The boss, wanting an update on the Allenhart case.

Her heart sunk. There was no update to give him. Which meant that he'd have nothing for his superiors.

For which he, political to his core, would blame Rachel Ferguson.

She'd worked long and hard to be assigned to homicide. *Be careful of what you wish for*, wasn't that the old saying? Rachel Ferguson had joined the Seattle Police's homicide section, her long awaited dream, only one day before the Allenhart killing.

A murder in the kitchen of one of the biggest estates in the Pacific Northwest. And after two months of an intense investigation Detective Rachel Ferguson had nothing to show.

She stood up with a sigh, tugged at the bottom of her suit jacket to straighten the hem, and glanced at her watch. With luck the reaming out, the demands that she and her team *do something*, wouldn't take too long and she'd be able to get to dinner on time.

But the nap was probably a lost cause.

Molly Smith left the Lizard Lounge through the door onto the alley. Thin lights from the back of the bar and the nearest intersection showed her a woman pressed up against the wall. Her shirt was shoved up around her throat, her shorts were in a puddle on the ground, and her legs were wrapped around the grunting man holding her up.

"Take it inside," Smith said.

The woman screamed. The man dropped her.

"Fuck," he said.

"Not here," Smith said. "You have one minute to be out of my sight or I'm taking you in. Public indecency, we call it. Might even make tomorrow's papers."

The woman scooped her pants up, but her partner was already disappearing into the night, zipping his fly as he ran.

"That is not a gentleman," Smith said.

The woman was young, too young to be allowed into the bars. Her hair was long and straight, and her pants barely reached her pelvic bones. She pulled her T-shirt down over breasts not yet completely developed.

"Dyke," she said to Smith.

"Go home, Lorraine. Please. You don't need this. Why don't you go to the support center tomorrow? You know my mom works there sometimes. You can talk to her."

"I do that, I'll turn into a dyke cop. Screw you, Molly."

Smith watched as Lorraine walked up the alley, wiggling her hips as she struggled to fasten the zipper on her shorts. She wasn't a hooker, just a lost girl whose neighbors were always calling the cops to come break up the battle raging in her kitchen. She was looking for a man to love her.

Smith wanted to spit.

Instead she kept walking. The rest of the alley was quiet. Something rustled in the hedges on one side. A cat mewed softly and she caught a flash of yellow eyes.

She passed behind Rosemary's Campfire Kitchen, the store next to her parents' place, and Wolf River Books. She crossed Elm Street. The scent of the day's baking still lingered in the air from Alphonse's bakery. Ahead of her, she could hear laughter coming from *Feuilles de Menthe*, the new, expensive, highly fashionable restaurant.

The sun was setting and the light over the back door of the restaurant was weak.

A black shape lay in the alley. At first she thought it was a garbage bag. Then it cried out. She ran forward. It was a man, small and slight. He'd wrapped himself into a tight ball. He gripped his stomach, and moaned. She dropped to her haunches beside him and shouted into the radio at her shoulder asking for an ambulance. The scent of ripe vomit overpowered that of bread and garlic. "Hold on, buddy. Help's on the way."

Round white eyes stared up at her. "No," he whispered. "Fine."

"I can see that. But let's get a second opinion, okay?"

"No," he said, as he passed out.

She heard the siren of the ambulance and jumped to her feet to guide them down the alley.

Then she saw it. A needle, lying in the gravel beside his arm.

Chapter Eight

John Winters heard it over the chatter of the busy restaurant, the clink of good stemware, the pouring of wine, loud laughter, and the meaningless conversation of his dinner companions.

As planned, he'd joined Eliza and her group around nine, full of apologies for his tardiness. They'd been there an hour, but the appetizers were only just arriving. Wine glasses, he suspected, had been refilled more than once. Eliza smiled her secret sexy smile as she caught sight of him making his way across the crowded dining room.

Frank Clemmins nodded, barely suppressing a glower, as Eliza introduced her husband to the table. Clemmins looked like a tough guy, with hair shaved right down to the scalp, black bristles making a crescent pattern around the naked dome of his head. Winters knew that under the man's summer dress shirt, his arms bulged with muscle and a rattlesnake was tattooed around his upper arm. They'd met not long ago when Clemmins' partner, Reginald Montgomery, had been murdered. Clemmins had been a suspect, although not for long.

José, the model, was a darkly tanned, pouting man looking to be in his well-preserved fifties, with cheekbones so sharp you could cut meat with them and lips like a pampered woman. A lock of thick black hair, highlighted by a single silver strand, fell over his forehead. He wore a tight white T-shirt and a small gold earring in his left ear. A denim jacket was tossed over the back of his chair. He was sitting down, too close to Eliza, so Winters couldn't see too much of him, but José's chest was broad under the T-shirt and his arms were muscled.

Winters was introduced to the people he didn't know. José, the model, who, unfortunately, was not with a date. And the new partner, Steve Blacklock. In this casual town, in high summer, Blacklock was the best dressed of them all. He wore a gray business suit with a starched white shirt and a gray tie shot with thin pink threads. His face was well worn with tired brown eyes sunk into bags you could carry to the Laundromat. A woman with badly dyed blond hair, small eyes outlined in thick black eyeliner, and sagging breasts revealed by a deeply scooped blouse, sat beside him. She was Blacklock's age at least, maybe a bit older. Clemmins introduced her as Nancy Blacklock.

Winters ordered a draft, and, without looking at the menu, said he'd have whatever Eliza was having for her main course.

She lifted her wine glass and smiled at him over the rim. He was about to settle into his chair, ready to relax and try to enjoy himself when he saw her give José the same salute.

Conversation swirled around him. Mostly about the problems of building a resort in this environmentally correct age. Frank Clemmins babbled on about the importance of his project in maintaining the viability of the Grizzly bear habitat. He was mainly directing his arguments to Eliza: clearly he was aware that she wasn't entirely convinced of the virtues of the project. José sighed heavily and announced that people rarely appreciated true beauty. He was looking into Eliza's cleavage as he said it.

Winters leaned back to allow the waiter to place his meal in front of him. Oops, he'd ordered a spinach salad. Clemmins and Blacklock were being served with steak and ribs respectively. Both had Caesar salad on the side and baked potatoes piled high with sour cream and crumbled bacon.

"Where are you from, Mr. Blacklock?" he asked. Merely for something to say.

"Call me Steve, please. My family's from Washington State, but I've been living in Vancouver for five years or so. Not much on earth outside of Dubai hotter than Vancouver real estate these days, John. Now it's the Interior's time. I hope you own property, John."

"A small place outside of town."

"Expand, if you can," Blacklock said.

His wife giggled, and finished her glass of wine. Without waiting for the waiter to assist, she reached across the table and grabbed the bottle by the neck and poured herself another. The glass was large, and she filled it almost to the rim.

"Buy, before it's too late and the boom's passed," Blacklock continued. "Isn't that right, Nancy? Take the plunge, now, when you have the equipment."

Mrs. Blacklock laughed out loud. Winters got a better view of her poached salmon than he wanted.

He looked at own his wife. Eliza stuffed a spinach leaf into her mouth, trying to avoid his eye.

"Good advice, I'm sure," he said.

A siren. Getting closer. Ambulance, not police.

Blacklock also heard the siren. "I've been told you're a police officer, Mr. Winters." He cut into his blood-red steak.

Winters shrugged, spearing a mushroom. He'd just about kill for a piece of that meat. "Desk job mostly. Filling in time 'till retirement. You know how it is."

"Tell you the truth, John, I don't. I wake up every day, pumped, can't wait start making things happen. Right, honey?"

His wife rolled her eyes and drank more wine.

There it was—the police siren. It was coming from the alley, getting closer, and, instead of passing, stopped right behind them.

"Sounds like business. Gotta go. Sorry folks."

"What have you got, Smith?" Sergeant Winters said, emerging from the single light at the back of *Feuilles de Menthe*.

The paramedics had gone, the patient loaded into the back of the ambulance, heading for Emergency. At the sight of the abandoned needle, she'd called for police backup. "Heroin, at a guess. Look at that," She pointed to the ground.

A man broke out of the shadows. "Heroin. Are you sure?"

Winters stepped in front of him. "Who are you?"

"I'm a drug counselor. I heard the ambulance, overheard what the officer said, and thought I'd offer my help. Moonlight, great to see you."

"Sir?"

"Julian Armstrong. Remember me?"

She didn't.

"I used to help your mom out, down at the homeless shelter. Left eight years ago to set up a counseling practice in Victoria and then Vancouver."

She vaguely remembered. She'd also volunteered at the homeless shelter when she was in school. Part of her mother's attempts to get her doing good works.

Armstrong held out his hand. Smith shook it. She felt his eyes on her bruised mouth. Someone else who'd assume her boyfriend knocked her around. "Yes, I remember. Welcome back."

"Thanks."

He offered his hand to Winters and the men shook as Smith made the introductions.

Armstrong was in his late forties, although he tried to look younger, with brown and gray hair tied into a short ponytail, a small black goatee, and a tie-dyed T-Shirt stuffed into loose camouflage pants with plenty of pockets. Smith thought the kids would respect him more if he didn't try to look their age, but what did she know?

Constables Evans and Solway got out of the car. They stood in a small circle, looking at the needle on the ground, as if it were a cobra curling and ready to strike.

"Did you recognize him, Moonlight?" Armstrong asked.

"Seen him around. But I don't know his name and I've never had reason to stop him."

"Can you describe him? It might be one of my clients, and if so I'd better follow that ambulance. If not, I might be able to convince him to seek help. I work at the Mid-Kootenay Methadone Clinic." He reached into his jacket pocket and pulled out a card.

"Right now, I'd rather you left, Mr. Armstrong." Winters ignored the card. "This is a crime scene."

"I'm only trying to help."

"I'm sure you are. Constable Smith, can you escort Mr. Armstrong to the street. You can answer his questions there."

"Yes, sir," Smith said.

As she walked away, Winters began issuing orders. "Get that thing into an evidence bag. And be goddamned careful. Dave, take it to the Mounties fast. Tell them I want an analysis and I want it yesterday."

"Just a kid, Julian," Smith said. "Like any other. A boy, small, thin. A white guy. Longish brown hair. I wasn't concentrating on his face."

"You think it was heroin?"

"It could of been soda pop in that needle for all I know. Maybe he's allergic to it."

"Your mom's got me helping out down at the women's support center. She looks good."

"She's got a new project to keep her out of trouble." A baby. If they didn't find Miller's family soon, Lucky'd be wanting to adopt the kid. Molly Smith did not want a brand new baby brother, thank you very much.

It was time, she reminded herself, once again, to find a place of her own. It was just that she never had the time, and rents were ridiculous for what you could get in the Kootenays these days.

She and Graham had planned to buy a condo in Victoria, once Smith had graduated, and Graham finished the job in Vancouver that had killed him. He'd had a small inheritance from a grandmother, and was keeping it for their home. He didn't have a will and when he died, Smith had no idea what happened to the money. His parents got it, probably.

She hadn't bothered to find out. It was intended for them to build their life together. If there was to be no life, then she didn't want the money either. Let Mr. and Mrs. Buckingham spend it.

Armstrong's eyes were on her face.

"Sorry, just thinking about my mom."

He held out his card. "I'd better be going. See you, Moonlight."

She took it. "See you."

"Constable Smith," Winters called.

She stuffed the card into her pocket and turned. Winters walked toward her. Evans was holding an evidence bag as if it were full of dog poo, and Solway was doing her best to keep out of his way.

"You're with me," Winters said. "Let's get to the station and pick up the van. I want to go to the hospital and find out what that kid's been up to. If he's lucky he'll live, and if I'm lucky, he'll be ready to give me his source. Dave, get that thing to Ray Gavin, and Dawn, take the streets while Molly and Dave are occupied."

If they'd been in the army they would all have leapt to attention, saluted, and cried, "Yes, sir!"

Lucky was feeding the baby when she heard footsteps coming down the stairs. "You're up early, dear."

"Like I can sleep through that racket. Geeze, Mom, I had a hard shift, I got home late, and here it is," Moonlight looked at the clock over the stove. "All of eight, and he's screaming the house down."

"You should've heard him at two," Lucky said. "I thought he was a good little boy to sleep this long."

"Oh, God, shoot me now. Where's Dad?"

"Went to the store early."

"I wonder why."

"Miller's quiet now," Lucky said. "Go back to bed."

Moonlight filled the kettle. "You know me, Mom. If I'm up, I'm up. I'll try and have a bit more sleep later. I've got the three-to-three shift again today." She cut two slices off a loaf of whole wheat bread and tossed them into the toaster.

"As long as you're up… Dad brought in the paper when he left."

"So?" The *Gazette* was delivered to a red newspaper box at the bottom of the driveway six mornings a week.

Lucky turned the paper over. A nice picture of the organizing ladies taken at the Catholic Church's annual August tea and rummage sale, graced the front page.

"Charmed, I'm sure." Moonlight barely glanced at it.

Lucky stabbed a forefinger at the story below the one about the church tea. "It says that you, it mentions you by name, arrested a tourist for smoking a single marijuana cigarette. Really, dear."

"Let me see that," Moonlight snatched the paper and read quickly. "Oh, look. Meredith Morgenstern reporting. *Quelle surprise.*" She tossed the offending object into the recycling box by the back door. "I saw Meredith there, digging through garbage like a rat looking for a rotting tomato."

"I'm no fan of our local Brenda Starr…"

"Who?"

"Before your time. I don't like Meredith any more than you do, but let's forget about her and look at the content of the story."

"Let's not."

"It sounds as if you reacted with, shall we say, a bit too much enthusiasm."

"Please, Mom," Moonlight said. "Let's not go there."

Miller stopped feeding, and Lucky lifted the baby to her shoulder, upon which she'd already placed a small towel. She patted his back. Eat and sleep, burp and poop. That was all a baby required out of life. Why did children have to grow up and become so difficult?

"You arrested a man for smoking marijuana."

"I am not going to have this conversation, Mom." Moonlight stood over the kettle, encouraging it to boil.

"He's from the States. A promising athlete at a good university. You know what they're like in the States. A conviction for something as harmless as pot could destroy his entire life. Marijuana is no more harmful than tobacco, or alcohol. Less harmful, in fact. I thought the police here had more sense than to ruin a young man's life for something so trivial."

"For heaven's sake, Mom. The jackass practically begged me to arrest him. I bet Meredith doesn't mention that." The kettle switched off and Moonlight poured hot water into her cup with such force that it splashed onto the countertop. "Whether you like it or not, marijuana is illegal. That means not allowed. Some indulged frat boy on summer vacation gets the wrong impression of what we're like here in B.C. and puffs smoke into my face, I'm not gonna turn my back and walk away.

"Come on Sylvester, let's go for a walk." She made clucking noises with her tongue. The dog ran out from under the table, ears up, tail waving, tongue lolling.

"If they asked me to arrest every black person in town I might object. But the law is the law and there are a lot of reasons for keeping marijuana illegal. I'm not going to stand here arguing about them with you." She took her tea cup and headed for the back door. "Particularly not this morning. I spent a good part of last night in the hospital watching the doctors saving a kid from a heroin overdose. Sadly, he wouldn't tell us a thing about where he got the stuff."

"Marijuana isn't a gateway drug to heroin. The situations aren't related."

Moonlight threw open the back door. "Ask Miller what happened to his mommy."

"Are you saying Ashley died of a drug overdose? I don't believe it. I never saw any signs of her taking hard drugs. Or even soft drugs for that matter."

Color drained from Moonlight's face. "Forget I said that, Mom. Just forget it, please."

Confidential police information, Lucky suspected. "Forgotten. However, as we all know, marijuana, regardless of whether Ashley used it or not, isn't a killer drug."

"I'm going for a walk."

"You're still in your pajamas."

"Call 911 and have me arrested for public indecency." The door slammed behind her. Sylvester barely escaped with his tail intact.

Lucky looked at Miller. The baby stared back, his face twisted in disapproval at all the noise. So Ashley's death had something to do with drugs. The poor thing. Lucky hadn't known the girl, not well. She'd only had contact with her a few times, down at the center, but surely she would have noticed if Ashley had a drug addiction. The police got things wrong all the time.

"Repeat after me," Lucky said to Miller. "The patriarchal, military-industrial-corporate establishment is to be resisted at every turn."

Miller's eyelids flicked twice, and then they closed and he drifted off to sleep. Lucky lifted the baby to her shoulder.

Early Sunday morning, John Winters drove to the Trafalgar Women's Support Center to meet the morning class on infant and child hygiene. He parked the van beside the only other car in the parking lot, thinking that this was going to be a big waste of his time. He'd gone to the hospital last night and waited to question the boy found in the alley. That had certainly been a waste of time. He should have stayed in bed, with Eliza, watching the hot, yellow sun play with the curtains, eating pancakes running with butter and maple syrup, and doing whatever else seemed like a good thing to do in bed on a lazy summer morning. Instead he'd stopped at Big Eddie's for a large coffee to go and driven to the center.

But the house wasn't empty, and he remembered that in Trafalgar, people, particularly young people, generally walked rather than drove. They were gathered in the kitchen. Six young women sat at the table, watching a middle-aged woman holding up a jar of baby food. A pot boiled on the stove behind her. She stopped talking when Winters came in. "Can I help you?"

He held up his badge. "I'm Sergeant Winters, Trafalgar City Police."

"I know who you are." Her voice wasn't hostile, but neither was it welcoming.

"Please, finish your class. I'd like to talk to your clients, just some general questions. I'll wait until you're finished."

Her eyes narrowed, but she didn't object. The students had turned to stare at the intruder. Some of them were visibly pregnant, one held a sleeping baby to her chest. Strollers lined the walls.

He leaned against the back wall of the kitchen and watched while the instructor showed the class how to heat pre-prepared baby food. She was hugely overweight, dressed in a shapeless flowered dress reaching almost to her ankles, which were two or three times normal size. Her gray hair was tied in a long braid that touched the small of her back. Steam rose from the pot on the stove. A fan on the kitchen counter did nothing to cut the heat. Old buildings such as this had been built to keep warm in winter, not cool in summer. The instructor stopped for a moment and wiped the back of her neck with a dish towel. Not, Winters thought, a lesson in sanitation.

The students didn't pay him much attention. No doubt they knew who he was, and also why he'd come.

The baby in the young woman's arms grizzled, and she, very casually, opened her blouse, pulled out her right breast and stuck the nipple in the child's gaping mouth. It settled immediately and began to feed. Winters looked away. He was just too old to take a woman's naked breast in stride.

At last the speaker droned to a halt. "Any questions?"

There were none.

"Thank you for coming," she said.

Winters stepped forward. "Before you leave, I'd like to take a few more minutes of your time, if I may. I'm Sergeant John

Winters with the Trafalgar City Police." He smiled. The women didn't smile back. He leaned up against the kitchen counter, trying to appear casual, chatty, friendly. And not look at the feeding baby. "Have you heard what happened here on Thursday evening?"

They nodded.

"Did any of you know Ashley?"

The women glanced at each other. A pregnant one shifted her belly. It looked like she had a basketball stuffed up her shirt. *That must be so uncomfortable.* He smiled at her. She cracked a trace of a grin in return.

"Anyone?" he asked again. "You've seen her here in the center. How about around town?"

Quiet.

"Why do you want to know?" Someone spoke at last. She had hoops running up both ears, a silver bar stabbed into the top of her nose, between the eyebrows, and a hoop, which looked as if it were intended to hold a cow bell, through her nostrils. Her bare arms were covered in colorful tattoos.

"She wasn't murdered, was she?" another woman said. "The paper said it was an accident."

The paper hadn't mentioned murder because the police weren't releasing the details of Ashley's death. Let the killer think they believed it was an accidental overdose.

"We investigate any unusual death. Ashley was young, found dead in the woods. That's unusual. We want to know what happened to her. It would help if we knew more about her. Did any of you ever speak to her?"

"I did," the basketball girl said. "This," she rubbed her stomach, "is my first." She looked about sixteen: Winters certainly hoped it was her first. "I come here to meet the other moms. Find out what it's like. You know, giving birth. Having a baby." She blushed and looked down.

"Were you and Ashley friends?"

"Not really. We talked, a bit. She said childbirth was as easy as sneezing."

Cowbell Girl snorted, and a couple of the others laughed.

So Ashley hadn't told the girls Miller wasn't her natural son. Even Lucky had been surprised to hear that. "Do you know her last name?"

"No. Don't you?"

He answered her question with a question. "Can I ask your name?"

"Carlene."

"Carlene, thanks. Anyone else?"

No one answered. Winters let his question linger. The women began to shift in their seats.

"She didn't talk much," Cowbell Girl said, breaking the silence. "Not to anyone. About a week or so ago she was here, wanting to get some baby clothes."

"We run an infant and child clothing and accessories exchange," the fat woman explained.

"Beowulf's bigger than her baby, so I said she could have some of the things he'd outgrown," the young mother said. For a moment, Winters thought she was talking about dog dishes and the like. Fortunately before he could ask, he understood that Beowulf must be the name of her baby. "She came over to my place and got them. And that's about the only time I spoke to her."

Winters asked the same questions in different ways. But no one had anything more to add. He thanked the women for their time, and asked Cowbell Girl and Basketball to stay a while longer.

The nursing mother pulled her baby's mouth off her nipple, stuffed her breast back into her shirt, and the baby back into its sling. The young women left quietly, their mood somber and quiet. When the others had gone, Winters pulled a chair up to the table and sat down with Basketball and Cowbell Girl. The fat woman joined them.

But the young women could tell him nothing more. They'd talked to Ashley; she hadn't talked back. She didn't tell them where she was from, didn't talk about Miller's father, not even to badmouth him. They'd tried to make friends, but she didn't want to be friends. And so they'd dropped it.

"She wanted to be left alone," Cowbell Girl, whose name, he'd found out, was Paula. It didn't suit her. "So I left her alone."

"Me too," Carlene said. "She wasn't rude, like. But she made sure you got the hint."

"Did you know Ashley at all?" Winters asked the fat woman. "Sorry, I didn't get your name."

"Betty. She came to my classes a few times. But she didn't ask any questions, and didn't stay to chat after. The girls usually linger for a social time after class. Sometimes, we go out for coffee. My treat. The girls look forward to that." Clearly she was telling Winters that he had spoiled their coffee klatch.

He handed Paula and Carlene his card. Paula read it, but Carlene put it into her pocket without looking at it.

"If you can remember anything, I'd appreciate it. We need to find Ashley's family, otherwise Miller will have to go into foster care."

Paula looked up. Her lips were dark with purple lipstick, her eyes heavily rimmed in black eyeliner. Water filled her eyes as if a dam had been opened. "Foster care," she whispered. "The poor thing."

There was a story there. But it wasn't his business. "Almost anything Ashley told you might help us find her family."

Paula gripped the card. "I'll try to remember. I will, Mr. Winters."

And he knew she would.

"Thanks." He stood up.

They gathered their things. Paula reached into a stroller against the kitchen wall, and gathered up a baby. "This is Beowulf," she said to Winters, bursting with pride. Beowulf burped and opened his eyes.

"How old?"

"Nearly six months."

"Wow," John Winters said, "he's a big one." Good thing too—with a name like that, the kid would need to be big when he got to school.

Paula smiled and tucked the baby in amongst his blankets. "We'd better get moving. Now he's awake, he'll be wanting to be fed. And fast."

Winters smiled back. Beowulf might curse his mother for his name someday, but he'd not grow up unloved.

The front door opened as the two young women reached it. Carlene was asking Paula if Beowulf was sleeping through yet.

A man stepped aside to let them pass.

It was Julian Armstrong. Armstrong had been at the hospital last night, but left when told he couldn't see the overdose patient.

"John," he said with jovial familiarity. "Great to see you again." Betty held out her arms and Armstrong enveloped her in an enthusiastic hug.

"What brings you here, Mr. Armstrong?" Winters asked when they'd separated.

"Drumming up business, I'm sorry to say."

"Julian's setting up a counseling practice in town," Betty said. "I thought he'd like to meet some of our clients. You're late. They've left already."

He gave her a sheepish grin. "I apologize, got tied up. Sorry to say, I met Sergeant Winters last night. Heroin overdose in an alley."

"How awful."

"It was. But the boy's going to be okay, right, John?"

Winters didn't reply.

"The girl I particularly want you to meet didn't come today," Betty said, taking Armstrong's arm. "Let me fill you in on her situation and we can come up with a plan of attack."

Winters let himself out.

Staff-sergeant Al Peterson met Smith and Evans, the duty constables, when they came on shift at three.

"Hot time in the old town tonight," he said.

"Huh?" Evans said.

"He means we'll be busy," Smith said. Her dad used that expression when he was all fired up about something. Fortunately, these days her dad got all fired up about things like the scoring record of the latest Toronto Blue Jays' prospect. Not about marijuana laws and whether or not his daughter should be enforcing them.

Peterson led them into the constables' office. It wasn't used as much as in the old days, Peterson had told his younger officers many times. These days, constables were expected to be out on the streets, in the cars, using their computers to write up reports and whatever other paper work needed to be done.

"At three-forty-five you're both to be sitting in a patrol car at the back. Any problems between now and then, I'll handle it."

"You?" Evans said.

Peterson raised one overgrown gray eyebrow. "You have a problem with that, Constable Evans?"

Smith kept her face even. Evans had been on the force longer than she. He was out of probation, and she wasn't. But he was such an arrogant prick that she did get a chuckle, sometimes, at seeing him slapped into place.

Of course he, Evans, liked nothing more than to watch Smith shoved back into line.

"Just curious, that's all," he said, his voice deep and smooth.

"Well don't be. You must have reports to finish up. If not you can eat lunch until then."

Paul Keller, the Chief Constable, nodded to them as he walked down the hall to his office. A miasma of cigarette smoke followed in his wake. Smith wondered if the CC had ever done surveillance work. Unlikely, as anyone within a hundred yards would be able to smell him out. Something was up. Keller wasn't an office-hours only, keep-to-the-book Chief, but it was unusual to see him on a Sunday.

The boss stopped in his tracks and turned around. "Molly. If you have a moment."

"Yes, sir."

"My office."

"Catch you in the car," Evans said.

Her heart tightened in her chest as Keller asked her to shut the door behind her. He walked around his desk and dropped into the big swivel chair. Here it was—the Chief was in on a Sunday to tell her she was sacked. He'd seen her name in the papers once too often and didn't want an officer who attracted so much local media attention. She stood at attention, and gripped her hands behind her back.

"I've had a complaint about your mother," he said.

"What?"

"Informal, fortunately. Not through channels. Just a private e-mail telling me that Mrs. Lucy Smith is refusing to hand over the Ashley Doe baby." He rubbed the bit of hair that remained on the top of his head. The afternoon sun streaming in from the window behind him reflected off pieces of scalp floating in the air.

Smith hadn't even known that child services wanted the kid.

"I don't know what I can do, sir."

He waved his hand in the air. "I'm not asking you to do anything, Molly. Please take a seat."

She plopped herself down.

"I wanted to let you know what's happening, that's all. Your mother and I have known each other for a long time."

Smith shifted uncomfortably. With all the equipment around her waist she had trouble settling into the chair. She'd recently wondered if the CC had a thing for her mother: she'd instantly closed that line of inquiry. But his eyes were turning all soft and dreamy as he talked about Lucky Smith. He looked like a sixteen year old boy thinking about Pamela Anderson.

"Of course, I can't take sides." He glanced at his watch. "Tomorrow's Monday and it's possible that child services will be back. I wanted you to be aware of what's going on, that's all."

She stood up. "Thanks, sir. But my mom isn't likely to listen to me, you know."

Keller again rubbed his hand across his bald dome. "And she isn't going to listen to me either, Molly. But we can try. Take care."

"Sure," she said, not knowing if he was asking her to take care of herself on the streets, or her mother if things didn't go Lucky's way.

She went to the parking lot at the side of the building. It was three-forty-three and Evans was behind the wheel of a patrol car.

"What was that about?"

She fastened her seat belt. "Everything and nothing. Everyone in this town knows everyone and everything there is to know about them."

"Which is why," Evans said, "I can't wait to get the hell out of here."

Small towns had their disadvantages, Smith was about to agree. But if you wanted a life outside of work, someplace to relax, to calm down, there weren't many places better than Trafalgar.

"Two-five. Where are you?" The radio cracked. It was Sergeant Winters. Smith glanced at the clock. Three-forty-six.

"Office," Evans said.

"Go to Vancouver Street, park between Redwood and Cedar. Remain in the vehicle until notified. No noise."

"On our way." They pulled out of the parking bay onto George Street. Sunday traffic was light and no cars were coming their way.

"What do you think, Mol?" Evans said, his foot hard on the gas.

"Grow-op raid, for sure. Either that or an Al-Qaeda cell."

"I'll put my money on the grow-op," Evans said. "Although it'd be nice to tackle those Al-Qaeda guys. It's pretty nasty the way they treat women."

They took a corner and Smith's head shook, as much with the centrifugal force as with Evans' remark. Hard to know, sometimes, if men wanted to help women in distant places, or if they wanted to be seen as powerful and macho as they offered their help to women in distant places. There was a profound difference, Lucky had taught her. One approach cared about the result of their interference. One did not.

Evans slid the car up against the crumbling curb on Vancouver Street. An elderly lady was grooming her lush perennial garden.

She approached the car, scissors in liver-spotted hand.

"Oh, goodie," Evans said. "We have backup."

Smith rolled down the window. "Afternoon, ma'am."

"If you're here about them." The gardener waved her shears, which were, Smith noticed, well sharpened. "You're too late. They're gone. For good I hope, but I don't expect my prayers to be answered."

"I'm afraid not, ma'am."

"It's those cats. I've complained and complained about what they're doing to my plants, but does anyone listen. No. I'm just an old lady. Who cares what I think? An old lady, I'll remind you, who's lived in this town since 1938. How about that?"

"Wow," Smith said. For lack of anything else to say. "That's a long time."

The woman peered into the window of the car. Her eyes were clear and sharply focused. "I know you. You're the Smith girl. Moonbeam. What a ridiculous name. And now you're with the police. What could your father have been thinking, allowing you to take a man's job?"

Evans almost busted a gut trying not to laugh. Smith refrained from slapping him.

"Pardon me, Ma'am. Police business." John Winters was beside the car, and the gardener bustled away after giving him a simpering smile.

"You're with me Smith. Evans, pull the car up in front of that alley. This is the only way out. Anyone comes down it, stop them."

Chapter Nine

Meredith Morgenstern was sitting in her living room, painting her toenails and wondering if she should spend the afternoon at the beach or just sit here on her miniscule balcony. The phone rang, but she was in no hurry to answer it. Nothing of importance would be happening in Trafalgar on a Sunday afternoon.

"Too bad you're not there," a voice said into the answering machine. "Interesting stuff happenin' on Redwood Street." It was a man, probably, the sound muffled, the words indistinct.

Meredith tossed the bottle of polish onto the low coffee table and grabbed the receiver. "I'm here, I'm here. Who are you? Why are you calling me?"

"Just bein' friendly. It's no concern of mine if you go. Do what you like. But you might see an old school chum of yours there." He hung up.

Redwood was a residential street in the lower east end of town, an area of crumbling older homes and weed-choked gardens. If anything would be happening in Trafalgar on a Sunday afternoon it would be likely to happen on Redwood Street. Meredith ran into her bedroom, not noticing the blood-red polish dripping into the carpet.

◇◇◇

Smith scrambled out of the car. She plopped her hat on her head and settled the gun belt around her waist.

Winters was dressed in jeans and his raid jacket. "You're to do nothing but follow me," he told her. "Understand?"

"Yes."

They walked up Vancouver Street and turned into Redwood. A casually dressed man tossed a cigarette butt onto the sidewalk and ground it under his heel. Smith had seen him around—RCMP.

429 Redwood Street was a dilapidated shack. Weeds choked the life out of a yard that once-upon-a-time had boasted a pleasant garden. The brick walkway was buried in more weeds and recently laid piles of dog dirt. Paint peeled from gingerbread edging. Particle board covered basement windows.

Meredith Morgenstern watched from across the street. She was dressed in black shorts, red T-shirt, and sandals with heels, a camera bag tossed over her right shoulder.

Meredith saw Smith and Winters arrive. She held up her right hand, index finger pointed out, thumb folding back the other three fingers. She threw them a bright smile, along with the implied threat.

"That woman's with the paper," the Mountie said. "If they've spotted her, we might as well be home playing tiddlywinks."

"Someone's informed on us," Winters said, his voice low. "Can't worry about that now."

The three police officers walked up the weed-choked pathway. Winters and the Mountie looked like they were heading for their mothers' homes to escort the ladies to church. Smith's heart pounded so hard in her chest, she wouldn't have been surprised if the residents of the house heard them coming and ran out the back into Dave Evans' waiting arms.

Winters knocked on the door.

Nothing.

He knocked again.

The door opened, just a crack. A head, all uncombed hair and unkempt beard peered up. He looked at the men first. "Yeah?" Then he saw Smith, in uniform. "Jesus," he said.

The Mountie stuck a heavily booted foot into the door before it could be slammed shut.

"Police search warrant," Winters yelled. "We're coming in."
He flipped the flaps on his jacket and the word 'Police' was
displayed. "Smith, secure the street." He disappeared into the
house.

Other cars were arriving. Trafalgar City Police's non-descript
blue van. Mounties in a truck painted with the logo of a horse-
man carrying a lance. A uniformed officer leapt out. It was Adam
Tocek, who'd saved their asses in the riot last month. He opened
the back for a gorgeous German Shepherd.

Orders cracked over the radio.

Evans ran around the corner. No one had come out the back
door into the alley, to his apparent disappointment. He checked
out the street and went back to his post.

It would be great to be in on the action, but from now on
Smith was only here to keep the curious back. Onlookers,
mostly, neighbors going about their Sunday afternoon business
of firing up the barbeque or cracking open a two-four. And the
occasional pot customer wandering down the street and, grate-
fully, escaping the raid.

"Go home. Keep this road clear." Smith said as she stretched
yellow tape between the bushes on either side of the sidewalk.

"What's happening?" the elderly lady who'd been caring for
her hosta asked.

"Go home, ma'am. There's nothing to see here."

"Don't be ridiculous, young lady. There's obviously a great
deal to see. Otherwise you wouldn't be here, now would you?"

Can't argue with logic like that.

The man with the filthy hair and beard was hustled out and
stuffed into a car.

Nothing more appeared to be happening, and Meredith
Morgenstern and the rest of the onlookers were getting restless,
when John Winters and his Mountie pal came out of the house.
They went to the blue van, climbed into the back, and soon
came out carrying suits that looked as if the men were preparing
for an exploration of the moon.

That got the crowd whispering to each other.

Meredith ran up to Sergeant Winters, notebook and pen in hand. He walked past her as if she wasn't there. Meredith's face settled into dark, angry lines. She looked up and saw Smith watching her. "Screw you," the reporter's lips said.

She went back to interviewing the good citizens of Trafalgar.

◇◇◇

Constable Tocek waved at Smith as he walked down the front steps. She lifted her hand with a smile. Tocek led his dog toward her. By now the onlookers had either gone home or knew there was no point in asking if they could get closer to have a look. The big German Shepherd sniffed at Smith's boots.

"Nice dog," she said.

"This is Norman. The best nose in B.C."

"Nice to meet you, Norman." Smith leaned forward to let the dog sniff her hand. He did so, and then lifted his enormous head and looked at her. His ears were not much smaller than satellite dishes; his brown eyes warm and intelligent.

"Can I have a minute, Constable Smith?" Tocek said in a low voice. He twitched his head toward the onlookers, brimming with curiosity. The lady who'd lived in Trafalgar since 1938 dared to edge closer.

"Sure."

She followed man and dog a few yards down the road. "Norman's a strange name for a dog."

A bio-suited figure carried out a large paper bag full of... something. Smith wondered if she should be offering protection, but as the citizens only whispered amongst themselves, she decided not to.

Tocek dug the toe of his boot into the ground. "That was the name he had when we got him. Someone's dad, maybe. Or ex-husband."

Smith laughed. Norman peed against a bush.

"I'm glad to see you looking okay," Tocek said, following a long pause. "After that business last month."

"I'm sorry, Adam. I never thanked you for the flowers. That was nice of you guys. Thank everyone at the detachment for me will you?"

"Uh, sure. I was wondering… well, I've got a couple of days off starting Tuesday, and I'm going hiking in Kokanee Glacier Park."

"That'll be fun," she said. "Weather's supposed to stay good."

"So I was wondering… uh… if you'd like to come with me. Just a day trip. No more than you'd like to do."

She hadn't been into the wilderness since that last break with Graham. Before he moved to Vancouver to take up the new job. And after Graham's death, she'd simply not wanted to go alone, with nothing accompanying her but her memories. A day hike would be nice. When she and Sam were in high school they worked for the family business guiding kayaking and backcountry hiking trips in the summer, skiing expeditions in the winter. She missed the wilderness. She usually worked four days on/four days off. She'd be free starting tomorrow. She smiled at Tocek, all ready to say yes.

But the color was high in his cheeks and he was staring at the ground. He'd dug a neat circle in the dirt with the toe of his boot. His own business finished, Norman sat politely at his master's side.

And Molly Smith knew why Adam Tocek had suddenly come over all awkward and embarrassed.

He wasn't asking her to be his hiking companion. He was asking her on a date.

She swallowed, trying to throw back rising panic. "Sorry, Adam. I can't. My mom's sick and I said I'd stick around to help out if she needs a ride to go to the doctor or something."

What an awful excuse. As if everyone in the Kootenays didn't know Lucky Smith and know that she'd slit her throat before asking for help.

He gave her a weak grin. "Sure, Molly. I understand. Maybe some other time."

"Yeah, some other time."

"Call me, if you can get away. Come on Norman, time to go."

She watched them walk toward their car. Tocek held the back door open and the dog jumped in. As they drove past, Norman looked at her. Adam Tocek did not.

Molly Smith felt like dirt.

"Wouldn't mind being clapped in handcuffs by that one."

Smith whirled around. "You're on the wrong side of the street, Meredith," she barked, her voice loud in her own ears. Get back over there."

"Just wondering if you've got a word for the press."

Smith opened her mouth.

"Not that word."

"You know the rules. Get behind the line or I'll arrest you for interfering in a police investigation."

"And I'll bet you'd do it too. Time to get over yourself, Moonlight. You're not as tough as you think you are." With that Meredith picked her way back across the street.

The sun had dipped behind the western mountains and the onlookers had decided they had better things to do and Smith was tired of standing in the road. Evans had been called RTO—return to office—but Smith was left guarding the door. She carefully noted in her log book the time and name of anyone who entered or left the premises.

At last Sergeant John Winters et al left the house. They unwrapped themselves from the bio suits—it was only pot they were after so the suits weren't good ones—and stuffed whatever evidence they'd gathered into the back of the marked truck.

The only person still standing on the far side of the street was Meredith Morgenstern. She approached Winters.

"Do you have a statement for the press, Sergeant Winters?"

"Not at this time." He climbed into the truck, almost slamming the door in her face.

Smith's radio cracked. "RTO, Smith." It was Winters. "Show's over."

Chapter Ten

Miller had had a bad night. Awake every two hours, screaming to be fed, needing to be changed, hard to put back down once he'd had his bottle. Andy rolled out of bed and took his pillow to Sam's old room at the end of the hall. At six, Moonlight had come banging on their door saying that if she didn't get some sleep she'd throttle someone.

Lucky put the kettle on the stove. *Surely it hadn't been this hard when Samwise and Moonlight were babies?* Of course she'd been thirty years younger, and Andy had been an eager, willing partner in the great task of child-raising.

One of Lucky's friends had brought Miller a beautiful white wicker bassinet, and she'd set it on the top of the bedroom dresser. After shoving all their odds and ends into a drawer.

By nine o'clock, she'd finally gotten the baby settled into the pram by the stove, which he seemed to much prefer to the bassinet. Sylvester was asleep beside him and Miller lay still, his round fat bottom pointed toward the ceiling.

Lucky took a container of blueberry yoghurt out of the fridge. Andy had marched through the kitchen, remnants of blond hair sticking up all over, unshaven, shirt tail untucked. Face like a thundercloud. He said not a word as he grabbed his keys off the hook by the back door.

Fortunately Moonlight appeared to have gone back to sleep.

Lucky got a spoon out of the drawer, placed it and the container of yogurt on the table and sat down. She rested her head in her hands and her eyes drifted shut.

A car pulled up. Lucky's eyes did not want to open. She hoped it was Andy coming back to give her the farewell kiss he'd given her every morning for more than thirty years. Every morning except when they were arguing, that is.

A door slammed. Lucky forced herself to stand up. She looked out the window.

Jody Burke got out of the car and marched up to the front door, a woman on a mission. Lucky greeted her visitor with a smile and arms baring the entrance way.

"Ms. Burke."

"May I come in?"

"No. The baby's sleeping, very peacefully, I might add, and I'd rather he wasn't disturbed."

Burke was dressed in a long skirt, all possible shades of blue swirling through the fabric, a sleeveless red T-shirt, long silver earnings, and a pendant featuring a heavy red stone. She studied Lucky, and Lucky could imagine what she saw. The lined face, dark with lack of sleep, hair like a crow's nest, summer pajamas consisting of shorts and a bra-fitted tank top. A thin streak of baby vomit running across her left breast.

"There's no need for this to escalate into a legal argument, Mrs. Smith." Burke smiled.

"I agree. So, as I'm caring for the child, we have no reason for an argument, do we?"

"Please, Mrs. Smith. Why don't you put on the kettle and we can discuss this. You must know that I have obligations, legal obligations, if I'm to do my job properly. My boss wants to know what's happening here. I'm new, only arrived last week. I can't afford to look totally incompetent." She gave Lucky a lopsided grin, and shrugged her shoulders, seeking empathy.

Lucky didn't have any. Burke's armor hadn't been up the first time they'd met, and Lucky had seen her character for what it was.

Sylvester came to the door. He walked past Burke without a glance and trotted across the yard to sniff at her tires. He lifted his leg.

"I don't have time for a social visit. And it wouldn't accomplish anything in any event," Lucky said. "It's not in Miller's interest to be shuffled from one foster home to another. I've agreed to care for the baby until his family can be contacted. I would have thought that'd be the best possible situation at this time."

"I was hoping you'd see reason. Although from what I hear about you, Mrs. Smith, reason seems to be…"

"When you have a court order, you may return."

Burke stepped forward. Her forefinger touched Lucky's chest, and Lucky took a step back. "How dare you." Burke's voice was low and threatening. The voice she used, Lucky suspected, to intimidate poor, frightened young mothers. "I demand you hand the child over to me. This instant."

Lucky took a breath. She settled her feet into the ground and steadied her legs. "You take one more step, and I'll have you arrested for trespassing. And assault. As it happens, my daughter, who is in the house, is a police officer. And that's no lie—ask anyone in town."

Burke blinked, and her eyes shifted to one side.

Lucky took a step backward and slammed the door in the woman's face.

"I'll be back," Burke shouted. "With an officer who isn't a member of your family."

Footsteps crunched against gravel, and the car's engine came to life.

A low howl sounded from the kitchen. Lucky leaned against the wall, trying to take deep breaths, as it turned into a full throated cry.

Why don't I simply hand Miller over to Burke and get myself a good night's sleep?

Because she hadn't liked the woman from the moment they'd met. Jody Burke did not have Miller's best interests at heart.

There were lots of good people working in the social services. And a few who weren't so good.

Jody Burke, Lucky knew, was a bully.

And at last the bully had come up against someone stronger than she.

◇◇◇

Big Eddie's Coffee Emporium pretty much kept John Winters going. The coffee was high-octane, the muffins loaded with fat as well as a sprinkling of berries so he could convince himself he'd had a nutritious snack. Monday afternoon the place was almost empty. As soon as he walked in, Eddie poured a coffee. After Winters' first visit, the day he'd joined the Trafalgar City Police, Eddie had never again asked what he wanted:

"I was visiting friends on Redwood Street yesterday afternoon," Jolene, stunningly beautiful with midnight black skin, heavy hair gathered into colorful beads, and a Princess Diana accent, smiled as she handed him a blueberry muffin. "Find what you wanted?"

"Sure did." Yesterday's raid had been a big success. A house full of marijuana plants. Much of the crop only days away from being harvested. Two people charged. The house was rented, as most of them were. The owners had been contacted, and were heading back from Mexico.

They'd have an unpleasant surprise when they saw the condition of their house.

British Columbia in general, and the Kootenays in particular, had the reputation of being soft on pot.

Which was, John Winters knew, not always the case. He hoped this time it wouldn't be.

He carried his coffee and muffin back to the office.

He was settling down, ready to type up his report on the grow-op bust when Denton called him. "Lady here to see you, Sergeant," the dispatcher/front desk officer said.

A young woman stood in the waiting area between the front door and the security door. Winters watched her for a moment.

She ripped at the nail on her right thumb while looking at the posters of wanted and missing people from jurisdictions across Canada displayed on the bulletin board.

He opened the door. "I'm Sergeant Winters. You wanted to talk to me?"

She was skinny to the point of emaciation; her clothes much too big for her. Her face was dotted with spots and her brown hair hung in lifeless strands. Dull brown eyes skittered in a pale face. "I heard you're asking about Ash."

"Ashley," Winters held the door open. "Please, come in."

Like a mouse offered access to the cat's cage, the girl almost bolted.

"Miss," he said. "What's your name?"

"Amy."

"Would you like a drink, Amy? Coffee, tea, hot chocolate?"

"Coffee'd be nice."

He kept his smile in place as he held the door open. With great hesitation, she stepped through. No cats leapt out to devour her, and so she relaxed, just a fraction.

"Two coffees please, Jim. How do you take your coffee, Amy?"

"Uh, cream. Sugar?"

"Get muffins as well. We'll be in the guest room." Denton had probably never served coffee in his life, and he was unlikely to know what the guest room was, but he should be able to guess that it was the witness interview room.

Molly Smith came out of the constables' office, carrying a file folder. "Hey, Amy," she said. "How you doing?"

"Okay, Moon, okay."

"Constable Smith," Winters said, making a decision out of no where. "You're with me. Interview room one."

"Huh?" she said.

"One. Follow up with Jim on our coffee and then join us."

"Sure."

Winters settled Amy into a comfortable couch in the witness interview room. Unlike the suspect interrogation room, not intended to be a pleasant place to pass the time of day, this space was decorated in gentle pastel colors and furniture that didn't look like it was mass produced with the intent of being as ugly and uncomfortable as possible. A large box of tissues sat on the coffee table in the center of the room. He told Amy he'd be recording their conversation and left the door open for Smith, who soon arrived with two cups of coffee and a bag of muffins.

She held the bag out to Amy. The girl took one and dug in. The food was followed by a deep slug of coffee. "Nice," she said.

Winters lifted one eyebrow toward Smith. The constable knew the girl. Let her start the questioning.

"It's been a while, Amy." Smith's voice was hesitant at first, but it soon found its strength. "Whatca been doing?"

"This and that. Hanging around. You know."

"Yeah, I know. How's that baby doing? Robbie, right?"

Amy smiled, and settled against the back of her chair. "He's such a character, Moon. He makes me laugh, all the time."

"Where's Robbie now?"

"At the support center. They said they'd look after him so I could come here and talk to you, like without interruptions. Your mom wasn't there. I wanted to leave Robbie with your mom."

"Mom's like so busy right now." Smith said. Winters looked at her, amazed. Her voice had shifted. It was naturally high pitched, too high, Winters sometimes thought, to make her an effective voice of authority. But now it moved even higher up the scale, and casual slang slipped into her conversation. The way she spoke, she might not have been wearing the blue uniform with the Kevlar vest, the heavy, deadly, black Glock at her hip, handcuffs and baton around her waist.

"What brings you here, Amy? It must be important if you've left Robbie, eh?"

"It might be nothing, Moon. It's about Ashley. Like I heard she'd died. They said at the center that the cops want to talk to anyone who knew her."

Smith gave Winters a glance. He nodded.

"Tough, eh?"

Amy sipped her coffee. "Yeah. She had a kid, just a baby. I don't know where he went."

"Miller's being cared for, Amy. Don't have to worry about that."

Winters leaned across the table and gave the girl what he hoped was his best non-threatening smile. "Is there something you can tell me, Amy? About Ashley?"

Amy rubbed at her head. Deep scratch marks, old scars, ran down the inside of her arm.

"Ash didn't have many friends. She could of had friends. She was friendly, pretty. And real smart. She hung around town, most of the time, with the baby. She went to the support center sometimes. She liked your mom, Moonlight, she told me so."

Smith smiled. "Everyone, well almost everyone, likes my mom."

"Yeah."

"Was she your friend, Amy?" Winter asked, trying to get the conversation back on track.

"We talked, like a couple times. Down at the center."

Smith picked up the brown paper bag, and held it out to Amy. The girl took another muffin, dark, streaked with orange of shredded carrot, and broke off a section. She popped it into her mouth.

Winters was beginning to think he'd be here all day.

Amy chewed and Winters thought he'd lost her.

"Clark told me not to come," she said at last, wiping crumbs off her fingers onto her thighs. "But they said at the center that someone killed her. That's not right, is it?"

The town's grapevine was working hard. No one had said anything officially about Ashley being killed. Yesterday's paper ran an editorial on the danger of bad drugs. "It's not right to kill someone, no," Winters said.

"This person who killed Ashley, you need to find him, right?"

Winters chose his words carefully. "If Ashley was killed, then yes, I would very much like to find the person who did it."

"I thought so. Clark said I'd be stirring up trouble. I don't wanna do that, but I wanna help. Okay, Moon?"

"That's great, Amy," Smith said, sounding positive, and enthusiastic, and cheerful.

"Ash was real interested in that new social worker."

"Interested, how do you mean?" Winters said. "Had she met this woman before?"

"Not a woman. A guy. She told me she knew him, back in Victoria. Or maybe it was Vancouver. Might have been Vancouver."

"What's this social worker's name?"

"I don't remember exactly, but it's something like my friend Julie's, but a guy's name. Old fellow. Thinks he's all cool. Tries to look like a hippie."

Smith glanced at Winters and raised one discreet eyebrow. He nodded telling her to ask the question. "Might it have been Julian, Amy?"

Amy smiled. "That's it. You're so clever, Moon."

Julian Armstrong who he'd met at the site of the overdose and again at the women's center. Not that Winters thought of the social worker as an old guy. "What did Ashley have to say about him?"

The girl looked directly at Winters for the first time. "I'm sorry, Mr. Winters. But I get confused sometimes, and don't remember things."

"That's okay, Amy," Smith said. "I couldn't find my car keys today. I was late for work and everything. I got in so much trouble."

Winters doubted that any such thing had happened, but Amy appreciated the words and smiled in her slow, gentle way. "Not just me then. Ashley was all excited seeing him."

"Excited? How do you mean?" Smith asked. "Excited happy or excited mad?"

"Not mad, I don't think. She said he was the key to her future. I don't know what that meant. I figured you'd wanna know. That's all."

They got nothing more out of the girl. Winters asked if she knew Ashley's last name: Amy shook her lifeless hair. Smith told her to take the remaining muffins with her, and she clutched the bag to her skinny chest as she walked out of the police station.

Winters let out a long breath as he watched her pick her way across the street. "God, but that was sad. How do you know her, Molly?"

"Amy? Believe it or not, she's only a few years younger than me, though she looks like a kid. When I was in high school, she was in a special program, and I helped out for extra credit." She shrugged, and the right corner of her mouth turned up. "And because my mom made me. Amy's moderately functioning, able to get along on her own, with assistance. Some asshole knocked her up, and skipped out on her. By the time Clark knew she was pregnant it was too late to do anything about it."

"Who's Clark?"

"Her brother. The knocker-upper was singing falsetto for a while, I heard. Clark looks after Amy and Robbie. Their parents were bad druggies when the kids were growing up, the sort who had no concerns about letting the kiddies enjoy the stuff too. Family values, you know. No loss to anyone; they died in a car accident a few years ago. Clark works as a bouncer at The Bishop and Nun. He's a good guy. He makes sure Amy takes the baby to the support center."

"She was hungry, Molly."

"Clark does what he can. I'll talk to my mom later. Ask her what can be done to help out." A cloud moved behind the constable's blue eyes. "Sometimes, try as you want, you just can't make things right."

Winters blew out a lungful of air. "You should be on the street."

"You'd better tell the Sarge why I'm not."

"This Armstrong. What Amy told us? What do you think, Molly?" Smith was only a probationary constable. As wet behind the ears as one of the ducklings swimming down the Upper

Kootenay River. But she knew these people, and he didn't. He wanted to hear what she thought.

She looked around. Officers were coming and going. Jim Denton was sitting at the console, watching them. Barb came out of her office carrying a gigantic handbag, and bid everyone a good night.

"My office," Winters said.

He pulled up his desk chair, and Smith stood by the door, arms crossed over her chest,.

"I don't know Julian very well. I meet him a few times before he left for Vancouver, about, oh six or seven years ago, when I worked at the homeless shelter, the summer before I went away to University. My mom was involved with him on some project or other. And that's all I know. I don't know why he left town, and I don't know why he's come back."

"I need to talk to this guy. You know where we can find him?"

"No. But if he's helping out at the support center, even unofficially, they'll have him on file."

"Call them. Hopefully they'll have his number. Then phone Mr. Armstrong and tell him we'd like a few minutes of his time. ASAP."

Someone from her past. That was the second time that phrase had been mentioned regarding Ashley. Hadn't she told Lucky the same thing—she'd run into someone from her past and he'd take care of her.

Winters swung his chair back to face the computer.

Smith shifted her feet and her equipment rattled.

"Is there a problem, Molly?" He wiggled the mouse to get rid of the official Trafalgar City Police screen saver and bring up his unfinished report on the grow-op bust.

"I am supposed to be on the street, John."

"Sorry. I'll clear it with Al." He reached for the phone, and heard Smith's boots tramping down the hall.

Peterson was not pleased at having one of his constables reassigned at the last minute. Smith was needed on the beat, he told Winters. Winters reminded him that it was a Monday night.

Peterson reminded Winters that convoys of RVers from all across the Western United States were arriving for their annual gathering this weekend.

Winters rolled his eyes at Lopez's African violets. Hell's Angles, the RV bunch were not. "Any trouble, I'll send her back right away."

Peterson grumbled something and hung up.

Peterson was right, of course. Smith should be out on the beat. Patrolling the streets of Trafalgar. She was a probationary constable, not a detective. But he was lost in this small town. Only ten thousand people, everyone of them connected to everyone else by a myriad of invisible threads.

He should be using Ray Lopez for this sort of thing. But Lopez was working all out on another file, and anyway, today he was off. Winters had no compunction at all about asking his people to work on their days off. They weren't bankers.

But in this case, he figured that Molly Smith's local contacts would be of more use to him than Ray Lopez's. Ray had been in Trafalgar for more than ten years, but he didn't have the family roots that threw out even more of those invisible threads.

Chapter Eleven

Julian Armstrong rented a studio apartment in the basement of a house high above town. The views from the road and the driveway were spectacular, but from Armstrong's windows all that could be seen was bush and the bottoms of trees. A sofa bed, unmade, sheets and pillows tossed half onto the floor, filled most of the room. A desk and a computer were pushed up against a wall. The computer was switched off although the cup of coffee beside it let off a gentle plume of steam. Smith had obtained his number easily enough from the support center. She'd called, and found him at home. He'd sounded helpful, a concerned citizen, unfortunately not able to see the police at this time due to pressures of work. His tone changed when she insisted. He tried not to let his annoyance show, but it had. Not that she particularly cared.

There was no place for the police to sit in the main room, other than on the unmade bed. Armstrong had had plenty of time to tidy up for visitors. That he hadn't spoke volumes about the attitude he was going to take.

He dropped into the office chair in front of his computer, and swiveled around to face Smith and Winters. "I'm afraid I can't offer you coffee, Moonlight, Sergeant Winters. But I have an appointment in half an hour so let's get right down to it, shall we? I'll help any way I can, without breaking client confidentiality, of course."

His words were friendly, but his attitude was not. Smith hadn't told him on the phone why they were coming over. Did he have some reason to be concerned about their visit?

"You worked in Vancouver?" Winters had taken the only other chair in the apartment, a ripped vinyl thing pulled up to the scratched Formica table in what tried to pass as a kitchen.

"Yes."

"What did you do there?"

"Substance abuse counseling, mostly. Relationship abuse as well. Women in trouble, you know the scene."

"Work the Downtown Eastside?"

"Some of the time."

"I didn't know you. And I would have, if you'd been in the area when you say you were. I was on the Vancouver force until recently. Working mostly the Eastside."

Armstrong flushed. He glanced at Smith, seeking support, and then looked away. "Okay, you got me. A little white lie. Not the Eastside. My practice was in West Vancouver. Spoiled rich bitches with too much money and a hubby who was enjoying something tasty on the side."

"You were quick enough to lie to me about your work experience? Did you lie to the people in Trafalgar as well?"

Armstrong wiped beads of sweat off his forehead. The room was warm, but not hot. He kept glancing at Smith out of the corner of his eyes, although she was doing nothing but leaning up against the wall, holding her hat in her hands.

"Help me out here, Moonlight," he said at last. "You studied to be a social worker. You know what it's like in this business."

She blinked. Surprised he'd known what she'd been up to a few years ago, and not knowing if she should answer him or not. She was only here to lean against the wall and remind Armstrong that this was an official matter. "I…"

"Are you addressing Constable Smith?" Winters asked. "If so, I'd suggest that you talk to me instead."

Armstrong rubbed his forehead, keeping his eyes hidden. Seconds passed in silence before his hands moved down to massage his cheeks. "Sorry if I stepped out of line, but I was only looking for confirmation that there are some things you have to have on your resume to be taken seriously. It's nothing to do with the police,"

"I'll decide what's police business and what isn't," Winters snapped.

Unusual for Winters to break his cool. Armstrong was getting under the Sergeant's crocodile-tough hide.

"This won't get back to your mother, will it?" Armstrong asked Smith.

"Goddamn small towns," Winters said. "Constable Smith does not gossip about police business around the breakfast table. Spit it out, man." Smith hoped she wasn't blushing. At least once she had, completely against rules and ethics, gossiped to her mother around the breakfast table about police business.

Armstrong swiveled his chair a quarter turn so he was looking out the window at the expanse of green. A starling looked back at him. And then, not interested, it flew away.

"It sounds better, in some circles, certainly in Trafalgar circles, to say you've tried to help women who're in desperate conditions, rather than idle rich women with anxieties as big as their husbands' bank accounts. That's all."

Smith was amazed that he'd try to get away with fudging his credentials. Surely anyone could find out soon enough where he'd been practicing. But maybe no one here bothered to follow up. A lot of people in Trafalgar, people like her own mother, took things on face value. Honest, well meaning to a fault, they assumed that everyone else was as sincere as they.

"What brought you back to the Kootenays?" Winters asked.

Armstrong mumbled something to the window about love of the area, the fresh air, hiking in the mountains, nice people.

"Look at me when you're talking to me," Winters said.

Armstrong turned, slowly. He made an attempt to hold Winters' eyes, but broke off to study the worn carpet at his feet.

Winters looked around the room. "Not terribly nice accommodation for a professional such as yourself," he said.

"It's temporary, okay. And I don't give a flying fig if it doesn't meet with your approval."

"Merely making an observation. Tell me about Ashley. You knew her?"

"I saw her a few times at the support center. I didn't have much to do with her."

"I've been told she liked you."

Armstrong shrugged. He'd stopped trying to catch Smith's eye. "I'm glad to hear that, but I have to say I probably wouldn't even remember her if she hadn't died. Just another sad, lonely young girl, forced to grow up too fast."

Winters said nothing. Armstrong moved some papers on the floor with his feet. Smith shifted from one foot to another and looked out the window.

Somewhere on the property above them an electric lawn mower started up.

Armstrong was a social worker—a counselor. He should be comfortable with long meaningful pauses. But he broke first. "If there's nothing more, Sergeant?" He checked his watch as if the audience in the upper balcony needed to see him doing so.

Winters wasn't interested in the play. "She told people you were important in her life. Why do you think she'd say that?"

Armstrong flushed. "I don't have the slightest idea. I told you I barely knew her. She was just one of the young women who came to the center. I haven't been back in town for long, but I'm trying to get my practice up and running. It helps if I do volunteer work. Make contacts. I thought I could offer some of these girls substance abuse counseling, if that's what they need. I also have experience with homeless issues. But Ashley didn't want my assistance. We don't make them take help, you know." He pointed at Smith. "Her mother knew the girl better than me. Ask Lucky these questions."

Winters stood up, so suddenly he caught Smith by surprise. "I'll be in touch, Mr. Armstrong."

◇◇◇

"Call Rose Benoit in Vancouver," Winters said as Smith maneuvered the van down the steep residential street toward town. Benoit and Winters had been partners for a long time; she was now the inspector in charge of commercial crime. "Tell her I need to talk to someone who can fill me in on this Julian Armstrong."

"You think he has a police record?"

"Won't know until I ask, will I? I can check, easily enough from my own desk, but there seems to be more here than a record search will tell. He left Vancouver in a hurry, something to do with 'rich bitches', I'll venture to guess. You may have noticed that he doesn't have a respectful attitude toward his clients."

"Still, I don't see what you're looking for, John. So Ashley told her friend she liked him. It's his job to be friends with these kids. He likes to think he's a local, but he's not. Not any more. He doesn't know what's wrong and so he's trying too hard." She coughed. "Well, that's my take anyway."

"Ashley told Amy that he was quote, the key to her future, unquote."

"Perhaps to her he was. Even though she might not have gone to him for help yet, in her mind he might be the one who'd help her unlock the solution to her problems."

"I asked you to contact Rose for me. I didn't ask you to analyze my reasons. But you may remember that, according to Amy, Ashley knew Armstrong in Vancouver. Note that he didn't mention that."

Chapter Twelve

When Winters got back to his desk the coroner's report on Ashley Doe was ready.

Killed, he already knew, by an overdose of heroin. Restraint marks on wrists and ankles, but no other signs of recent trauma. Then, with as much emotion as a butcher's order, came a lengthy list of previously broken bones. Left arm twice, collarbone once, cracked cheekbone. Old wounds on a pre-pubescent body.

"Shit," Winters said to the empty room. He rubbed his hands over his eyes. Hard to interpret this report as anything other than sustained abuse when the girl was only a child.

In light of that evidence, it was a good possibility Ashley'd been on the run. He'd met plenty of girls in Vancouver for whom life on the streets was preferable to what they got at home. For many of them life on the streets soon turned into a death sentence. One way or another.

Ashley might have been on the run from a bad family life. Understandable.

But why did she have a baby—who wasn't hers—with her?

They'd put the question out, but so far hadn't heard any reports of a white male newborn kidnapped over the last couple of months anywhere in Canada. Reports from the States would take longer to come in. Europe longer still.

His phone rang. Eliza's cell. He answered with a smile.

"Lunch," she said.

"Work," he said.

"I'm standing on the pavement outside of the station. It's very hot. A young man is walking up the hill toward me. He's not wearing a shirt, and his long, burnished hair is flowing around his shoulders. He looks like Daniel Day-Lewis in *the Last of the Mohicans*. I wonder if he'd care for some nourishment."

Winters laughed. "I've only been on duty three hours."

"And I've been in discussions with Barney and the Grizzly Resort people for what feels like weeks."

Barney was Bernadette McLaughlin, Eliza's long time agent. Now approaching seventy, she'd celebrated her sixtieth birthday by giving up her habitual pack of smokes a day, and the sixty-fifth by jettisoning the single malt whiskey. As tough as they came, Winters wished Barney'd join the police.

"He's almost here, John, what do I tell Daniel Day-Lewis?"

"Tell him he's out of luck. I'll be right there."

"Love you," she purred, as the call disconnected.

His friends had warned him against taking up with Eliza. Woman like her, they'd said, beautiful, indulged, wouldn't last a year as wife of a cop. But Eliza had proved them wrong. She was a great police officer's wife. If he'd said he wasn't free for lunch, she would have laughed and let it go.

He put a light jacket on and left his office.

They ate at a trendy, pocket-sized bistro on Front Street. The patio extended into the road and took up a lane of parking spaces. It was surrounded by a white picket fence draped with boxes overflowing with white geraniums and purple lobelia. Umbrellas that could have been chosen to match the purple flowers shaded them from the sun. The street was heavy with summer traffic. Next door a guitarist sat outside the bank, playing Beatles tunes and collecting coins in his guitar case. Koola Glacier loomed over the town, snow shining in the sun.

"Barney's mad for me to take this job," Eliza said, as the waiter brought her glass of white wine. Winters was having a Coke, heavy on the ice. "At my age it's becoming harder and harder for her to find me good jobs."

"You're going to take it then?"

"I still haven't decided, John. It pays well, close to home."

"Is, uh, José still around?" Ice cubs clinked in his glass.

"He's signed. Now they're waiting for me to decide. Barney says they won't wait long. She thinks they have someone else in mind if I keep stalling."

"Just a negotiating ploy. They want you."

"You're always so loyal. But let's face it, John, there are hundreds of women out there, thousands, every bit as good as me, all anxious for work because we're too old for most stuff."

He snorted.

"There's an abandoned building on the property. They're doing it up inside to look like a finished suite, something to show prospective investors who don't want to put their money down on nothing but a set of blueprints. Frank and Steve want to use it for the photographs. They'll do the shoot in the faux-condo, relaxing in front of the fireplace, sitting on the balcony admiring the view. Laughing over drinks beside the roaring log fire. All the usual poses. They've planted grass and flowers and built a path that goes nowhere to provide a backdrop, but I think the river and the mountains should be all the backdrop they need."

"Tell me again what's bothering you about it."

She wrapped cold soba noodles around her fork and took a bite. "Um, good. I like it here, in Trafalgar. If I take this job, I'm taking sides in the argument over the resort. And I don't know if we can fit in once my airbrushed face is trying to seduce people into buying a condo at Grizzly resort."

"This is a passionate town," he said, picking up a ketchup-drenched French fry. "Look at that demonstration last month over the Garden. Half the town was on one side, half on the other."

"Yes, people like your Constable Smith's mother. People who've lived here for most, if not all, of their lives. But we're newcomers. I wonder if that will make the difference."

Newcomers. Ashley Doe was a newcomer. And, according to Marigold, she'd been interested in the Grizzly resort.

What did he know about Ashley, other than she was dead from a heroin overdose, apparently not self-inflicted? That she was opposed to the Grizzly resort. As Eliza pointed out, lots of people were. That she thought Julian Armstrong was the key to her life. Did Armstrong have a connection to the resort? He'd better find out.

"John."

He blinked. Eliza was looking at him. The fine lines radiating from her green eyes and pink mouth crinkled into a gentle smile. "Like a TV show when it breaks for commercials, I know when you're back on the job."

He grabbed another fry, and stood up. "Sorry."

She sipped at her wine. "Oh, look. Here comes Daniel Day-Lewis, perhaps he'd like a half-eaten burger."

Winters kissed her firmly on the mouth, and went back to work.

Molly Smith was dreaming about Graham. They were on the beach at Tofino. They were lying on the sand, white moonlight washing over naked bodies, surf pounding the shore. She was settling into his embrace, preparing her body to accept his when she realized it wasn't Graham above her, but the man she'd almost slept with earlier in the summer. Norman, Adam Tocek's police dog, was barking, barking frantically, trying to push the man off her, but Molly's legs were wrapped around his hips, holding him tight.

Her eyes opened, and she exhaled, heavily. The sound was not the Mountie's dog, but the screaming baby. For once she couldn't be too angry at Miller. Waking up after, she looked at the clock, two hours' sleep was better than living through that dream.

Again.

Her bedroom windows were open, and a cool early morning breeze stirred the lace curtains. She went downstairs in search of coffee.

Her mother was sitting in the kitchen, rocking the pram with one foot. Her hair was a mass of unwashed and uncombed red and grey curls. Puffy black circles that hadn't been there last week turned her eyes into slits. Lucky usually opened all the windows and lifted the blinds after sunset, to let the cool night air into the house to act as air conditioning the next day. But last night she hadn't, and even this early the air in the kitchen was heavy with impending heat.

Smith looked toward the hook by the door—not yet seven, but her dad's car keys were gone. Even Sylvester, who loved Lucky above all, was nowhere to be seen. Smith poured herself a cup of coffee, and added a splash of cream.

"When do they stop crying?"

"With luck, by the time they go to Police College."

Smith briefly considered telling her mother that she'd mind Miller for a while so Lucky could get some sleep. But the impulse didn't last. Lucky would have to deal with her own problem.

"This is putting me off having kids of my own."

She'd meant it as a joke, a match to her mother's crack about Police College. Instead, Lucky's face settled into angry lines. "Babies cry, Moonlight. That's what they do. Better you find out now before it's too late to send it back."

"If you want me, I'll be on the computer, checking out the apartment-for-rent ads."

It was supposed to be her day off. But the last thing Smith felt like was hanging around this house. She thought of Adam Tocek and his offer to go hiking. A good tough hike, deep into the old growth forest would do her a world of good. She considered trying to get a call through to him, ask if the offer was still open. Maybe they could camp overnight—in separate sleeping bags, of course. But the image of him, his soft brown eyes downcast, his ears pink with embarrassment, digging patterns into the dust with his boot, burst into her mind. Better not to go there. Instead, she'd head upstairs and check out places for rent. She had to get out of this house before her parents drove her mad. Never mind the cost. If she lived in town she could get a ride to work every day, so she wouldn't need a car.

Chapter Thirteen

Lucky rocked the cradle with one foot, and drank coffee with one hand. She was taking the baby to the doctor for a check-up this afternoon; she might ask if there was something she could do to get Miller to sleep better. Surely things had improved in the child rearing department since Samwise and Moonlight were babies. She could call Sam for advice, but, to her disapproval, he didn't seem to be involved in the rearing of his own children, and Lucky didn't care much for his wife, Judy.

Moonlight's bedroom was directly above the kitchen. Lucky could hear her slamming doors and stomping about. Andy had brought yesterday's paper in, but she hadn't read it yet. Miller's cries were slowing down, but although the muscles in her leg begged for mercy, Lucky didn't dare stop rocking.

She picked up the paper and turned it over.

'Grow-op Bust' screamed the headline. And there, in living color, for all the citizens of Trafalgar to see, was a picture of Constable Molly Smith in the foreground, while in the background men walked out of the building carrying large bags.

The front door opened. "Moonlight," Lucky yelled.

The blond head rounded the kitchen door. Moonlight's short hair stood on end; she looked like a frightened porcupine. "What now? I'm going into town. I didn't think you'd be wanting the car."

The swelling on her daughter's beautiful face had gone down and the bruise was fading. This morning, the cut lip looked like nothing more dramatic than the remains of a cold sore. But the wounds reminded Lucky that Moonlight did have a dangerous profession. Even here in peaceful little Trafalgar. "Miller and I have an appointment at the doctor at 1:30."

"I'll have it back by then."

Lucky tapped the paper with one chewed fingernail. "What is the meaning of this?"

Moonlight glanced at the headline and sighed. "Meredith again, I'll bet."

"What are you doing putting a hard working entrepreneur out of business?"

Moonlight's blue eyes grew wide. "Are you kidding? It was a freakin' grow-op. Right in the middle of town. Of course we put them out of business. And a nice long stay in prison'll do them good."

"Don't swear around Miller."

Moonlight rolled her eyes.

"And don't give me that look either."

"Bye, Mom. Have a nice day."

"I read a letter in the paper from a former police officer saying that in all his years on the job he had never once been called to an incident caused by a person smoking pot. How does that compare to the consumption of alcohol? You're a policewoman, answer that."

"The house was rented. When the owners get here, you can come and talk to them, Mom. Ask them how they feel that their house is so full of toxic mold that the officers wore bio-suits. They'll have to gut the place before they can even dream of living there again. Ask the neighbors if they're okay with having a rat's nest of uncovered wiring and illegal electricity consumption next door. There's a school on the street over. The place was a potential bomb."

"They wouldn't have to go to such lengths if their product wasn't illegal. There's lots of good land in the mountains, suitable for growing marijuana. Why…"

"Tell you what, Mom. When the Prime Minister calls to ask for my opinion on the legalization of pot, I'll tell him to talk to you. Until then I'll do my job and protect the citizens of this town, whether they want me to or not. Got it?"

Moonlight slammed the door on her way out.

Lucky peered into the pram. Miller was sound asleep.

"Good boy," she said, "If you want to be part of this family you have to sleep through the occasional thunderstorm we call a discussion."

The phone rang, and Lucky struggled out of her chair to answer before it woke the baby.

"I've heard from my source," a woman said, "that trouble's heading your way. I'll be there in half an hour."

She didn't identify herself, and didn't need to. Lucky went upstairs to get dressed. Best to look mildly presentable. Good thing Moonlight had decided to go into town. She would not want to be here.

Chapter Fourteen

Jim Denton raised one eyebrow as Smith punched in the security code to let herself into the body of the police station.

"What brings you round, Molly?"

"I work here, remember. They pay me the big bucks to show my smiling face once in a while."

"You're not on shift today."

"Some paperwork to catch up on."

"I admire your dedication." Denton looked back at his monitors. "Oh, for god's sake. There he goes again."

"Who?" Smith walked behind him to have a look. In five, a man was standing facing the cell door. His hand was at his crotch and his feet were spread about two feet apart. "Is he blind?" she asked. "Can't he see the toilet in the corner?"

A howl came from below. Not a bad imitation of a wolf.

"Every couple of hours he pisses in the corners of his cell, while barking like a dog. He's marking his territory or something."

"Most of our clients don't want to lay claim to their cells." Smith laughed and went to the constables' office.

Sure enough there was a voice mail message from Inspector Benoit. The strong New York accent provided a name and number of someone in the Vancouver police to contact regarding Julian Armstrong.

Smith scribbled the information on a scrap of paper. She leaned back in her chair. Winters had only asked her to get the contact info for him.

She walked down the hall to the GIS office. The door was open and Winters was typing with two fingers.

She knocked lightly.

He looked up and she thought she saw a ghost of a smile on his face as he caught sight of her. But she probably imagined it.

"Come in." He pointed to his computer. "The kid you found in the alley on Saturday? The heroin overdose?"

"I remember."

"Before they'd release him from the hospital, they made him agree to start going to the methadone clinic."

"Did he say where he'd gotten the stuff?"

"On the street. Doesn't remember what street. Medium sized guy, no identifying features. Come to think of it might even have been a woman. It was dark, blah, blah, blah."

"Let's hope he sticks with the program anyway."

"What's up?"

"I came in to check if Inspector Benoit had returned my call." Smith held the paper up as evidence. "She did, and said to contact a Constable Czarnecki."

"Thanks, Molly, but you could have checked for messages from home."

"Home," she said, "is not exactly a relaxing place, now that we have an infant in residence."

Winters held out his hand, and Smith was about to hand over the paper, when Lopez came in.

"Morning all," he said, with his usual cheerful smile.

"Ray," Smith said. "You have kids. How come you're still sane?"

"Normal people say hello to their co-workers first thing in the morning."

"Hello. My mom's looking after this baby, and it screams all night long."

"There's your answer," Lopez said. "Your mom's looking after it. Madeleine looked after our kids. I worked nights for seven years straight, sometimes had to beg the other guys to switch with me. Sorry to tell you this, Molly, but you're the wrong gender."

"Don't believe a word he says," Winters said.

Smith smiled. She'd seen Lopez with his daughters. Hard to imagine a more involved father.

"You coming?" Lopez asked his sergeant.

"Yeah," Winters got to his feet. "I have to go, but as you're in anyway, Molly, do you mind giving this Czarnecki a call?"

Of course she didn't mind. That's why she was here on her day off. "Okay."

"Find out what he knows about Armstrong, if anything. I'll call you when I'm done and you can fill me in."

She went back to the Constables' office to make the call. If they had to play phone tag, Smith feared that Winters would take over. As she'd hoped, Czarnecki answered on the first ring. She identified herself and told him why she was calling.

"Hold on a sec," Czarnecki said. Smith heard the click of a computer keyboard. She looked out the window onto George Street. A middle-aged woman, overweight, dressed in a red Bermuda short set and a wide-brimmed purple hat, struggled to walk up the steep hill. The woman stopped to catch her breath and fan herself with a tourist map of Trafalgar. The EMTs would be busy in this heat, what with over-eager, out-of-shape tourists wanting to climb mountains. It was so hot that one of the constables had almost fainted yesterday while patrolling the streets in the early afternoon.

Czarnecki came back on the line. "Oh, yeah. I remember him. Not a crime to be a sleazeball, unfortunately."

"What do you mean?"

"Couple complaints about sexual impropriety toward his clients."

Smith's stomach turned somersaults. "Go on."

"Complaints were laid that he offered his sexual favors as part of the healing process." Smith heard papers shuffle. "Nice work if you can get it."

"Kids? Youth?"

"No. The complainants, there were two, were adult women. Very adult women, if you get my meaning."

"Any charges?"

"Due to the age of the complainants, it was decided that there was no reason to lay criminal charges. If we could charge every sleazeball who calls himself a therapist, we'd run out of room in the jails. In one case the complaint was laid by the husband, and it looks like the wife wouldn't back it up. No names here, Constable Smith, but between you and me, I'd suggest this complaint came to us because the husband, is... ahem... an esteemed member of the police board of a community in the Lower Mainland. You might want to talk to Armstrong's professional organization. My notes say that that at least one of the women intended to take her story to them. That's all I know."

Smith said her thanks, with promises of a beer next time she was in the big city, and tried to cover up her disappointment. She'd hoped to dig up a rash of charges by teenagers and young mothers. Something she could use to confront Armstrong and have him confessing to an inappropriate relationship with Ashley Doe.

Still, Armstrong had come to the attention of the police, even though charges were not laid, which might indicate that, as Sergeant Winters suspected, he'd left Vancouver under less than favorable conditions. Plus, if two women went to all the trouble of reporting his behavior to the police, odds were good there were plenty others who hadn't complained.

She typed up a report of the conversation for Sergeant Winters.

Report filed, she leaned back in her chair and checked her watch. Ten o'clock. The day stretched in front of her. She could go hiking, alone. She could go home and fight with her mother. She could look for an apartment and/or a car. But it was too bloody hot to be tramping around town.

She picked up the phone and dialed a number from memory.

To the consternation of her cloth-coat Republican parents, Lucy Casey had been involved in progressive politics almost since she began to talk. When she and Andy came to Canada, Lucy Casey morphing into Lucky Smith, she hadn't changed her stripes. And over the years, she had made many friends of like mind.

A car pulled into the Smith driveway. Three women got out. They all had well-earned lines carved into tanned faces, much gray in their hair. One back was heavily stooped, and one proud woman walked on a cane, refusing any and all assistance.

They didn't bother to knock on the door to announce their arrival, but found comfortable seats on the wide veranda at the front of the Smith home.

Miller was, at last, sleeping soundly.

Lucky stood at the living room window and watched her friends take up their positions. She looked beyond them toward her garden. She kept a large vegetable patch on the south-facing slope leading down to the river. The land surrounding the house and garage was lined by overflowing perennial beds and terracotta pots of varying sizes filled with colorful annuals. Over the years, she'd constructed arrangements of stone and rock to add accent to the gardens. Lately the heat had been so intense, the rain so infrequent, and Lucky so busy with the baby, that the plants were calling out for water, dying like a remnant of the Foreign Legion, lost in the Sahara.

She made iced tea from the pot of English Breakfast prepared earlier, and the women outside chatted amongst themselves. But before the ice cubes had melted, and the last of the grandchild photographs had been admired, a dark SUV came up the driveway. It was followed by a white truck with Trafalgar City Police painted across the sides.

Jody Burke jumped out of the car and Constable Dave Evans emerged, without much enthusiasm, from the police car.

They walked toward the house.

The women on the porch rocked rocking chairs or settled back into cushions. One woman had brought her knitting—balls of white wool spread around her feet like the ground beneath a copse of cottonwood in spring.

Jody Burke stopped about five yards before the stairs. "I'm here to see Mrs. Smith."

"She's busy caring for a baby." An elderly woman peered at the intruders through thick, black-trimmed glasses. Her gray hair was thinning on top and a network of deep lines carved through the skin of her sharp-boned face. She wore Birkenstocks with white socks pulled up to her knees, colorful shorts and a matching top. Her right arm was wrapped in a cast. Jane Reynolds, former professor of physics, was retired from active teaching and research, and these days spent her time visiting her grandchildren and traveling the world as an internationally known peace and environmental activist.

Burke planted her feet into the ground. Dave Evans fingered his belt, adjusted his hat, and watched a large black raven cross the blue sky.

Jane had suggested that Lucky stay out of sight and let her handle things. Lucky peeked out from behind the living room blinds. Sylvester was shut in the pantry, howling.

Burke looked at Jane. "I'm here to speak to Mrs. Smith."

Moving with great care and deliberation, Jane got to her feet. She walked stiffly toward the steps, as if her old bones were hurting her. "Mrs. Smith is busy, as I may have mentioned."

Burke took a deep breath. She stared at the three aging women blocking her way.

Jane held out her hand. "May I see your authorization to take the child, please?"

Burke shifted. "I was hoping we could do this without any fuss."

They were so desperate for good foster families in the province, Lucky almost expected a call asking if she'd like to take another baby, or maybe two. Why Burke had it in for her, Lucky couldn't imagine. She'd never met the woman until the other day.

A good friend of Jane's worked mornings at the lawyer's office directly across the street from the police station. From her office she had an excellent view of the front door, the door that members of the public walked in and out of all day. Jane's friend didn't seem to get too much work done (she was the mother of the senior partner) but she was a mine of information about the comings and goings of the police and public. When Lucky told Jane about Jody Burke and her determination to take Miller, Jane said she'd ask her friend to keep an eye out for any attempts to involve the police in the custody of Miller Doe. Jody had marched into the police station this morning; the lawyer's mother called Jane, and Jane called her supporters and ordered them into position.

"Without any fuss," Jane repeated, her voice pitched as if she were lecturing to a hall full of first year students. "Or legally? Dave, it's nice to see you, dear. I hope you're well?"

"Yes, M'm," Evans mumbled, looking as if he wished aliens would descend from the skies and kidnap him from this very spot.

Dave Evans had broken Jane Reynolds' arm when he'd shoved her to the ground to protect her from a fire bomb. *Small towns*, Lucky thought, feeling a small knot of pleasure in her chest. There was no way Dave would ever arrest, or even speak firmly to, Jane.

"Ms Burke?" Jane said, her hand still outstretched. "May I see your legal papers ordering the surrender of the child in question?"

Burke stood her ground. "As you may not be aware, I am authorized by the province of British Columbia to act on its behalf. I don't need a court order."

"You mean you couldn't get one," Jane said. "Dave, why are you here?"

Evans shrugged. "Ms. Burke came into the station and asked for a police escort. She, ahem, said the baby might be in danger if Mrs. Smith wouldn't hand him over. Sorry, Mrs. Reynolds, but the Sarge told me to come. I don't know anything more about it. But, well, if you don't have a court order, Ms. Burke, you can't go into Mrs. Smith's house, and I can't ask her to bring out the child."

A light breeze rustled the tops of the cottonwood trees by the river, and a hummingbird hovered in the air, its wings moving to a beat faster than the eye could follow, searching for nectar in the feeders Lucky had hung on either end of the porch. They were empty, and the tiny bird darted away.

The door opened and Lucky stepped outside. The heat enveloped her like a *burka*. No one said a word. The windows of the police truck were down and they could hear the radio crackle to life as Evans called in, asking—begging—for instructions.

Burke stared at Lucky. Her eyes were cold and hard.

She turned and walked back to her car.

Chapter Fifteen

"Hey Chris, It's me."

"Oh. Hi." Not the warmest of greetings.

"I'm in town, not working today, and thought it would be fun to have breakfast and catch up," Molly said into the phone.

"I've eaten."

"Okay, it's late for breakfast. How about meeting me at Eddie's for a coffee?"

Christa hesitated. "I don't know. Today's the day I planned to get started reading for my courses. Class starts next week."

"That's great, Chris, I was… well, after what happened I was afraid you'd drop out of school."

"You mean after Charlie beat the shit out of me because you wouldn't help me?"

Smith closed her eyes and saw her friend's body after John Winters had found Christa lying in the stairwell of her apartment: face like the butcher's best steak, hair thick with drying blood, broken teeth. Paramedics loading her into the ambulance.

"I'm sorry, Chris. I'm so sorry," Smith said, so softly that Christa might not have heard. "I tried."

"Not hard enough."

Smith hat begun to say goodbye when she heard Christa whisper "wait". The phone didn't disconnect and after a long pause Christa said, "Dad's agreed to pay whatever the dentist charges, so I might end up better looking after this." She had a minor overbite; lots of guys thought it cute, but Christa figured it made her look like Bugs Bunny. "Have you heard anything about Charlie?"

"Nothing new. He was refused bail because John, Sergeant Winters, said he was a danger to you. You'll be notified of what happens."

"Will I have to testify? Will I have to see him?" Her voice sounded small, and very frail.

Smith hesitated. If Bassing decided to fight the charges, Christa would have to go to court. But Christa didn't need to worry about that now. Wait and see how it turned out. If she did have to testify, Smith would accompany her friend. And sit in the front row, in uniform, all body armor and attitude. "Probably not. It could be six months or more before the trial. And it might not even come to that. You just worry about getting those courses under your belt."

"Okay."

"Sure you don't want a coffee?"

"I have one here. Eddie's been sending Jolene around every morning with coffee, size *gigantico*, and two bagels with cream cheese."

"That's nice of him."

"Yeah, it is. People are nice, aren't they Molly?"

People in Trafalgar *were* nice. Winters had told Smith that Eddie was upset because Christa'd been attacked on her way home from his shop. Her breakfast bagel, tossed onto the lawn, had alerted Winters and Smith that something was wrong.

"But I can't be relying on Eddie and Jolene forever, can I?" Christa said.

"No." Smith cleared her throat.

"Maybe we could have coffee tomorrow? Or another day this week?"

"Tomorrow would be good. How about I call you in the morning?"

"Okay, Molly. Bye."

"Bye, Chris."

Smith hung up the phone as Brad Noseworthy came into the constables' office, laughing at something that had been said out in the hallway.

Tears were gathering behind her eyes and she blinked rapidly, wishing them away.

"You okay, Molly?"

"Yeah, Brad. Couldn't be better." She turned to him with a big smile. "Except that I'm starving."

"Speaking of methadone," Ray Lopez said. "I heard you talking about Julian Armstrong earlier, before we were interrupted. He's new to town and is helping Amin out at the clinic. What's your interest?"

"Just interest. Let me know if you hear anything."

"Never would have thought of that, Boss. Glad you reminded me."

"You don't have work to do, Ray? Keeping trouble from the streets of our town?"

They waited for the light to change, watching as a man, blond-streaked dreadlocks tied into a series of knots at the top of his head, beard half-way down his chest, strolled across the street, against the light. Winters considered giving the guy a warning, but he let it pass. He'd taken his detective out for a coffee, although Lopez was trying to reduce his intake and had instead ordered a carrot juice. His doctor had told him to cut down on caffeine, sugar, and fat. Lopez had managed to get down to one cup of coffee a day, surviving for the rest of the day on what he hoped were healthy enough drinks to compensate for the fact that he had no intention of giving up his daily lunch of Chinese take-out, or a hearty dinner followed by something from Madeline's repertoire of desserts. Lopez filled Winters in on the state of his investigation into the hard drugs dripping—slowly, but still coming—into town. Not much, was the essence of the Detective's report. The undercover officer had been shown the morgue photo of Ashley, but didn't recognize her. Which meant nothing except that they couldn't prove she'd been hanging around the heroin dealer they were after. It had been a long shot anyway.

Molly Smith walked by on the other side of the road, fair hair standing on end, long, muscular brown legs topped with khaki shorts, feet wrapped in sturdy sports sandals. She caught sight of the detectives and lifted her hand in greeting before continuing on her way.

"Now she," Winters said, "would be a great plant."

"If everyone between here and Vancouver didn't know who she is," Lopez said with a grin. "Can you imagine Molly trying to work undercover, while her mother and her pals burst into the deal, telling everyone to just get along."

Winters exhaled. "That wouldn't be so bad, would it?"

The light changed and Winters crossed the street, back to the station.

A welcome blast of frosty air hit him as he opened the door. Dave Evans was leaning on the counter by the dispatch desk, Kevlar vest undone, rolling a can of Coke back and forth across his red cheeks. His underarms and the front of his uniform shirt were so wet, he might have put them on directly out of the washing machine. "Waste of time," he said to Denton as Winters came in. "Should have known that woman wouldn't have a chance in hell against Lucky and her bunch."

"What's Lucky Smith up to now?" Winters asked.

"Stupid social worker tried to take that baby found at the Ashley Doe scene away from her. She came in here and led the Sarge to believe that Mrs. Smith was in contempt of court so she needed a police escort in case Lucky resisted."

"She didn't have an order?"

"She had absolutely nothing. Not even any moral authority. No reason Mrs. Smith can't take care of a homeless baby as well as a foster family. Made me look like a damned fool."

"Not that that's a first, Dave," Denton said.

"Ha, ha," the constable replied. He popped the tab on his can of pop. "You try taking on Molly Smith's mother. I'd rather go up against Tony Soprano. Tell Molly that and you're a dead man."

Denton laughed. "I had a few run-ins with Lucky Smith in my early days in Trafalgar. I'd show you my scars but the Sergeant's watching."

"Don't let me interrupt," Winters said. He walked down the corridor to his office.

After taking off his jacket and hanging it on the back of his chair, he sat down and started up his computer. The phone rang, routed from the central number by Denton.

"John Winters."

"Yeah, hi." It was a male, probably young, the voice tending toward the higher end of the register.

"Can I help you?"

"Are you the guy in charge of the investigation I read about in the paper?"

Winters restrained a sigh. "Can you tell me what investigation you're referring to, sir?"

"The girl, Ashley, found dead behind the women's support center?"

"Did you know her?"

"Kinda. We weren't friends, you understand. I mean I've seen her around town, her and her baby. In the coffee shops, on the streets. You know."

Of course Winters knew. A lot of people had seen Ashley walking around town, but no one could tell the police anything worthwhile about her. The girl might as well have been a ghost. But there must be some reason Denton put this call through to Winters, rather than just taking down the caller's information.

"Do you know something about her?" Sometimes he thought he might as well have made his mother proud and become a dentist. This job could be like pulling teeth.

"About how she died, no. I was sure sorry to hear about it."

"Then why are you calling?"

"Uh, well. It's like this. I saw her arguing with a man a day or so before her death. I thought maybe you'd like to know."

Winters stopped drawing circles on his notepad. "Arguing?"

"Like really intense, you know."

"Can I ask your name?"

The man hesitated.

"I like to know who I'm talking to, that's all. I'm John Winters."

"Yeah, I know. I'm Mike. Mike Jergens."

"I'd like to hear about this argument you overheard, Mike. But first of all, can you be more specific about the date? Did you notice the time?"

"Tuesday or Wednesday, maybe? It wasn't Monday, cause I'm closed on Monday. Most days, I go for coffee around five, when Debbie, my assistant, comes in. They were standing outside Big Eddie's, the coffee place?"

"I know it."

"I saw Ashley arguing with a man. It was, like I said, real intense. She was shouting. I particularly remember because the baby was crying. That was pretty unusual. Ashley's baby's always so good."

Not, Winters thought, *according to Molly Smith*. "Do you know what they were arguing about?"

"Only what Ashley told me."

Winters wanted to reach down the phone line and wrap the other end around Mike Jergen's neck. "You spoke to her about this?"

"For a couple of minutes. She was upset, so I bought her a coffee."

Winters looked at the ceiling. There was nothing of interest there so he looked at his computer. The logo of the Trafalgar City Police skipped around the screen. He took a breath. "I'd like to talk to you in person, Mike. Where can I find you?"

"Well, uh, I'd rather not. I'm kinda busy."

"It sounds like you have information I need."

"Well, I guess. I'm at Mike's Movie Mansion. I'm Mike."

"I'll be there in ten. Don't go anywhere, Mike."

◇◇◇

Before going to George's for breakfast, Molly Smith put five quarters into a sidewalk box and took out a copy of the *Trafalgar Daily Gazette*. The popular restaurant was almost empty, breakfast rush finished, lunch crowd still to come. She took a table at the back, away from the windows, ordered coffee and scrambled egg hash, and flipped the paper to the back section. The classifieds.

'Shared accommodation. Female, N/S, N/P, Private bath. Riverside.' And a phone number. Smith dug in her bag for a pen and came up empty. On the job, she kept herself well organized: her personal life was another matter.

"Sorry," she said to the vaguely-familiar waitress who brought her coffee. "Do you have a pen I can borrow?"

"Sure, Moonlight. How's things?"

"Good." Smith struggled for the girl's name. Inconveniently she wasn't wearing a name tag above her right breast. "How are things with you?"

The waitress pulled the stub of a pencil out of her shirt pocket, handed it to Smith, and shifted one hip to take a rest. "Jimmy'll be seven next month, and Rachel's five. Time flies doesn't it? I read about you in the paper sometimes, Moonlight. Sounds exciting, what you do."

"Naw. Deadly boring most of the time." Helena, that was the woman's name. Helena. She'd run with Meredith Morgenstern's crowd in high school. "Thanks for this." Smith indicated the pencil, and turned her attention to her open newspaper.

Helena leaned close, holding the coffee pot. "What really happened with that Ashley girl? Some of the customers are saying she was murdered, but the paper's saying nothing."

"Did you know her?"

"No. I don't remember her ever coming in here. Just wondering." She lowered her voice. "I won't tell anyone. Honest"

"I'm just a constable, Helena, still on probation. I don't know anything more than the paper does. Sometimes less."

Helena lifted the coffee pot and walked away.

Smith began circling ads. Sharing a flat with someone might not be too bad. She leaned back to allow Helena, no longer interested in engaging in chitchat, to place her breakfast on the table and top up the coffee.

Or she could look for a room in a house, like Julian Armstrong had. She stirred cream into her coffee. Armstrong. He had to have something to do with this. He arrived in town only a few weeks ago. He'd set himself up in practice as a drug counselor, and worked at the Mid-Kootenay Methadone Clinic. Ashley Doe had died by heroin overdose. Methadone was used as a substitute drug—it supposedly helped junkies get off heroin. Armstrong would meet plenty of hard-core users at the clinic. What better place for a dealer to find his customers? Conveniently, Julian also helped out at the Women's Support Center. Where Ashley sometimes showed up.

Smith poured ketchup onto her hash and stirred eggs around the plate with her fork.

Ashley had told Amy that Armstrong was the key to her future. Or some such garbage that at the time Smith assumed had dreamy romantic implications. But was she saying instead that Armstrong and she would make a financial partnership?

Smith swallowed most of the hash, not noticing how it tasted. She left the newspaper on the table for Helena to clear away with the dirty dishes.

The site of the proposed Grizzly Resort was situated about ten kilometers outside of Trafalgar, off Number 3 highway, heading north on the way to the town of Nelson.

John Winters took the department's unmarked van, and had barely left the town limits when his cell phone rang. He pulled over, mainly because cell phone reception would die in another kilometer or two.

"Winters."

"Hi." Eliza. "It's me. Time to talk?"

"Sure. What's up?" He pushed his sunglasses onto the top of his head. He switched off the car, hating to kill the air conditioning, but simply talking on the phone to Eliza would make him feel guilty if he left the engine idling.

"I've just hung up from Barney. She said they want me, very much, and have upped the offer. Considerably."

"That's good," he said.

"Well, yes."

"You don't sound too sure. Still worried about what the townspeople will say?"

"That's part of it. You know I don't care about the money." That, he knew, was true. Before she'd even finished high school, Eliza had been a top-of-the-line runway model. She'd hated it with a passion, and decided that if she was going to do something she hated as a career, she'd make sure it paid off in the long term. She took courses in finance, and read everything she could get her hands on. Winters still smiled when he thought of what a stir the eye-poppingly gorgeous teenager would have made in classes of middle-aged men trying to brush up on their investment skills. The result, almost thirty years later, was that Eliza Winters was a wealthy woman who only took work that interested her.

"You see, John, well, it's nice to be wanted. Frank told Barney that I was so perfect for their campaign they'll pay whatever I ask."

"I'm surprised a hardnosed businessman like Frank Clemmins would put all his cards on the table like that."

He could almost hear the shrug of her thin shoulders. "I suppose he doesn't know anything about dealing with temperamental artistic types."

Anyone less temperamental than Eliza would be hard to find. "Are you going to take it?"

"I think I am, John, I think I am. But I want to know what you think."

"Me?"

"Of course, you, silly."

"Well, if you're asking for my advice: take it. Chances are no one will recognize you in the ads, anyway. Half the time I don't even recognize you in print."

"Okay! I'm going to do it." Her voice was tinged with pleasure. "I'm calling Barney. Right now. Love you." She hung up.

He started the engine, and turned the fan up a notch to give him a good gust of air conditioning. She was going to call Barney *right now*. If Barney was available, and considering that she had been one of the first people in Vancouver to get a Blackberry and a Bluetooth, chances were that she would be, Barney would be contacting Clemmins at the Grizzly resort, right about... the time Sergeant John Winters arrived on police business.

Small towns.

An RCMP vehicle came toward him, heading into town. The driver slowed down, recognizing the TCP's van. Winters gave thumbs up and the driver nodded and sped away.

It was a different sort of policing here, to be sure, from the streets of a city like Vancouver. Winters had been in the grocery store with his wife one day last week. While she struggled to decide between organic tomatoes from the coast or non-organic locally grown ones, Winters spotted a man he'd arrested for masturbating in an alley behind Front Street in the middle of the afternoon heading toward them. Winters edged away from Eliza and prepared for a confrontation. Instead the man greeted him heartily, and even introduced his own wife, a tall buxom redhead who laughed like a horse. With a cheery 'see you next month'—presumably in court—the man continued on his way, pushing a cart piled high with meat and frozen foods.

Eliza's professional life had nothing to do with him, or the Trafalgar City Police. He pulled his sunglasses down, checked his side mirrors, and pulled onto the highway.

There were no protesters at the entrance to the resort site, and the sign was un-defaced. The chassis of the van and Winters' back teeth shook as he maneuvered the vehicle, slowly and carefully, down the gravel road.

Hoping to catch Blacklock in the office without warning, he hadn't phoned to say he was coming. There were three cars in the parking area beside the site office trailer: an ancient Toyota Tercel, a black BMW convertible, and a black Ford F150 so clean that it must have been washed moments after coming down the dirt road.

Bernice, the company secretary, sat behind the reception desk. The doors to the partners' small offices were closed. Architects' drawings, blueprints, and site-plans were pinned to the walls. Disconcertingly, a large picture of Eliza and José, posing with the river behind them, hung behind Bernice's desk. Eliza smiled up at the male model, her face radiant, full of happiness and, if one looked closely, sexual desire. It was, of course, her professional face. But John Winters still didn't care for that José character.

"A pleasure to see you, Sergeant Winters," Bernice said. "How can I help you?"

"Is Mr. Blacklock in?"

"He's just arrived. I'll check to see if he's free."

"I'm free." The door to the left opened and Blacklock came out. He crossed the room in three strides, hand outstretched. "How about some coffee, Bernice? Come on in, John. It was nice to meet you the other evening. How's Eliza? I hope she's considering our offer. My wife insists that absolutely no one else will do."

"She's well," Winters said, wishing the conversation hadn't started on such a personal note.

Steve Blacklock had removed all evidence of the office's former inhabitant. The furniture, even the window coverings, was new. The desk, solid, dark wood, pretty much filled the room, leaving only enough space for Blacklock to squeeze sideways past it to reach his leather swivel chair. Pictures of luxury resorts hung on the walls. Winters recognized Whistler easy enough, but one of the others was in mountains that were probably the Alps, and the third was near a beach: palm trees, infinity pools, and azure waters.

Blacklock gestured, and Winters took a seat in one of two armchairs. Its leather was the color of drying blood and the texture of melting butter.

A photographic display filled the back wall. Blacklock shaking the hands of smiling people, including the mayor of Vancouver, the premier of British Columbia, and the celebrity Governor of California.

The developer took his own seat and picked a pen up off his desk. Other than a computer monitor as thick as Winter's credit card, but probably more valuable, and a framed photograph of Nancy Blacklock, twenty years, at least, out of date, the desk was bare, gleaming with polish.

This was a man, Winters thought, who very much wanted to give the appearance of status.

But a man whose office was still in a trailer.

A small, square air-conditioning unit was set in the window. Trying to keep the heat out, it wheezed and rattled like a ninety-year old on the *Tour de France*.

"How can I help you, John? Or should I say, Sergeant, as you're here in your police role, right?" The bags under Blacklock's eyes jiggled as he talked.

"John'll do." Winters got to the point. "Your name's come up in one of my investigations."

"I'm glad you're paying attention at last, John. Those damned, pardon my French, environmentalists. I can't keep a sign in place, untouched. Makes we worry about what'll happen when we start building, eh? Where's the line between spray painting a sign and burning down a construction site? Can you tell me?"

"The RCMP will help you with any security concerns you might have. I'm with the Trafalgar City Police, and your property isn't within town limits. Tell me about this woman." Winters took the morgue photo of Ashley out of his pocket and handed it across the desk.

Blacklock took the picture, and studied it for a long time. Furrows of concentration gathered in the space between his eyebrows. "Not a nice picture," he said at last, handing it back.

Winters didn't accept it, and Blacklock tossed it onto his desk. It lay face up, watching them. Winters said, "It was taken in the morgue. Tell me about her."

New leather creaked as Blacklock leaned back in his chair and made a pyramid of his fingers. "I might have seen her around town. Girls like her," he waved a hand over the picture, "they're everywhere. Usually carrying a baby and dragging a toddler dripping snot by the hand, with another one in the oven. Three kids, three fathers, most of them. Why get a job when there's welfare to collect?"

"Take another look."

Blacklock shrugged and picked the picture up again. "Like I said, I think I've seen her around. Trafalgar's a small town, even smaller than it looks, I've come to understand. Don't tell me that you, a Sergeant, are planning to show this picture to every person in town? And then what? Through the whole Mid-Kootenays, up the Valley, then to Nelson, Castlegar? Christ, man, you'll be a hundred and ten before you're finished." He slapped the picture back onto his desk.

His point was a good one, Winters hated to admit. In a town the size of Trafalgar you passed the same people all the time, sometimes every day. You noticed them, if they looked or acted strange, or were particularly attractive or unattractive, or wore clothing out of the ordinary—which in Trafalgar in the summertime could be a three piece suit or a tailored dress with stockings and pumps. But Blacklock, who loved to pose for photographs, had been identified by Mike, of Mike's Movie Mansion, as having argued with Ashley Doe. A pretty good identification too: before Winters even arrived at the video store, Mike had pulled out a back copy of the *Gazette,* ready to point out a picture of Blacklock and his partner, Clemmins, smiling and chatting with the mayor.

"I have a witness who tells me you engaged in conversation with the woman recently."

The air-conditioning unit was emitting more noise than cool air. Against the leather chair, the back of Winters' shirt soaked up moisture. Blacklock opened a desk drawer, rummaged inside and pulled out a tissue. He used it to wipe the back of his neck. "Is that so?"

The office door flew open with so much force it struck the wall.

Winters whirled around, rising out of his seat, his hand automatically reaching for the weapon strapped to his waist. Bernice stood in the doorway carrying a tray set with a blue coffee carafe, two mugs, a small bowl, and a tiny pitcher.

Bernice gasped. "Sorry to startle you, Mr. Winters. I keep forgetting that the hinges on this door are broken. You should get them fixed, Steve," she scolded, arranging the coffee things on the desk. "You'll have a little old lady in here one day, about to buy a group of suites for her whole family and pow! She'll drop dead of a heart attack."

"For God's sake, Bernice," Blacklock shouted. "Will you shut up for once."

The woman's wide, cheerful face collapsed in on itself. She took a deep breath, and her prodigious bosom rose like Poseidon leaping out of the sea. "I am," she said, holding her head high, "only attempting to help. Reginald knew that guests appreciate coffee served properly. Call me when it's time to clear away the tray."

The door closed beside her, nothing but a whisper on the warm air.

"God, but she gets on my nerves. Acts like she's the Queen presiding over a tea party. Never mind Reginald this and Reginald that. She'd get the sack, fast enough, if she didn't know everything that's happened here since the resort was a twinkle in Saint Reginald's eye."

"The woman in the picture," Winters said, tired of fencing. "Did you know her or not? Did you recently have a public altercation with her or not?"

Neither of them bothered to serve the coffee. Blacklock studied the picture some more. Beads of sweat were building across his forehead. Winters might have taken that as a sign of a man with something to hide were his own body not perspiring. "Now that you remind me, I think I did have a run in with her. I don't remember the day, a week ago maybe. I was heading for that coffee shop on George Street. Should know better than to frequent a hippie hang out."

That Big Eddie's Coffee Emporium was also a police hang-out, John Winters didn't bother to mention.

"This girl approached me. I'm pretty sure it was her. She was young, carried a baby in that sort of satchel around her hip that girls here have. I stopped to talk to her. Before I knew it she was haranguing me about the resort. All that new age nonsense about the sacred earth and protecting the environment. Look, John, Sergeant Winters, I'm not too proud of myself, okay. Instead of just walking away I tried to argue with her. The earth's so sacred, I said, why'd she pollute it by producing another human parasite. She didn't like that much."

No kidding. "And?"

"And? And nothing. That was the end of it. I told her she was a spoiled welfare brat who didn't have a clue how the real world works and went to get my coffee somewhere else. I never saw the girl again, and I can't say I'm sorry about that."

"You hadn't met her before that day? On any other occasion?"

"I told you no. Sorry." Blacklock leaned forward, picked up the carafe and poured coffee into two mugs bearing the logo of M&C Developments. "Cream?" he asked. His hands shook slightly, and his professional smile was forced.

"Black." Winters had learned a lot about body language, and how to read unspoken signals, in his career.

According to Mike, Ashley had been upset at the encounter with Blacklock for what seemed to be personal reasons; she hadn't even mentioned the Grizzly Resort. They hadn't been friends, Ashley and Mike, so she hadn't confided in him. She just said something to the effect of, "I really need someone to help me out, but the bastard brushed me off." She sipped at the latte Mike bought her, and attempted to quiet the crying baby. Ashley's face, he'd said, was red, and her fists were clenched, and, sensing her agitation perhaps, Miller cried all the harder. Mike made his escape. She was a cute chick, he told Winters, and he'd briefly wondered if he could offer himself as the one to help her. But no way, he'd said, with a shake of his head, was he going to get involved with a woman with a kid and a truckload of personal issues. That's just asking for trouble.

Winters accepted a mug from Blacklock, leaned back in his chair and sipped his coffee. It was surprisingly good.

"Sorry I can't help you further, John," Blacklock said, looking as if he meant it. Drops of sweat gathered across his forehead. "The girl was opposed to what we're trying to build here. That was her right as a citizen. She was mistaken, and I'm sorry she didn't live long enough to realize it. She had a baby with her. Sad thing, to grow up without a mother."

Silence stretched between them. The window air conditioner continued to wheeze and emit lukewarm air. A phone rang in the outer office, to be answered before the first ring died away.

"I'd like to ask, if you don't mind," Blacklock said, "what's your interest in the girl? Accidental death, the paper said. Tragic, of course, for one so young, but not the business of the police. Don't tell me there's more to the story than was in the papers?" His laugh was tight.

The second time the door flew open, Winters rose from the chair, but didn't reach for his gun.

Nancy Blacklock stood there, smiling cheerfully. "What a pleasure, John," she said. The heavy black liner around her eyes had run as she sweated, giving her the appearance of a raccoon. Or an old-time movie bandit. She slipped a tiny pink cell phone into a pocket of her cavernous bag. "I've just heard the news. I'm so dreadfully thrilled." She rushed forward and enveloped him in an enormous hug. The force of her perfume was almost enough to bring water to his eyes. "Everything is working out perfectly. You're ahead of me; we don't have the contract printed yet."

Blacklock lumbered to his feet. "You remember, dear, that Sergeant Winters is with the Trafalgar City Police."

Nancy put her hands to her cheeks. "Oh, dear. I quite forgot. Have I said something I shouldn't have?" She tipped her head to one side and batted her black-rimmed eyes between her husband and their guest like a junior high girl trying to decide between the captain of the football team or the student council president. The expression did not suit her.

"Nancy, we're conducting a business meeting here." Steve Blacklock's voice was deep and firm, as suited a man of business not pleased at the indiscretion of a fluffy-brained wife. But he couldn't quite carry it off, and Winters knew the man was pleased at the break in conversation. "Anyway," Blacklock said, "I have no idea what you're talking about."

Nancy giggled. "Oops. My bad. I'll be on my way. Sorry to interrupt. I got a call from Frank. Mrs. Winters has kindly accepted our offer, Steve. This is all so exciting. Toodles." She waved her fingers, the nails long and red, at them both, and backed out of the crowded office, reaching into her bag for her phone as she went.

Toodles?

"That was somewhat off topic," Blacklock said. "But welcome news nonetheless. My wife has excellent taste, and I'm pleased she's pleased your wife's going to work with us. Why, that pretty much makes us partners, John." He beamed.

"I have no involvement in my wife's business affairs." Winters pulled his card out of his pocket and passed it to the developer. "Thank you for your time, Mr. Blacklock. If you remember anything about Ashley, no matter how insignificant it seems, please give me a call."

Blacklock accepted the card. With his other hand, he picked up the photograph and attempted to pass it over.

"Keep it," Winters said. "It might help you remember."

The developer put the picture down. "Okay."

In the outer office Nancy Blacklock was pacing up and down, phone clamped to her ear. Bernice rolled her eyes at Winters. He said his good-byes and Nancy wiggled her fingers in his direction without pausing to take a breath in her conversation. "A coup, my dear, this is quite the coup. They said she'd retired and wouldn't be interested in our little project for what we could offer. But let me tell you, I know…"

Small towns. In Vancouver he'd be taken off a case that had a personal involvement as intense as this one. But in Trafalgar? If the city tried to employ only officers who didn't know anyone who might be related to someone who was involved in an investigation, or who played golf once a week with a potential witness, or who had once upon a time asked the suspected perp to replace the water pump, they'd be hiring new officers every week.

The arrival of Nancy Blacklock had pretty much put a halt to any confession Steve Blacklock might have been about to make to Sergeant Winters. Not that a confession had seemed to be imminent. Unless he arrested Blacklock, upon no grounds, there was nothing more he could learn here, today, about the secretive Ashley Doe.

Blacklock wasn't going to say why the girl had thought he'd help her. It had been suggested earlier that Ashley might have been involved in prostitution, but nothing had come up. Not even a whisper of a suggestion that the girl had been hooking. It was possible that she'd specialized in exclusive relationships, or even had a secret lover, but so far Winters had no reason to believe that.

Blacklock might, quite genuinely, not have a clue about anything Ashley had told Mike Jergens. They might have been arguing about the resort, as Blacklock said, and Ashley wanted to make it all sound much more dramatic as a reward to Mike for buying her a coffee.

A teenager trying to sound dramatic, to make herself important—what a concept.

Everything Winters had heard from Mike, of Mike's Movie Mansion, was third hand.

In a web of lies and half-lies, wishes and dreams, made up names and unclaimed babies, who could tell what was the truth?

There was, Winters reminded himself as he turned the key in the ignition, one incontestable truth: Ashley Doe was dead and someone had killed her.

Chapter Sixteen

Wearing the tiniest of bikinis, Eliza Winters let her body soak up the hot Hawaiian sun. She sipped a coconut-flavored drink with an umbrella in it and watched her grandmother swimming in the sea. An airplane flew overhead, low, much too low, the noise of its engines as irritating as a swarm of mosquitoes. Then Eliza remembered that not only could she no longer wear an almost-nonexistent bikini, but her beloved grandmother had died many years ago. And it wasn't a plane: it was the damned phone.

The light from the clock on the night table said two.

"Winters," John said into the phone. "Go ahead, Dave." He sat up.

Eliza rolled over, suppressing a groan.

"That's okay," she heard John say. "What have you got?"

It wasn't okay with her. But she'd never say so. Her husband was a cop, middle of the night phone calls were part of the job.

When she met John, more than twenty-five years ago, she was seriously involved with a fashion photographer. When she broke it off, because she'd fallen in love with the handsome, serious Constable John Winters, the fashion photographer, Rudy, short for Rudolph, Steiner, had taken it badly. When the news got around that she was engaged, Rudy took her out for a drink and warned her against marrying someone with that job. It would never work, Rudy, and all her friends, said. But it had worked. A great deal better than it would have with Rudolph, no longer called Rudy, whom Eliza still heard about now and again. He was at the top of his profession, and on his fourth—or was it fifth?—wife. Eliza doubted things would have been any different if he'd married her: every wife had been a good deal younger than her predecessor. The current one was even younger than Eliza had been when she and Rudy had been an item.

Tonight, wrapped in a light summer duvet, buried deep in the big bed in their house on the side of the mountain, Eliza tried to control her breathing. There was no point in getting mad at her husband.

"Stay there. Tell the woman… What's her name?"

Yup, he was going out.

"If she looks to be ready to leave, ask her to wait. I'll be there in twenty minutes."

John slipped out of bed and went to the bathroom. When he came back, she asked, "Trouble?"

"Just someone who needs me. Go back to sleep."

"I need you."

He leaned over and snapped the spaghetti strap of her summer pajama top. "As long as you still need me when I get back." He touched her sleep-tussled head and went to the closet.

She rolled over and pretended to be asleep when he left the room.

As the sound of his car disappeared into the night, she got out of bed and went downstairs.

In all the years of their marriage, she had never slept well when he was called out at night. She had never told him so. What would be the point; he wasn't going to say he couldn't go to work because his wife worried. And it was an irrational worry anyway. He could be hurt on the job during the day, or when he had a regular night shift. It was just the middle of the night phone calls that upset her so much.

She poured a small Drambuie and curled up on the living room couch with a magazine.

At least it was better in Trafalgar than in Vancouver, where some weeks she didn't get much sleep at all. Eliza loved Vancouver, loved living in the heart of the city. But the job had been killing her man. For the last couple of years the strain of the things he saw one person do to another had started getting to him, and she'd had more to worry about than an incident on the job. He was drinking so much that she worried whenever he was out late.

It all came to a head with the Blakely murder. John had seriously considered ending his career, consumed with guilt over what he saw as an error in judgment, exasperated, she suspected, by the quantities of booze he was consuming. He heard about an opening in tiny Trafalgar, and he'd brought the suggestion of moving to her. She told him to try for it, and before she could blink, here they were. Six months out of the big city, and his drinking was way down. No more going out with the boys (and girls) after work. No more stopping in bars for a solitary one, which always lead to many more, before heading home.

Eliza opened the magazine and tried to concentrate on an article about what one could do with summer's bounty of tomatoes.

◇◇◇

Molly Smith had also been dreaming. But her dreams were not as pleasant as those of Eliza Winters.

She swung her legs out of bed, barely avoiding stepping on the big warm bulk that was Sylvester, curled up, breathing deeply, on the floor of her bedroom.

She hadn't said anything to her parents about the trouble she was having sleeping. Lucky would insist on talking it out and Andy would bury his head deeper into the newspaper.

It was still dark, and the house was quiet. For once, Miller slept. A soft breeze ruffled the lace curtains, cool and welcome after the heat of the day.

The night-light at the top of the stairs lit her way and Smith didn't bother to flick on any lights. She went downstairs; Sylvester, who'd pulled himself out of sleep, ran on ahead. Like her mother had done for her when she was a child, bothered by monsters hiding under the bed, she'd heat up a cup of milk to take upstairs. Hopefully she'd soon be able to fall back into sleep. And Miller would stay quiet.

She flicked the kitchen light on. Lucky was in a chair at the big pine table. Her arms were crossed over a pile of papers, making a pillow for her head. She started, and her head jerked up. Smith threw the light switch off. Too late. "Sorry, Mom. Didn't know you were here."

"Quiet," Lucky snapped under her breath. "He's sleeping." She nodded toward the pram, so old it should be in a museum, by the stove. The baby blanket rose and fell in a gentle rhythmic motion. Sylvester nuzzled at Lucky's hand.

"Well pardon me for living. I'm looking for a glass of milk, if that isn't too much to ask in my own house."

Lucky sucked in a breath. She scratched the ridge between Sylvester's eyes. His favorite place. "Sorry, dear. You caught me napping, that's all." Her voice was a whisper. Suited for the hour and the night.

"Like napping at," Smith looked at the clock on the wall, "four in the morning is something to be guilty about."

Lucky placed her hands on the table and pushed herself up. "It'll just take a minute."

"Sit down, Mom. I can heat a cup of milk. They taught us that in Police College on day one. Right after donut eating class."

Lucky seemed not to hear. She took a jug of milk out of the fridge and a packet of chocolate chip cookies from the cupboard.

Resigned to being waited on, Smith took a seat at the table. She pulled the stack of papers her mother had been sleeping on toward her. A Revenue Canada tax form was on the top. Smith flicked through the papers. Lucky turned on the light over the stove, which provided enough illumination to read the bigger print. Accounts payable, government forms, staff expense sheets, accounts receivable. The books that ran Mid-Kootenay Adventure Vacations, her parents' business.

Lucky turned, holding a pottery mug in swirls of blue and gold. The handle was chipped. "Things were simpler when your dad and I started the business. No employees, not much stock."

"And," Smith said. "You were young and enthusiastic. That was before I was born, right?"

"Samwise was three. Clients thought he was cute, toddling around the unfinished room we called a store. Your dad took the trips, leading city-people into the wilderness. He'd be gone for a day at a time usually, three or four days at the most. I minded the store, while Samwise ran underfoot. Then your dad would come back. To help with Samwise, to help run the business. Our timing was perfect and we caught the demand for adventure vacations, kayaking in the summer, skiing in the winter, hiking all year long, as it all took off. By the time Samwise was in school our business was picking up so much we needed larger accommodation, and even staff."

"Then you had me."

"I carried you to work in a green corduroy satchel across my front. I remember pounding away at that old typewriter while you slept under the desk. We began to stock adventure books, particularly children's books because your brother dived into everything we got in. From there we branched out, into maps, clothing, camping supplies. And things began to bloom." Lucky took a cookie out of the bag and bit into it. "Good times," she said.

"But life goes on. Children grow up."

"And business gets bigger and bigger and more prosperous than you ever expected. I thought that the more profitable the company got, the easier it would be."

"Not so, I guess."

The microwave pinged and Lucky took the mug out. She sprinkled cinnamon across the top and handed it to her daughter. The scent whispered soft pillows and sweet dreams. Smith stood up, the mug spreading warmth into her hand, and grabbed a fistful of cookies.

"You know, Mom, no one can recapture the joy of youth. The world doesn't work that way. People age. Life goes on."

The blanket shivered, and Miller let out a tiny whimper.

Lucky exhaled, heavily. She dragged her fists across her eyes. Her shoulders slumped and her knees buckled.

"Thanks for the milk, Mom. I'm off to beddie bye," Smith didn't try to cover her enormous yawn. She left the kitchen with her nose to the mug of warm milk.

All cinnamon, warmth, and mother's love.

Chapter Seventeen

So Julian Armstrong was, as they said, known to the Vancouver police.

John Winters read the file on the counselor. Inappropriate relations with clients, reports of sexual advances. There had been two complaints made, but no charges laid. The alleged victims failed to back up their complaints.

Armstrong had had a busy practice in fashionable West Vancouver, working with wealthy women. He gave it up to volunteer at a woman's center and a methadone clinic in the Mid-Kootenays and live in a shabby basement apartment.

Ashley Doe had said he was the key to her life.

It would be tricky to interrogate Armstrong with no evidence other than John Winters' own gut feelings.

Last night he'd been called out to a heroin overdose. Jeff Matthews, the novelist, hugely famous for the only piece of work he'd ever produced, would have died had not his wife taken ill at dinner with friends and come home early. The call should have gone to Ray Lopez. But, as Ashley Doe had died of an 'accidental' heroin overdose, Winters had ordered that he be kept informed of any similar incidents.

As he'd been leaving the hospital, he'd seen Julian Armstrong crossing the parking lot.

He picked up the phone and punched in numbers. It was answered on the first ring.

"Hope I haven't disturbed you, Ms. Matthews. It's John Winters here," he said into the phone. The wife, a far better woman than Winters thought the novelist deserved, had told him she'd do everything in her power to see her husband's dealer behind bars.

"Not at all, Sergeant. I'm sitting at my kitchen table watching the herbs in the garden grow."

"Sounds exciting."

A sigh came down the phone line. "I'm done with excitement for this week. I'm trying to work up the courage to go to the hospital and visit my husband who almost died last night. Does that sound uncaring of me?"

"It sounds like a woman pushed to the edge."

"You're a sensitive man, Sergeant Winters, if I may say so. To my surprise I find that I'm getting more empathy from the police officer than the supposed drug counselor."

This was an opening he hadn't expected. "Ms. Matthews."

"Please, call me Susan. I've told you things I can't tell my own mother."

"Susan. Can I buy you a coffee, if you have time before going to the hospital? How about Eddie's?"

"The plants may die without my constant supervision, but I'll risk it. Give me half an hour."

Winters paid for the drinks—a plain coffee for him, a chai latte for her. The breakfast and heading-to-work rush was over and they found a private table in the back corner.

He got straight to the point. "I'd like to talk to you about Mr. Armstrong, if you don't mind."

"Julian?" Susan Matthews raised one eyebrow. "I thought you asked me out to demand that I leave my husband and run away with you. Or failing that wanted to know more about Jeff."

He grinned at her. She was dressed in beige capris and a blue T-shirt. Thin gold earrings looped through her earlobes, but otherwise she wore no jewelry. Smudges of strain lay under her eyes and lines that hadn't been there last night stretched between her manicured eyebrows.

"Julian Armstrong. Had you met him before yesterday?"

"No. He showed up after you left. Why are you asking? Is there something wrong?"

"Not at all. It's only that I need to know all I can about every person involved in this business. Mr. Armstrong's new to town, and I don't have a feel for him yet."

She looked into the depths of her mug. Winters let the silence stretch between them. Jolene came out from the back with a watering jug. She poured water into plant pots and snipped at dead leaves, her body moving all the while to whatever sound was coming out of the iPod in her ears.

"I got the feeling," Susan said at last, concentrating on the depths of the mug in front of her, "that he was more interested in impressing me with his credentials than discussing how we might work together to help my husband."

"Did he have anything to offer, being from the methadone clinic, I mean?"

"John, I don't want to venture too much into conjecture. Do you understand?"

"Of course." Although he was trying very hard to nudge her into the realm of conjecture. "Impressions matter, I've learned. Impressions can be wrong, 180 degrees wrong, but they can be right as well. It's my job to gather up all the impressions, and sort them out as best I can. And sometimes I make a mighty mess of it all."

She smiled. "Okay, John. Just between you and me, if I didn't know better, I'd say that Julian had come on to me. I might sound like a hysterical female, suspecting evil male intentions behind every innocent gesture, but I have been around the block a few times." She stuck her index finger into her cup, scooping up milk foam. "And I'd say that Julian Armstrong is a predator."

She put the cup down and in one fluid motion, got to her feet. "Past time I was at the hospital." Her voice fell to a whisper. "I've decided to give Jeff one more chance, although he doesn't deserve it. But for some strange reason, I love him very, very much."

She walked out of the coffee shop. Her head high, her back straight.

"Pretty lady," Eddie said. He picked up the empty cup.

"A strong one, too," Winters said.

The hot milk had helped, and for the rest of the night Smith's dreams were so sweet she couldn't remember them, but only knew that she got out of bed feeling warm and happy.

When they met outside of Big Eddie's, Christa had, at first, been reserved, very much a different person than her former bouncy self, but she'd been through a great deal of trauma. Mental as well as physical. Her face was slightly misshapen, and she spoke with a lisp, largely a result of the smashed-in mouth. Anger against Charlie Fucking Bassing boiled up in Smith's chest, but she pushed it down and hugged her friend with genuine enthusiasm.

They ate bagels and drank coffee, fussed over by Eddie and Jolene, and talked about family.

"I've an appointment at the dentist tomorrow," Christa said. "He's going to make me beautiful."

Smith laughed. "More beautiful than you are now? The sun will be hiding its face in shame. Who are you seeing?"

"Tyler."

Smith stuffed her face into her mug.

"Okay. Something's wrong with Doctor Tyler. What?"

"As a dentist, there's nothing wrong at all. He'll do a good job."

"But?"

"But, nothing." Hard to explain that after questioning Doctor Tyler last month regarding the killing of his lover's husband, Smith wouldn't allow her long-time family dentist to approach her with a ten foot dental pick.

She changed the subject and told Christa about Miller. Christa laughed. It was a good long deep laugh and it made Molly smile to hear it. "Sounds like what she did with me," Christa said, "Lucky wants every child to be happy."

"Yeah, but you were ten years old when Mom took you under her wing. And she was a lot younger then. This baby's taking her to the edge and she's too proud, and too stubborn, to admit it. The kid doesn't know the meaning of the word sleep. Dad's not being supportive of her at all, and he's always in a bad mood."

As usual, Smith had taken the chair that put her back against the wall; over Christa's shoulder she could see the woman at the table across from theirs not even trying to conceal her interest in their conversation. "Can I help you?"

Christa turned to see who Molly was talking to.

The eavesdropper was thin, her heavy make-up tinged with orange. An untouched slice of cheesecake and a coffee sat in front of her. Silver bangles jangled as she lifted her hand. "I apologize if I appear to have been listening. I couldn't help but overhear." She dug in her pocket and pulled out a card. "You must be talking about Mrs. Lucy Smith."

"What of it?" Molly Smith said.

The woman pushed the card forward. Jody Burke. The logo of the Province of British Columbia. Something to do with children and family.

"I've been attempting to persuade Mrs. Smith to give up the child. Perhaps we have a common goal."

"Perhaps not. If my mother wants to care for the baby, as much as I might not be happy about that, I support her."

Jody Burke smiled. "That's good of you, dear. But considering your mother's age, I'm sure we can find a more suitable foster family for the child, until his parents' families can be located."

"I'm sure of no such thing. Foster families are not lying on the ground, you know, waiting to be picked up like lost coins."

"I assume you're Moonlight Smith, otherwise known as Constable Molly Smith."

"That's hardly a secret." Christa burst into the conversation. "And Lucky's a wonderful mother. There's no one kinder, more generous. I resent you implying that she isn't."

"My dear girl." Burke smiled at her. "I'm only saying that considering Mrs. Smith's age, and her other responsibilities, the care of an abandoned infant might be too much for her. In which case it obviously isn't in the child's interest to be left with her. You yourself, Constable Smith, said it was causing problems in your parents' marriage."

Christa leapt to her feet. "How dare you," she shouted. Jolene and the woman she was serving turned and stared. Eddie's head popped out of the back room. "You can't eavesdrop on a private conversation and throw it back at us.

"I've finished my coffee, Molly, and I need to get to work. Let's go."

Smith stood up. She gave the card back to Jody Burke.

"Keep it," Burke said, "you may need it."

"I doubt it."

"A pleasure meeting you, Constable," Burke said.

Smith didn't reply as she followed her friend out the door, tossing the card onto the table. They walked toward Christa's apartment. The sun was hot on her face and bare arms and shoulders. "That was strange."

"What a busybody." Christa was virtually dancing under the force of her indignation. "Imagine. Someone trying to imply that your mom can't look after a child. I don't know what would have happened to me, Mol, if your family hadn't taken me in when my mom died. Dad was hardly up to the task, now was he? Not that my life's this huge success story, but it would be a lot worse without your mom."

"Have you told her that?"

"Of course not. Have you told her you owe everything you are to her?"

"Of course not. Don't be ridiculous."

They laughed, and wrapped arms around each other. It felt like old times. B.C. Before Charlie.

They arrived at Christa's building. A heritage house whose glory years were long past, now divided into upstairs and downstairs apartments.

"Thanks for the coffee, Mol. I needed to get out."

"It was fun. Well, it was fun until that woman popped up."

"Catch you later."

Smith headed back toward town with the feeling that a great weight had been lifted off her chest.

She was walking back to her car—her mother's car—when her cell phone rang.

Constable Dawn Solway was in a state of high excitement. She needed a big, big favor. Fast. Smith knew that Solway was having an Internet-based relationship with a sailor in the U.S. Navy. They'd met a few months ago at a rock concert in Spokane and spent, what was by Dawn's account, the most fabulous weekend in the history of instant relationships. The sailor had shipped off to some exotic locale, and Solway returned to Trafalgar. They'd kept in touch by e-mail and hot and heavy phone sex. All of which had been much, much more than Molly Smith wanted to know. But now, as Dawn said over the phone, the sailor had gotten leave unexpectedly and wanted to come to British Columbia TODAY for a couple of days of not-much sightseeing. Unfortunately Solway had one more afternoon to do before getting four days off.

"Please, pretty please, Molly. If you take my shift I promise you my first born daughter."

It wasn't as if Smith had anything better to do. "I don't want your daughter, Dawn. There are enough infants in my life right now. But you can be sure I'll think of something."

"You're the best, Molly. I knew I could count on you. Bye."

The sailor was, in fact, a lawyer doing whatever job lawyers in the U.S. Navy did. That she was also a female was not generally known in the department. Smith wondered how some of the old guard would react if Solway ever introduced her lover around.

It was time, Winters had decided, to put pressure on Marigold, Ashley's roommate. None of his other lines of enquiry were going far. Marigold knew something. Something she was keeping secret.

At three o'clock Molly Smith came into the station as Winters was heading out.

"Thought you were off today," he said.

"I switched with Dawn."

"Check in and join me in fifteen minutes. I'll square it with Al."

She smiled, clearly pleased at being taken off the beat, if only for a while. Peterson grumbled, as expected, but when Winters promised to have Smith back before the evening started to heat up, he reluctantly agreed.

"I'm going to see our pal, Marigold," Winters said when Smith joined him. "And as you were with me the last time, I thought I'd take you along."

"Any particular reason?" she asked, as they walked down the steps.

At the bottom of the stairs, she turned right and he turned left.

"She lives this way," Smith said.

"I had Dave drop into The Bishop earlier and check. She's working. Marigold's real name is Joan Jones."

"I'm not surprised she changed it," said Moonlight Legolas Smith, who probably knew a thing or two about undesirable names.

"Under the name of Joan Jones, she's got a record in Vancouver for possession and dealing."

"Pot?"

"Good old B.C. Bud. No matter what name she's using, Marigold's been less, much less, than forthcoming with us, and I've decided it's time to come on like a tough guy. You know how well I play the bad cop, Molly."

At three o'clock on a Wednesday afternoon, the bar was empty of customers. The Bishop and Nun had been decorated by someone who had probably never been in a traditional English pub. Heavy red paper, tearing in places, covered the walls, dotted with cheap replicas of paintings of foxhunts, pre-industrial farm life, and gently rolling landscapes. A gas fireplace was set into the back wall, turned off in the heat of a Kootenay summer. A portrait of Queen Victoria hung over the fireplace. The blinds were down and the room was dark and gloomy.

The bartender stood behind the wooden bar running the length of the room, flicking through a skiing magazine. Marigold was reflected in the large, gilt-framed mirror that filled the wall behind the bar, the reflection broken by a crack in the glass. Her back was to the door, and she was examining her nails. Her matted hair hung down her back in thick ropes. The bartender gave Smith a friendly wave. As a beat constable she was in here almost as much as some of the regulars.

"Not you again," Marigold said, not turning around.

"Me again." Winters walked down the single step into the room. Smith's boots hit the floor behind him. "How's it going, Morris?" she asked.

"Boring," the bartender said. "And not likely to get much busier. There's a big act playing at the Potato Famine tonight and tomorrow. They'll suck our customers away like leeches on a swimmer's leg."

"Ugh. That is so gross." Marigold half-turned toward the police. Her eyes slid over Smith and she looked at her nails. "I can't talk to you now, Sergeant Winters. I'm working." She wore a short denim skirt cinched by a wide white belt and a white cotton blouse that left her plump shoulders bare. An order pad was tucked into the back of the belt. White running shoes were on her feet.

"And working very hard indeed, by the looks of it." Winters took a seat on the stool beside her. Smith hovered at his back. "But I'm sure you can spare me a few moments."

"You have to order a drink."

"Happy to. Ice water for me. Constable Smith?"

"Water'd be good."

"Two ice waters. Heavy on the ice. I've been thinking about Ashley, Marigold. And I'm sure you have too." She turned her head, leaving him looking at the back of her neck. A blue and yellow butterfly spread its wings on either side of her vertebra.

"Tell me a bit more about Ashley. She must have talked to you about her family, where's she's from. Did you get the impression, for example, that she was new to B.C.? Did she ever mention Vancouver?"

"Maybe. Yeah, I think she'd spent some time in Vancouver. Look, I told you, Mr. Winters, she didn't want to talk about her family and her past and all that shit."

"I find it hard to believe that she didn't say anything. People talk about themselves. Whether they want to or not, they reveal things."

The girl shrugged. "Guess I'm not a good listener."

"Look, Marigold," Smith said. "You might not care much about what happened to Ashley, but surely you have some consideration for the baby. Miller'll spend his childhood in foster care if we can't find his family. Is that what you want for him?"

Winters bit back a retort to the probationary constable. She wasn't here to interrupt his interrogation. But it was a good question, and had an interesting effect. Marigold turned around, lifted her chin, and fastened her eyes directly on Smith.

"Precisely my point. Family isn't all it's cracked up to be. Ashley didn't want anything to do with her family, and that's all I know."

The door opened with a groan and a group of bikers spilled in. Graying hair or balding scalps shook with laughter as they pulled off leather gloves and unzipped unseasonable jackets. Men pulled tables together and women gathered chairs.

"Gotta go," Marigold said. "But I'll tell you this. If Ashley didn't want anyone to find that baby, neither do I."

Chapter Eighteen

Lucky Smith was making up baby formula when she heard the familiar car turning off the road into their long driveway. She looked out the kitchen window. The tomato plants were heavy with red fruit—if she didn't get out there soon, they'd be nothing but a rotting mess—and the lettuce beds overflowed. Weeds were moving in on the spinach and chard, like an army that's discovered the enemy's sentinels sleeping. Andy's car rounded the corner and parked in its usual place beside the big red cedar. It was early for him to be home from the store. She was pleased to see that he wasn't carrying an armload of work for her to do.

Miller was awake, but for once he wasn't screaming, just watching the sunlight play with the mobile Lucky had strung over his bed. Sylvester was taking his afternoon nap beside the pram. Alone in the Smith family, Sylvester seemed to like having the baby around, and Lucky had moved his bed from its usual place in the master bedroom into the kitchen.

Without even bothering to shut the door Andy gathered Lucky into his arms in a big bear hug. He tired to lift her, as if he was about to swing her off the ground in the way he used to. But he was too fat, and too unfit, to pick her up and Lucky was too heavy to be picked up. Instead he patted her ample bottom.

"What on earth?" she said with a laugh, "has gotten into you? And what are you doing home in the middle of the day?"

"Molly here?"

"No. She took an extra shift."

He gripped her by the buttocks and pulled her hips toward him. "I knew that. I saw her in town. She was in uniform and with John Winters. I realized that my luscious wife was at home. Alone." He nuzzled her neck and lifted one hand to grip her breast.

To Lucky's considerable surprise she felt a bulge in Andy's pants. "You dirty old man," she said with a laugh. It had been a long time since they'd had sex outside of their bedroom after the ten o'clock news. In the early days they lost customers when Andy would put the closed sign on the shop door and join Lucky in the storage closet. But soon they accumulated children, and employees, regular hours and responsibilities.

Lucky loved having her nipples stroked. She pushed her chest forward, as Andy's fingers tightened their grip. "Do you remember the first time," she murmured in his ear, "on the side of the hill, the lights of the city."

"Where you wouldn't let me do it, because I didn't have a condom?"

"But you made me happy, anyway. I remember that."

They had been students at the University of Washington. Young, in love, with each other and with radical anti-war politics.

She kissed him, deeply, full on the lips. He wasn't exactly the handsome, thin student, with hair as long and pale as that of a fairy princess, whom she'd fallen in love with long ago. But she still loved him, not with a fever, but with maturity.

She reached for his belt buckle, and he groaned. It had been a long, long time since they'd done it on the floor.

Miller cried. He didn't even bother to warm up, simply let loose with a full throated howl.

What on earth do I think I'm doing? I'm an overweight gray-haired grandmother who gets hot flashes, not a sex kitten. Lucky grabbed Andy's hand. "You left the door open."

"So. If someone drops by they'll get an eyeful."

She stepped back, out of range of his reaching arms. "The baby's crying." She scooped Miller up. "How about later?"

"Later? When later? When you fall asleep before your feet are off the floor? When you stay awake long enough to come to bed? When our daughter's in the house, not sleeping because of her dreams?"

"What dreams?" Lucky tucked Miller to her chest and bounced on her toes.

"Ever since that goddamned mess, Moonlight cries out in the night, Lucky. And it's getting worse, not better, since that baby's been here. She thinks we don't hear her, yelling in her dreams, crying when she wakes up. Prowling around the house instead of sleeping."

Lucky thought of the hot milk, the circles under her daughter's eyes. Moonlight wasn't sleeping. And her mother hadn't noticed. "Moonlight's an adult. She wouldn't be pleased if her mother came into her room and asked what was wrong."

"She's your daughter, no matter what her age. Or her occupation."

"Pass me that bottle, will you, dear."

Andy grabbed the baby's bottle off the counter without looking at it. It slipped out of his hand and fell to the floor. It rolled under the table.

"Oh for heaven's sake," Lucky yelled, frustration boiling over. "I can't use that one. Get another out of the fridge."

Andy held out his arms. "Give him to me."

"What?"

"Give him to me. I'll hold him while you get a bottle ready. Don't look at me like that. I'm not going to bake him into a gingerbread house."

Lucky passed Miller over. Andy took the screaming bundle awkwardly. The baby looked into the man's face and stopped crying.

"Isn't that nice," Lucky said. "He likes you."

"I doubt that very much. He's been struck dumb, that's all. Get the bottle. You can't keep him, sweetheart. If nothing else, I'm too bloody old. I don't get a hard on like that much any more."

Lucky rummaged in the fridge and pretended not to hear him. Tears pricked the back of her eyes.

Barb was heading out the door as Smith and Winters walked into the police station. "You still haven't told me what you're bringing on Sunday, John," she said.

"Sunday?"

"The pot luck. My house. You haven't forgotten have you?"

"Of course not. I'll check with my wife tonight and get back to you tomorrow morning."

"You're bringing lasagna, right, Molly? Your mother's lasagna is to die for."

"For sure," Smith said.

"See you guys later." Barb skipped down the steps.

"What?" Winters said to the expression on Smith's face.

"You know this is a command performance, don't you? Barb hasn't forgiven you for not coming to Ralph's retirement party."

"I'd been working here two weeks. I didn't know Ralph from the occupant of Cell Number One."

"Irrelevant. Barb is big on department socializing. She believes it builds teams and helps morale. The CC believes what Barb tells him to believe."

"I almost forgot about poor little Miller," Winters said, changing the subject and punching the buttons to let them in the door. "Your mom still has him?"

"And it's killing us. Mom most of all. She's so ridiculously stubborn. Won't admit that she can't manage. It doesn't help that that horrid woman from family services is bouncing around trying to make Mom give the baby up. All that's done is get her back up."

Winters kept his smile to himself: *Like mother, like daughter.*

"Is anything happening about finding out who Ashley is? And thus getting Miller to his own family?"

"We're working on it," he said, automatically.

Ray Lopez was at his desk, typing away. "Chief wants to see you," he said, without looking up from the keyboard. "Said soon as you get in."

Winters went in search of Paul Keller, the Chief Constable. The office door to the corridor was closed, but the side one that joined Barb's office stood open. Keller looked up at the sound of footsteps.

"John, come on in. Have a seat."

Winters sat. "Ray said you wanted to see me."

"The Ashley Doe murder. Fill me in." Keller reached behind and opened the bar fridge where he stored his daily supply of diet coke. He drank about ten to twenty cans a day; judging by the contents of his wastepaper basket it had been a heavy drinking day. The staff assumed the boss needed the pop to keep his mouth occupied because he couldn't smoke in the building any more. "Want one?"

"No, thanks."

"What about the girl herself? Any leads on who she is, where she's from?"

"Not a thing. I have to tell you, Paul, outside of the witness protection program I've never seen anyone disappear so cleanly."

Keller's eyes lit up. "You think that's it?"

"No. If she was in the program she'd have been given ID. A background. Ashley Doe appears to have been plopped down in Trafalgar B.C. by a spaceship. We've checked all the local banks—she doesn't have an account. Every restaurant or store she's been in says she always paid cash. Who does that any more? My wife doesn't believe in paying with debit, she says it's too easy to lose track of how much you're spending, but even she runs out of cash and uses her card now and again. Ashley gave her roommate cash to contribute to the rent. We've talked to the women at the support center; they all say she was friendly, but quiet. Kept to herself and never shared confidences. Not one of them could remember her mentioning a thing about her past. And when the women talked about the fathers of their babies— Ashley stayed mum."

"Strange."

"Very strange. We've circulated her fingerprints, of course, but come up with nothing so far. And the baby's a real complication. Miller isn't Ashley's child, but we can't find a stolen or missing baby that matches. Although it's early days for a continent-wide search." Winters blew out his cheeks. "Two people at least know more than they're telling—Marigold, the roommate, and Armstrong, the supposed counselor. You read my report on him?"

"Yes." Keller crunched the pop can in his right hand. "Shady character."

"Shady past to be sure. You think it's time to haul him in for a turn under the bright lights?"

"It might be."

"We've been told that Ashley seems to have had some contact in the past with Armstrong, which he isn't admitting to. And that she seems to have been opposed to the Grizzly Resort: enough to have an angry public confrontation with Steve Blacklock, the new partner, about it. A lot of people in town are, opposed that is, and it's hardly unknown in Trafalgar for citizens to express their political opinions passionately."

"Never noticed that myself," Keller said, tossing the pop can into the garbage. It rattled as it fell in amongst its predecessors.

"But that doesn't fit with Ashley's persona, as I see it. Why did she care about the resort, but only that? One of the times I dropped into the center, the young mothers told me they're trying to get a protest going against the use of pesticides at the golf course. They said it's bad for their kids, but Ashley wasn't interested."

"Who knows why people care about one thing and not another. My wife won't eat veal—says it's barbaric—but she digs into lamb readily enough."

Winters grinned. "You trying to play devil's advocate, Paul?"

"Just speculating. Maybe because we were out for dinner last night with friends, and when Jay considered ordering veal, Karen gave him a stern talking to.

"We need to lean on Armstrong. Hard. If he's spinning us a line, reel him in on it." The Chief made fishing gestures with his hands. He was an avid fisherman. Pictures of himself, proudly displaying salmon of various size, covered his desk, crowding out the single family photo. Winters had been fishing a few times, trying to be one of the boys with his sisters' husbands or the guys from work. He'd been bored to tears, and hadn't gone fishing since he stopped pretending to be one of the boys.

Keller spun his chair in a half-circle and looked out the window. In the foreground, the red maple leaf snapped in the wind; in the background the bottom of the sun touched the top of Koola Glacier. Even in late August, the mountain was heavy with snow. Keller cleared his throat.

"Murder's a rare crime in this town, John, very rare. We hadn't had a murder in years until that business last month. I don't want an unsolved on our sheet."

"Nor do I," Winters said, but he doubted that he'd been heard.

"I've called the IHIT."

"I could use them." Although it bothered him to admit that he needed help, he did. The Integrated Homicide Investigation Team was an RCMP unit out of Surrey that could be called upon to help local forces with murder cases. Winters was floundering, and with Lopez tied up in the drug case, he wasn't getting the help he needed. "When will they be here?"

"Tomorrow," Keller said, turning his chair back so he faced his lead detective. "Sometime in the afternoon."

"Good." And he meant it. His ego wasn't so big, at least he hoped not, that he'd wish failure on IHIT where he'd failed.

They talked for a while longer, about other cases, before Winters was dismissed and headed back to his own office. The red message light on his phone blinked.

"Six o'clock," Eliza purred. Her voice always made him think of sex, even if she were calling from Wal-Mart to report on the price of pencils. "And all is not well. This is a reminder that we're due at M&C at seven for drinks to kick off the advertising campaign. If you've stubbed your toe and can't make it, let me know, eh? Love you."

It was only six fifteen. Time to get home, shower and change into suitable cocktail party attire and be smiling, clean, and presentable by seven. No one arrived at fashion parties on time anyway.

He wrote *Armstrong* on the note pad he kept beside the computer and headed out the door.

"Five-one, five-one?"

That was her. "Five-one. Smith here." Molly Smith spoke into the radio. Tonight she was in the car. Blessed relief. Air conditioning, bottles of cold water in the cup holders. Dave Evans was on the streets. Lately Evans had been getting the car and Smith sent to pound the pavement. Maybe Sarge noticed, at last, and decided to balance the load. Whatever. Smith had simply been grateful to be out of the heat. It was after midnight, the cool night air should be sliding down the mountains, but there was no sign of it yet.

"484 Aspen Street. Neighbors report a disturbance. Not the first time."

"On my way." She flicked on lights and sirens and punched the address into the car's computer.

The house had a string of complaints. Noise violations, dangerous dogs, blocking the street, him threatening to kill her, her threatening to kill him. Even a complaint of peeing in the neighbor's foxgloves. And that was her, not him.

A small crowd was gathered on the sidewalk when Smith pulled up. She switched off the engine and climbed out of the car. A man approached her, dressed in a red velour robe, with Tevas on his feet. "I think this is it, Constable," he said, "He's going to kill her this time."

"Let's hope," a woman said. "Then we can all get some sleep."

Everyone, including Smith, ducked as a bottle flew out the open door and crashed into a walkway so weed-choked it was almost invisible. Inside the house a woman screamed, and glass broke.

"Five-one," Smith said into the radio at her shoulder. "I'm entering the residence and I need assistance. Fast." Her heart beat in her chest. She was pleased that her voice held steady; it had an embarrassing tendency to squeak when she was under stress.

"Trafalgar City Police." She pounded on the open door. "I'm coming in." In the back of her mind she listened for the sound of a siren, coming her way. Nothing. She fastened her right hand around the solid butt of her Glock, took a deep breath, and stepped through the door. She was in the kitchen. Dirty dishes were piled in the sink, bits of shattered crockery littered the floor. The scent of overripe fruit lingered in the stifling air. A fly threw itself against the window, going mad in a frenzy of buzzing. The air was foul—meat kept out of the fridge for too long on a hot day, most likely. From the back of the house, slightly muffled as if it was behind a door, thank you God, a dog barked.

"Police," she shouted again. "I'm…"

"Hey, they sent the pretty one. Nice o' them." A man walked into the kitchen. He carried a bottle of beer. His black T-shirt was stained with sweat and dust and the remains of meals past. His gray hair hadn't seen shampoo in a considerable period of time; his beard was thick and long and unkempt. He smiled at Smith—he was missing his bottom plate—and stepped forward. He slipped in something and collapsed against the counter. "Woopsie," he said, with a high-pitched giggle.

"You're drunk."

"He's always drunk." A woman stood in the doorway. Her face was heavily made up, and her hair was dyed too black, emphasizing the wrinkles dragging down her face. She wore a short white denim skirt with a blue tank top and four-inch heels. Drying blood ran from her left nostril, mingling with lipstick the same color. Her lip was beginning to swell. She smelled of good perfume, applied with too heavy a hand. Her voice, also, was none too steady, probably due to the glass she held. It was large, half-full of liquid the color of honey. "He's had a good look at you, so you can leave now, girlie. There'll be no more trouble. Once the fuzz arrives he crawls into a corner and sleeps it off."

"Did your husband hit you, ma'am?" Smith asked.

"Nah. I fell into a door. Nothing to worry about, so you can leave now." She lifted her glass to her mouth and swallowed.

"This is the second call we've had this month to this address. What's your name?" Smith asked the man, although she knew it. Jake LeBlanc. His wife was Felicia and his daughter was named Lorraine. Lorraine who screwed men in the alleyways because she needed affection and she had nowhere to take them.

Instead of answering the officer's question Jake took a long pull from his bottle.

"Forget about it, will ya," Felicia said. "Like I said, I fell into a door. No harm done. I'll put him to bed." She took a step toward her husband, tripped on the edge of a ratty rug and fell against him. They both tumbled to the floor in a fountain of flying whisky. The brown bottle broke, spraying shards of glass and beer across the room.

Smith danced nimbly out of the way. As if this kitchen didn't smell bad enough, spilled liquor was now added to the mix. "You're coming with me, Mr. LeBlanc. Get up."

Felicia got to her feet, using her husband's head as a point of leverage. He slid further down, and she reached toward the open whisky bottle on the counter. A fly buzzed around their heads.

"Help him up," Smith said to her. "And let's go."

"Where we goin' honey?" Jake said. He put his hands flat on the floor and pushed himself to a standing position. His belt buckle was undone and his fly at half-mast. He thrust his crotch toward her. "Your place, I hope."

She wanted to gag. "My place of work." Although she couldn't see behind her, she was conscious of neighbors gathered around the open door. She felt that she was on stage, performing before a particularly difficult audience. Sweat dripped down her back and between her breasts. There wasn't a window open and the air was close and heavy. Two flies circled around the liquid on the floor, their buzzing audible even over the noise from the kitchen, the street, and the dog, its barking approaching the point of hysteria.

Jake headed toward the fridge. "Great. I'll get us something to party with. Okay, honey?"

"You've had enough. Do up your pants or you'll be getting a charge of indecency."

He leered at her, and Smith reached out, grabbed his upper arm, swung him around, and snapped handcuffs on him. "And," she said to Felicia, who'd picked a dirty glass out of the crowded sink and was about to pour herself another slug of whiskey. "So have you. Put that glass down."

"Who the hell do you think you are?" From out of nowhere, Felicia, who had been all calm excuses and trying to make sense, turned on Smith. She began screaming a stream of obscenities that had Smith blinking in shock. Ugly words, sour breath, cheap whisky, and expensive perfume washed over the young policewoman. Spittle gathered in the corners of Felicia's mouth; her face contorted, and her eyes flared, bloodshot and mean. "Think you can come into my house and tell me what to do. You bloody well better get your hands off my husband, if you know what's good for you, you bitch."

"Calm down, Mrs. LeBlanc. I have no interest in your husband."

Her radio cackled. "Five-one. MVA with injuries downtown. Car is delayed. Sergeant coming."

"Ten Four. And tell him to hurry." Smith wasn't sure if she said the last sentence loud enough to be heard.

Felicia launched herself at Smith, her fingers aiming for the soft, vulnerable eye sockets. Smith leaped back, pulling Jake with her, and Felicia stumbled across the room. She collapsed like a rag doll into a drunken heap on the floor. Where she sat, legs stuck out in front of her, screaming more abuse.

"Bummer," Jake said.

A motorcycle engine roared up the hill. It was cut off. Someone yelled, "Hurry, hurry. They're killing her."

Smith heard pounding footsteps and Sergeant Caldwell, the shift supervisor, burst into the kitchen. He grabbed Felicia and hauled her to her feet.

"I didn't touch her." The woman's purr was as soft and sweet as a kitten. "Ask anyone."

Caldwell snapped cuffs on Felicia.

"My husband struck me," she said to the sergeant, her voice soft and pleasant. A solid, reliable citizen explaining what had happened. "It was an accident, but your lady officer overreacted. I understand, and I won't lay a complaint, if you let me go. Although Jake could use a night in the drunk tank."

Smith choked back her indignation.

"Bring the man," Caldwell ordered Smith, as he led Felicia out the door. "Then call the humane society to send someone around to take the dog."

Caldwell had come on the motorcycle, so the LeBlanc family was stuffed into the back of Smith's car.

She walked around to the driver's door.

"I hope you'll finally put an end to this." The neighbor in the red robe stepped in front of her, blocking her way. "We live next door." He pointed—the big old house had been broken into a duplex. "My wife and I haven't had a moment's peace since we moved here."

Smith looked at the circle of faces watching her. Dressed in an assortment of nightwear, the street lights casting heavy shadows on their faces, the neighbors stood silently behind him.

"If you'll excuse me, sir."

He stepped out of the way. Inside the car Felicia was speaking to Jake in soothing tones, telling him that she'd sort everything out. Jake was making choking sounds. Smith prayed that he wouldn't vomit until they got to the station.

She moved to get into the car, but a spark caught her eye. Lorraine stood under a huge old walnut tree. Her shirt barely touched the bottom of her breasts and her jeans barely covered her pubic bones. The fake gem through her navel threw off light from the street lamp above her. Her eyes were wet. Seeing Smith watching her, Lorraine turned away and melted into the darkness.

Chapter Nineteen

Winters avoided long boozy evenings with police officers: he'd struggled too hard to get out of that trap. For the same reason he wasn't too keen on department social functions, such as Barb was forcing him into. But at affairs to do with Eliza's business, or her associates from the fashion world, he was never in danger of over-consuming. He was having too much of a miserable time to be able to forget how much he was drinking.

He clutched a glass of beer—some sort of expensive imported European thing that was, he'd admit, pretty good—and watched the party. They were at the M&C Developments' Mid-Kootenay office. The night was clear and warm. The mountains a black bulk against a pale blue sky. Teak patio furniture had been laid out around the grounds; a bar and tables holding canapés stood in the shelter of the couple of trees that hadn't been felled in the clearing of the construction site. In place of a view of what had once been heavy forest, posters with the logo of M&C marked the perimeter of the party area. Small groups of guests were escorted by rented staff, all young, pretty, thin, and female, down a chipped wood pathway to view the model suite. Winters followed, because he could think of nothing better to do.

What had once been an old barn had been given a fresh coat of red paint and new window frames and shingles. Inside, the barn had been fitted with dark wood, good carpet, and ceramic tile. Light fixtures sparkled, and wide windows looked over the dark, brooding forest. The kitchen might have served a four star restaurant. The master bedroom, filled with candlelight, coyly hinted at illicit passion in an enormous four poster bed and décor in shades of deep red and silver. Potted plants surrounded the Jacuzzi in the bathroom, and sliding doors led out onto a deck, larger than some people's houses, where a hot tub sat, dark and cold. It was all for show: he suspected that the plumbing didn't even work.

Guests made appropriate noises of approval. John Winters headed back to the party. He'd like to have gone for a walk in the woods, but beyond the party, the old barn, and the path leading up to it, there was no lighting. It would be somewhat embarrassing to get lost.

Back at the party, Winters stood off to one side, watching Eliza. She wore a simple skirt of pale blue cotton shot with silver threads that swirled around her shapely calves, blue sandals with flat heels and thin straps, and a white blouse with turquoise and silver jewelry he'd bought her on a vacation in Arizona. She was laughing and smiling at everyone, nibbling on a smoked salmon canapé, sipping at her *Veuve Clicquot*. 'Work the room' was the phrase. Eliza had made a success of the highly competitive world of modeling as much because she could play the game as for her looks. She would rather have spent the evening at home, on the deck with a good book, watching the sun set. But to watch her, which all the men were, anyone would have thought the M&C party was the most fun she'd had all year.

"Impressed?" Steve Blacklock appeared at Winters' side.

For a moment, Winters thought the man was talking about Eliza. "The suite was very nice."

"Frank needs help, now that Reg has left the building." Winters thought that was rather a harsh description of a man's death. But, to be charitable, perhaps Blacklock had never met the late Reginald Montgomery. "I'd been thinking about investing in this place for some time. Property in the lower mainland's gone through the ceiling. Nice for those of us who own some of it, but the smart money needs to find property still undervalued. Right?"

"I guess so."

"Your wife has some money behind her, I've heard."

Winters said nothing.

Blacklock's voice dropped. "If you're looking for a wise investment, this place has it all. I'm talking about partners in the business, understand, not property owners."

"I'll keep that in mind."

"You do that. And don't be put off by a scattered bunch of protesters. Can't put up a chicken coop these days without them wanting to put their two cents in. We've got all the required permits and authorizations, so there's nothing they can do to stop us. Soon as we start building they'll find some other poor schmuck to torment. Until then, I've got security guards around this property day and, especially, night. Think about it, John, think about it."

"I will." He would do nothing of the sort.

Blacklock walked away, tossing greetings to guests left and right.

Winters watched the guests. Meredith Morgenstern was there, lovely in black and gold, fluttering from one guest to another. Her long black hair was secured at the sides by gold pins. She carried a notebook, and didn't try to hide the microphone in her hand or the tape recorder stuck in the belt of her wide-legged black satin pants. She started to head toward John Winters, recognized him, and spun on her heels. He'd last seen her at the grow-op bust the other day. She'd arrived at the scene mighty fast. Someone had called her as soon as the police began to move in. Which meant that someone had been watching the house. Someone who was keeping an eye on the competition's operations, probably, and decided to gloat in their downfall over the morning paper. Falling out amongst thieves always made John Winters' heart happy. He'd suggest that Ray pay close attention to some of the other houses in that block.

A beautiful, exceptionally skinny redhead who didn't look old enough to drive had attached herself to José. As he chatted to his hosts and their guests, his hand occasionally wandered to plant itself on her bony butt. Winters was pleased to see it—if that was José's type, the sophisticated, *older*, Eliza, wouldn't be.

He'd thought the party was going to be for the partners, the ad agency, and the models, but there must have been two hundred people crowded around the open air buffet. He recognized the deputy mayor of Trafalgar and several prominent citizens from other towns in the area. The MLA was deep in conversation with Frank Clemmins. The only person looking less comfortable than John Winters was Pete, husband of the secretary Bernice. Pete's collar was too tight, his white shirt marked by sweat stains, and his tie was too colorful and too short. Winters headed toward Pete. But Nancy Blacklock intercepted him, and he settled his smile into something appropriate for mindless social chitchat. She was dressed in a colorful outfit of long green blouse over billowing blue pants. A paisley scarf in purple and yellow draped her shoulders. It was not a pleasant combination. "Enjoying yourself, Mr. Winters?" she asked.

"I am."

She drank deeply from her glass of champagne. No plastic glasses here. Nothing but flutes of lead crystal. "I always organize my parties down to the last detail, even the weather. Steve wanted to rent a room at a hotel, but I knew it would be perfect outside. I love my husband with a mad passion." She fluttered her eyelashes and Winters wondered if she was trying to send a message in code. "But he's a bit of a stick-in-the-mud sometimes. It doesn't bother me, of course." In more than twenty-five years as a police officer, John Winters knew that 'of course' usually meant the opposite. "His sister thought an outdoor party was taking too much of a risk. For once I stood my ground. She's not supposed to have anything to do with the business but never stops interfering. With my ideas mostly. And whatever Jamie says is pure gospel to Steve." She tossed her head back and the last half glass of the Champagne disappeared.

Her arm flew up, and a waiter appeared at her elbow. She held her glass to one side; he filled it and slipped back into the crowd. Not a word had been exchanged.

Nancy Blacklock took another swallow and then reached out—her fingernails were chewed almost to the quick—and touched Winters' arm. "If it had rained, they'd be all 'I told you so'. But as I said, I plan everything perfectly, so screw them, eh?" She cackled. Her laughter did not invite onlookers to join in. "You're not eating."

He held up his half-finished glass of beer. "I'm fine with this."

"Nonsense." She pulled at his arm and he could only follow. She handed him a plate and began piling it high with jumbo shrimp, smoked salmon, smelly cheese, and assorted things he didn't recognize.

"There," she said at last. "A growing boy needs his sustenance." She touched his chest with a chewed fingernail, giggled, and left him as she spotted the far more important person of the deputy mayor, momentarily standing by herself.

As the guests of honor, Eliza and José had to stay until the bitter end. While Blacklock and Clemmins waved goodbye to the last of their guests, Winters pulled himself out of the uncomfortable chair he'd managed to snag half an hour ago. Eliza's smile hadn't faded in the slightest, but his back was about to give out on him.

"That was a great party," he lied to his hosts, as Eliza slipped off to the bathroom. "Thanks."

"Don't be in such a rush, John," Nancy Blacklock said. She waved a hand over the party detritus all around them. "The caterers will clean up. I've made reservations at Flavours. Off we go." For lack of anything better to do, Winters had watched Nancy's champagne consumption. She'd had a prodigious amount, and other than a slight slur to the edges of her words, didn't seem too much affected by it. The sign of a serious drinker.

As if following Winters' line of thought, Steve Blacklock said, "If you've had too much to drink, *Sergeant*, I'll consider it my public duty to call the police if you try to drive." He laughed heartily at his joke. Winters forced out a smile. He'd nursed the one beer all night, and hadn't even finished it.

"He's a cop?" José's date said, to no one in particular.

Winters considered asking to see her ID. But then Eliza was slipping her arm through his. "Did someone mention Flavours? What a delightful suggestion. John and I'll join you for a quick drink and maybe an appetizer, but then I have to be getting home. I can't do with too many late nights any more, I'm afraid." She smiled up at her husband, all warm eyes and white teeth. "You don't mind, do you dear, if we don't stay long?"

"If you'd rather not," replied the caring husband. If he had to sit through another dinner with these people, he'd go into the kitchen, find the sharpest chef's knife they had and slit his throat.

Eliza settled into the car and slipped her shoes off. "God, what a bore."

"Present company?"

"Don't be silly. Nancy Blacklock can out-drink the U.S. Army, but she has to have some real organizational skills behind her to pull that party off so quickly. And where she got all those people with so little notice, I can't imagine. She and Steve have a rather unorthodox marriage, I'd suggest. Have you seen the way she talks to him? Somewhat like Momma and Baby."

"That's rather harsh."

"He's a wimp. A moneyed wimp, but a wimp none the less. I do not like it when there's a power concealed behind the curtain. I don't know what's going on."

"Is dinner going to be Dutch?"

"The company'll pick it all up. Your tax dollars at work. Although…"

"What?"

"What what?"

"What are you thinking? That was a meaningful *although*."

"To get a catering company that good in the height of summer on a week or two's notice, and all that fabulous food and drink, must have cost a bomb."

Winters smiled to himself. Trust Eliza to calculate the cost of the whole thing.

"And now dinner for, what, fifteen counting the ad company people, Bernice and her husband, José and his girlfriend, and is she a ditz—tell me I wasn't that vacant when I was starting out—and not counting us. Dinner at Flavours, the most expensive restaurant in town, with the best wine, and you can be sure everyone'll order the most costly things on the menu. Two and a half, three thousand bucks, maybe."

"You make it sound as if that's a lot to pay for a dinner."

"I'll say it's more than the company can afford. I told Barney I suspect they're on shaky financial ground, and she's to make sure I get a good chunk of my fee up front. They're spending money they don't have."

"Come on, it was just a fancy party and now dinner." The forest crowded the road. The mountains all around them had disappeared in the darkness. The red backlights of José's BMW convertible were ahead of them, the sturdy while headlights of Bernice and Pete's Ford Focus station wagon behind.

"It's not just tonight, John. Didn't you tell me that the late Mr. Montgomery was in charge of the books?"

"Reg ran the business side. Frank scoured the world for investors. Maybe he's come up with a big investor."

"Maybe." She exhaled softly. "But big investors want to see their money producing product. Not fancy parties and over-the-top ad campaigns."

Chapter Twenty

"Good morning, sweetie. It's going to be a lovely day."

"It's going to be a lovely day for sleeping. Bye, Molly."

"Hold on, Chris. I have something I want to talk to you about. Let's have breakfast."

"I don't want breakfast."

"How about George's?"

"George's?"

"Ten o'clock?"

Christa eyed the bedside clock. It was nine now. That would give her forty-five minutes to snooze and fifteen to get dressed. "Ten fifteen." Then she could have an hour to snooze.

"See you then."

Christa gathered her duvet from where it had bunched up around her feet and pulled it to her chest. Her upstairs apartment was too warm for cuddling under the blankets, but she didn't mind. She needed to feel warm and cozy. Protected. If only by a Wal-mart duvet.

She was still sleeping when Molly Smith pounded on the door.

"Aren't you going to get that buzzer fixed," Smith asked, following her friend's pajama-clad butt up the steep stairs to the second floor apartment.

"I told the landlord." He'd brought a bunch of white carnations, browning around the edges, to the hospital. The bad-tempered downstairs neighbor, who made Christa's life a constant misery, had complained about the noise that day, police breaking down the door, paramedics trampling the flowerbeds. The landlord had told her if she wasn't happy she could move. The neighbor hadn't moved, but neither had she stuck her head out of her window to yell at Christa since. For about a week, the landlord had been around all the time, asking if there was anything she needed. Then life returned to normal, and he hadn't fixed the doorbell.

She left Molly looking out the window and went to get dressed. Christa's bedroom was barely large enough for her double bed and an old dresser with broken drawers piled high with cardboard boxes used for storage. The closet doors didn't open fully. She reached in and grabbed whatever came to hand. Beige capris with a tomato stain on the lap and a black T-shirt bought at a concert by the popular tribute band from Nelson, BC-DC. She ran her fingers through her hair and avoided looking at herself in the mirror over the dresser.

Molly was scratching at a mosquito bite when Christa came out. "Don't do that. It'll scar."

"I'd settle for amputation if the itch would go away." A droplet of red blood rose on the inside of Molly's arm, and she pulled a tissue out of her pocket.

Christa turned her head away. They'd taken the clothes she'd been wearing when Charlie attacked her because they were covered with blood. Her blood. She thought she remembered seeing blood spraying out, drenching the walls of the entranceway. But perhaps that was only in her dreams.

"Your pants are dirty," Molly said.

"So what? You're not buying me breakfast to congratulate me on my fashion sense. Let's go."

Molly looked hurt. As Christa planned. Molly was a cop, wasn't she? If she'd done her job better she, Christa, wouldn't have been beaten up, would she?

She scooped her keys off the side table. In the back of her mind she knew it wasn't her friend's fault. Molly couldn't have followed Christa everywhere, gun out and at the ready. And only that would have stopped Charlie. But someone had to be held accountable. She had to blame Molly. Otherwise the only person Christa had to blame was herself.

Yesterday, Christa'd added an extra course to her next term's load: the psychology of survivor's guilt.

Lucky's old Pontiac Firefly was parked at the bottom of the street.

"I love this car," Christa said, climbing in. It was the first words they'd spoken since leaving the apartment.

"*This* car? It's a wreck."

"It is so your mom. If Lucky was a car, this would be her. Do they laugh at you at the police station when you come to work in it?"

"Tell you the truth," Molly said, "they do. Dave Evans wants to use it for target practice. Practice stopping a fleeing vehicle. He has images of himself in a car chase a la *Bullitt* and bringing down the bad guys in a hail of gunfire. Oops. I shouldn't have told you that. Really, Chris. Don't repeat it. I could get in real trouble talking about a fellow officer like that. And he's higher up the food chain than me."

"I've no one to repeat it to. What's *Bullitt*?"

"An old movie. One of my dad's favorites. Starring Steve McQueen, the bad boy of his day."

George's was a popular place. They got the only empty table, in the back corner next to the kitchen door. One of their school classmates was waiting tables. He threw menus in front of the two women and took coffee orders, with a muttered "How ya doing?" his eyes sliding away from Christa's face in embarrassment.

A red fist closed around her chest. "Jerk," she said to herself.

But Molly heard. "Who? Kyle? What'd he do?"

"He's still here, isn't he? He's been working here since we were all in Grade nine."

"His dad owns the place. You know that."

"So. He's a no-account."

Molly concentrated on the menu, although she probably knew it by heart. Christa scanned the price list. Crab cakes was the most expensive breakfast item. So that's what she'd have.

"How's things with the baby?" Christa asked. Talking about Lucky seemed to sooth some of the anger always threatening to choke her.

"The same. It screams instead of sleeping. Mom doesn't sleep. I don't sleep. Her friends from yoga class came around the other day, wanting to help. All they did was pace around with the screaming kid, one after another."

Christa looked at her friend. The delicate skin under Molly's tired blue eyes was dark.

"Dad's sorta getting into the parent thing a bit. He was feeding the monster this morning so Mom could have a long soak in the bath. It's just plain weird."

Kyle brought plates piled high with crab cakes and *huevos rancheros*. He smiled at Molly, who was always pretty no matter what sort of night she'd had, and avoided looking at Christa. *Idiot.*

"This coffee isn't very good. Take the cup away, and I'll have a cappuccino instead."

"Sure, Christa." He picked up the unwanted mug.

Molly applied salsa liberally to her food. "I have something to tell you, Chris."

"I knew it. Charlie's out, isn't he. He's coming back to town. Back to me. To finish the job." She pushed her plate away.

"No. It's good news. Sergeant Winters called me this morning. He asked if I wanted to tell you what's happening rather than him. And I do." Molly smiled at her, a mess of tortilla, beans, egg, and cheese speared on her fork. "The prelim was yesterday and Charlie pleaded guilty."

"Guilty?"

"Yup. Guilty as sin."

Tears rose behind Christa's eyes. A great weight lifted off her chest and for the first time in weeks, she felt that she could breathe. "That is so great."

"He got six months."

She should have known it was be too good to be true. Her burst of enthusiasm shattered as if someone had popped her birthday balloon. The tears dried up. "Six months?"

"Hey, that's good, Chris. Good."

"He'll be back in six months?"

"He's got no reason to come back—he doesn't have any family here, and no job to speak of. But listen to me. Sergeant Winters told the judge Charlie's an ongoing threat to you, and that if he was released on bail, the Trafalgar City Police had reason to believe he'd be back after you. So no bail. I'd guess Charlie's lawyer told him it would be six months to a year before his case came to trial, so he might as well do the time straight up."

Kyle brought the cappuccino. Cinnamon had been sprinkled across the top. "I hate cinnamon," Christa shouted. "Take it away and bring me another. Fast."

The people at the next table looked up.

"Who anointed you belle of the ball?" Kyle said, picking up the cup.

"Christa, listen to me, and stop taking all your anger out on Kyle," Molly hissed across the table.

Christa pushed her chair back. "I don't have to listen to you."

"Don't you dare walk away until you've heard me. John Winters went to bat for you, Chris." Molly waved her fork in the air. "He fought, hard, to keep Charlie behind bars. Six months for an assault that did not result in permanent injury or disfigurement is not a bad sentence. You don't like that, take it up with the Justice department, but don't take it out on Kyle or on me. Six months isn't a lark. You used to watch *Prison Break* on TV, right? Well six months in provincial jail isn't like that for sure. But it isn't a Girl Guide picnic either. After six months guarding his ass, or maybe not, Charlie'll have forgotten all about you."

Christa felt as if she'd been stung by a wasp. Molly was genuinely mad. She was keeping her voice low, but the anger was so close to the surface that Christa would have preferred it if she were yelling and screaming and making a scene.

Molly threw her napkin on the table. The end dipped into a puddle of refried beans and soaked up sauce. Her chair scraped against the floor as she stood up. She pulled two twenties out of her pocket and threw them on the table. Far more than the meal cost. "Finish your breakfast. You've made enough of a scene over the coffee, you might as well be here when it comes. A nice thank you note to John Winters would be the polite thing to do. But I won't hold my breath waiting for that to happen."

She walked out. The entire restaurant, staff and diners, watched her go.

Kyle put a fresh cup of cappuccino, without cinnamon, in front of Christa. He nodded toward Molly's unfinished plate.

"Guess I can take that away, eh?"

"This interview is being recorded. Do you understand?"

"Yes."

"Then we'll begin. This is Sergeant John Winters of the Trafalgar City Police with Julian Armstrong. It is August the 31st at 11:00 am. Is that correct?"

"Yes. Can I say something?"

"Say whatever you like."

"This is a farce and a travesty of justice. I've done nothing at all to have been brought here."

"Which is what this interview will determine, Mr. Armstrong. Tell me about the woman known as Ashley Doe."

"You don't even know her last name, and you're trying to pin something on me."

"I'm not trying to pin anything on anyone. And it's because I don't know her last name that I have to resort to bringing you in, Mr. Armstrong. Because I think you know more about Ashley than you're telling me. Do *you* know her last name?"

"I do not."

"Tell me what you do know about her."

"Ashley is, was, a client of the Trafalgar Women's Support Center. I volunteer there on a casual basis to provide counseling, particularly but not exclusively addiction counseling, to women who request it."

"Did Ashley request counseling?"

"She did not. And I did not provide counseling to her. But she was a client of the center and so I saw her there sometimes."

"Sometimes?"

"Sometimes."

"How many times?"

"I don't remember. Once or twice. No more than twice. I've only just arrived in town. She had a baby, a young baby, and so she came to the center. They provide formula, diapers, that sort of thing. Plus support and education for new mothers. A most worthwhile endeavor."

"I've no doubt about that. So that was your only contact with Ashley? When she was a casual visitor to the center?"

"Yes."

"Since Vancouver?"

"Huh?"

"That was your only contact with Ashley since you were both in Vancouver?"

"I don't know what you're talking about. It's no secret that I moved here from Vancouver in July."

"Did you have contact with Ashley in Vancouver?"

"No. I would have told you if I had."

"When was the first time you met Ashley?"

"I can't remember. I don't keep a log of every person I meet. Do you?"

"When was the first time you met Ashley?"

"Let me think, will you? I got here, to Trafalgar, on July 21st. I went to the support center almost straight away to volunteer my services. That was maybe the 23rd or 24th. I don't remember what day it was that I saw Ashley for the first time. A week after that, maybe? Hey, you know who might remember? You can ask Mrs. Smith. Lucky Smith. Ashley and her baby were with Mrs. Smith when I came in one morning. I remember now.

Mrs. Smith introduced us. Lucky and I knew each other when I lived in Trafalgar a number of years ago."

"I'll check with Mrs. Smith. That was the first time you met Ashley? I don't mean the first time in Trafalgar, or the first time since the moon was in the seventh house. The first time, ever?"

"On my mother's grave."

"I don't care about the state of your mother's health. Was that the first time you encountered the woman we know as Ashley?"

"Yes. Yes. Sometime in late July in the presence of Lucky Smith."

"Okay. Can you think of any reason Ashley told a friend she knew you in Vancouver?"

"What the hell is this? I told you how it happened. I don't care what some addle-brained, drug-soaked, purple-haired friend said. Maybe Ashley confused me with someone else. You of all people should know what the minds of these druggies are like. Mush. Pure mush."

"Ashley was not a druggie. By all accounts she was a sober, clean, responsible mother."

"Whatever. Can I go now?"

"Soon as you've told me about your involvement with the Vancouver police. I gather you've come to their attention before. Something about inappropriate advances in your professional capacity."

Sound of a chair falling to the floor.

"What the hell? That has nothing to do with anything. The bitches pulled back, soon as court and judge and proof and all that legal stuff were mentioned. Women of a certain age, they get, well, I hate to say delusions, but they're seeing a counselor for a reason, you know. Risk of the job. Come on, John, you must know how it is."

"No, I don't know how it is. I've always trusted middle-aged women more than I do most people. You're saying these women made up the accusations against you?"

"Proof is in the pudding. Did it go to court? No. Were charges laid? No. That's all I need to say."

"Tell me once more about your relationship with Ashley."

"I'll tell you once more that I had no relationship with her. She came to the support center for tips on saving money on diapers and how to milk the welfare system. I smiled and said hi 'cause I'm a friendly sort of guy. Got that through your thick cop brain?"

"It's a struggle, I'll admit. You're free to go, Mr. Armstrong. But please, if you plan to leave Trafalgar for any reason, let us know where you can be contacted."

"I'm not going anywhere."

Winters settled into an uncomfortable chair and reviewed the audio tape. It didn't show the degree of Armstrong's nervousness, the twitch of his right eye at certain questions, the way his left knee had of shuddering when he was lying. When he talked about Ashley in Trafalgar he was calm, as calm as anyone can be in a stark police interview room under interrogation. But when it came to Vancouver, Armstrong was as jumpy as the frog in the proverbial pot of water set to boil. Whether or not Armstrong had screwed his female clients was not Winters' concern. If Vancouver had decided, for whatever reason, not to pursue the allegations, neither would he.

One phrase stood out from the interview as if it was highlighted in yellow marker: *milk the welfare system*.

Milk the system: a good indication that Armstrong, supposedly the caring counselor, didn't have a whole lot of sympathy for the women who were his clients. Or at least not for Ashley. Was Ashley *milking the system*? Winters could only wish she had been—any involvement with government agencies would leave a paper trail. She'd never applied for benefits, or even left a full name at the center through which they could contact her.

Ashley.

It all came back to Ashley. Of course the victim was the center of any murder investigation, but this one was different. The girl had no past, almost no present. And certainly no future. Except for one tiny, screaming little thing.

Miller. Miller wasn't going to open his petite pink mouth and say "my mommy was killed by…" Nevertheless, Winters needed to see him again. And he could talk to Lucky Smith at the same time.

"What's up?" Lopez said, walking into the interview room.

"You ever had reason to come across a girl calls herself Marigold? Waits tables at The Bishop and Nun?"

"I know her. I suspect she's a low level dealer. Why?"

"She's Ashley Doe's roommate."

"I know. You think she knows something about the killing?"

"Just fishing. Ashley died a week ago. We've had officers circulating her picture all around town, to every community in the area. But no one's come forward as recognizing her other than as a girl they'd seen hanging around. She doesn't seem to have had a boyfriend. No friends to speak of. Her roommate barely knew her. No mementos in her room—no pictures of happy days with Mom and Dad. No letters from home or old school friends. No boyfriend, no girl friends either. Just Ashley and Miller. And Miller isn't talking."

"It takes time, John, you know that. To find the right person who, when they see the picture, will recognize her straight off and know everything there is to know about her."

"Time isn't usually on our side. We can't keep flashing her morgue picture forever."

Lopez glanced at the tape recorder on the table. "Interview?"

"Armstrong. Right now, Julian Armstrong is my number one suspect. Listen to this when you have the time. Let me know what you think. The guy's lying, no doubt about it. He knew Ashley in Vancouver. That doesn't mean he killed her, of course. But it makes me wonder why he's so determined to lie to me."

"Some people lie to the police soon as breathe."

"Let the Yellow Stripes sort it all out. Chief's put in a call to the IHIT."

"I don't imagine they'll be in a rush to get here."

"Huh?"

"You haven't heard?"

"Heard what?"

"Shooting at a playground. All over the news. Two children dead, three critical. Between the ages of four and six." Brown freckles stood out on a face white with anger. "A mother died shielding her daughter with her body."

"Jesus."

"You got that right. Not one of the shooters apprehended. Every cop in the province'll be on it like white on rice. That plus the suspected gang-connected lawyer knifed in the washroom of his office building yesterday, and the IHIT has enough on the go. A week-old death of a heroin junkie will be a minor pea on their plate."

"Ashley wasn't a junkie."

"Prove it," Lopez said. "I'll listen to that tape later."

Chapter Twenty-one

John Winters wiped steam off the bathroom mirror so he could have a good look at his face. He held his index finger up to cover his mustache, wondering what he'd look like without it. He'd had a mustache since the '70s. Then it was trendy, not to mention black. Now it was old-fashioned and mostly gray.

But Eliza liked it.

The mustache would stay.

It was past time for Armstrong and Marigold to account for themselves.

He often thought he did his best thinking in the bathroom in the morning.

Time to bring Armstrong in again, and lean on him hard. Winters didn't see the counselor as a killer, but he'd been wrong before. And even if Armstrong hadn't been involved in Ashley's death, he knew things about the girl he wasn't telling. And as he'd claimed he'd never been her counselor he couldn't hide behind client privilege. Winters couldn't charge Armstrong with withholding evidence based on his gut feelings. But Armstrong needn't know that.

And then he'd deal with Marigold.

He called the station and asked to have a uniform and marked car pick him up at home.

Eliza sat on the chair at her dressing table applying pink polish to her toenails. She had amazingly unattractive feet, all bumpy joints and long skinny toes. As far as he was concerned her feet were her only physical flaw. He had never told her so. She raised one well-shaped eyebrow as he hung up the phone, and pointed the bottle of polish at him.

"No breakfast?"

"I'll get something in town. I want to see someone before his day starts."

"And thus before your day starts, too." She turned back to her feet. "Grab yourself a coffee, anyway. It's ready."

Dave Evans pulled into the driveway in less than ten minutes. Winters ran out carrying a full travel mug.

He opened the car door and was about to jump in when something caught his eye. He walked over to the edge of the garden. Most of the pale blue berries on the elderberry bushes were gone; the smaller plants around its base trampled. A pile of fresh bear scat.

"Big one," Evans said, coming up behind him. "And probably a mom. Look over there." He pointed and Winters looked. It had rained in the night, just enough to wet the ground. Small prints wandered over themselves and underneath a larger set. They disappeared into the bush.

"Wish I'd seen her," Winters said.

"Me too."

They went back to the car.

"I want to pay a visit to Julian Armstrong," Winters said, as Evans put the car into gear. "We'll try his home first."

"Christ, not you again," was Armstrong's greeting.

"Your lucky day. I'd like to ask you a few more questions, Mr. Armstrong, if you don't mind."

"And if I do mind?"

"Then I'll leave. And I'll mention that to the judge at your trial."

Armstrong stood back and let the police into his apartment.

"As a matter of fact, Sergeant Winters, I was about to call you."

"Were you indeed?"

"I don't care whether you believe me or not, but it's true." Armstrong was dressed in a white T-shirt and baggy track pants, elastic loose, hem ragged, pocket torn. Probably what he slept in. The door to the bathroom was closed.

Winters looked toward it. "Are you alone, Mr. Armstrong?"

"Sadly, yes. Have a seat."

Winters took the only chair in the room. Evans stood by the door, and Armstrong walked to the window. Morning sun shone through gaps in the trees.

"I don't have much of a fondness for the police."

"I'm not here to ask for your vote in a popularity contest."

Armstrong spoke to the window. "I had some problems, back in Vancouver. That's why I gave up my practice there and moved to Trafalgar. They were personal problems, nothing at all to do with the law. But the cops interfered."

Mentally Winters rolled his eyes. He'd heard that before—from every abusive husband he'd arrested when he was in uniform. What happened in a man's home, they insisted, was a private matter.

Armstrong didn't turn around. "Far as I'm concerned what an adult woman wants to do with an adult man is her business. Women often form a bond with their therapists. And often it's that bond which gives them the strength to make the changes they need in their lives."

Over their heads, footsteps crossed the floor of the main house. A radio was switched on. A blast of music, quickly turned down.

"But some people don't see it that way. Political correctness and all that rubbish. I had a relationship with a client outside of office hours."

"One client?"

Armstrong pulled at the edges of the drawstring on his pants. "More than one over the years. But only one that matters here. She was a nice lady. Attractive, rich, spoiled. And so sad." He turned away from the window. Light shone through his thin hair, gray and greasy. He hadn't shaved yet, and the edges of his goatee were ragged. Winters couldn't possibly imagine why a wealthy, mature woman would find Julian Armstrong attractive. But as he, John Winters, wasn't a wealthy, mature woman, his opinion was of no consequence.

Armstrong sat down, heavily, on the unmade sofa bed. Springs squeaked. He turned his head back toward the window.

Winters admired the décor. Late eighties cheap. Other than the furniture there wasn't much to look at. The art on the walls was tasteless and mass-produced; the counter in the kitchen alcove was piled high with dirty dishes. Silence stretched between them. Outside a car engine came to life, and someone shouted to someone else to "hurry the hell up, or I'll leave without you." Doors slammed and the car pulled away. Far down the mountain, an ambulance screamed.

"Her husband, suspecting she was playing outside the school yard, hired someone to follow her. When faced with it, she told him about me. Who I was." Armstrong said at last.

"That must have been difficult."

Armstrong jumped to his feet. "Difficult, you don't know the half of it. The husband's on the goddamned police board. He was like thirty years older than her. Gave her lots of spending money but not much else except a fist when he couldn't get it up. Which was most of the time. He wasn't too pleased to learn that the trophy wife went in search of a bit of outside excitement because she wasn't getting it at home, was he?" He rubbed his hands across his face. "From then on it was out of control. She gave him the names of her friends who were clients of mine. The husband, let's call him Mister F, for a word I always think of when I remember him. Well Mister F went to them, leaned on them, made them lay complaints about me. Say that I'd made inappropriate advances."

"Had you?"

Armstrong went to the kitchen and poured water into a beer-encrusted glass. He didn't offer his guests a drink. "Them? Hell, no. Credit me with some taste. It was a bit ironic, because the ones who complained weren't ones I was friends with."

"You're saying that this man asked women to lay charges against you knowing that they weren't true?"

"Yup. That's what I'm saying." Apparently water didn't satisfy the need, because Armstrong reached into his fridge and pulled out a bottle of beer. He twisted off the top, tossed the cap into the sink, and took a deep slug. Again, not bothering to offer one to his guests. "They tried to charge me with raping the wife, said I talked her into it by telling her that sex was part of the counseling process. Nothing could have been further from the truth. Guy doesn't often meet a woman so desperate for it." He lifted his beer toward Winters. "So I gave it to her. Tell me you wouldn't have."

Winters said nothing.

Armstrong took a deep drink. "First examination she fell apart. Prosecution knew they couldn't put her on the stand. Couldn't even pretend she was too traumatized to testify, because I had the foresight to keep an e-mail she sent me apologizing for causing so much trouble, saying that her husband threatened to divorce her if she didn't go to court, and asking when we could meet up again. After all that, she kindly tossed in a highly graphic description as to what she'd like me to do to her at our next meeting. The other lady... well it was her word against mine, and considering that she was lying outright... Case closed."

"All nice and clean and settled," Winters said. "So why are you here," he waved his hand around the cheap room. "In Trafalgar?"

"Look Mr. Winters. I'm going to tell you how it is. Straight. You can believe me or not." Armstrong rested his hip on the windowsill opposite Winters' chair. His chin was up and a fire burned in his eyes. "My professional body wasn't too happy at the threat of legal charges being laid, and, no matter that said charges were dropped, the climate was decidedly chilly."

He looked at Winters, who had gotten to his feet some time ago. "It was time to leave town. And leave counseling people, women, who could solve most of their life's problems by throwing enough money at them. Believe it or not, Sergeant, I do want to help people."

"An interesting story, Mr. Armstrong. But I'm afraid it has nothing to do with the matter at hand. I have more than enough witnesses telling me that you knew Ashley and knew much more than you're telling me. I've no doubt you're aware that obstruction of justice is a crime."

"Don't you understand, man? Mr. F, the policeman's friend, has his knife sharpened for me. Julian knows a girl who's died, ergo Julian is the killer and we can call him up before a judge without having to worry about the girl's emotional state. The firing squad will assemble at dawn."

"It doesn't work that way. I'll lay charges as and when I see fit, whether your Mr. F approves or not." Armstrong, Winters thought, had been watching far too many conspiracy movies.

The counselor sucked on his bottle of beer.

"Okay, I've heard your story of woe. Now tell me about Ashley. Fast. I know you knew her in Vancouver. I know you meant something to her, and I know she saw you here, in Trafalgar. I'm tired of beating about the bush. You make one false statement and we're off to the cells."

John Winters didn't like Julian Armstrong. He had no doubt that Armstrong used his position as trusted counselor to lure needy women into his bed. Some women, with money, influence, age even, could handle it. But what about others, more vulnerable?

Armstrong finally admitted that he'd met Ashley in Vancouver. About two years ago, give or take a couple of months. She was a serious heroin addict, but young enough, pretty enough, blond enough, and able to turn the sweet, blushing virgin on at will, that she worked the better hotels and convention centers. Which was where he'd met her. At a convention for the directors of shelters for battered women.

He wasn't admitting to paying Ashley for her services, and Winters let that go, although cold fingers crept up his spine at the thought that Armstrong went to a feminist conference to pick up abused girls.

"She was unhappy with her pimp," Armstrong said. "And trying to get away from him. But she was too hooked on the drug to make the break. You know how it is, Sergeant. The pimp controls the supply. He hands it out in doses according to how well she performs."

Winters knew.

"She asked me to help her. And so I did. The next morning." Armstrong coughed, recognizing his mistake. He looked away. Winters wanted to hit the man. Instead he sat in his chair and listened. "I drove her to a shelter for hookers and druggies. They took her in. She was there for a couple of weeks. I checked on her regularly." Winters could guess at the nature of this checking in. But he still said nothing. If it would take everything he had, he'd see that Julian Armstrong did not set up practice in Trafalgar.

"But then I was… well… called away. Things got busy. And we lost touch. I'm sorry about that. I should have followed up. But you know how it is. Life just gets busy."

Found an easier screw, Winters interpreted. "And in all that time, she never told you anything about herself. Her name, her family, her hometown?"

"We aren't the police," Armstrong said, letting a touch of arrogance creep into his voice. "We don't pressure. If the girl chooses not to reveal those details, I wouldn't dream of trying to make her."

Unlike trying to make her drop her pants.

Winters nodded at Evans, who took down the name of the shelter that had taken Ashley in, and the dates.

"There was one thing," Armstrong said. "That I heard about later… well, after I got busy with my own practice. Around that time an eager young guy showed up. Right out of school. All set to make the world a better place." Armstrong almost sneered. Winters had no doubt that Armstrong would hold anyone still in possession of their principles in contempt. "All fresh-faced and full of ideals. Graham Buckingham. Don't know why I remember the name, except that I have a brother named

Graham, and Buckingham, well that's the palace, so it's easy to remember. It was a while after, but one day I ran into a woman who worked at the shelter. She told me Buckingham helped Ashley a lot. Got her to make the break, get rid of the pimp, stop taking the drugs."

Armstrong shrugged. "But, no matter what a great job we do with them, they always go back to the stuff. Never fails." He gave Winters a grin, like they were long time pals or something. "Addicts and hookers are swimming around at the bottom of the barrel for a reason. What can I say, eh?"

"And then you ran into her again, in Trafalgar?"

"I told you about that. It was at the women's support centre. Lucky Smith was there. I scarcely recognized Ashley at first. She was looking nice, cleaned up, it suited her, so I guess young Graham Buckingham had accomplished something. Miracles happen. I said hi, and she turned away. If she didn't want to admit to knowing me, that's part of client confidentiality, isn't it? Her choice."

"What happened the next time you saw her?"

Armstrong opened his mouth to protest. To deny there was a next time. Instead he closed his eyes as well as his mouth and took several deep breaths. "A couple of days later. On Front Street. She was standing outside the bakery when I came out with a croissant for breakfast. No preliminary conversation. No 'hi, Julian, how's it been?' Just told me right out that I was going to help her. I said I didn't have an office set up yet, but she could make an appointment at the center. She said she didn't want my professional help. She'd changed since Vancouver, I can tell you. She was much more confident for one thing, held her head up instead of always looking at the ground. She spoke to me, well, as if she were ordering me around."

Winters found himself feeling pleased at the idea. "Go on."

"She'd run into some difficulties, she and Miller, and she needed help with someone who knew how the world worked. That's what she said: 'how the world worked'."

"What did she mean by that?"

"I honestly don't know. Someone came by, a girl with a baby in a stroller and toddler by the hand and stopped to chat. The girl started chattering, on and on. Obviously we couldn't talk, so Ashley told me she'd explain everything later. I swear to God, there was no later. Next time I heard about her, it was in the paper."

Winters got to his feet. Time to leave. Being in the same room with Julian Armstrong made him want to have a long, hot shower before touching his wife.

About the only useful thing that Armstrong contributed, and the only thing Winter believed, was that Ashley went into that shelter prepared to do whatever it took to get herself clean, off the streets, and free of her pimp. Julian Armstrong was interested in nothing more than getting his libido satisfied, but his intervention might, just might, have put her on the track to meet someone who could truly help her make the break. According to Dr. Lee's report, Ashley had, until the overdose that led to her death, been clean for a good long time.

As soon as they got back to the office, Winters called the shelter in Vancouver.

He was prepared for a couple of days of phone tag, and hopping from one shelter worker to another. But sometimes the gods are in a good mood, and the woman who answered the phone, after a bit of description, and mentioning that she'd arrived with Julian Armstrong (A snort of "*Him!*"), remembered Ashley.

"One of our success stories," she said in a warm voice. "A nice girl. I haven't heard from her for, oh, must be well over a year. And let me tell you Sergeant, in my line of work that's a good thing."

"I'd like to know whatever you know about her," he said, "But you'll tell me it's confidential."

"As it is."

"Just one question then. What was her last name?"

"That's an odd question. But an easy one. Can't be anything confidential in that, I guess. Watson. I don't think Ashley was her legal name, but off hand I can't remember why I thought that. Why are you calling, Sergeant? I do hope she hasn't fallen back into the old life."

"No. She didn't. I can assure you of that. Armstrong mentioned that a man by the name of Graham Buckingham helped Ashley when she was at your center. Do you have a number for him?"

"Oh," All the warmth and humor left her voice, and he knew what she was going to say before she said it. "Graham, such a dear, died. Not long after Ashley left us, in fact. It was terribly sad. Tragic."

"I am sorry to hear that," Winters said. "Thank you for your time."

"We miss him dreadfully. He had a real gift for this work. He was about to get married. I wasn't able to get to Calgary for his funeral, so I never met the girl, but I would have liked to tell her how much good Graham had done."

Something niggled at the back of Winters' mind. Fiancée— Graham—social worker. Wasn't Graham the name of the man to whom Molly had been engaged? He might mention it to her later.

"I appreciate your help," Winters said, hanging up. He'd already forgotten Graham Buckingham.

Now that he had a name, he had someplace to start searching. He punched Ashley Watson into the computer and let it do its work. If Julian Armstrong had given them this days ago, he could have saved them a lot of time.

Chapter Twenty-two

Molly Smith watched Graham as he attempted to nail a roof to their house. The house was situated at the very pinnacle of a mountain, and there was so much snow that only the roof stood out. But for some reason Graham needed to secure the roof right now. Molly laughed from inside a tunnel of warm snow.

Graham laughed back. A deep laugh that sounded almost like a dog barking.

It was a dog barking.

Sylvester. Smith punched her pillow, rolled over, and tried to fall back into her dream.

But Sylvester kept barking.

The Smith home was out in the country, situated between a mountain and a river. Lots of wildlife passed through in the night, and sometimes the dog tried to warn them away.

At last the barking stopped. But the gossamer threads leading her to the lovely dream were gone. The first pleasant dream she'd had about Graham in months.

Awake, she could no longer bring his face into focus behind her eyes at will, and asleep he was drifting further and further away. She worried that the day would come when she couldn't remember why she'd loved him so much.

Her bedside clock read three o'clock. Time for another hot milk.

She scrambled out of bed and crept down the stairs feeling like a jewel thief. Miller was sleeping. There'd be hell to pay if she woke him up.

About half-way down the steps, she heard Sylvester whining. It was his welcome whine. She expected to see him rush across the hall to greet her.

The hinges on the kitchen door squeaked.

She stopped. Other than the nightlight at the top of the stairs, the house was fully dark. The living room blinds were open, but no light came in from outside. Everyone in the Smith family liked to sleep without a trace of light. Only once Miller took up nightly residence in her parents' bedroom had Lucky dug a nightlight out of the depths of the junk drawer.

And Andy moved down the hall to Sam's old room.

"Sylvester," Smith called. "What on earth are you up to?"

More of his welcoming whine, but he didn't appear, eager for a scratch behind the ears.

A floorboard creaked.

Smith took the remaining stairs very carefully. She reached the bottom and her fingers felt for the light switch. "Is someone there. I am a police officer. I'm armed, and backup's been called."

The back door rattled shut.

Smith jumped off the bottom step and ran.

She knew exactly where the kitchen light switch was located, and hit it, keeping her body tucked out of sight. She probably should have gone back upstairs for her gun, but it was too late for that now. Lights on, she darted into the kitchen, keeping low, heading for the gap between the refrigerator and the wall. No shots rang out; no one shouted or threw anything.

"This is the Trafalgar City Police," she said. "Step into the light, with your hands up."

Only Sylvester obeyed. The big dog stuck his face into Smith's crotch. She almost screamed.

Footsteps on the stairs. "What on earth is going on?"

"Don't move, Mom," Smith yelled.

"What do you mean, don't move?" Lucky came into the kitchen. She was dressed in her pajamas, her hair wild around her head, blinking at the light.

Smith jumped out from her hiding spot. She shoved her mother into a chair. "When I say don't move, I mean don't the hell move. You got that?"

"Moonlight?"

"Sit there, and *don't move*."

Smith checked the pantry. Empty. The kitchen door was unlocked, which wasn't at all unusual. Lucky often didn't bother to lock up at night. Smith threw the dead bolt. No one had passed her in the hallway, and she'd heard the kitchen door close. But she checked the house anyway. Sylvester ran beside her, and she knew he'd sniff out anyone hiding in a closet or under a bed.

"What's going on," Andy said, when she threw the light on in Sam's room.

"Downstairs, Dad. Now."

Only in her parent's bedroom did Smith not hit the lights and check the closet. Miller was sleeping and Sylvester didn't seem too concerned, so she let the baby dream.

Her parents sat at the kitchen table, sleep-befuddled, confused.

"Did you leave this door unlocked when you went to bed, Mom?"

"I don't remember. What's the matter?"

"Might be nothing. I thought I heard someone come in."

"Into our house?" Andy said. "I didn't hear anything. Did you, Lucky?"

"No."

"Must have been the wind. Or a bear trying to get into the garbage bin. Bill next door told me that a black bear tossed his garage the other day, after he'd forgotten to shut it."

"A bear," Smith said. "Perhaps."

"Much ado about nothing." Lucky yawned. "Try to be quieter in the night, will you, dear. Miller sleeps so lightly." She stood on tip toes to kiss her daughter on the cheek. She smelled of fresh baby power and baby vomit going rancid.

"You think someone tried to break in?" Andy said, as Lucky's feet echoed on the staircase.

"I don't know, Dad. I thought so. It sounded like someone had come into the house. But I don't see anything." There were no muddy footprints on the ceramic floor, no signs of anything in the house being disturbed. She'd taken a look outside, but nothing seemed to be out of the ordinary. The motion light over the garage was on: something had triggered it. "Maybe it was a bear. I'm sorry to bother you. Go back to bed."

He held her close, for just a moment.

"Dad?"

"Yeah?"

"Let's make sure we lock up, eh? I know Mom wants her friends to be able to come and go, but at least at night we should be a bit more careful."

Saturday morning, Winters had Jim Denton call the owners of The Bishop and the Nun and check the staff schedule. Marigold started her shift at four.

At three thirty he was at her door. He'd also checked the staff schedule at the station, and brought Molly Smith along with him. The young policewoman seemed to rattle Marigold even more than he did. Probably a generation thing—she'd be suspicious of him no matter what he did for a living. But Molly, when not wearing the uniform, looked just like Marigold and her friends.

Smith rang the bell.

"Go away," Marigold said from behind the door. "I don't want to talk to you."

"Nevertheless, I want to talk to you. May we come in?"

"No."

"I can take you down to the station, if you'd rather talk there."

"You can't."

"Don't tell me what I can't do. I'm not playing around any more, Marigold."

"Okay, okay. I'll talk to you tomorrow. I have to get ready for work."

"The faster we talk, the sooner you'll get to work."

The door of the next apartment opened. A young woman with long straight brown hair, dressed in sleek yoga wear, stuck her head out. A wave of incense surrounded her. Winters couldn't stand the stuff. "Keep it down, will you. I'm meditating here." She slammed the door.

"I don't want to bother your neighbors, Marigold," Winters said. "But I will place you under arrest if I have to."

The door opened. Only Marigold's dreadlocked head emerged. "I'm not dressed."

"I'll wait here while you get dressed. Constable Smith will come in in the meantime."

"How do I know she's not gay? Probably is, being a cop."

"Marigold, I suggest you start cooperating before my patience runs out."

The door opened fully. Marigold was dressed in the short skirt and white blouse she wore to work. The blouse didn't fit very well, and the space between the buttons gaped in an attempt to contain the fat around her middle. Black socks were crumpled around her ankles and she wasn't wearing shoes. "You might not have anything better to do, but I do. Come in if you must."

"Thank you," Winters said.

Smith stood with her back against the door, as he'd instructed her to do, her arms crossed over her chest.

He walked to the window. Marigold couldn't keep them both in sight, so she turned to follow Winters.

"Watson," he said. "Name mean anything to you?"

The girl's eye twitched. "No."

"I think it does. Is there a first name to go with it?"

Marigold threw up her hands. Her silver rings flashed in the light from the window. "Ashley. It was Ashley's name, okay, as you obviously know. Can you leave now?" She looked at her watch. "If I'm even a minute late, they dock me fifteen minutes pay."

"They'll dock you a lot then," Smith said. "If you're spending time in our cells."

Marigold turned around. "Are you on a power trip or something, cop lady? They say your mom's okay. What the hell happened to you? Go away, and take The Man with you. I told you people what you want to know."

"Watson, what?" Winters said. "Or rather what Watson?"

Marigold threw up her hands. "Jennifer. Boring name. Ashley hated it. I don't blame her. Reminds me of cheerleaders and pom-poms and rah rah and rich bitches blowing football stars behind the bleachers at school."

Now that Marigold was letting it out, Winters hoped she might be ready to let a lot of other things out as well.

"So Jennifer changed her name. Who cares? You wanna make a big deal out of it?"

"Changing her name? No. Keeping information from the police that's relevant to their investigation? Yes, that is a big deal."

A door slammed in the hallway and a man shouted at someone not to forget the recycling. Outside a child laughed. The apartment was very warm. He could smell the incense next door. But it didn't cover up the smell of pot, recently enjoyed, inside the apartment.

Marigold glared at Smith. Smith hooked her thumbs through her gun belt and stared back.

Winters allowed the silence to fill the apartment. He could wait all day. But, he'd guess, Marigold couldn't. Smith's boots creaked as she shifted her feet.

Marigold paced in front of the couch. Her eyes kept straying to the wooden box containing her stash, and she gnawed at her fingernail.

"Ashley died," he said, "under what we call suspicious circumstances. That means that everyone she knew, everyone she had contact with, falls under the scope of our investigation. It's not fair, sometimes. But you know what, dying wasn't fair to Ashley."

Marigold looked directly at him for the first time. "You got that right."

"Did Ashley have a problem with you dealing drugs?"

"I don't deal anything."

"That's not what they say on the streets," Smith said.

"I don't care what anyone says." Another longing look at the box.

"You're known to deal in what's sometimes called soft drugs, Marigold," Winters said. Blood flooded into her face, and she looked very angry. "But that's not my concern. I'll let the drug squad worry about it." That there was no drug squad in the Trafalgar City Police, and that, if there were such a thing, Winters and Lopez were it, he didn't bother to mention. Sometimes people's impression of police gleaned from U.S. television shows could prove helpful.

"Did you kill Ashley because she objected to you selling marijuana behind The Bishop and Nun?"

"No!" Her eyes opened wide with fright, and she suddenly realized that this was not a game. She fell onto the couch. The springs weren't very good and she wasn't watching where she was going. She slid onto the floor. "You're going to pin Ashley's death on me so you can screw me for helping a pal out and making a few bucks in the bargain."

"I'm not going to pin anything on anyone. But I am going to find out what happened to Ashley the day she died. You can count on that."

What pictures there were in the apartment looked like calendar art, or postcards, stuck into cheap frames and hung on the walls. But there was one picture of Marigold, looking young, and pretty, and happy. He picked it up. It might have been taken on the East Shore of Kootenay Lake.

"Put that down," she said in a soft quiet voice, "please."

He put it down.

"Ashley cared about that baby." Tears gathered behind Marigold's eyes and overflowed. She didn't lift a hand to wipe them away. "Miller. He wasn't her baby, not physically. I asked

her what it had been like, and she told me she wished she'd
brought life to Miller, but she hadn't. She didn't tell me where
he'd come from, and I didn't care. She loved him, and looked
after him. Isn't that enough?"

Winters glanced at Smith, still leaning up against the door.
She was a dark threat in the equipment laden uniform, but her
face was drawn, her blue eyes questioning.

When Winters looked back at Marigold, her makeup had
began to blend with her tears into a black river. A river with
nowhere to go.

"We tack on extra penalties for dealing around children."

"I only ever sell behind The Bishop," she said, her voice so
soft he had to lean forward to hear. "I swear. And not much.
Just a toke here and there. Ashley didn't know. When I came
home with extra cash, I told her I'd had a big tipper." Her nose
ran, and mingled with her tears. "As if that ever happens. I liked
to buy the occasional thing for Miller, when I could. The day
Ashley moved in, I knew she'd leave if she found out I dealt. So
I didn't ever tell her."

"Thank you, Marigold," Winters said. "You've been helpful. Take this as a warning: stop selling. Stop now. We will be
watching you."

He nodded to Smith, and she opened the door.

They left the apartment and walked down the steps to the
street.

Smith let out a deep breath. "You believe her?"

"I'm not sure." They walked up the hill, heading toward the
police station. The sun was hot on his face. Smith wiped the
back of her neck. He didn't know what he thought. So he sorted
out his impressions, using Smith as a sounding board. "I believe
Marigold truly cared about Miller. But Ashley? Hard to say. I'll
have someone drop into The Bishop tonight, looking to make
a buy, looking for something stronger than B.C. Bud. Ashley
was killed by a heroin overdose, not marijuana. Marigold can
turn on the tears, fast enough. I don't quite have a feel for how
smart she might be. She confessed, when confronted with it,

to selling pot. Was she clever enough to be trying to turn my attention away from her other product? I don't know. But she makes no bones about needing money, more money than she makes at The Bishop. Maybe more than she even makes selling small quantities of locally grown produce. There's an avenue I've failed to explore. Marigold seems to live simply. No car, cheap apartment. But she puts in long hours at The Bishop and it's a busy place most nights. What's she do with the money she earns? And how much does she earn, in all of her occupations?"

Chapter Twenty-three

"What are we going to take to the pot-luck?" John Winters asked, peering into the depths of the stainless steel refrigerator.

Eliza looked up from her toast and coffee and yesterday's paper. "Pot luck?" She shivered at the very mention of pot luck. The most dreadful of all social occasions. Food, prepared hours (days!) ago and trucked to the party in the back of a van with failing air conditioning. Macaroni salad. Chili finished with too heavy a hand on the spices (or not enough). Reheated pasta. Spinach dip in a bowl carved out of bread. Iceberg lettuce browning around the edges, drenched in supermarket-brand bottled dressing.

"The pot luck at Barb's place this afternoon. For the whole department. Remember?"

If he'd told her they had to go to a pot luck, she would have remembered. "John, you haven't said one word to me about a party."

"Sure I did. Didn't I?"

"No." She dragged out the word as if it were polysyllabic.

He ducked his head and looked sheepish. Toast popped out of the machine and he grabbed it. "Guess I forgot. I can't get out of it. Barb's been on my case for weeks, demanding to know what I was going to bring."

"What did you tell her?"

"That I'd sort though the multitude of Winters family favorites and let her know. I need to go, sweetheart. Show the flag, so to speak. It starts at four. I'll get there around four-thirty and I should be able to escape by six."

Police functions. Booze. Shop talk. More booze. And more booze. They'd come to Trafalgar to get away from that.

It wasn't hard for John to read her mind. "I swear, on the grounds that you are the most understanding woman in the whole world, that I'll have one beer and be out of the place by six, five-forty-five, if I can make it. Call my cell at six. Something about an emergency at home. The toilet is overflowing. That'll do it."

Eliza put down her toast and pushed back her chair. A soft breeze came in the open window and lifted the edges of the newspaper. "Most people bring casseroles, salads and desserts to a pot luck, potato chips if they can't cook, and forget about appetizers. I'll get some smoked salmon and cream cheese. Mix that with a bit of chives for color, paprika for kick, roll it all into a tortilla and slice it thin. Voila. We have a tasty, pre-dinner treat."

"You're coming?"

She put her hands on his shoulders. "In Vancouver I avoided everything to do with your profession, John. That was a mistake. I left you alone to battle your demons."

"You didn't...."

"Now that we're here, making a new start, I'd like to meet your colleagues."

And she meant it. In Vancouver they lived separate lives, and were content to have it that way. He was a police officer—long hours, crazy job. She was a model with her own long hours, crazy job. She had been in Florida when the crisis she'd been too pre-occupied to notice arrived and John had fallen apart. She'd been helping her parents after her mother fell when an absent-minded rollerblader ran into her and broke her leg, but she might as well have been on the catwalk in Milan. John had needed her. Badly. And she hadn't been there.

"The other wives are coming?"

"And the husbands, yes. Barb told me specifically that I was to bring you. Are you sure? I know you hate those things."

"Almost as much as you hate the parties I take you to. Like that awful thing at the Grizzly Resort. Incidentally, I heard that José's girlfriend had way too much to drink at the restaurant, made a play for one of the ad execs, and José told her to make her own way back to the hotel and be out of town next morning."

"I'm so sorry we missed that." Sarcasm dripped off his tongue as thickly as the marmalade he was spreading on his toast. "You finished with the paper?"

She handed the *Gazette* over. He took his reading glasses out of his pocket and popped them on the edge of his nose. He hated the glasses, but she thought they looked good on him. Sophisticated, mature.

"What are you staring at?"

"I can't look at you?"

"Not like that." He wiped at his face, trying to remove non-existent crumbs.

"I'd better decide what I'm going to wear," she said. "Then I'll go shopping for the food."

Molly Smith was also thinking about Barb's party. She checked out the big freezer in the basement. A few packages of summer fruit and vegetables—last summer's—lay at the bottom. Enough bags of bagels to see them through a nuclear winter. Frozen waffles. Packages of the sausage rolls and small frozen pizzas her father loved.

Nothing she could take to the department pot luck. Smith had told Lucky about the party a week ago. Whereupon she'd assumed her mother would prepare a casserole that would be the hit of the event.

Lucky had a recipe she'd cut from *Martha Stewart Living*. It was expensive, complicated, wordy. And it made a meal that tasted like something served in heaven to angels fluttering their wings on fluffy white clouds. Lucky named it Five Hour Lasagna because of the time involved.

Smith had sort of hoped that her mom would get up in the night and make Five Hour Lasagna for the City Police's pot luck.

Apparently not.

What was the point of living at home if you couldn't count on your mom to cook for you?

She'd signed up to bring lasagna, so she'd have to head over to the supermarket and buy a frozen slab of mass produced product.

At least none of the older guys would ask if she'd made it herself.

She didn't bother to get a shopping cart. She was here for one thing only. A package of frozen lasagna.

Smith stood in front of the freezer case and stared. The variety was impressive: seafood lasagna, vegetable lasagna, chicken lasagna, three mushroom lasagna, four cheese lasagna. Nothing called five hour lasagna, unfortunately, so she settled on the package with the simple label of: *Lasagna.*

The line at the checkout was long. To pass the time, Smith read the label on the container.

Defrost overnight.

Otherwise, three hours to bake from frozen.

Who knew frozen food was so time-consuming?

Eventually she was allowed to pass her money over and leave.

She had to get this thing home. Three hours of cooking and she'd barely make it to Barb's on time.

It wouldn't do for a probationary constable to be late.

When she got home, she let herself in through the kitchen door. Neither Sylvester nor the big blue pram were at their usual place. Lucky must have taken the baby for a walk. Smith removed the packaging from the frozen meal, put the lasagna into the oven, and turned the dial to set the temperature.

For once the house was quiet. A nap would be nice, while the party food cooked.

◇◇◇

They'd had little more than a sprinkling of rain for more than a week, but somehow the wheels of the pram found the only patch of mud between here and the coast in which to get stuck. Lucky wrested the awkward carriage back onto firmer ground. Miller didn't seem to mind, and he slept on. Movement seemed to be about the only thing that put the child to sleep. At fifty-five years old, feeling every day of it, Lucky figured she could provide the baby with just about anything except constant movement. *What is the one thing that money can't buy?* Youthful energy.

Sylvester brought up the rear. His step was slow and his tongue hung almost as low as his tail. Even the dog was getting tired of all these walks.

Why am I doing this? Lucky asked the trees.

She parked the carriage beside the vegetable beds and took her canvas shopping bag out of the pram. She'd promised to bring fresh produce to a sick friend, and even though she might be ready to drop to sleep on the soft ground between the spinach and cabbages, she would deliver fresh produce. She set the brake on the pram. Miller didn't move, and Sylvester collapsed in the gentle shade of a large maple. The garden smelled of good dark soil and ripening vegetables. A cloud of white butterflies rose into the air from the compost heap. Lucky moved among her tomato plants, lifting green leaves, and selecting brilliant red cherry tomatoes. Many, too many, were overripe, split and spoiled or fallen to decay onto the ground, but there were still plenty good for eating. She also selected two fat beefsteak tomatoes and placed them carefully in her bag.

She picked a variety of greens from the lettuce beds. The zucchini plant was overflowing, some of the vegetables too large to be any good, but she she found one a nice size.

Lucky's garden had been sadly neglected, but at this time of year it pretty much took care of itself.

Her bag full, Lucky returned to the pram, and walked slowly back to the house. The sun was warm on her face, the vegetables fragrant in her arms, Miller dreaming happy baby dreams. Lucky was content.

Moonlight opened the kitchen door. Sylvester ran ahead and dove face first into his water bowl. "Thanks, Mom. That'll go nicely with the lasagna."

"Lasagna?"

"The pot luck? Today?"

"I forgot about it, sorry, dear. Help yourself to the garden, there's lots left, and the zucchini's running rampant." Lucky put the produce bag onto the counter. "Eileen's having a hard time since her stroke, so I thought I'd take something from the garden to her. I was going to go after our walk, but Miller's sleeping so peacefully, I hate to disturb him."

Moonlight looked into the pram. The baby's pink face was crunched in sleep. He shifted slightly and then lay still. Watching her daughter, Lucky felt something move in her chest. Instead, she said, "What's in the oven?"

"I bought a lasagna to take to the pot luck."

"I suppose I'll have to wake Miller, if I'm going to go. I told Eileen what time to expect me, and she has to keep to a strict schedule."

"Oh, all right." Moonlight threw up her hands. "I'll look after him while you're on your errand of mercy. But don't be long, I have to get ready for the party."

Lucky stood on her tiptoes to kiss her daughter's cheek. "You're a dear."

"No, I'm not. I don't want Eileen to feel she has to entertain you and Miller. That's all."

Lucky picked the bag of vegetables off the counter. "I'll wash these at Eileen's. Don't want to give you the chance to change your mind. If you need it before I get back, there's a bottle made up in the fridge. Be sure and warm it up first." She grabbed her keys and, calling "car" to Sylvester, left. Sylvester was never too tired to go for a ride in the car.

◇◇◇

Molly Smith cracked the oven door open to check the lasagna. It sat on the shelf like the lump of frozen preservatives it was. The coil at the bottom of the oven burned red hot.

She looked into the pram. "I'm sure you'd be very happy with family services, right?" she whispered. "After all, you're just a baby. I don't know why Mom can't see that."

Still, she thought to herself, he was a cute wee tyke. At least when his mouth was shut. She carefully maneuvered the pram out of the kitchen. The oven would soon be heating up the house. She took Miller into the family room and parked him beside the black eye of the TV, before running upstairs to get a book.

The baby hadn't moved while she was away. She settled into an armchair to read, curling her legs up under her.

Smith was deep in the book, one of the historical mysteries her mother loved, when the bell at the kitchen door jerked her out of the foggy, gas-lit streets of London and back to the present. She stretched her neck to peek into the pram; cuddled in his yellow sleeper suit, Miller slept on. The bell rang again. A friend of Lucky's, probably. Smith ignored it, and returned to the book. Might be Jody Burke coming back to try, again, to talk Lucky into giving Miller up. Smith had no interest in getting involved in that business. Let her mother sort it out.

The bell rang again, harder. Miller began to stir. Smith cursed under her breath and tried to breathe quietly, willing him back to sleep.

She felt ridiculous. Hiding in the back as if there were a Jehovah's Witness, or an unwanted suitor, at the door. But she had no interest in exchanging the time of day with one of her mother's friends, or in receiving another lecture from Jody Burke.

The ringing stopped.

Miller cried.

Smith swore.

The kitchen door was old, original to the house. The hinges needed oil and they always squeaked when opened.

They squeaked.

Of course Lucky hadn't locked the door behind her. She never did.

Miller cried again. Not a soft whimper this time, but a deep throated bellow. He was warming up to his full, impressive, repertoire.

"We're back here," Smith yelled, deciding that there was no point in trying to be quiet any more. The visitor had well and truly woken the baby up.

As she leaned into the pram to pick him up, she heard footsteps on the old wooden floorboards in the hall and sensed someone behind her.

"You've woken Miller," she said to whoever was there.

"Too bad."

The voice was hard, cold. Not one of Lucky's friends to be sure.

Molly Smith turned around.

All she could see was the business end of a .22.

Chapter Twenty-four

Eliza Winters knew a thing or two about making people feel at ease. She marched up to Barb's front door, carrying her tray of canapés. Her husband followed.

"Hi. I'm Eliza. This is such a pleasure," she said to their hostess. "Thank you for including me. What a fabulous view you must have. Do you mind if I take a look?"

Barb beamed, and took the food. "Of course not. Please, come in. We're all out back. Glad you could make it."

Eliza exclaimed over the décor and went with Barb into the kitchen. Winters walked through the house, following the sound of men's voices.

As he stepped onto the deck, Ray Lopez handed him a beer. The smell of fresh cedar, newly laid, still hung over the deck. The view, as Eliza predicted, was spectacular. Far below the town of Trafalgar was tucked into the curve of the river. Only the glacier had snow, sparkling in the afternoon sun. A few more weeks and the white stuff would dust the peaks like icing sugar sprinkled on chocolate cake.

Most of the department was here, accompanied by wives and husbands or friends. Winters felt a soft hand on his arm and turned to see Eliza smiling at him. "Please introduce me to your colleagues," she said. She wore khaki capris with a blue shirt, a simple silver chain and earrings. Her sandals were flat and she'd tied her thick hair into a casual knot at the back of her head.

He made the introductions. He'd met the Chief Constable's wife, Karen, previously, but none of the other spouses or companions. Dawn Solway had come alone. Dave Evans, dressed as if he were about to catch a wave in Hawaii, was with a pretty young woman Winters recognized as the shop assistant at Rosemary's Country Kitchen. Properly introduced, Eliza melted into the crowd. She touched her lips to the rim of her wine glass and looked fascinated at what everyone had to say. Winters leaned on the railing of the deck, holding his beer. The air was warm, and close, but the promise of fall, and winter, to come, lingered about the edges of the day. A cat screamed a warning in the woods.

Barb offered him another beer and he took it. One more wouldn't hurt.

But then Eliza was beside him. "No one," she said to Barb, "is eating my lovely salmon rolls. John, you have to take one for the team. If you don't drop dead on the spot others might dare to give them a try." She pulled the bottle out of his hand. Her smile was radiant. He'd have preferred to have the beer, but he could hardly wrestle her for it.

He went to the table where appetizers had been laid out and filled a small plate. What happened to his beer he never did discover.

Jim Denton's wife, Gale, joined him at the railing. "Aren't these good," she said, munching on Eliza's offering.

"Very," he said.

Gale chatted on about the view and the company. The deck was filling up as late-coming guests arrived.

Gale Denton was a bit of a bore. Winters had finished his salmon rolls long ago and was wondering how to excuse himself. Going for another beer would be a legitimate excuse. Paul Keller was lecturing Barb's husband, Carl, on the finer points of operating a barbeque as Barb hovered with a plate of hamburger patties.

"I work for the government," Gale said in answer to Winters' question. "Don't we all? I'm with Children and Family

Development. It's a hard job, let me tell you, and getting harder. I could tell you some stories. It was only last week when…"

"You must know about the baby Miller Doe situation then," he said, not wanting to hear what happened last week. He looked around, searching for an escape route. Eliza was chatting to Dave Evans; the young constable almost drooling under the force of her charm. His date clung to his arm and pouted. "What's your take on Jody Burke?"

"Burke?" Gale's eyes covered over as she searched her memory banks. "Can't say I know her. She must be new, although I would have expected to have been told if someone new was coming. But we're so busy that things don't always happen as they should. Why just last week…"

"If you'll excuse me, my wife's signaling to me." Eliza was doing nothing of the sort. But Gale's back was to her, so she wouldn't know that.

"It's unlike Molly to be late," Barb said as Winters escaped from the chatty Gale Denton.

"Maybe she took an extra shift."

"I know who's working today and she isn't. She was supposed to bring lasagna. Her mother's lasagna is famous over half the province."

Winters smiled. "I think you have enough food, Barb. More than enough, I'd say." The large patio table was set with napkins, cutlery, plates, and condiments. Bowls of chips and nuts sat on side tables, and the legal clerk was passing appetizers. Mr. Barb piled racks of ribs and burgers and hot dogs onto the sizzling barbeque. Al Peterson held the door open as Karen Keller and Dawn Solway brought bowls of salad out of the kitchen.

"There's never enough," Barb replied. Then she laughed. "Okay, time to confess. It's me I'm worried about. I can eat lasagna every night of the week and still want it for breakfast. I was hoping for one of Lucky's vast casserole dishes, enough leftovers to see me through the winter. Molly said she was coming."

Winters' cell phone rang. He dug into his jacket pocket and flipped it open.

"John Winters."

"This is Lucky Smith. I'm not sure where Moonlight is, but she left her cell phone behind, so I hope you don't mind that I found your number and am trying you."

"Of course I don't mind." Winters turned his back to the party and looked out over the valley. Purple shadows wrapped themselves around the black mountains. A red light flashed on the highest peak, warning airplanes away. Behind him the air was full of the scent of barbequed meat, pungent salad dressings, and warm casseroles.

"Can I speak to her, please?"

Winters hesitated at telling Smith's mother that she hadn't shown up where she was expected. "Why do you think she's with me?"

"I'm sorry. I assumed you're at the department party. I'll try Barb's house. I have the number here somewhere."

"I am at the party. But Molly isn't."

The silence was so complete that Winters thought he'd lost the connection. "Lucky?"

"I'm sure it's nothing. Sorry to bother you, John. Bye."

"Don't go, Lucky. Tell me what's worrying you. I'd guess she found something better to do than come to a work party. That's not hard for a young woman to do."

Lucky laughed, the sound nervous, broken. "Probably not. But not with a baby."

"Baby?"

"Moonlight's not here. And neither is Miller. I'd think she'd taken him out for some air, except that the pram's in the family room. And I found the casserole she bought for your party still in the oven and very overcooked."

"Let me ask around, Lucky. See if anyone's heard from her. You contact the hospital. If Miller took sick, she might have taken him there."

"I called them already. Nothing."

"You don't think she took the baby for a walk?" As he talked, Winters slipped into work mode. Molly Smith was not where she was expected to be—at the annual police department party. A young, highly ambitious, probationary constable would not pass attending a company function on a whim.

"Stay by the phone, Lucky. I'll find out what's happening and call you back. Will you do that?"

"Yes."

"Talk to you soon." He snapped the cover shut on his phone.

"Problem?" Eliza asked. The party swirled around them. People were lining up at the barbeque, paper plates in hand. Barb staggered out of the house under the weight of a casserole dish. Cabbage and onions and bacon by the scent of it. There wasn't much John Winters loved more than cabbage and onions.

He kissed his wife. *Thanks to you I'm sober.* "Nothing major. Help yourself to dinner. I have to make a call. Guard that cabbage with your life, will you, until I get back."

One perfectly formed black eyebrow lifted, telling him that she didn't believe him. Then she turned to Barb. "Is there anything more that needs to be brought out?"

Barb laughed, and the only word he heard was 'lasagna'.

Winters walked to the railing. The sun was moving west, toward Koola Glacier, the Upper Kootenay River a thin blue line carving a passage between the deep green and brown of the mountains on either side. Traffic moved on the highway. Motorcycle engines, a lot of them, heading out of town.

Should he worry about Molly Smith? Her mother didn't know where she was. If the police responded to every worried mother… But the baby was apparently missing as well. Daughters in their twenties might get up and walk out of the parental home, but infants didn't.

Molly had left a casserole in the oven, skipped the company party (for which he could hardly blame her, wanting to do the same himself) and headed off for amusements of her own. She'd probably taken the baby to give her exhausted mother some relief. The last thing in the world she'd want would be the entire complement of the Trafalgar City Police searching for her.

"These ribs are great," Dave Evans said, sucking on a bone. The pretty girl from Rosemary's Country Kitchen stood beside him, smiling, eyes shining. "Nice party. Where's Molly anyway?"

"Busy," Winters said. "Save me some of those, will you. Ray, give me a minute."

Chapter Twenty-five

Lucky was now getting seriously worried. Where on earth might Moonlight have gone? The thought crossed her mind, briefly, that the girl might have decided to take advantage of her mother's absence to hand Miller over to social services.

But she dismissed the idea. Moonlight wasn't happy at having the baby in the house, but she wouldn't do something that would upset Lucky so much. Besides, she didn't have a car, and all of Miller's things were still in the house.

Lucky called Christa.

The girl immediately launched into a complaint about Charlie only getting six months. Uncharacteristically, Lucky cut her off.

"We'll have coffee one day soon and you can tell me about it. But I don't have time right now. Is Moonlight there?"

"No. Why are you asking?"

"Have you seen her today?"

"No. Why?"

"Have you heard from her today?"

"No. Lucky what's happened? Why are you asking me all this?" Christa's voice rose in something approaching panic.

"No reason," Lucky said, realizing that she herself was starting to panic. Nothing spread faster than panic. "Just wondering. You haven't met Miller yet. I'll get Moonlight to bring you out for lunch one day soon. Bye, dear."

Lucky hung up without hearing Christa's cry of 'Wait!'

She called the store, this time trying to make it sound as if she needed to locate Moonlight for some inconsequential reason. Andy hadn't seen her. He had, however, lost the staff time sheets for last month, and Flower was complaining that she hadn't been paid for all the hours she'd worked, and did Lucky still have them at home?

"No," she said, hanging up.

Other than Christa, Moonlight didn't have any friends in town. At least no one Lucky knew about. Moonlight didn't see her school friends any more. Lucky didn't know if her job with the police had anything to do with that. She sometimes wished that Moonlight had a more normal social life. But, since Graham's death…

There was, however, one old acquaintance who seemed to keep up with what Moonlight was doing. Lucky reached for the thin Trafalgar and District phone book.

"Meredith? This is Lucky Smith."

"Lucky?" Meredith's voice was wary. And so, Lucky, thought, it should be after the way she'd disgraced herself by her recent involvement with that unspeakable television person.

Lucky tried to sound as if their past problems were forgotten. "Sorry to bother you at home, Meredith, but something's come up, nothing serious mind, and I need to find my daughter quickly. She's gone out and not taken her cell phone."

"Are you okay, Lucky? Your husband?"

"Yes, yes. Everyone's fine. I thought that well, being on the police beat at the paper and all, you might have heard from Moonlight recently. Today I mean. Sometime today. Since noon."

Lucky could hear Meredith thinking. "No. Sorry. But if I do hear from her, I'll let you know."

"Just ask her to call home. Thanks."

"Are you sure there isn't something I can help you with, Lucky?"

"Nothing at all. Everything's perfectly fine. Bye."

Chapter Twenty-six

Sergeant John Winters leaned on the railing and ripped a strip of meat off a rib with his teeth. Ray Lopez walked across the deck.

"Nothing," he said in a low voice. The party swirled around them. Eliza laughed at something Gale Denton said. "Not at the hospital, the station. The Mounties haven't heard anything. I even called the guys in Nelson. No luck. Do you know any of her friends?"

"Only Christa Thompson. Lucky might have called her. Check. Molly doesn't have a car, and they live outside of town. Find out if Molly took her mom's car, or anyone else's."

"Those sort of questions'll worry her mother."

"Almost as much as they're worrying me. I'll ask Barb if there's a quiet room we can use. No use in worrying everyone else."

Lopez pulled his cell phone out as he went back into the house.

Paul Keller crossed the deck carrying a paper plate wet with meat juices and salad dressing. "What's going on, John?"

"We need to talk, Paul. Let's find someplace private." He put his half-finished plate down, and wiped his fingers on the seat of his jeans.

Keller's plate joined his. Winters spoke to Barb in a low voice, and she led him to a room off the kitchen. "Problem, Paul?" she asked, holding the door open to the TV room.

"Work," he said. "Ray's out front, making a call. Show him where we are, will you, please."

"Sure thing." The door shut behind her.

"Explain," Keller ordered his lead detective.

"Molly Smith. It might be nothing. And if it wasn't for the fact that the baby's also missing, I wouldn't give it another thought." Winters rubbed the face of his watch as he filled the Chief Constable in.

The door opened. "Christa Thompson knows nothing," Lopez said. "Lucky called her already. She also called Meredith Morgenstern, who, as you can imagine, knows less than nothing, but that's unlikely to stop her from speculating."

"Lucky called the paper?" Keller sat on the butter yellow leather couch. A flat-screen TV filled one wall.

"She and Molly have a history. Lucky's getting desperate," Lopez said. "I can hear it in her voice."

Outside, the party had gone quiet. Everyone knew something was up.

"Lucky says there wasn't a car at the house when she left," Lopez said. "She checked Molly's gun safe—it's locked. Her cell phone is on a table in the family room. Her keys to the house are hanging on a hook by the back door where she usually leaves them."

"Someone might have dropped by and picked Molly up," Keller said.

"Looking at things one at a time, we have nothing," Winters said. "An adult woman who's been missing for a couple of hours, if that. She seems to have taken her foster sibling with her—nothing wrong there. But Lucky says the lasagna was burning in the oven, indicating that Molly intended to come to this party until something changed her mind at the last minute. Very last minute if she didn't even switch the oven off. No note from Molly saying that she had to take the baby to the hospital or something."

"I can't start a full-scale search based on that, John," Keller said.

"Agreed. But there is one thing we're overlooking."

"What?"

"Jennifer Watson. AKA Ashley Doe. The woman caring for the baby who is now missing was murdered not much more than a week ago."

"You think that has something to do with this?" Keller asked.

"We've come up almost completely blank on Ashley. After a week of digging, I don't know much more than her name. Jennifer Watson: a common name at that. She has no police record, no history, not much of an identity, thus no motive I can find for her death. We know one thing, and one thing only about her—she was caring for a child that was not her own."

"You think someone wants the baby?"

"I think I dropped the ball on this one. It never occurred to me to consider that someone killed the mother to get the kid."

"And Molly," Keller said, "has the kid."

"Last we heard," Lopez said, "she had the kid."

"All right," Keller said. "We start a search for Molly Smith."

"I'll get Vancouver trying to dig up more on Jennifer Watson. She was a druggie and a hooker at one time. It's possible, likely, that even if she was never arrested formally enough to be fingerprinted, the police knew her. I know people I can drag away from their Sunday evening. Ray, get back onto the baby angle. Someone must be missing him—he had to come from somewhere. Go around to the Smith's. Find out if anything unusual happened while Lucky had Miller."

"Something unusual at the Smith home," Keller laughed without humor. "That won't be hard to find. I'll notify the Mounties and the Trafalgar Police to be on the lookout for a suspected officer in danger. Do you want the Mountie's search dog out?"

"That might be an idea. Change of plan. Ray, you contact Vancouver. Drop my name all over the place if that'll help get some action. I'll take the Smith home. Ask the dog handler to meet me there, Paul. It's remotely possible that Molly left on foot."

"You know you're going to have egg all over your face if she comes home with the baby under one arm and a pizza under the other."

"Egg, I can handle. I'll ask Barb to call a taxi for Eliza. Ray?"

"Madeline too. I'd say this party is officially over."

"This is getting ridiculous," Al Jacobi said, slamming his foot onto the brakes at the last possible second to avoid rear-ending a cheerful yellow Mini.

"Traffic's always bad at this spot."

"Not talking about the damned traffic. I mean the Allenhart case. It's not as if we've nothing else to work on."

Detective Rachel Ferguson shrugged. It might be a Sunday afternoon, but Allenhart's lawyer wanted a personal update on the progress (or lack thereof) of the case. Allenhart Enterprises owned approximately half of the Pacific Northwest, probably owned half the politicians as well. And the politicals told the police when to jump.

The city was covered in low-lying clouds. They could see nothing but the road in front of them. Ferguson closed her eyes as Al cursed and swore at the traffic.

"And on top of it all, he'll complain that we're late."

Puget Sound lay off to their left, somewhere, hard to see in the fog. They reached their turn-off and the car jumped forward. Houses got larger and large properties spread themselves out. Soon the houses themselves disappeared from view, and all they could see were long winding driveways disappearing behind ghostly trees. Al slowed and pulled off the road, lowering his window. He pressed the buzzer at a tall, heavy gate. "Jacobi."

He might have said, "Abracadabra." The gates opened with silent majesty and they drove through.

Manicured lawns ran to their left and right, as far as Ferguson could see.

Ricardo Gallo, the chauffeur, was standing on the front steps of the house, waiting, when Ferguson and Jacobi drove up. "You're late," he said.

"You're lucky we came at all," Jacobi said.

Gallo's massive shoulders shifted under his black jacket. "Not my problem. He's waiting in the library." He turned and walked into the house, without waiting to see if the detectives would follow. They did.

The sound of Ferguson's heels clicking on the floors echoed through the empty, quiet house. Notably, she thought, Gallo had said 'he', not 'they' were waiting.

Gallo held the door open for the detectives and closed it, without a sound, behind them.

George Dowds, the family lawyer, looked up from the papers on his lap. "Please," he said. "Take a seat."

They did so. The library was decorated in calming shades of mauve and sea green. Most of the books lining the walls appeared to be well-thumbed.

"Mr. Allenhart would like an update," Dowds said.

Rachel Ferguson cleared her throat. "We've not yet managed to locate the girl."

"If we'd been allowed to circulate her picture and description…" Jacobi said.

Dowds waved a well-manicured hand. "I shouldn't have to keep reminding you, Detective, that Mr. Allenhart has requested that this affair be handled as discreetly as possible."

Ferguson jumped into the conversation before Jacobi could, once again, offer his opinion of that 'request'.

"Will we be meeting with Mr. Allenhart?"

"I'm afraid he had a very bad night. I will, of course, make a full report of this conversation to him later. People don't just disappear off the face of the earth, Mr. Jacobi, not in this age of hyper-security. I'd like to be able to report to Mr. Allenhart that you've made some steps toward finding her."

Detective Rachel Ferguson knew that some people could disappear quite well if they wanted to, but she refrained from saying so, and let Al dance around Dowds' questions, while trying not to admit that they hadn't made a single bit of progress since their last meeting.

Murder amongst the ultra-rich would normally have thrown the newspapers into a frenzy. But so tight was Richard George Andrew Allenhart's empire's control over the media and the legal profession that little more than the bare details got to the attention of the public. R.G.A. Allenhart was 92 years old, bedridden after a stroke, and lived in paranoiac isolation approaching that of the fabled Howard Hughes. Protected by almost as much money.

She'd only met the old man once. He'd been dressed in a somewhat tattered multi-colored robe, with leather slippers on his feet, reclining in a comfortable armchair beside the big bedroom window. He had said nothing, and his body didn't move once, but he had kept his piercing black eyes on her face the entire time as his lawyer answered the officer's questions. A nurse hovered at the old man's shoulder, and in the distance Rachel could see boats sailing on the blue waters of the sound.

Richard Allenhart had been married to Eleanor Browne for sixty-four years. The union had been childless, yet, by all accounts, happy. When Eleanor died of cancer, Allenhart, trapped in his grief, became a recluse. Eleanor had done good works all her adult life, and was particularly involved in charities helping homeless and drug-addicted women and their children. Richard continued to support Eleanor's causes, without ever leaving his house.

One night about a year ago Ricardo Gallo, the chauffeur, came across a young woman awkwardly trying to pick up johns on the street corner. He'd brought the girl home to his boss. Katie was her name. Katie Watson.

Young Katie had liked the old man, and he'd liked her, and so she moved in. Allenhart was more than ninety years old, and supposedly mourning his wife. Nevertheless Katie was soon pregnant.

The day Katie gave birth, at home, to a healthy boy, the lawyer was summoned. The will rewritten. Everything left to the baby, who was graced with the name Richard George Andrew Allenhart II.

On the day of the birth, the day Allenhart instructed his lawyer, he was in very sound mind. Although not all together sound body. Imagine screwing the old guy. Must have been like making it with King Tut. Ferguson couldn't repress a shudder. She glanced up to see if anyone had noticed her mind wandering. But Jacobi was still talking, and Dowds was watching him.

Whether Allenhart, or his sperm, had been up to the job —Ferguson suspected the chauffeur had a hand in the business— didn't really matter. Allenhart was the name written in the line for father on the birth certificate, and the baby was named in the will. Paternity, and thus inheritance, was legally cut and dried.

Less than a week later Allenhart suffered a massive stoke. It didn't kill him, but left him severely physically incapacitated and unable to speak. Round-the-clock nursing staff was hired. Katie and Richard Jr. continued to live in the house. One of the nurses told the police she suspected the girl nursed the old man as well as her baby. Ferguson shuddered again.

Then, one sunny afternoon, an intruder broke into the house, while Katie and her baby were there alone, except for Allenhart upstairs in the bedroom suite he never left. Katie's head had been bashed in. Her baby hadn't been seen since.

Jacobi got to his feet. His cheeks were burning. "You can tell Mr. Allenhart," he said, loudly and distinctly, "that we are confident of apprehending the suspect shortly." Ferguson also suspected that upstairs, trapped in his failed old body, Allenhart was listening.

He was old enough, rich enough, influential enough, to indulge his whims, even when it comes to the police.

But he did want the person who had murdered his young lover caught.

And most of all, his son back.

Chapter Twenty-seven

A few yards before the road reached the Smith driveway there was a small lay-by, half hidden by bushes and thick undergrowth. Meredith Morgenstern pulled her Neon in as tightly as she could. She climbed out, pushing aside grasping twigs and dead branches. The rear end of her compact car stuck out, but the path dropped sharply into the bush, and she daren't drive in any further.

So Molly Smith had gone walkabout. And not only her mother, but the police were worried. After talking to Lucky, who hadn't fooled Meredith for a minute that she wasn't desperately worried about her daughter, Meredith decided to take a drive past the police station. Where she saw cars gathering; Detective Lopez running in. Meredith knew that the police department pot luck was today. It should still be going on. But Lopez had left the party in one big hurry.

What, Meredith wondered, was Smith up to? Maybe she'd gone bad and the cops were looking for her to arrest her. That would be a juicy story. Although, to be honest, Meredith couldn't imagine Moonlight Smith turning dirty after less than a year on the job.

Meredith had pulled into a parking spot across the street from the station, wondering what to do next. As she watched, uniformed men ran for a patrol car, and it pulled into the street, siren breaking the peace of the afternoon, red and blue lights flashing. Meredith followed.

The car had gone straight to the Smith house.

◇◇◇

Lucky Smith opened the kitchen door for the police. She was glad John Winters had come. Glad that he'd taken the strange, sudden disappearance of Moonlight seriously. As he walked into the kitchen she head a patrol car, coming down the highway and turning into their road. It was a Trafalgar City Police car. More sirens and an RCMP SUV pulled into the driveway. A Mountie leapt out, and opened the back door of his vehicle. A dog, a big German Shepherd, jumped to the ground.

Sylvester threw himself against the kitchen door with a chorus of aggressive barks. The old wooden door was heavily marked with scratches.

"Better put your dog away, Lucky," Sergeant Winters said, "as long as the police dog's here."

Lucky felt the blood draining from her face. Cadaver dog. She'd recently read something about cadaver dogs—whose job it was to search for human remains. She felt Winters' hand on her arm. "And then you can have a seat," he said, his voice gentle. "Would you like a glass of water?"

She shook her head. "That dog…"

"That's a search dog," he explained. "It's possible Molly left on foot, and if so, he'll try to track her."

Lucky sucked in a lungful of air. She felt foolish at the way she'd leapt to assume the worst. She grabbed Sylvester by the collar. He resisted at first, but she spoke to him sharply, and he allowed himself to be dragged away from the door. She pushed him into the pantry off the kitchen. Packages of dog food and treats were stored there. When he finally calmed down and realized where he was, he'd have a grand feast.

"Where do we start?" Lucky asked.

"You searched Molly's room? Found nothing out of the ordinary?"

"Nothing."

"Does she often leave her cell phone behind when she goes out?"

"Never. You'll be wanting something of Moonlight's for the dog to sniff. I'll be right back." She ran out of the room. Clumps of hair had worked themselves loose from the clip and flowed around her head.

Winters opened the door at the dog handler's knock. He was tall, bulky, young, and good looking. His black hair was cut short, and his brown eyes were dark and troubled.

"Thanks for coming," Winters said. "Mrs. Smith's gone to get something of Molly's to show your dog."

"We don't work that way."

"I know, but it gives her something to do. I'm not going to tell her it isn't necessary."

Lucky came back, waving pink cloth in her hands. "Moonlight's pajamas. Will they do?"

"Sure," the Mountie said with a smile that didn't reach his eyes. "Thanks, Mrs. Smith. I'm Adam Tocek."

"You have a dog?"

"Yes."

She'd run out of the room, repeating to herself, over and over, that she had a task to do. Find something of Moonlight's. Give the dog something to follow. Don't stop and think. Don't cry. She'd grabbed the bottoms of Moonlight's summer pajamas, the ones with a Winnie-the-Poo motif.

She handed over the pajamas. Constable Tocek's face might have colored, just a little, as he accepted the clothing.

Winters and the Mountie headed toward the door. Lucky began to follow, but Winters turned to her and suggested she wait by the phone.

She filled the kettle, plugged it in, took out the big old tea pot that she only used when she had lots of visitors, threw four bags of tea in, took down mugs, and filled bowls with milk and sugar. There were peanut butter squares in the freezer. They'd been there all summer, but they should still be good. She laid the squares on a colorful ceramic plate.

The store-bought lasagna, scorched across the top and blackening around the edges, sat on top of the stove. Lucky's stomach turned over and tears filled her eyes. She tossed it into the trash.

A car pulled up and she looked out. Paul Keller, the Chief Constable. There might not be enough squares. She'd have to open a bag of store-bought chocolate chip cookies. Police officers were said to have hearty appetites. Perhaps she should make coffee as well as tea.

The phone rang and Lucky grabbed it before the first ring ended.

"Moonlight?" she shouted into the receiver.

"Just me, Jane. I was wondering if you've given any more thought to what we're going to do about the war-resister petition. It seems to me…"

"Sorry, Jane. Gotta run." Lucky hung up.

The kettle called for attention, and she filled the tea pot. She'd had the big brown pot almost as long as she'd had Moonlight. Perhaps longer. There was a chip in the handle, and the top had been replaced with one that didn't match.

Paul Keller came in without knocking.

"Tea?" Lucky said.

"Tea?" he repeated.

"Would you care for some?"

"Oh, tea. Don't go to any trouble."

She waved a hand across the counter. "It's all made."

"Then tea would be nice."

"Sit down. Please."

He sat. Lucky Smith had been a thorn in the side of Paul Keller since he'd come back to his hometown of Trafalgar to take over as Chief Constable. She hoped that now, today, he wouldn't remember all of that. They'd been at loggerheads many times, over a variety of issues. But she liked to think that, like warriors of old, they'd come to respect each other. As much as she hadn't wanted Moonlight to become a police officer, Lucky'd feared that Paul would be opposed to hiring the girl because of her mother's history. To his credit, he'd accepted Moonlight on her own qualifications.

She poured tea.

"Good dog," Keller said.

Lucky blinked. Sylvester was still trying to force his way out of the pantry. "He's upset at having his home invaded."

Keller smiled. "I meant the Mountie dog. He's got a good nose. They've taken him into the woods. Hopefully he can pick up a scent. If there's anything fresh out there, human fresh, he'll find it. Did you know that all police dogs are male? They've found that female dogs just don't have enough aggression."

"I remember that in '68, the dogs were more than aggressive enough, thank you." Now why on earth had she said that? It had nothing at all to do with what was happening outside, in her own backyard, right now.

"Is your husband home?" Keller asked.

"Andy? He's at the store. It's the busy season." Even busier since Lucky hadn't been coming to work.

"Did you, uh… tell him… about Molly?"

"He hasn't heard from her. I thought it best not to worry him."

"I see. Oh, tea. Yes, sugar. Thank you. No thanks." He said to the offer of a square. "We've just come from the pot luck. Too much food. Although we didn't get to dessert." He reconsidered, took a square and bit into it.

As always, the scent of tobacco smoke radiated from Paul Keller like an aura. Lucky wondered if his wife had ever gotten used to it. Did his pajamas smell as bad?

Lucky stopped thinking about what the Chief Constable wore to bed, and started as someone shouted outside. But the shout wasn't answered by other calls and her heart settled down.

She sipped her own tea. When she looked up, Paul was watching her. His brown eyes were full of sympathy. And something else, something she wasn't sure she recognized. The moment passed and he looked away and said, "Call your husband, Lucky. He won't be happy if he comes home to find us all here and not knowing what's going on. Good cookie, this."

"I guess you're right," she said.

It hadn't been affection in his eyes, had it?

"I don't think she went into the woods, or down to the road, recently," Constable Tocek said. "Norman doesn't seem to be getting a strong scent out here at all."

Winters studied tire tracks in the gravel driveway. Lucky's Firefly was parked in front of the garage. Andy Smith drove a compact Toyota. Fortunately the driveway was wide, and Lucky's car hadn't covered the set of tracks laid earlier. They were much larger, from an SUV or a pick up. He'd asked Ron Gavin, the RCMP forensics officer what he made of them.

"Lucky Smith's a popular person," Gavin said. Before coming out, he'd put on whatever clothes were at hand on his Sunday evening: uniform shirt over jeans that had once been worn to paint something white. "This is a busy home. Lots of people coming and going all the time."

"I'm only interested in today."

"We'll do what we can."

It was almost dark. There was a full moon, hanging bright and white in the western sky, and so far the sky was clear, which helped. But the search would have to be called off soon.

Winters called The Bishop and Nun and asked if Marigold was working. She was. He hung up. He hadn't expected her to have anything to do with this in any event. He was pretty sure he'd put the fear of God, or himself, which was almost as good, into her. He'd sent their undercover guy to The Bishop Saturday night looking to make a serious buy. But Marigold had batted her eyelashes and pretended not to know what he was talking about. She hadn't even told him where he could buy some pot.

Winters went into the kitchen. Lucky and Paul Keller were sitting at the big, scarred, wooden table. They weren't looking at each other, but the air so full of emotion he could almost see it, like flashes of lightening jumping from one mountaintop to another.

Lucky lifted her eyes. They were heavy with worry.

"I'd like to ask you some questions, Lucky," Winters said, pulling up a chair.

"Anything. Would you like some tea? I've made lots."

"No, thank you. Tell me about Miller."

"Miller?"

"I've a feeling he might be the source of all of this."

"But he's a baby."

"You took Miller in when Ashley died. Have you had any unusual situations since then?"

Her laugh was tinged with panic. "Apart from not getting any sleep, and driving my daughter and my husband to distraction?"

He didn't return the laughter. "Apart from that, yes. Think carefully, Lucky."

She lifted her cup to her lips. She breathed in the scent of the tea but didn't take a sip. "Moonlight thought someone might have been trying to break in one night."

Keller sat up. "What?"

"Sylvester started one heck of a racket. Moonlight got up to see what was going on, and she said she'd heard the kitchen door. The motion light over the garage was on. Andy thought a bear had been in the yard. I've heard of bears getting doors open and into houses, we all have. I don't lock up before we go to bed, not usually. Moonlight suggested I start locking the doors at night."

"A good suggestion," Keller said.

"Anything else?" Winters asked.

"Nothing I can think of. Other than that fool woman trying to take Miller."

"What fool woman?"

"Jody Burke, from the Ministry of Children and Families. You sent her out here, Paul. That wasn't nice."

Keller colored. "I didn't send her, Lucky. I merely asked Dave Evans to escort her, as she'd requested."

Winters' nerve ends stood to attention. Jody Burke. The woman whom a long-serving district social worker had never heard of.

"She wanted you to relinquish the baby?"

"Yes. It was quite odd, I thought, how much she wanted me to surrender Miller. I know enough about these things to know that the province is desperate for good foster families. I thought they'd be happy I'd taken him in."

"Do you know why she wanted him?"

Lucky shook her head. Strands of red and gray hair flew around her face. "I assumed she doesn't approve of my anti-war or anti-development stance. People are getting too polarized these days. I wasn't entirely surprised that someone would try to take the baby because I want to see the Grizzly Resort shut down."

"Excuse me." Winters almost ran out the door. He flipped his cell phone open and punched in the number. "Ray, I want everything you have concentrating on a woman by the name of Jody Burke." He spelled the name. "Start with the Department of Children and Family Development. I want to know if they have an employee by that name, and if so where she can be contacted. If they can't help you, find her. She has to be staying somewhere in the Trafalgar area. Call Dave Evans, he's searching the woods with the Mounties. He accompanied Burke to the Smith home a few days ago. She might have mentioned where she's living."

"It's a Sunday, John. No one who works for the government is going to be answering the phone."

"Then call the Minister and put him on it, if you have to. Burke has Molly. I'm sure of it." He hung up.

Now all he had to do was find Jody Burke.

Chapter Twenty-eight

Constable Molly Smith could have taken him out, easily. A kick to the knees or the balls and he'd be down for the count. But his partner, by far the more dangerous of the two, still held the gun as well as the screaming baby.

A man had come out of the trailer as soon as they drove up, as if he'd been expecting them. The setting sun was in his eyes, and he lifted a hand to shade them. Smith recognized him, but she wasn't sure from where. He was in his forties, heavyset, hair too thick and too black. His face was tanned and deeply lined and the bags under his eyes cast deep shadows.

He saw Smith, behind the wheel. Tense and no doubt pale in the driver's seat. He looked in the back, and color drained from his face. "Are you out of your mind?"

Which was pretty much what Smith had been thinking ever since she'd turned from Miller's pram to see a person standing in the doorway to the family room, pointing a gun toward her with a steady hand.

"This is a surprise. And not a pleasant one." The voice had been calm. "When I saw that your car, and your father's, was gone, I expected to find your mother here alone."

"It's not my car," Smith had explained. "It's Mom's. She's gone out. I don't have a car."

"Wish I'd known that earlier, but it can't be helped now." The .22 pointed straight at Smith's chest. She gave a thought to her own weapon, bigger and more powerful than this one, locked away in the safe in her room.

It might as well be buried in Lucky's vegetable garden.

"Back up. Stand by the window."

"Why?"

"Never mind why. From now on you do everything I tell you, no questions. Move."

Smith did as ordered. She felt the wall press against her back.

Without moving her eyes, or her gun hand, from Smith, Jody Burke crossed the floor to the pram. Her right arm shot out and she pointed the weapon directly at Miller's head. "You twitch without permission, you do one thing I don't tell you, and I'll shoot him."

Smith believed her.

"Turn around."

"Look, you must know this isn't a good idea. You want Miller, take him. What do I care? The kid's a nightmare."

"You got that right. If your mother was here, where she should be, I'd end it all now. But you, Constable, are another problem all together."

Meaning, Smith surmised, that the search for the killer of a police officer would be much more intense than what appeared to be a robbery gone wrong, and would spread far beyond the boundaries of the Kootenays, or even British Columbia.

"I'll tell them I didn't see who it was. I'll go upstairs…" to where her gun was… "and tell them I was sleeping and when I got up, he was gone. Poof. Like magic. You'll be doing me a favor."

"Don't want him taking your inheritance?"

"I don't have anything to inherit. I'm talking about something much more valuable—a good night's sleep and home cooked meals."

"You talk a good line, lady. But somehow I don't believe you. You'd be happy to be rid of the brat, I don't doubt that. But you won't let me walk. You look like a cop with too much dedication to the job.

"Now turn around, like I said."

"What do you want with him, anyway?"

"Enough talk. Turn around. I could shoot you now, but I'm thinking a change in strategy might be required. So you come with me. You're a complication I don't need, but easily remedied, I'm sure. Turn, or I'll shoot the baby."

Smith turned. She heard the springs of the old pram squeak as the weight inside shifted, Miller's tone change as he was lifted up. Smith looked out onto the woods at the back of the house. A jay sat on the branch of a mountain ash. The tree was heavy with red berries.

"I'm holding him, and I have the gun against his fat head. You twitch and he's dead. And then you'll follow him to the sweet hereafter. Do you understand?"

"I understand."

"Good girl. Now you can turn around. Walk through the kitchen. My car's outside. Don't look back and don't do anything but walk. Get in the driver's seat. The keys are in the ignition. I'll get in the back with the monster. And off we'll go."

"Where?"

"Never mind where. I'll tell you where. And cop?"

"Yes."

"Don't doubt for a minute that I'll kill him. You want to be responsible for that, bring me down in a heroic confrontation, go right ahead. I'll plead shock and fright and say that you misunderstood me, and be out in three years, if that. But Miller'll still be dead. And your career along with him, after I've painted you as an overly eager rookie grabbing the chance to look heroic."

Burke stepped back, taking herself well away from the path between Smith and the door. "Now, let's go."

They walked past the stairs, through the kitchen, and out the back door. As ordered, Smith got into the driver's seat, and Burke and Miller climbed into the back. Smith adjusted the mirrors. Burke had lowered both the baby and the gun, so they were below the level of the windows.

"You do anything to draw attention to us, he's dead. Go through town, toward Highway 3. I'll tell you where to go from there."

They drove down the narrow winding road through the forest to the highway. Across the black bridge over the wide Upper Kootenay River, toward the bustling town of Trafalgar. Smith's heart pounded in her chest. What would she do if she saw a police car? Nothing. Burke's voice was cool and calm, her hand steady on the gun. Smith had no doubt she'd kill Miller. That was probably her intention all along.

What could a three month old baby have done that would make an adult woman want to kill him?

That, she'd worry about later.

If she lived long enough.

The town faded behind them. The Trafalgar City Police would be gathering at Barb's home for their end-of-summer pot luck. Eating good food and drinking good booze. Unlikely anyone would notice Molly Smith's absence. No one but Barb cared if Smith brought lasagna or not.

Lucky might briefly wonder where she'd gotten to. But she'd be so grateful that Moonlight was looking after Miller, she'd fall into bed and sleep until morning.

"Take a left," Burke said.

Miller had stopped crying almost as soon as they got into the car. He'd fallen back to sleep and only gurgled to himself occasionally. Smart kid. It was as if he knew that Burke would smother him rather than listen to his noise.

"Now a right."

They'd come to the billboard announcing that this was the location of the future Grizzly Resort. *Eighty percent sold!!!* Smith turned. The car rattled down the washboard road.

She stopped where the path ended. She'd been here before, the trailer that served as the offices of M&C Developments. One car was parked in the lot. A black BMW convertible, clean, slick.

"Turn off the engine," Jody Burke said.

The man walked down the trailer steps. His greeting turning to shock at the sight of the young policewoman. "Are you out of your mind?"

Burke got out of the car; Miller nestled in one arm, the gun in the other hand. "Shut the hell up. I don't see you having any brilliant ideas."

"Here's one. You don't involve the cops. You do know who you've got there, right?"

"Too late." Burke showed Smith the gun, and then stepped back. "Get out of the car."

"This has gone way too far, Jamie," the man said.

"It'll have gone too far when I say it has. Get her out of the car."

He opened the door. Smith stepped out. She tried to look the man straight in the eye, but his gaze slid to one side.

"This wasn't my idea," he mumbled. "I want you to know that."

"Then don't make it any worse. You and your wife…"

"My sister."

"Whatever. You know I'm a police officer. Kidnapping is a serious offence."

"Shut up," Burke said. "Or there'll be a more serious offence here. The brat's right in front of me, and you know I won't hesitate to shoot him if you try anything funny. Right in the fat, bald head."

"Jamie, I…"

"I've changed my mind. If we kill the kid now we won't inherit a plugged nickel. Lucky Smith was supposed to be in the house with him—two dead birds with one stone, so to speak. No reason for anyone to think we were involved. But Lucky'll remember me; she'll give the police a good description. Even if we fight it—she can't prove anything, all circumstantial—you can be sure that goddamned lawyer'll turn heaven and earth to guarantee we're cut out. End of all our expectations. Instead, I've decided to settle for a good chunk up front. Trade the kid for the money and split. New identities, a beach house in Rio, sun and sand, the good life. Not what we've been waiting for all these years, but it'll do."

"I don't know."

"For you, hookers on tap, flowing like hot water. Sound good, bro'?"

"Jamie, I don't think…"

Burke turned her attention from Smith, but the gun was still held to Miller's temple. "You weren't put on this earth to think, Steve. Don't you know that by now?"

He mumbled to the ground. "What about her?"

"That's my boy. I knew you'd agree. We'll throw her in as part of the deal, not that she's worth much. You should see her house. What a dump." Miller began to squirm in her arms. Burke was not holding him with much care.

"Put them in the model suite. No one comes there unless Nancy brings them. Nancy is well out of the way until this is finished, isn't she? You managed that at least?"

"Several bottles of *Veuve Clicquot*, courtesy of my partner Frank, were delivered to the house this afternoon. A thank you for doing such a good job organizing the ad campaign party. She won't be coming up for air anytime soon."

"Good."

Miller cried.

"He needs to be fed," Smith said.

"He can wait."

"No, he can't. Babies are small, their stomachs don't hold much. He'll die if he isn't fed regularly."

"Not your concern. Steve, fetch some rope. I saw some earlier behind the secretary's desk."

"Why?"

"Because I said so, okay? Do it."

Miller let out a full strength yell.

Steve ran into the trailer. Smith remembered him now: the Grizzly Resort's new partner. She'd seen his picture in the paper, proud and beaming, shaking Frank Clemmins' hand to seal the deal.

"I'm guessing you're going to hold Miller in exchange for money. Not worth much if he's dead. He needs to be fed."

"With what? You got tits that work?"

"Stores in town sell bottles and formula. Buy some."

"I'll see."

Steve ran down the trailer steps, carrying a length of thick rope. His face was flushed red, perhaps from the exertion, perhaps from the tension. He did not look happy at the direction events had taken.

"You should know that your sister's not half as smart as she thinks she is," Smith said to him. "Nothing could possibly have made my mom dig her heels in more than throwing her weight around and ordering her to give up Miller. If she'd just left things the hell alone, he would have been gone in a day or two."

"Wrap her hands," Burke said. "She's making me nervous."

Smith held her hands out in front of her, like a good obedient girl. As she hoped, Steve began wrapping rope around them. If she'd let him have the initiative, he probably would have turned her and tied her hands behind her back. Bad enough to be wrapped up like a Christmas parcel. But worse if her arms were behind her. She knew she could take him out in a moment. But his sister would have all the time she needed to shoot Miller. And then Smith.

Burke snorted. "You were so easy, cop. Too bad I don't fancy women."

Chapter Twenty-nine

Eliza Winters hated being abandoned at a party. But tonight wasn't the first time, and probably wouldn't be the last. The whole thing had been a dreadful bore, but she'd managed to make polite chit-chat with the wives-of, and the boss, and the underlings. She kicked off her shoes as she came through the door, and the cab kicked up gravel as it spun its wheels down the driveway.

Barb had insisted that 'the girls' take home leftovers. Eliza stuffed hastily-wrapped foil packages into the fridge. At least they'd have dinner for a few nights.

If John would be home to eat it.

She'd heard more of what was going on than he probably realized. His constable, the young Smith woman, was missing. Eliza hadn't met Molly Smith, and didn't particularly care if she ever did, but John did seem quite concerned. The party broke up very early. Officers returned to duty; spouses escorted home.

Home early. That was nice. She'd have time to do the week's laundry and relax with a glass of wine.

Laundry! She'd forgotten to buy laundry detergent. It was Sunday evening; she could leave the wash until tomorrow, or go out now. No, tomorrow she was busy all day with preliminaries for the Grizzly shoot. And the plain white shirt she planned to wear was in the hamper.

She picked up her keys.

◇◇◇

Meredith Morgenstern stepped out from behind a bush.

"Lots of activity tonight," she said.

"Go away, Meredith."

"Come on, Dave. I know this is Molly's house. And you're all over it like ants at a picnic. I know Molly can't be found; her own mother told me that. This is serious stuff. The citizens of Trafalgar want to know."

"The citizens of Trafalgar can…"

"Careful Dave. You don't want to say anything you wouldn't want to see in print."

"Go away, Meredith." Dave Evans, dressed in wildly patterned board shorts, sandals, and a T-Shirt announcing that it had been bought in San Celemente, California, walked away.

Sergeant Winters came out of the Smith kitchen. He pulled out his cell phone, and talked into it while looking into the woods at the back of the property.

Meredith walked up the driveway. If you act as if you belong, she'd been told by a famous reporter one drunken night, most people will assume you do. A heavy-set man she knew to be the RCMP forensic expert had his head in the back of his van. He straightened up and watched her pass, but said nothing.

Meredith marched up to the house. Shadows in the yard were long, the sky purple with the approach of night. The full moon stood over the dark mass of Koola Glacier. Lights were on in the kitchen, and through the uncurtained windows Meredith could see two people sitting at the table.

She opened the door and stepped into the house. "Hi, Lucky. You called me so I hurried over soon as I could. Hi, Chief."

"Did you call Ms. Morgenstern?" Keller asked Lucky. Not a very polite greeting, in Meredith's opinion.

Lucky's eyes were unfocused, and she wasn't listening closely to the CC. Just as well, or she'd throw Meredith out on her ass. She nodded.

He got to his feet. "I'll leave you then. Need to find out what's happening." He headed for the door. His glance at Meredith was not friendly. "Phone Andy, Lucky," he said, as he stepped out into the gathering night.

Keller had been sitting across the table from Lucky. Meredith pulled up a chair beside her.

"I can't imagine," she said, "what you must be going through."

"I have to call my husband." Lucky pushed herself out of her chair.

"Sure, you go right ahead. You need some support right now. What with the dog and the RCMP van and all those officers out there beating the bush. Looking for your daughter."

Lucky fell back into her chair and swallowed a sob.

Meredith patted her hand. "What do you think happened to Moonlight? What do the police think happened?"

At least her jail was nicely decorated.

She had been shoved onto a bed in what was apparently the model suite of the Grizzly Resort.

Steve hadn't brought any more rope, causing Burke to scream at him for his incompetence. But, unfortunately for Molly Smith, he found a roll of duct tape in a drawer in the model suite's kitchen. He wrapped the silver tape around her bound hands, securing her to a bed post. It was a nice bed, king sized, English country house four-poster type. The mattress was thick and soft, but not too soft. The wooden frame, posts, and large headboard were carved out of warm red wood. The duvet was blood red satin shot with silver threads, and the bed was piled high with matching pillows of all shapes and sizes.

Perfect for kinky games. And for securing a kidnapped police officer.

Burke threw Miller onto the bed at Smith's feet. He bounced, and began, again, to cry.

"You want her to kill him?" Smith asked Steve Blacklock.

He glanced at Burke. Questioning, hesitant.

"He's no good to us dead," Burke admitted. "Go to town and get baby stuff."

"This is going too far, Jamie," he said. "Let's just go. We can…"

She spun around. The gun was no longer pointing at Smith, or Miller, but at Blacklock.

"We can," she said, "get what we're owed. And that's what we're going to do. You will go into town, like I told you, right, Stevie?"

He swallowed heavily. "Yeah."

"While you're doing that I'll make a couple of calls. I've got a plane standing by, and we'll be out of here before anyone knows they're missing."

"You'll let her go, the cop, right?"

"Sure. I'll let the cop go. Now beat it."

Steve scampered, like he'd been told. The bedroom door shut behind him.

Burke smiled at Smith, and winked.

Winters watched Tocek load the dog into the truck. Nothing, he'd said. Nothing. Ron Gavin had set up big lights and was photographing tire tracks on the driveway while his partner prepared to take casts. Even if he got good prints, they had nothing to match them with. Officers came out of the woods, shrugging their shoulders. Dave Evans was here, dressed like a surfer dude but helping out. Although it was in the middle of her days off, Dawn Solway had gone back to the station, to help Lopez work the phones.

Paul Keller stood on the kitchen porch. A flash of red light as he ignited a match and bent to light a cigarette.

Winters' phone rang. He answered before the ring tone finished.

"John, I…"

"Sorry, Eliza, I have to keep this line clear."

"I understand. But I have something you'll be interested in."

"What?"

"I went to the supermarket to buy laundry detergent."

Why on earth she'd think he'd be interested in her shopping habits when he was in the middle of a case, he had no idea. "Get to the point," he snapped.

"I'm doing just that. You remember Steve Blacklock, from the Grizzly resort?"

"So?"

"He was there, at Safeway. With a cart piled high with baby formula and diapers."

His mind began to click into gear, to follow hers.

"And that would be..."

"Most unnatural for a man in his forties, whose wife told me they don't have children."

"Did she now."

"And even if they do have grandchildren, by some circuitous route, Steve did not strike me as the type to be out buying diapers."

"Nor me."

"I heard a bit of what you were saying, John, on the phone at the party. About a missing baby. So I thought you'd be interested."

"Did Blacklock see you?"

"I don't think so. I didn't want to make mindless chit chat, so I darted down another aisle. Then I started thinking."

"Thank you," he said, hanging up.

He made another call. "Ray, I want everything you can find on Steven Blacklock. He's the new partner at the Grizzly Resort. Dig, and dig deep."

"I have to remind you, boss, again, that it's Sunday night."

"I'm working. You're working. Get everyone else working. He's not local, hasn't been in town more than a few weeks, so he probably doesn't have a Trafalgar address on file. But his partner, Frank Clemmins, should know where he's staying. Send someone around. If Blacklock's home tell them they're to wait with him until I get there. What have you found on Burke?"

"Nothing. I'm waiting for some calls to be returned. I'll let you know soon as I know."

"Okay. In the meantime, I'm going to the Grizzly Resort, check out the situation. I'll call you when I get there."

Winters looked around. Evans was nearby, but he couldn't help, not dressed like that. No uniform. No firepower. Gavin was pointing out something in the driveway to his partner. Paul Keller was standing on the doorstep, smoking, looking troubled.

Adam Tocek, the Mountie, the dog guy, walked toward him. Head down; steps heavy. Disappointed, Winters thought, at his dog's inability to help.

"Want to come for a ride?" Winters asked.

"Where?"

"Probably nowhere, but I have a lead. Not much of one, but it's something. We'll take your car. Bring the dog. He might still be useful. I need to swing by my house first and pick up my equipment. It's not far out of the way." Badge, handcuffs, collapsible nightstick. Gun.

Someone had kidnapped a police officer, and Winters wasn't going in unarmed.

◇◇◇

"That was a waste of time. We should be out catching the bad guys, not letting rich men's lawyers tell us how incompetent we are." Al Jacobi tossed his empty coffee cup at the trash can. It missed and rolled under his partner's desk.

Rachel Ferguson made a face. "Don't bother trying out for the NBA." Jacobi ignored her. He was a small man, short and lightly built. He'd spent a good part of his youth in the gym, trying to bulk up. He hadn't been able to do anything about his height, and with all the weights he never managed to look like anything but a scrawny man with some muscles. Ferguson had known him when she was a rookie patrol officer and had not been happy to have him assigned years later as her partner when she joined homicide. But to her surprise, the man had mellowed and accepted himself and his body and had turned into an effective police officer and a good man.

"However, I was thinking on the way back," he said. "Thought I smelled something."

"I still have my doubts about Jennifer being the killer, and as time goes by they're getting stronger."

"She was seen, Al, running from the scene. Carrying the baby. At least carrying something that was probably the baby. And seen not only by Jamie Blacklock but the neighbor's gardener. And then she disappeared. Why would she disappear if she didn't do it?"

"Jennifer had no reason to kill her sister, Rachel."

"We don't know that they were sisters. Mrs. Sanchez assumed they were because of a slight resemblance." And Mrs. Sanchez, who'd finished work for the day at the time in question, tried so hard to be of help to the police, Ferguson suspected that she was making a lot of stuff up rather than admit that she didn't know. "Anyway, people kill all the time, with no reason anyone one else can understand. Maybe Jennifer wanted a baby of her own without all the mess and bother of going the usual route."

Jacobi didn't look convinced. "I still have my eye on Jamie Blacklock, with or without her brother's help."

"Come on, Al. And as much as you might not like Jamie, your gut instinct just isn't proof enough."

"Where she's these days anyway?"

"New York. Visiting friends. We can't send the NYPD around knocking on the friend's door to check that she made curfew just because you've got a bad feeling about Jamie."

"How do we know she hasn't come back? Got on a plane with a fake ID and a false moustache? It would suit her."

"We'll know soon as she gets back to Seattle. She'll be at the lawyer demanding something."

"Speaking of the lawyer. What'd he say about Allenhart? The only thing keeping him alive is hope that he'll see his son one more time." Jacobi shook his head. "Not gonna happen. The kid's at the bottom of the sound."

"And until we can prove that, we keep on looking." About the only thing Ferguson and Jacobi agreed upon was that the killing of Katie and the disappearance of her baby wasn't done by a random intruder, the story they'd fed to the press.

"Wanna grab some supper?"

Ferguson thought about the remains of last night's salad dinner she'd put in the office fridge. "Sure. Mickey D's?"

Allenhart's only sibling, a sister to whom he had apparently been close, had two children. She, the sister, died about thirty years ago. His sister's two children, Jamie and Steven Blacklock had been his sole heirs. Until Katie popped.

The previous heirs, shoved out of the will in favor of the by-blow of a fledgling hooker, put up a good front and chattered on about respecting their beloved uncle's wishes. Jacobi didn't trust either of them for a moment. But, no matter how hard he tried, he'd never been able to put them solidly in the frame. Steve had been in Canada for a business meeting. Jamie had found the body, but he couldn't prove she'd had a hand in it.

Ferguson argued that the killer was more likely to be Katie's supposed sister, Jennifer, who had recently become a regular visitor. But Jennifer had turned the corner at the bottom of the street and disappeared.

They bought Big Macs and milk shakes and ate at Ferguson's desk, going over the story one more time.

The day before Allenhart's stroke, his lawyer left on an extended vacation to Tuscany. The new will, changed just a week before leaving everything to Richard Junior, gave Jamie Blacklock power of attorney. Why Allenhart didn't realize that might present a problem—from heir to half the fortune to babysitter—was hard to imagine. But Allenhart had always been very close, and very loyal, to the women in his life. Katie was provided for, more than adequately, but not left with any power over the estate.

After the stroke, Jamie announced that she was moving in—to help out. She fired the cook and the housekeeper who'd lived at the house almost as long as Eleanor and replaced them with staff from a temporary agency.

A month later 911 was called. Jamie had found Katie dead in the kitchen.

Jamie said she'd been out. Taking a walk around the grounds. Allenhart had been upstairs, in his bedroom, where he now spent almost all of his time. He had a full-time nursing staff, but the shift changed around that time. And, according to Jamie, it was Katie's responsibility to watch the old man if there was a gap in the nursing coverage.

Which there had been. The scheduled nurse had called to say she had a dentist appointment and was running about half an hour late.

Jamie, red-eyed and weeping into a torn tissue as she was being questioned, said that Richard Junior had been sleeping, and she'd assumed Katie could handle the old man in the nurse's absence. So she went for her walk.

Katie, of course, couldn't tell them anything.

Jamie said she saw a woman running from the house, carrying something she thought was a parcel, when she returned from her walk. Whereupon she ran into the kitchen, found Katie dead on the floor, Richard Junior missing, and called the police.

The police found prints of a woman's shoes on the kitchen floor, and running down the driveway to the road. They were very small, almost child sized.

They searched, hard, for the small woman, without luck. But they were sure that it was Jennifer, Katie's sister, who was very short.

Jacobi threw his wrappings toward Ferguson's trash. They joined the coffee cup under her desk, and Jacobi sauntered back to his own desk. Ferguson swung her chair around to face the computer and scanned her new e-mail.

"Al, get over here. Fast."

Not only Jacobi but several others gathered to peer over her shoulder.

"Police in some town in British Columbia are trying to identify a baby boy. The age is right. I think this might be it. Wait, there's more."

She finished reading, and lifted her head to look at Jacobi. "Baby was found beside the body of a murdered woman."

Chapter Thirty

There wasn't a sliver of light from moon or stars. The wind had picked up. A branch brushed against the roof. A dog, maybe a wolf, barked once.

Burke had followed Blacklock out, switching off the light as she went. It was as dark inside the suite as out.

Smith couldn't see Miller, lying at the foot of the bed where he'd been tossed, but his breathing was deep, ragged with crying, so she knew he was still alive.

How long could a baby go without being fed? She tried to determine when Lucky had last given Miller a bottle. She'd probably fed him before taking him out for his walk. Two o'clock maybe? Three? It was after ten now. So eight hours, at least, since the last feeding. Molly Smith knew nothing about babies, but when she'd been doing her practicum toward her BA in Social Work, she'd heard mothers bragging that their babies slept through the night at three months—Miller's age. She'd also heard mothers bragging that their child talked in full sentences before their first birthday and were potty trained before they could sit up. And, no one knew better than she, Miller was nowhere near sleeping though the night.

She worked at the tape securing her hands to the bed frame. If she could loosen it, just a bit, she might be able to pull her hands free. They hadn't tied her feet—if Steve or Burke got close enough she could kick out. And then do what? Hope they'd drop dead of a heart attack?

Steve had secured the tape very loosely. His heart not fully in it, Smith guessed. There was some pretty weird stuff going on between brother and sister—if they really were brother and sister. Steve obviously spent his life squashed under Burke's thumb. He was doing what she ordered, but reluctantly. Was he reluctant enough to balk when it came to murder?

Perhaps. He seemed to need reassurance from Burke that Smith wouldn't come to any harm. And he was gullible enough to believe her.

Or he wanted to convince himself that he believed her.

Smith needed to puncture his delusion. If Burke would leave them alone long enough.

Which, she guessed, was highly unlikely.

And what about Miller, now sleeping the sleep of the exhausted?

Burke thought he was worth something, a great deal of something, in ransom. To whom, didn't matter.

A sliver of pale light crept in the window, as a cloud slipped to one side, allowing the moon to give the world a flirtatious peek. At Burke's orders, Blacklock had drawn the silver blinds across the windows, but not all the way. There was enough light for Smith's eyes to gradually start getting accustomed to the dark.

She worked at the tape. It could stretch, a little. A bit more and she might be able to slide her hands out. Her hands were bound together by the rope, but she could at least run like that.

She couldn't carry Miller, but she could go for help.

How far she could get, trussed up like the Christmas turkey, in the woods, at night, before being overpowered, was another matter.

She felt a soft swell of optimism as she remembered that she'd grown up running through woods exactly like these. Before he'd allow Moonlight and Sam to lead camping and kayaking parties, her father made them spend time, at night, alone in the forest. Molly Smith would bet her life—literally—that Jody Burke and her brother had never done so.

She returned her attention to her hands.

◇◇◇

She hadn't planned it that way, but Meredith found herself sitting across from the Smith's big kitchen window. Pots filled with fragrant green herbs lined the windowsill, and a dangling construction of colored glass strung along a thin rope hung from the top of the frame. It was too late for the sun catcher to catch any sun.

She had a clear view to the driveway where it rounded the house toward the garage.

Sergeant Winters was talking to Adam Tocek, the cute Mountie. Tocek climbed into his car. Winters spoke to Paul Keller, waving his hands to indicate the woods behind the Smith property. The mountains had disappeared into the night. Black upon black. Too dark to continue with the search. The search Meredith suspected was coming up empty anyway.

In one part of her heart Meredith hoped that Molly had gone on a bender. All this fuss and bother, and they'd find her passed out behind some low-life bar. Maybe with her pants around her ankles and her face buried in dirt and her own vomit. That would end her career. But for some reason Meredith hoped that wouldn't happen.

"Andy," Lucky said suddenly. "I have to call Andy. I can't let him come home and find all this." She grabbed the phone, resting beside her hand. Her fingers hesitated over the buttons. Some of the life returned to her face, and Meredith knew that the feisty old Lucky was coming back. "This is a private matter, Meredith."

She hadn't opened up. Not even a little bit. She was a smart one, Lucky Smith. She'd been fooled once by a journalist's pretend sympathy. She wouldn't let it happen again. She held the phone in the air and regarded Meredith pointedly. "You can let yourself out."

Meredith stood up. She'd been told to leave. If she stayed, it would compromise any story she'd want to file.

She let herself out, as ordered.

Winters was climbing into the RCMP car. Tocek at the wheel. Tocek threw the vehicle into gear and it pulled away, spitting gravel, before Winters had his seatbelt fastened. The police dog watched Meredith out the back window.

She followed at a run, heading for her own car.

Her hands were almost free. They hurt like hell, but she'd worry about that later. The duct tape was stretching. Just a bit more wiggle room, and she'd be free of the bed post, at least. This building was a resort show house; it wouldn't be outfitted like a jail. She should be able to simply unlock the door and walk out.

The moonlight had faded again as more clouds moved across the sky. She couldn't turn on any lights—that would be a sure sign that she'd gotten free. The model suite was a good distance from the construction trailer, and the forest between was heavy, thick with summer foliage. But in this deep dark any sliver of light would show through the trees like a search light at a Hollywood opening. She couldn't chance that.

Could she leave Miller behind? She'd have to, although it would hurt to do it. She wouldn't get far carrying him if she couldn't get the rope off her wrists. Even if she managed to bring him, the woods would give her no protection if he cried. He was Burke's ticket to the good life—she wouldn't harm him. Would she? But Burke's original intention had been to kill the baby. She might be so enraged by Smith's escape that she'd turn her anger on Miller.

Could Smith chance that?

She was getting way ahead of herself. She wasn't going anywhere if she didn't get her hands loose.

The bedroom was at the back of the cabin, so she hadn't heard anyone coming. The door opened. A thin beam of light danced into the bedroom. Smith tried to settle into the pillows.

"You'll be pleased to know," Burke said, "that even my fool of a brother can shop." She held up a baby's bottle. "Happy?"

"Yes," Smith said, meaning it. No point in escaping if Miller starved to death. "You want me to feed him?"

Burke laughed. Smith didn't care for that laugh. It was ugly and mean. Smith imagined that as a child Jamie used that laugh when she pulled the legs off flies.

She picked Miller up. Roughly. His head flopped, and he let out a cry. She stuffed the bottle into his mouth. It was probably unsanitary, and not warm enough. But it was nourishment. He fussed for a moment, before settling into the rhythm of sucking.

"Miserable thing." Burke carried the feeding baby to the window and looked out into the night.

"So what's your real name?" Smith asked. "Your brother calls you Jamie."

"You don't need to know my name, cop."

"Okay. What do you have in mind now? For us, I mean, me and Miller?"

Burke turned from the window. She looked at the baby in her arms. Her face shuddered, as if she'd found herself suckling a giant slug. "Hideous creature isn't he? But this bundle of joy is worth more than your miserable little town and everyone in it."

"His mother didn't seem to have two nickels to rub together."

"His mother was a whore. She served no purpose in this life other than as an incubator. And, like an incubator, no one much cared whether she kept working or not. There's always another. But I assume you're thinking of Jennifer. Or Ashley or whatever she wanted to call herself. She, by the way, was not Miller's mother. She was a thief and a junkie. Once a junkie always a junkie. They never get over it, do they?"

"Some do."

"To answer your question, Miller here, his real name is Richard by the way, Richard George Andrew Allenhart Junior, is the goose who lays the golden egg. And thus he gets to live. But you, cop, are worth nothing to me. And so you will die."

Smith had known Burke's intention. But to hear someone announce her imminent death, so calmly, so efficiently, so lacking emotion, made her heart close.

When she'd sat in the alley in Vancouver, where Graham had died, she'd wanted to join him. If, during that long vigil, Jody

Burke had stepped out of the shadows and handed her a gun, she might well have used it.

The light from the other room threw a thin beam into the bedroom. It shone into Burke's eyes but no light was reflected back. They were like black holes, sucking energy, returning nothing.

She cradled a feeding baby in her arms.

The devil's version of Madonna and Child.

Molly Smith looked at Miller. His face was in shadow, but she guessed that his own eyes were closed as he fed, doing what he had to do to live.

She might see Graham again some day.

But not today.

Burke pulled the bottle out of Miller's mouth. "That's enough."

"He needs more."

"I said that's enough. He'll live for a while longer. Christ, he stinks."

"He needs his diaper changed."

"Well I'm not going to do it. And you're in no position to. Let him stink." She threw the child back onto the bed.

"I made a couple of calls. Good thing this place is on the river. A floatplane's going to land, pick us up. It won't have a lot of range, but it'll take us to where we can get a bigger ride. And then South America, here we come. You'll not be coming along for the ride, of course."

"So why am I still here?"

"When that plane hits the water, you're one dead cop. Until then, you might be of some use. I plan for every eventuality."

"If Ashley isn't Miller's mother who is? And why did you have to kill her?"

"Innocent little me? I didn't kill her. My brother dearest got carried away. She was a junkie, right? It was his idea to give her a shot of the stuff, make her willing to see things our way. He bought some in Vancouver for the purpose. I guess he gave her too much. No loss. But I have no interest in explaining myself to you. Sweet dreams."

She left, taking the light with her.

Weak it might have been, but the light had ruined Smith's night vision. But she could still feel. She worked at her hands, as Miller whimpered at her feet.

"No lights, no siren. Come to a stop at the turn off, and we'll go in on foot. Can the dog stay quiet?"

"For the most part. Until he finds the person he's looking for."

"Then he can come with us."

Winters could barely remember the days before cell phones, and sometimes he wondered how they'd managed. The Trafalgar City Police had Frank Clemmins' number on file, because of the incident involving the death of Clemmins' partner, and had contacted him driving home after a movie. He'd given them the address of the house Blacklock was renting. Brad Noseworthy paid a visit.

Mrs. Blacklock, Noseworthy reported, was happily riding the train to alcoholic oblivion. Where her husband might be, she'd told the officer, she neither knew nor cared. He'd been instructed to ask about a baby. Whereupon Nancy Blacklock had burst into tears, and confessed that she'd had three miscarriages as a young woman before her first husband left her to find more robust breeding stock. She and Steve hadn't tried to have children. Too late in life, she'd said, but it didn't matter much because Steve needed almost as much care as a child. She smiled at Noseworthy, tripped over her shoelace, and invited him in for a drink. He declined and radioed Winters.

The RCMP SUV pulled to the shoulder and slid to a stop. Cars passed them on the highway. Away from the beam of headlights, the woods were black, the mountains invisible.

"We might need backup," Winters said. The clasp of his seatbelt unfastening was loud. "Put them on stand-by."

"You think Molly`s here?" Tocek asked.

"I think nothing. Blacklock was observed buying baby stuff. He isn't at the place he's supposed to live in, with the wife he's supposed to be with. For all I know he might be cuddled up in a house in the country with his bigamous wife and their ten children.

"But, until that's proved to me, we're going to act under the assumption that, for some unknown reason, Blacklock has brought Smith and the baby here. If it's for a party, we'll leave. Embarrassed, but with our balls still intact. Let's go."

Winters had his hand on the door when the radio crackled to life.

Ray Lopez. "I've just had a call from Seattle. They're missing a baby boy. And it's one heck of a big story." Lopez quickly explained what he'd learned from an excited Rachel Ferguson.

"Start working on a search warrant for the offices of the Grizzly resort. Remind them that we have an officer missing. And get everyone looking for Steve Blacklock. Send Brad back to the wife to question her again, this time with an eye to finding out what she knows about the business in Seattle and the Ashley Doe case." Winters thought for a moment, then turned to Tocek. "This is no longer just a guess. From now on I'm operating under the assumption that Steve Blacklock murdered Ashley Doe, sounds like there's a big inheritance involved. Somehow he lost the kid and it ended up with Molly, so he had to grab Molly. Who Burke is, I don't know, but Blacklock's sister is a suspect in the murder of the mother of a missing baby boy and is currently unaccounted for. Might be the same woman.

"Take care. If we're right, these people have killed before. And probably more than once."

They got out of the SUV. Tocek fastened the lead onto his dog, and the animal jumped down. For such a big creature, he moved with the grace of a ballerina.

"Unlikely she walked down this road," the Mountie said. "In which case there's nothing for Norman to find."

It was fully dark. Moon and stars hidden behind thick cloud. But the wind was high, and clouds could move. Winters touched the gun in his belt. "Have a light?"

"Yeah. Want it on?"

"Not unless we need it. We need surprise, first. Let's go."

They walked carefully down the gravel road, keeping as much as possible to the edge of the forest. Branches reached out to grab them; rocks tried to trip booted feet. Norman pulled on his lead, making no sound save for the depth of his breathing. An owl hooted, and both officers started.

"This is a construction site, right?" Tocek said.

"Yes."

"Strange that there isn't any light. Would have expected the place to be lit up like the SkyDome. Discourages thieves and vandals."

The Grizzly Resort had been a lightning rod for controversy since the day M&C Developments had applied for a permit to build. Protesters were regularly found outside the perimeter, marching along the edge of the highway. The big sign on the road was defaced continuously. Winters should have noticed how quiet it was. When he and Eliza had been here for the party, Blacklock had bragged that security guards patrolled round the clock. He pulled his gun out of his belt. "You're right, Adam. Call it in. I want full backup. ASAP."

Tocek spoke into the radio at his shoulder. His voice was low and soft, but clear.

Norman lifted his ears, and whimpered.

"He's got something," the Mountie said. "Hey, it's worth a try." He pulled Smith's pajama bottoms out of his pocket. Police dogs weren't trained to follow a specific scent. They went into a search area, and tried to find anything laid down recently, anything deviating from the expected. Tocek had stuffed Smith's pajamas into his pocket to make her mother think she'd been useful. He held the Winnie-the-Pooh pants in front of the dog's face. Norman took a sniff. A short sniff, as if he was merely refreshing his memory. He pulled on the lead.

The road bent to the right and they could see the trailer that was about all the Grizzly Resort amounted to. One light, no more than forty watts, burned inside.

An SUV and a BMW were parked outside.

Norman pulled on the lead. His ears stood at attention and the hair along his back bristled. He growled, low in his throat, as if he knew better than to let out a sound, but couldn't hold it in any longer.

"She's here," Tocek said. "He's found her."

Meredith followed as close as she dared. To her surprise the white RCMP SUV with colored stripes running down the side and the logo of the mounted policeman, turned left, rather than right at the highway, and headed north away from town. It traveled slightly over the speed limit for about ten minutes, before turning down a narrow road leading up into the mountains. Meredith knew that Sergeant Winters lived up that road. Everyone in the Mid-Kootenays knew that John and Eliza Winters had bought the beautiful, remote Richardson place. She drove past the road, and pulled off to the side of the highway.

They'd given up. Tocek was taking Winters home. Meredith considered her options and decided to go home as well. Nothing more she could accomplish at the Smiths'. Lucky had closed up, and the investigators were closing down for the night. She'd come back at first light. She threw her car into gear, ready to do a U Turn. A silver Cadillac passed, well under the speed limit, a large-brimmed hat behind the wheel. A long line of impatient vehicles followed. The highway was narrow and winding and it was a good distance between broken yellow lines. At last Meredith could make the turn. Her foot pressed the gas, ready to accelerate, when white headlights lit up the forest on either side of the road. She slowed to a crawl. The RCMP vehicle stopped at the intersection, checked that no one was coming, and pulled out. There were still two people in it. Meredith let them have some distance and fell in behind. They drove past the

Smiths' toward town. Across the big black bridge and through the dark streets of Trafalgar. To her surprise they kept on going; didn't turn up the hill to the police station. Past the Ford dealer and the animal hospital, past the Shell station, and the Catholic Church. Past the old mine office, now a museum. Out of the city limits. It was a Sunday night, and traffic was light. Once they left the city, Meredith feared she'd easily be spotted, so she dropped back and let the red lights of the SUV disappear into the curves of the mountain road. *Where were they going?*

If they were heading to Castlegar or Nelson, there wasn't much point in following. But the Grizzly resort was on this road. Lately, most everything seemed to center around the Grizzly Resort.

Meredith would head for the resort site. If Winters wasn't going there, or if he was and by the time she arrived it was all over, nothing would be lost. But maybe, just maybe, she'd get lucky.

She deserved a bit of luck.

Chapter Thirty-one

"How do you want to play it?" Tocek said, his voice no more than a rough whisper.

"There's one person, at least, inside the trailer. I can see him walking around. Pacing. There might be more, and we don't know if they have weapons. All's quiet. No need to be in a hurry. We'll wait for back up before we go in. Tell them to approach with full lights and sirens, the whole shebang. Shake things up. When they get here, I'll take the trailer; you give Norman his lead and let him take you where he wants to go." Winters bent over and gave the big dog a slap on the rump.

Norman whined, not happy. He'd been given a task—he'd succeeded in it—and he was being held back from leading his master to a successful conclusion.

Traffic on the highway was light; only the occasional vehicle passed. A small car came closer, it slowed, and, to Winters surprise, turned. It shuddered down the rough gravel track to the construction site. Headlights illuminated tree trunks and threw long shadows into the forest.

"Someone's coming," Tocek said, unnecessarily, lifting his hand to shield his eyes from the sudden light.

"Off the road," Winters said. They stepped behind large, ancient trees.

A green Neon passed their hiding spot. The door to the trailer flew open and a man ran down the steps. The light behind him was weak, but the car's headlights threw clear white light into his face. Steve Blacklock.

The driver switched off the engine, extinguished the lights, and got out of the car. "Hi." A woman's voice was sharp in the quiet night.

Meredith Morgenstern. Winters had run into her before: a young, hungry journalist with far more ambition than common sense. He didn't know what she was doing here, but it couldn't be good.

"I know her," Tocek said. "She was at the Smiths, just before we left."

"Get ready to move."

"Hi, Mr. Blacklock. Meredith Morgenstern, *Trafalgar Daily Gazette*. Remember me? We met at the party here the other night."

"It's late, Ms. Morgenstern. What do you want?" Blacklock's voice was angry, full of tension. Like any man's would be, cornered by a journalist on a Sunday evening.

"If I can have a moment of your time, Mr. Blacklock, I'm hoping you can help me with a story I'm working on."

A woman came out of the trailer. She was tall and lean, dressed in a loosely flowing dress, and a black cape. Her face hidden in the shadows. She pulled Blacklock's arm and he stepped behind her. "You may contact us in the morning," the thin woman said. "This is a most inappropriate time."

"Yeah, I know. But, well, there's all this trouble in town, see, and I'm following a lead. When I saw the RCMP car parked up on the highway, I thought you might know something about..."

Her words were cut off as a small aircraft flew low overhead. The Grizzly resort site was long and thin, spread out between the road and the river. Mountains lined the highway to the west; across the river, mountains filled the sky. Dangerous flying, in the dark, for a small plane.

The plane followed the river north, and then turned and headed back. It sounded as if it were coming down.

Blacklock lunged forward and ran down the steps. "No," the woman yelled. But either he didn't hear her or didn't care. He punched Meredith, still smiling, full in the stomach. With a started cry, she fell backward.

"That plane's coming for them. We can't wait." Winters gripped his gun and ran forward. Tocek and Norman at his heels.

"Trafalgar City Police. No one move."

A shot rang out. "Drop the weapon," Winters shouted.

The thin pool of light from the trailer showed Meredith attempting to stagger to her feet.

"Stay down," Winters yelled.

Blacklock grabbed the reporter and pulled her upright. He held her against him, while he let off several shots, blindly, uselessly into the woods. With one more step, Winters would be revealed by the light coming from the trailer. He stopped and yelled, "Throw down your weapon and release the woman. Do it, Blacklock. Now!"

The woman who'd stood in the door to the trailer leapt off the steps, dodged behind the man holding Meredith, and, using the Neon for cover, ran into the darkness.

"She's going for Molly," Tocek shouted. Norman streaked past Winters, head down, heading for the clear, strong scent he'd been instructed to follow. Tocek still had the lead in his hand.

"Wait," Winters yelled.

A shot rang out. Norman yelped, took two more steps and collapsed.

Shocked at what he'd done, Blacklock threw down his gun, and shoved Meredith aside, hard. She fell to her knees. "Sorry, sorry. I didn't mean it," he sobbed.

Tocek hesitated, for just a moment, above his dog. Then he jumped over the animal and pointed his own gun at the weeping Blacklock. "Where the hell is she, asshole?"

Beyond the line of trees, the airplane's engines accelerated as it ran down the river. It took to the air, and passed overhead.

Meredith screamed. Norman whimpered. Blacklock alternately sobbed and yelled, "It wasn't me. It wasn't me." Over and over.

Tocek ordered Blacklock to take two steps backward and turn around. Still crying, still apologizing, the man did so.

"Down. Flat on your stomach. Move!" Blacklock dropped as if his legs had been kicked out from under him. He buried his face into the gravel.

Winters lowered himself slowly and picked up Blacklock's gun. He stuck it into his belt. The woman had disappeared into the woods. He tried to listen for the crunch of dried leaves, breaking twigs, swinging branches. But nothing came to him over the cacophony in the clearing.

Chapter Thirty-two

With a sudden pull, Molly Smith's hands came free. The pain in her wrists was excruciating, and she took a moment, a precious moment, just to breathe, to let the agony ebb. The length of duct tape hung, empty, over the bed post. The next prospective owner to visit the model apartment would think this was the naughty boys and girls suite.

Her hands were still tied together, but at least she could get the hell out of here.

She couldn't see anything, but she thought Miller was looking up at her. His hero. Bugger that. All she had to do was get to the highway, flag down a car, flag down every car that passed, and tell them to get into cell phone range and contact the police. She didn't have her uniform, her badge, her gun. But she figured that the anger in her face, and the rope around her wrists, would have any civilian jumping to do as ordered.

A plane flew overhead. Low. Was it coming for Burke and Miller? Almost certainly. Small planes didn't usually fly in these mountains at night.

Which meant that she had no time to go for help. By the time the police arrived, the place would be empty, the plane long gone.

She'd have to get to the plane and try to convince the pilot that being an accessory to the murder of a police officer was not worth whatever he was being paid for this trip.

And then run like hell for help.

She crawled to the edge of the bed. The satin duvet cover felt smooth and cool against her bare legs. Miller sobbed. He smelled terrible.

"Gotta leave you, little buddy," she whispered. "But I'll be back, count on it. With all the milk you can drink and a nice clean diaper."

A gunshot. Smith launched herself off the bed before realizing that the sound wasn't at all close. Shots followed in rapid succession. A man yelled, but she couldn't make out the words. The cavalry. Oh, dear god, let it be the cavalry.

She ran out of the bedroom, toward what she hoped was the front door. She didn't dare turn on any lights. If help had arrived, light would guide them to her. But if the shots were a falling out amongst enemies, she didn't want them coming to check on her. She tripped over something blocking her way; glass fell to the floor and shattered. With outstretched hands, she guided herself toward what she hoped was the front of the suite. She found the lines of the door in the wall, and slid her fingers down to the smooth, cool metal of the doorknob. She grabbed, twisted, and pulled. Nothing happened. Locked. She used the fingers of her right hand to fumble in the gloom in an attempt to find the bar that operated the lock. They found it, turned it easily, and she let out a sigh of relief. But hope came too early. She couldn't twist the door knob, not with her hands crossed over each other. One hand on its own wasn't strong enough to give her a good grip. She was sweating so hard her fingers slipped on the smooth metal. She struggled desperately for purchase but couldn't find it.

She'd heard no more shots. What did that mean? That the police had arrived and taken control and she could relax? That Burke had killed Steve and now she had no chance at all of pleading for her life? Or that other baddies had arrived and were sorting out the situation? The engine of the plane roared, and she heard it taking off down the lake. The timber changed as it took to the air. Burke would be royally pissed at that, if she were still at liberty.

Smith was not going to get this door open. She ran back toward the bedroom. The furniture she'd knocked over had felt like a small, folding-legged, wooden table. The type of table a '60's housewife would set up to serve dinner in front of the TV to her well-scrubbed, beaming-faced family. She used her feet to feel for it.

Found it.

It was light enough, compact enough that she could lift it in her bound hands. A razor-thin sliver of moonlight touched the big picture window. She smashed the table into the glass. Again and again. Shards tinkled as they fell, a few onto the floor, most into the forest. She used the legs of the table to sweep away any glass that might still be clinging to the window frame. No point in escaping with a cut that would bleed her out before she got to the road.

Breaking glass, her own desperate breathing, the baby howling in the bedroom, all covered the sound of the door opening.

A bullet flew past her ear, followed an imperceptible moment of time later by the sound of a gun being fired. Smith fell to the floor and rolled onto her back.

A shape stood in the doorway, tall and thin. Black against the black of the night. At that moment the clouds moved aside and the strength of the full moon came through the window. Jody Burke's face, etched in lines of anger and hatred, shone white in the pale moonlight. Fabric flowed around her body, like a fairy flying though the air. Smith slithered on her behind toward the big leather couch she'd seen when she'd been brought in, bracing herself to feel a bullet penetrating her fragile body. When it didn't, Smith realized that with the light shining in her face, Burke couldn't see anything.

"Keep your head down, cop, and out of the way, and I won't shoot it off," Burke said. Her shape, all flowing robes, long silver earrings, and pointing gun, passed into the bedroom.

Chapter Thirty-three

"Keep that man down," Winters said to Tocek. A siren screamed its way up the highway, getting close.

"And shut her up," Winters said, meaning the screaming Meredith. How Tocek could handle both people at once, he didn't stop to consider.

Winters knelt beside Blacklock and rolled him over. The man's eyes were nothing more than frightened white orbs in a white face. The front of his pants was soaking wet, and the knees were torn. "It wasn't me," he repeated. "It wasn't me. I told her she'd gone too far."

"Where is Constable Smith?"

The woman who'd been inside the trailer had disappeared. The plane, which Winters could only assume had been called to take them out, had left in a big hurry. Winters thought he'd seen a gun in the woman's hand. Burke, it had to be Jody Burke. And, judging by the way this babbling fool was going on, Burke was the intelligence, if you could call it that, behind this business.

Norman could have found Smith, fast. But Norman lay on the road, bleeding into the gravel, breathing heavily and whining with pain. When Tocek had shouted the situation into his radio, he'd asked them to send a vet.

Steady white light, along with flashing red and blue, flooded the trailer and parking area. In the distance, more sirens sounded.

Winters had been here before. Drinking good beer and eating expensive canapés under the trees. Eliza had touched her pink lips to a glass of Champagne, all the drinking she ever did at business functions, and looked every inch the supermodel she'd once been. José, the Spanish stud, had hovered protectively over his date. Too protectively, Winters had thought, as if he were showing the woman he really wanted what a macho man he was. But Eliza had never much cared for macho. Tiny white lights had decorated the trees and terracotta pots filled with flowers and candles outlined the walkway. Party guests had been taken to view the model suite where the photo shoot would be done. John Winters had followed because he had nothing better to do.

An officer jumped out of the car. "Take that one," Winters told him. "There's one suspect still on the loose. I have reason to believe she's armed. I'm going after her."

"Sir, I don't think that's wise."

"Neither do I. But we still have an officer missing. And a suspect on the run. Adam, care to come with me?"

"Wouldn't miss it," Tocek said.

"Light the way."

Tocek switched on his flashlight. He didn't bother to ask where Winters was going. Just illuminated the path and followed.

Outside of the light cast by the patrol car, the path split into three. One way led toward the river. They could hear water lapping against the rocky shore. A logical choice for anyone wanting recreation. Or a waiting floatplane. One led left, trees cut down to make an easy walking trail, thick with a well-laid bed of chopped pine bark. The third went into the dark woods. Not a hospitable path, in the impenetrable night. Ancient trees, dark and quiet, heavy with pale green lichen, never still, loomed over the narrow corridor.

Without hesitating Winters took the third trail.

"This doesn't seem right," Tocek said.

"It has to be. It will be."

Chapter Thirty-four

Andy Smith drove a Toyota Corolla. A nice, reliable, respectable car. Tonight he might have been driving it in the Indy 500. The trees lining the road passed in a blur, as if they were running backward and he were going home at his usual law-abiding pace.

When he pulled into his driveway, he found a Trafalgar City Police car and an RCMP van blocking his way. He would have rammed into the van, but he figured his Corolla would get the worst of it.

He jumped out, leaving the keys in the ignition, the engine still running. "What's going on here?" he yelled.

A beefy man, about Andy's age, slammed shut the doors on the van. "Mr. Smith?"

"What about it?"

"Mr. Smith." A young man walked toward them, dressed as if he were about to catch a giant wave off Waikiki.

"Is someone going to tell me what the hell's going on here?" Andy said. He looked closer at the man. "Dave Evans?"

"Yes, sir. Your wife's inside. Come with me."

Andy followed Evans. Ten o'clock on a Sunday night in late summer, and he'd still been at the store. Trying to find the timesheets that ever since they started the business his wife kept at the tips of her fingers. Lucky had called, said something about Miller, the baby she'd so rashly taken into their home, and Moonlight. Their daughter now preferred to be known by the more sensible name of Molly. Lucky'd taken Moonlight's change of name as a personal rebuke, but Andy figured that she had to do it if she wanted to be taken seriously in the police world. You couldn't be called Moonlight when your colleagues had four letter names like Paul, Dave, John.

Moonlight was missing, Lucky had said. At the office, Andy dug through piles of paper without paying much attention to his wife. Molly was hardly a child. She should be able to go where she liked, when she liked, without her mother calling her father. The police were here, Lucky had said.

What the hell? Their twenty-six year old daughter had gone out without telling her mother, and Lucky had called the cops? Could that be Lucy Casey speaking? Lucky who, once upon a time, thought that cops were fascist scum?

She mentioned the Chief Constable, Paul Keller. Keller was a local boy. He'd joined the Trafalgar City Police as a probationary constable, a long, long time ago. Come to think of it, that was the same rank Molly now held. He'd once collided with Lucky Smith and knocked her to the ground in a protest over… Andy couldn't remember. There had been so many, in the early days.

Andy Smith had never cared for Constable Paul Keller. There was always something about the way he looked at Lucky. Andy had been happy when the man left Trafalgar for better opportunities in the big city of Calgary. Many years later Keller came back, back to his hometown, to take the post of Chief Constable.

In all these years the man had never come to the Smith home. Not until that business last month, and now here he was again. Andy found Paul Keller enjoying a smoke on his kitchen steps.

"Paul," Andy said, "is anyone going to tell me what's going on here?"

Keller threw his cigarette to the ground, and crushed it into the earth under his shoe. "You'd better speak to your wife."

Lucky's face was washed out. The only signs of her normally red complexion, her Irish heritage, were splotches of red on her cheeks. She stood up as Andy came in.

"Oh, my dear," she said. "This is all my fault."

"What's your fault?"

"Ever since I brought that baby into this house, it's all gone wrong. My Granny Casey used to tell us stories of the lost babies. Children called by the sea. Selkie children. They didn't belong on the land, she said."

Andy grabbed her hands. "No one," he said, "is ever lost. You know that, don't you? Lucky? Lucy, light of my life."

"Moonlight," she said, "wants to be with Graham."

"Of course she does. But she knows Graham has gone where she can't follow. And she's much, much too strong to try to go after him." Still holding his wife's hands, he pushed her gently back into her chair. "Moonlight is your daughter, after all. She comes from a line of strong women."

Lucky chuckled, the sound as soft as a feather falling from the sky. "A line that began with me. You've said that before, dear."

"No less true for being repeated. Now, please tell me why I've come home to find Paul Keller and all his people standing in my driveway."

◇◇◇

Smith crouched behind the sofa. The front door stood open. The door to freedom. Safety. No one would blame her if she took it. Something was obviously happening up at the trailer. She could hear men shouting, a woman screaming, the piercing, oh so welcome, sound of a siren coming up the gravel road. The floatplane had barely touched down, and then it had left. Wise pilot. Leaving Burke and her brother stranded.

Smith struggled to get to her feet. She tugged at the rope tying her hands together, but nothing happened.

Clouds moved across the moon again. But her eyes were accustomed to the shifting shadows of the dark. She could see Burke coming out of the bedroom, carrying Miller, gasping for breath. "You're not still here?" Her gun was pointed at Miller's temple.

"I'm a curious sort. I don't know what he means to you, and I want to find out. The police have arrived, and your plane left.

Give up, Jody, you've lost. You don't want to add murder to the charges."

Burke held up the gun. It was very steady in her hand. "I've heard it said that there's a place where we go when we die where the meaning of life is revealed. I don't believe that for a moment. And I don't imagine that you, Constable Smith, do either. But you are about to find out."

Burke looked as cool and relaxed as if she were sipping cucumber water at a garden party. Smith's heart raced, and her legs wobbled. Fire ran though her wrists. She really, really, needed to pee.

"You're not a stupid woman, Jody. Jamie. Put Miller down and drop the gun. Do the right thing and it won't go so hard on you at your trial."

The clouds cleared, and the full moon burst out of cover. Light hit Burke in the face, and Smith read her intention. She hit the floor.

Burke fired at the rolling body. Glass shattered.

Screams echoed through the model suite. Smith wasn't sure if they were coming from her or the baby.

Like a turncoat, the moonlight changed sides and was no longer her ally. Burke had tossed Miller to the ground like a naughty kitten, and stood few feet from Smith. She stared directly at the constable.

Molly Smith stared into the gun barrel. She tried to scramble backward, but didn't have the use of her hands, and besides, she had nowhere to go.

She closed her eyes.

The door hit the wall.

A man's voice. "Police. Freeze."

A shot.

Another shot. The second one from a more powerful weapon.

The wet sound of a body falling.

Silence.

Smith opened her eyes and attempted to scramble to her feet. Her legs wobbled beneath her; they couldn't find the strength to support her whole body. She'd landed badly and pain lanced through her shoulder. She fell back to the floor. For some strange reason she found herself admiring the bold blue strokes of the art on the far wall. A man stood in the doorway, to the left of the painting. His right arm was outstretched, the Trafalgar City Police standard-issue Glock in his hand. Another man stood behind him, tall and big, wrapped in shadow.

"Call for an ambulance." Sergeant John Winters stood over Burke. She didn't move, and he kicked her gun away from her outstretched hand before kneeling down. "See to Molly," he said.

The second man slapped the switch by the door. Bright light from the ceiling reflected off the yellow stripe running down his pant legs.

Adam Tocek fell to the floor. "Molly, are you there. Molly?"

"Hell, yes. Check on Miller, the baby. He might have been hurt when she threw him. But first." She held out her hands. "Have you got a knife on you?"

Officers guided paramedics down the path to the model suite. They used strong flashlights to light the way.

Inside the suite, Jody Burke lay on the ground, her lifeblood leaking out of her chest into the gleaming hardwood floor. Her eyes were open wide, but they saw nothing. Her black robe surrounded her like a funeral shroud. She groaned once, and died. Winters got to his feet.

Adam Tocek crouched on the floor, patting a baby on the chest with one hand, and trying to keep a protesting Molly Smith down with the other.

Smith repeated that she was okay. Her wrists were red and angry, and she rubbed at them as if they were infested with bugs.

"Keep still, Constable Smith," Winters said. "Until you're checked out."

The second paramedic headed for Burke. The first went to the baby.

"I'll take him now," she said, and Tocek handed her the stinking bundle, looking very pleased to be doing so. The paramedic felt the child's limbs and head. "He's breathing, but we'd better get this little guy checked out, and fast. Roy, what have you got there?"

"Woman shot to the chest. Dead."

"Possible head injury here. I don't like how quiet he is." She ran out of the room, carrying Miller, passing a second ambulance crew coming in.

Ignoring orders, Smith attempted to stand up. She bit back a cry of pain as her shoulder moved. Tocek half lifted her. "Some guy named Steve," she said. "He's in on it."

"We've got him. Crying harder than a baby."

"Good. Good."

"Check her out," Winters told the paramedics.

"No. I'm okay. Shook up, but nothing's hurt."

"Your decision. I can't make you go with them, Molly, but we've got a long night ahead of us."

"I'm ready," she said. Strength began to come back into her voice. "Thanks, Adam. I can walk by myself."

"I'll go check on Norman, then," he said.

"Is Norman hurt?" Smith watched Tocek leave the room.

"Shot. But alive."

"Poor dog." She took a step toward Winters, staggered and almost fell. He grabbed her. "You are not okay, Constable Smith."

She took a deep breath. "You'd better call my mom. She'll be wondering where Miller is."

Chapter Thirty-five

Sergeant Winters helped Constable Smith negotiate the path through the woods to the parking area. They went into the trailer for a quick minute and then he guided her into the back of a Trafalgar City Police vehicle.

Before getting in, she took one long look behind her. Then, with a shake of her blond head, she ducked and disappeared into the car. It pulled away.

First out had been an ambulance. Meredith had seen the paramedics running toward it, the woman carrying a yellow bundle. The ambulance spat dirt and gravel as it sped away, sirens screaming.

Then came a stretcher, carrying a still shape. It was loaded into the second ambulance, which took off after the first.

Meredith had hugged herself and watched. Her stomach ached like hell, but she knew if she mentioned it to anyone she'd be giving them the excuse they'd need to send her packing.

Okay, so she'd fallen to the ground and screamed like a '20's movie virgin tied to the railway tracks. Embarrassing, but no one from the paper had been here to see it. When she wrote up her article, she'd mention, prominently, the unprovoked assault on the reporter. If they'd let her get so graphic about a case still to come before the courts. She'd have to talk to the paper's lawyer about that. It should help that she was personally involved.

The excitement moved on once Blacklock was under guard, and Winters and Tocek disappeared into the darkness. Meredith had heard shots. She would never, ever admit, that she'd wanted to follow those shots, find out what was going on, but instead found herself curled up on the ground, moaning with pain, her head under her hands, too scared to move.

Rather, she'd tell everyone that the officer had told her to remain put.

And, under orders from the police, she had no choice.

A van passed the second ambulance as it left. Dr. Hughes, the vet, jumped out. He ran toward the dog lying in the gravel, moaning softly. After a quick inspection, Hughes settled back on his heels and put his stethoscope in his shirt pocket. He looked up at Constable Tocek, walking silently up the path.

"Flesh wound," the vet said. "Clean in and out the right foreleg. Bleeding's almost stopped. This dog won't be running a marathon soon, but he'll be fine after a bit of care."

"Thanks," Tocek said, trying to smother the sound of his voice breaking. "He's new. Cost a lot to train. Wouldn't want to lose him."

"Help me get him into the van. I'll disinfect the wound and bandage it up. Keep him overnight, under observation, but he'll be fine."

The big Mountie crouched down and gathered the dog into his arms. Norman moaned, softly, but let himself be carried to the van.

"I'll call later," Tocek said. "To check up."

"Anytime." Hughes climbed into the driver's seat. "He should be able to go home in the morning."

John Winters came out of the woods, walking beside and slightly behind Molly Smith. They moved very slowly as he led her toward a patrol car. She rubbed at her hands continuously, like Lady Macbeth trying to wash them clean of the king's blood.

Tocek stepped forward. He smiled at her, and held out his hand. "Can I help?"

Molly looked at the hand. "I'm fine," she said. She walked past the Mountie. A uniformed officer held the back door of the car open for her.

Tocek turned and walked away. Meredith watched as Molly looked behind her and hesitated, for just a moment. Then she ducked and got into the car. The officer slammed the door shut and they sped away.

Detective Ray Lopez stepped out of the shadows. He held out his hand. Without a word, Winters handed over his own gun and the one he'd stuffed into the back of his belt. He walked down the road toward the highway, disappearing into the darkness. Lopez dropped the weapons into evidence bags.

"Still here, Meredith?" Lopez said. "I'd suggest you be on your way. Constable Tocek, as Miss Morgenstern refused medical help, will you show her to her car."

"Glad to."

Meredith's green Neon was beside the steps to the trailer, where she'd parked it.

"Sorry," she said, the single word sticking in her throat.

"What?"

"I'm sorry, okay." She took a breath. "I screwed up."

The entire area was lit up by white lights. Police officers walked in and out of the trailer, and disappeared down the path through the woods. Sirens came from the road as more police arrived. Adam Tocek's brown eyes were unreadable, but the skin around his mouth was stretched tight. "I must be mistaken," he said. "I thought I heard a reporter apologize for messing up a crime investigation, and almost getting an officer, not to mention a good police dog, killed."

"You won't hear it again. Not from these lips. But I am sorry."

Chapter Thirty-six

Jody Burke was formally pronounced dead on arrival at the Trafalgar and District Hospital. Steve Blacklock was sent to the psych ward, muttering nothing but "it wasn't me," over and over. Miller Doe, who'd started to cry as the ambulance sped toward town, was fed, bathed, changed, and settled into a soft crib, whereupon, all of life's necessities provided for, he immediately fell asleep. For eight full hours.

"I'm going down to Seattle later," John Winters said to the Chief Constable the next morning as light from the rising sun touched the tip of Koola Glacier. "To meet with the detectives working the Kate Watson murder. Looks like we've solved their case as well as ours."

Keller rubbed his yellow fingers. "Is there any doubt about who killed the girl, Ashley?"

"Burke told Molly it was her brother, Steve, who did it. Misjudged the amount of heroin. But Jody was the one in charge, and if Blacklock did the killing, it was at his sister's orders. Accidental overdose or not, the result would have been the same. Ashley wasn't going to hand over Miller, and so they would have killed her."

"Why don't you take Molly with you to Seattle, John. She deserves to see where this mess all began. I can authorize the additional expense. How's she doing anyway?"

Keller's phone buzzed. He picked it up. "I said no interruptions, Barb."

"Constable Smith's here."

"Send her in." One side of the Chief's mouth turned up. "I guess that answers that question."

The door opened and Constable Molly Smith walked through. She was dressed in uniform. Her face was pale, much paler than usual, and her wrists were red. But her eyes were clear and her back was straight. She carried her hat underneath her arm.

"I thought you might want a debriefing, sir, before I hit the streets."

"Pull up a chair, Molly."

She did so, and gave Winters a slight nod. He was pleased to notice that the CC didn't condescend to Smith. Suggest that she needed some time off. Whatever feelings Keller might have for Lucky Smith, and thus for Molly Smith herself, he kept his relationship with the probationary constable as professional as with anyone under his command.

Smith's voice was strong and clear, breaking only when she mentioned the baby. Winters suspected that Smith had been more concerned about Miller, and more ready to protect him, than she let on.

But he let it go.

This was Smith's story to tell. So far.

She stopped talking with a deep sigh.

Winters got to his feet.

"Are you on patrol, Molly?"

"Ten minutes."

"I want you to meet someone first."

"Who?" she said, her voice tinged with suspicion. "I've already been told I have an appointment with the shrink this afternoon."

"Someone who has an apology to make."

A man was sitting in the lunch room. He was big, tough, ugly, with a once (or more) broken nose, and long, greasy hair tied into a rough pony tail. His white T-shirt was stained with brown marks and sweat and his thick arms bulged with tattoos. He put his coffee mug down, and stood up as Smith and Winters entered. He smiled, a slow smile that went a long way toward taking some of the toughness out of his face.

"What the…" Smith said.

"I think you've met," Winters said with a laugh. "But I thought I'd better make it more formal this time."

"You're the one who hit me," she said. "And you got off without even a…." She looked at Winters.

"Corporal Brian Atkins. Brian's transferred into the local RCMP from New Brunswick. I thought we could make use of him before he got known around town, to try to shake down some drug dealers."

"I am sorry, Constable." Atkins held out his hand. "I didn't mean to hit you, and I felt pretty bad about it. You sort of fell into my fist."

She looked at his hand, but made no move to take it. "I worked part-time at a battered women's shelter when I was a student. That's what the men all say." She burst out laughing and accepted the handshake. "I hope it worked. Because, if I may say, you look the part. My name's Molly."

"My wife won't sleep in the same bed with me until I do something about these tattoos." He lifted his arm and grimaced. "She has a phobia about snakes. I forgot that when they were applying the image."

"It worked," Winters said. "Brian was helping Ray, and even as we speak Ray's writing up a nice, detailed arrest warrant for a gentleman who's acting as a distribution point for heroin across the southeast of the province."

"Sweet," Smith said.

Atkins tugged at his ponytail, his expression rueful. "My wife also hates the hair, so I have an appointment at the barber. I think it makes me look like a hot dude, what do you think Molly?"

"I think you'd better not miss that appointment."

"Be seeing you." He walked out.

"How's Miller?" Winters asked.

"Starved, dehydrated, soaked in pee and poo, thrown on the floor, and this morning he's his normal hungry, screaming self.

He spent the night in the hospital, just for observation, but my mom's gone to pick him up. We should all be so supple." She rotated her left shoulder with a wince.

"Allenhart's lawyers have already arrived." Winters told her. "They've started procedures to get Miller returned to the States."

"It's going to be hard on my mom, giving him up. Tell you the truth, I kinda like the little guy. He's a fighter. But I don't want him moving in permanently."

"He owes you something, Molly. Something big."

"He owes me," she said, shifting her feet, adjusting her gun belt, and looking out the window, "a good night's sleep." Sunlight reflected off moisture in her blue eyes. "It's going to be another scorcher today, they say. I can't wait for winter."

She walked out of the lunch room, putting her hat on her head and pulling her sunglasses out of her pocket.

Chapter Thirty-seven

"Ninety-two years old and he wants to be a daddy. Are you crazy?" Andy Smith threw up his hands. "What's he gonna do? Toss a football from his wheelchair? Once, and then he'll fall asleep. How about swim practice. Learning to canoe or ski. That'll be fun. The facts of life. He won't even remember them."

"Calm down, Dad," Molly Smith said. "Allenhart might be old, but he named Miller in his will and the lawyer doesn't intend to allow a paternity test. So that's that. You should be happy that Miller's got a home. And he's going to be really, really rich. Like I would be if you guys had done better in life."

"Ha. Ha."

"I just want to know about Ashley. Poor Ashley," Lucky said.

"Poor Ashley indeed."

It was late autumn. The nights were getting longer, the trees turning yellow, a few red or orange. Snow touched the mountain tops in the mornings, and Koola Glacier grew, day by day. The last of the produce had been gathered and the rich, black earth of the garden turned over. Andy hired a high school student to chop wood for the stove, enough to get a start on the winter. And Molly Smith felt that she could breathe, once again, in her Kevlar vest and dark blue uniform.

Burke was dead; Blacklock in the loony bin awaiting a hearing to determine if he could stand trial. Frank Clemmins had put the Grizzly resort property up for sale the day following the incident at the site, swearing that he was leaving the Kootenays forever. Nancy Blacklock told the police that she thought the relationship between her husband and his sister was a bit *intense*, but she had ignored it in the interests of family harmony. And, John Winters had surmised, as long as she was given free access to the liquor cabinet and the advertising budget.

Miller, the baby, had left the Smith home. Back to Seattle, to what bit of family he had. The parents of Jennifer and Katie Watson had been located, in the affluent town of Oakville, Ontario. They hadn't shown much concern over the fates of their daughters and no interest in taking in a *'bastard child'*. Their words, not those of the Oakville Police. Although no one would be surprised if they suddenly remembered the importance of blood relations when they found out just how much Richard George Andrew Allenhart Junior was worth.

Lucky had waved good-bye from the front porch, as a big black rental car took Miller away, wiped her hands on a dishcloth, and announced that she was going back to work. The big, old-fashioned, awkward, incredibly ugly pram still sat in front of the oven. Neither Andy nor Molly dared to move it.

"Steve Blacklock's starting to make some sense. Between him and our investigations, we think we finally have the whole story. "Looks like Jennifer knew from the get go that Jody—Jamie—wasn't her friend. But she thought Steve was okay. Ricardo, the chauffeur, heard Steve telling Jennifer that he wanted to buy into a development project in the Kootenays. Steve had been here on vacation a year or so ago, and thought the area had lots of potential."

Lucky snorted. "Potential to be defiled. Raped. Invaded. Occupied."

"Mom, please. I'm telling this story."

"Carry on, dear," Andy said.

Lucky looked out the window. It had rained for days on end and the forest was sodden and inhospitable. Thick strands of pale green lichen hung from cedar and pine branches like party decorations left too long outside. The house smelled of wood smoke, wet dog, and the vegetable and tofu curry they were having for supper.

"As an aside, Steve was so deep in debt the whole house of cards was about to come crashing down around him anyway. He, and Jamie as well, received a nice tidy income from Uncle Richard's various companies, but he was just too greedy."

"An old story," Andy said.

"It is. Steve borrowed most of the money for his investment in the Grizzly based on his plans to inherit. After all, the old guy was in his 90s, he'd be dead any day now, and Steve would be rolling in the dough. He had expectations, as they say. *Great Expectations*, Charles Dickens called it, I believe. Anyway, when Jennifer found herself running from the body of her murdered sister, carrying her nephew, she knew she had to disappear. We don't know how she got him across the border, probably never will. Not only had she heard Steve talk about Trafalgar, but Julian Armstrong thinks he might have mentioned that he's from this area. She probably thought she was being guided," Smith made quotation marks in the air with her fingers, "to come to Trafalgar. Didn't hurt that this is a town full of transients, where no one looks twice at a homeless girl and her baby."

"Speaking of Julian," Lucky said, "I've been told he left town quite abruptly. Complaining of police harassment, some say."

"Some say the moon is made of blue cheese. But, speaking of Julian, if we must, we would have gotten to the bottom of all this mess much quicker if he'd come out and told us what he knew."

Not to mention, Marigold—Joan Jones—who thought her roommate deserved her privacy 'even in death' and who, they'd finally found out, worked hard because she had credit card debts piled on top of student loans.

"Do you want me to continue or not?"

Lucky leaned over and scratched behind Sylvester's floppy ears. His tail wagged in contentment. "Sorry dear. Carry on."

"Jennifer figured she could hide the baby here, in Trafalgar, while looking for Steve and getting him to help her. Jennifer, our Ashley, either saw her sister murdered, or came across the body immediately after. Jamie, our Jody, killed the girl, and then she took a walk, probably to dispose of the murder weapon. The property's on Puget Sound. The Seattle police sent down divers, but didn't find anything. When Jody got back, no doubt intending to smother the baby, make it look like whoever killed the mother had killed the baby as well, Miller was gone."

"That must have given her a bad moment," Andy said.

"You think? It's all pretty horrible."

"Poor Jennifer. She came to Trafalgar trying to save the baby, thinking that Steve Blacklock would help her." Lucky looked up from her tea cup. Her eyes were rimmed red, as if she'd used a child's crayon as eyeliner.

"Blacklock. He's a piece of work. Whether he directly killed Jennifer or not, I don't much care. She came to him for help. And he turned his back on her and the baby. He deserves whatever he's going to get. But, back to the scene. Jamie left a hefty bundle of cash on the kitchen counter when she went for her walk. She'd probably made a withdrawal to be used to bribe the cops, if that became necessary. Although, judging by the detectives we met down there, I don't think any amount of bribe would have been enough."

Lucky stirred. "In Seattle," she said, beginning a story.

"Forget it, Mom. That was a long time ago. Anyway, Jennifer grabbed the money, and the baby, when she ran, probably not even aware of how much it was. Thus she was able to live for months with no income. We found a safety deposit box, under her real name, at a bank in Trail, stuffed with U.S. bills, and her Ontario health card."

"What about her own family? Why didn't she go to them?"

"The Oakville Police suspect the Watson parents are part of the problem. There were allegations of abuse when the girls were in school. Nothing proven. No action taken. They're a *very* respectable, old money family."

Lucky snorted.

"Jennifer, Ashley, ran away when she was 14. To Vancouver, where she found herself hooked on drugs and walking the streets to pay for them. But somehow, she must have been one strong woman, she got herself clean. Katie was a few years younger. She also left the parental nest at 14, and came west looking for her sister. One of Katie's friends back in Oakville told the police she received a letter at her house, addressed to her. Inside there'd been an envelope addressed to Katie. She gave it to her friend; the next day Katie disappeared. But something went wrong and Katie ended up on the streets of Seattle, not Vancouver, and then in the Allenhart house. Jennifer must have followed her to Seattle and the sisters were reunited shortly after Katie's baby was born. The story could have had a happy ending. It should have had a happy ending. That's what makes me so mad. When I think about those two girls, struggling so hard, Jennifer getting herself clean so she could send for her sister, finally finding each other. And then they meet Jamie, disinherited, vengeful."

"Sad," Lucky said.

"What a waste," Andy said.

"I can't get over the gall of that woman. She must have had nerves of steel. Pretending to be with Children and Family Development. Even asking the police to help her out."

"Who would ever think someone would pretend to be a social worker?" Andy said. "This isn't the big city. No one asks for ID."

"And no one thought to tell you that the public health nurse had filed a report recommending that Miller be left with you until his relatives could be located. Funnily enough, I suspect Jody's nerves were her undoing. Even after taking a stroll to dispose of Katie's murder weapon, and coming back to find the baby gone, she left Miller lying beside Ashley's body. He would have been dead by morning, if you hadn't found him, Mom. And all we'd find would be a junkie who went back to the stuff, leaving the baby she'd kidnapped to die at her side. Allenhart's will left everything to Jamie and Steve in the event that Richard Junior pre-deceased them."

The family sat in silence. Sylvester licked at his private parts with much enthusiasm.

"They said you can come and visit, Mom," Smith leaned across the table and touched her mother's hand. "Will you go?"

"I don't think so. He's going to be raised by hired help. No mother, a father who's not all there and will probably be dead before his next birthday. A big, empty house. Lots of money. Not much love. No, I don't think I'll visit." She stood up. "Tomorrow's the Peace Guild's Christmas Bake and White Elephant. I said I'd make something. My world famous lemon squares are always nice."

"Christmas," Smith said. "It's only October."

"Never hurts to start early, Moonlight. Andy, I don't have enough lemons. You'll have to go to town."

Chapter Thirty-eight

Meredith's story had not made the paper. Instead they printed something generic, mild, unprovocative, submitted by the pimply faced junior who thought he was Jimmy Olsen, Boy Reporter. All bases covered, all legal angles considered.

She needed to get out of this hick town.

It had been the best story she'd ever written. Consigned to the trash bin.

She pushed her chair back from the computer with a sigh and walked to the window. She grabbed her right foot in her hand, and folded her leg back to give it a good stretch. Nothing new on the Internet today in the way of openings for a reporter on a big city paper.

An RCMP car drove past, heading toward the city police station. Probably for a dull, routine meeting. She wondered who was behind the wheel.

Tocek?

For some reason thinking about Constable Adam Tocek always made her think about sex.

But she didn't have a chance with him, and so, for the first—and hopefully the last—time, she'd sent a man after another woman.

He'd walked her to her car, that night at the Grizzly Resort, after the ambulances had left, sirens screaming, and Sergeant Winters had surrendered his weapon, and Molly Smith, pale and on the verge of shock, had been bundled into the back of a police car.

Meredith had put her hand on the door frame of her own car. She began to step in, but stopped. "Okay," she'd said to Tocek, looming over her. "I'll tell you one thing. Moonlight Smith and I have never been friends. To be honest, we pretty much hate each other. You might not know this, but her fiancé was murdered by a druggie. I guess that's why she became a cop."

"If you're stopped at the highway, have them contact me," he said. "I'll tell them we want you out of here as fast as possible."

"Get as smart as you like. But first, I'm going to tell you something you can take to the bank." It would appear that, here tonight, all had ended well, and although Meredith might tell herself tomorrow morning, and in the years to come, that she'd helped to make it so, she knew, at this moment, deep in her heart, that she'd screwed up. She'd come across a great story, and she'd be heading back to the *Gazette* offices to file it. If she was lucky, one of the wire services or the major papers would pick it up.

But before she left, she'd try to make restitution, somehow. "I saw Molly watching you, after you turned away. I saw her look at you at the grow-op bust the other day, when you walked back to your car. Molly Smith carries around so much emotional baggage, it's burying her. You dig underneath all of that, Adam, and you'll find a woman who cares for you."

Meredith pulled the door shut and threw the car into reverse.

To receive a free catalog of Poisoned Pen Press titles, please contact us in one of the following ways:

Phone: 1-800-421-3976
Facsimile: 1-480-949-1707
Email: info@poisonedpenpress.com
Website: www.poisonedpenpress.com

Poisoned Pen Press
6962 E. First Ave. Ste. 103
Scottsdale, AZ 85251